I0642492

ECONOMIC ANALYSIS FOR BUSINESS DECISIONS

For

M.B.A. & P.G.D.B.M. (Semester - I)

As Per New Revised Syllabus, Effective from June 2016

Mrs. Kiran Jotwani

M.A. (Economics), B.Ed.

NIRALI PRAKASHAN
ADVANCEMENT OF KNOWLEDGE

N2952

ECONOMIC ANALYSIS FOR BUSINESS DECISIONS

Third Edition : **July 2016**

© : **Author**

Published By :
NIRALI PRAKASHAN
Abhyudaya Pragati, 1312, Shivaji Nagar
Off J.M. Road, Pune – 411005
Tel - (020) 25512336/37/39, Fax - (020) 25511379
Email : niralipune@pragationline.com

➢ DISTRIBUTION CENTRES

PUNE

Nirali Prakashan : 119, Budhwar Peth, Jogeshwari Mandir Lane, Pune 411002, Maharashtra
Tel : (020) 2445 2044, 66022708, Fax : (020) 2445 1538
Email : bookorder@pragationline.com, niralilocal@pragationline.com

Nirali Prakashan : S. No. 28/27, Dhyari, Near Pari Company, Pune 411041
Tel : (020) 24690204 Fax : (020) 24690316
Email : dhyari@pragationline.com, bookorder@pragationline.com

MUMBAI

Nirali Prakashan : 385, S.V.P. Road, Rasdhara Co-op. Hsg. Society Ltd.,
Girgaum, Mumbai 400004, Maharashtra
Tel : (022) 2385 6339 / 2386 9976, Fax : (022) 2386 9976
Email : niralimumbai@pragationline.com

➢ DISTRIBUTION BRANCHES

JALGAON

Nirali Prakashan : 34, V. V. Golani Market, Navi Peth, Jalgaon 425001,
Maharashtra, Tel : (0257) 222 0395, Mob : 94234 91860

KOLHAPUR

Nirali Prakashan : New Mahadvar Road, Kedar Plaza, 1st Floor Opp. IDBI Bank
Kolhapur 416 012, Maharashtra. Mob : 9850046155

NAGPUR

Pratibha Book Distributors : Above Maratha Mandir, Shop No. 3, First Floor,
Rani Jhanshi Square, Sitabuldi, Nagpur 440012, Maharashtra
Tel : (0712) 254 7129

DELHI

Nirali Prakashan : 4593/21, Basement, Aggarwal Lane 15, Ansari Road, Daryaganj
Near Times of India Building, New Delhi 110002 Mob : 08505972553

BENGALURU

Pragati Book House : House No. 1, Sanjeevappa Lane, Avenue Road Cross,
Opp. Rice Church, Bengaluru – 560002.
Tel : (080) 64513344, 64513355,Mob : 9880582331, 9845021552
Email:bharatsavla@yahoo.com

CHENNAI

Pragati Books : 9/1, Montieth Road, Behind Taas Mahal, Egmore,
Chennai 600008 Tamil Nadu, Tel : (044) 6518 3535,
Mob : 94440 01782 / 98450 21552 / 98805 82331,
Email : bharatsavla@yahoo.com

niralipune@pragationline.com | www.pragationline.com

Also find us on 🅕 www.facebook.com/niralibooks

Preface ...

The field of economics is very dynamic, characterised by continuous changes in its variables which have a deep impact on the business world of the economy. In the business world, with the cut-throat competition, the survival in the market depends on the managerial decisions. The entrepreneurs with borrowed funds cannot leap into the dark without forming the basis for a new venture.

It gives me a feeling of immense pleasure and gratitude when placing before the students of MBA and other readers, the book of Economic Analysis for Business Decisions. It is based on the revised syllabus, with effect from June 2016.

This book contains the terms and concepts of the modern business decisions. The basic principles of managing business in the modern times are explained in the most illustrative form. The changes in demand, a topic so important to analyse for business decisions, since it is ruled by known and unknown factors, is dealt extensively. It explains the various innovative, accurate methods of demand forecasting, the different types of markets, with their decisions analysis on output and price. The role and functions of Reserve Bank of India in Money Market has effectively kept a watch on the credit control and role of SEBI in Capital Market points out to the fact that the market is heading towards a systematic and organised functioning. Topics like Public Revenue and Public Expenditure extends knowledge on the working of the Government and its resource allocation to the different sectors of the economy.

The book contains Case Studies on the required topics. Various diagrams and flow-charts help to simplify the most complicated of the topics. The language used is simple and flows naturally.

I am thankful to my friends and long time publisher Shri Dineshbhai Furia, Shri Jignesh Furia and the entire staff of Nirali Prakashan, Pune without whose unerring support and sustained effect, this book would not have seen the light of the day. A special thanks to Mrs. Nirja Sharma for her ever-availability to me for solving the queries of the updated syllabus. I would also like to acknowledge here the contributions of the editorial and graphics team of Nirali Prakashan which includes Nirja Sharma, Prasad Chintakindi, Akbar Shaikh, Mrs Muley and Neha Deshpande.

I am ever grateful to Shri Suresh Jotwani, for his unconditional help and encouragement. I am sure that the book will be a good guidance to the students. Both, my publisher and I will be thankful and will welcome any suggestions for the improvement in any of the contents of the book. We are quite confident that this text book will receive the patronage of all for whom it is intended.

Kiran Jotwani

Syllabus ...

(With Effect from June 2016)

M.B.A. (Sem. I : Course Code 102)

(Number of Sessions)

1. Basic Concepts of Economics (7 + 2)

Introduction to Economics, Basic Economic Problems, Circular Flow of Economic Activity, Nature of the firm - Rationale, Objective of maximizing firm value as present value of all future profits, Maximizing, Satisficing, Optimizing, Principal agent problem, Accounting Profit and Economic Profit, Role of profit in Market System, Adam Smith and Invisible Hand.

2. Demand Analysis and Forecasting (7 + 2)

Determinants of Market Demand at Firm and Industry level - Elasticity of Demand - Market Demand Equation - Use of Multiple Regression for Estimating demand - Case study on Estimating Industry Demand (Formulating equation and solving with the aid of software expected)

Demand and Supply

Market Equilibrium - Pricing under perfect competition, Monopolistic competition, Case study on pricing under monopolistic competition, Oligopoly - Product differentiation and Price discrimination; Price - Output decision in multi-plant and multi-product firms.

3. Cost Concepts (7 + 2)

Cost Concept, Opportunity Cost, Marginal, Incremental and Sunk Costs, Cost Volume Profit Analysis, Breakeven Point, Case Study on Marginal costs.

Risk Analysis and Decision Making

Concept of risk, Expected value computation, Risk management through Insurance, diversification, Hedging, Decision Tree Analysis, Case Study on Decision Tree Technique.

4. Money and Capital Markets in India (7 + 2)

Role and Functions of Money Markets, Composition of Money Market, Money Market Instruments, Reserve Bank of India - Functions, Regulatory Role of RBI w.r.t. Currency, Credit and Balance of Payment, Open Market Operations.

Role and Functions of Capital Markets, Composition of Capital market, Stock Exchanges in India, Role of SEBI, understanding of stock market quotations in financial press expected.

5. Public Finance Infrastructure (7 + 2)

Familiarity with important Terms/Agencies/Approaches/Practices related to National Income (such as GDP, PPP, Growth Rate), Foreign Trade (such as GATT, WTO) and Union Budget (such as Revenue Account, Capital Account, Revenue Deficit, Fiscal Deficit, Plan and Non-plan expenditure) is expected.

Understanding of Summarized budget for the current financial year is required (knowledge of detailed budget provisions not required).

Contents ...

$\mathcal{C}hapter$ **1**...

Basic Concepts of Economics

Contents ...

Learning Objectives ...

➢ To equip the students of management with time tested tools and techniques of managerial economics to enable them to appreciate its relevance in decision making.

➢ To understand the generation of national income in the country by means of circular flow of economic activity.

➢ To understand the basic concept of microeconomics, i.e. a firm, its rationale and its objective.

➢ To know the importance of 'profits' operating as a signal to a firm to enter or exit an industry.

➢ To understand the importance of intervention of government in a free economy.

Introduction

It is important to understand what managerial economics is about. This subject includes decision making, and thus it will be quite helpful, if we identify and understand some of the basic concepts underlying the subject. The various decision problems are based heavily on these concepts, methods and models.

In Management studies, the terms 'Business Economics' and 'Managerial Economics' are often synonymous. However, both the terms involve 'economics' as a basic discipline useful for certain functional areas of business management.

Managerial economics is essentially, applied economics in the field of business management. It relates to all economic aspects of managerial decision making. Managerial economics is the integration of economic principles with business management practices. A course in managerial economics, thus, provides an understanding of the framework and economic tools needed by managers or businessmen as an aid to better business decision making.

1.1 Meaning of Managerial Economics

Managerial economics is concerned with the application of economic theory and methods of decision sciences to analyse decision making problems faced by business firms. Thus, Managerial economics is both conceptual and practical. The first important problem faced by a business firm is the choice of a product to be produced or the service to be provided. The second important problem to be taken by a firm is about price and output of the product so as to maximise profits or to attain some desired goal.

Managerial economics draws heavily on the decision sciences for the techniques used for decision making. The techniques of decision sciences used especially for business decision making are optimisation techniques, methods of statistical estimation, game theory of decision sciences. These techniques help managers in achieving firm's objectives. Thus, *"managerial economics refers to the application of economic theory and methods of decision sciences to arrive at the optimal solution to the various decision making problems faced by managers of business firms."*

- Managerial economics has both descriptive and prescriptive roles.

- It not only, explains *how* various economic forces affect the working of a firm but also *predicts* the consequences of the decision made by the firm. This is its *descriptive role*.

- Managerial economics prescribes the rules for the improvement of decision making by the firms or managers so that they can achieve their objectives efficiently. This is its *prescriptive role*.

- Managerial economics deals with not only *private firms* but also *public enterprises*. This is because managers of all types of organisations face similar problems.

1.2 Definitions of Managerial Economics

(a) According to **McNair and Merriam,** *"Managerial Economics consists of the use of economic modes of thought to analyse business situations."*

(b) Managerial Economics can be defined as, *"the discipline which deals with the application of economic theory to business management."*

(c) In words of **Spencer and Siegelman,** Managerial Economics is, *"the integration of economic theory with business practice for the purpose of facilitating decision making and forward planning by management."*

(d) According to **Mansfield***, "Managerial economics is concerned with application of economic concepts and economic analysis to the problems of formulating rational managerial decision."*

1.3 Nature of Managerial Economics

The characteristics of Managerial Economics sum up the nature of Managerial Economics:

(a) Managerial Economics is Micro economics in character, as Managerial economics does not deal with the *entire* economy as a unit of study.

(b) Managerial Economics is pragmatic (practical) in nature. It tries to solve complications ignored in economic theory to face the overall situation in which decisions are made. Managerial economics considers the particular environment of decision making.

(c) Managerial economics largely uses those economic concepts and principles which are known as 'Theory of the firm' or 'Economics of the Firm'.

(d) Managerial economics belongs to normative economics. That is, managerial economics involves value judgements. It tells how best to achieve these aims in particular situations.

(e) Nowadays, managers and entrepreneurs' make it their business to have a good working knowledge of managerial economics.

(f) Thus, we summarise the salient features of managerial economics as follows:

- It involves an application of economic theory, micro economics analysis, to practical problem solving in real business life, i.e. it is essentially applied micro economics.
- It is a science, as well as an art facilitating better managerial discipline.
- It is concerned with firm's behaviour in optimal allocation of resources. Thus it provides tools to help in identifying the best course among the competitive activities in any productive sector.

1.4 Scope of Managerial Economics

The following topics may be said to generally fall in the scope of Managerial Economics

(a) Demand analysis and forecasting: A major part of managerial decision making depends on accurate estimates of demand. Demand analysis includes demand determinants and demand forecasting. Before production schedule can be prepared and resources employed, forecast of future sales is essential. Demand analysis is essential for business planning and occupies a strategic place in managerial economics.

(b) Supply analysis: Important aspects of supply analysis such as supply schedule, supply function, law of supply and elasticity of supply and factors influencing supply are subject matter of managerial economics.

(c) Cost Analysis: Cost analysis includes cost concepts and classification, cost output relationships, economies and diseconomies of scale and cost control and cost reduction. The factors causing variations in costs must be recognised and management is to arrive at cost estimates which are significant for planning purposes. Discovering economic costs and being able to measure them are necessary steps for more effective profit planning, cost control and sound pricing practices.

(d) Pricing Decisions: The success of a business firm largely depends on how far the pricing decisions taken by the firm are correct. Pricing decisions involve price determination in various market firms, pricing methods, differential pricing, product-line pricing and price forecasting.

(e) Profit Management: Business firms are generally organised for the purpose of profit-making and in the long-run profits provide the chief measure of success. The element of uncertainty existing in estimating profits is because of variations in costs and revenues which in turn, are caused by factors both internal and external to the firm. If the future could be predicted with perfection, profit analysis would have been a very easy task. However, with uncertain conditions, expectations are not realised and hence, profit planning and its measurement constitute a difficult area of managerial economics.

(f) Capital Management: The most complex area for any business manager is that relating to the firm's capital investments. Capital management implies planning and control of capital expenditure. Capital management covers cost of capital, rate of return and selection of projects, etc.

In recent years, techniques such as Linear Programming, Inventory models, Game theory, and so on are a part of Managerial Economics to integrate managerial economics and operation research.

1.5 Features of Managerial Economics

(a) Micro Economic in Character: Managerial economics is micro economic in character, as the unit of study is a firm. That is, the problems of a business firm are subject matter of managerial economics. It does not deal with the entire economy as a unit of study.

(b) Economics of the firm: Managerial economics mostly uses that body of economic concepts and principles known as "Economics of the firm". It also seeks to apply profit theory which forms part of distribution theories in economics.

(c) **Avoiding abstract issues of Economic Theory:** Managerial economics avoids difficult abstract issues of economic theory but involves complications ignored in economic theory to face the overall situation in which decisions are made. Thus, managerial economics is pragmatic.

(d) **Normative Economics:** Managerial economics belongs to normative economics rather than positive economics. It is prescriptive rather than descriptive. Managerial economics has been described as normative economics because it is concerned with what decisions ought to be made and hence, involves value judgements. In managerial economics, decision making involves two aspects: (i) it tells what objectives a firm should pursue; (ii) once these objectives are defined, it tells how best to achieve these objectives in a particular situation.

(e) **Understanding of the Business Environment:** Macro economics is also useful to managerial economics, since it provides an intelligent understanding of the environment in which the business must operate. The important topics included are trade cycles, national income accounting and economic policies of the government like taxation, foreign trade, and so on.

1.6 Micro and Macro Analysis in Economics

Modern economists have clearly divided the study of economics into Micro Economics and Macro Economics.

"Micro" means **individualistic** and "Macro" means **aggregative**. When we analyse the problems of an economy as a *whole*, it is macro-economics. While an analysis of the behaviour of *any particular decision making unit*, such as a firm, an industry is micro economics.

Micro-Economics

- The word 'micro' means a millionth part. Micro economics is some small part or component of the whole economy that we are analysing. For example, an individual consumer's behaviour, or that of an individual firm. In micro economics, it is the demand of an individual which is studied and not the aggregate demand of the entire community. Likewise, the income of an individual and not the national income of a country is the scope of micro economics.

- Micro economics is concerned with the behaviour of micro-variables or micro-quantities such as individual demand, individual supply, etc.

- A noteworthy feature of the micro-approach is that while conducting economic analysis on a micro basis, generally an assumption of full employment, in the economy as a whole is made. On this assumption, the economic problem is mainly that of resource allocation or of theory of price. That is why, till recently, economics concerned itself mainly with the theory of value and distribution and it ignored the study of the economic system as a whole.

- Thus, micro economics is referred to as 'Price theory' as pricing system is the core subject of micro economics.
- Micro economics studies with the help of an indispensable tool namely 'marginal analysis.

Macro Economics

- The analysis of economic system as a "whole" is macro economics. It is concerned with **aggregates** and **averages** of the entire economy, such as national income, total output, aggregate demand, aggregate supply and the general level of prices.
- In macro economics, we study how these aggregates and averages of the economy as a whole are determined and what causes fluctuations in them.
- In macro economics, the theories are based on the basis of empirical knowledge, hence, the assumption of full employment stays invalid. It is very vital that we should investigate how these aggregates of an economy are determined and having known their determinants, how to ensure the maximum level of income and full employment in a country.
- Macro economics deals with how an economy grows. Thus, it analyses the chief determinants of economic development and the various stages and process of economic growth.
- It is generally argued by Classical economists as to why there is need of a separate macroeconomic approach? The justification of a separate macro approach to the study of several economic problems lies in the fact that micro approach is not only inadequate but may lead to altogether misleading conclusions. In economics what is true of a part, is not necessarily true of the whole. After all the problem of the aggregate is not merely a matter of adding or of multiplying what happens in respect of the various individual parts of the whole. It may be quite different and far more complicated than a mere summation. For example, savings, in times of depression while savings by an individual may be beneficial to him, but savings on the part of the entire population will deepen the depression further as aggregate demand will decline.

1.7 Managerial Economics and Micro Economics

(a) If economics deals with the body of the principles itself, Managerial economics deals with application of economic principles to the problem of the firm.

(b) Economics has two approaches, i.e., it is both micro-economic and macro-economic and managerial economics is micro-economic in character.

(c) Micro- economics as a branch of economics, deals with both economics of the firm and the economics of the individual. On the other hand, though Managerial economics is micro-economic in character, it deals with the economics of the firm and does not have economics of the individual as the unit of its study.

(d) In Economics, the theory of distribution studied under micro economics, includes theories on wages, interest and profit. Whereas, under Managerial economics, mainly Profit Theory is used; other theories of distribution have practically no significance in it. In short, the scope of economics is wider than the scope of managerial economics.

(e) Micro economic theory hypothesises economic relationships and builds economic models, but managerial economics adopts, modifies and reformulates economic models to suit the specific conditions and provide solution to the specific problem. In other words, economics gives us the simplified model, whereas managerial economics modifies and enlarges it.

(f) Micro economics is based on certain assumptions, whereas managerial economics introduces certain feedbacks such as objectives of the firm, multi product nature of manufacture, environmental aspects, constraints on resource availability, etc. In short, Managerial economics embodies a combination of complexities assumed away in economic theory and then attempts to solve the real life, complex business problems with the help of tool subjects namely mathematics, statistics, econometrics, accounting and so on.

1.8 Role of Managerial Economist

In a knowledge-based economy and business, those who continue to get expertise in managerial economics are referred to as managerial economists.

A managerial economist is an economic adviser to a firm or businessman. The business economist, by virtue of his expertise, helps the businessman or the manager in arriving at correct decisions in the nature of the product to be produced, the quantity of it to be produced, its quality, cost, price, diversification of business, renewal of worn-out equipment and machinery, modernisation etc.

A managerial economist in a business firm may carry on a wide range of duties, such as,
* Demand estimation and forecasting;
* Analysis of the market survey to determine the nature and extent of competition;
* Advising on pricing, investment, capital budgeting policies, etc.;
* Assisting the business planning process of the firm;
* Directing economic research activity;
* Briefing the management on current domestic and global economic issues and emerging challenges.

The business economist has to keep an eye on the fast changing technological developments, because the decision taken will be within the framework of such developments. The business economist has to keep pace with modern times as innovation of new products may adversely affect the business of the firm.

A business economist should work in harmony with the policymakers, because he identifies constraints and alternatives in decision making. He should help the management in identifying long and short-run objectives and in reconciling the conflicting ones.

In modern business, particularly, big firms, employment of a business economist has become inevitable. However, the role of business economists depends on the type or nature of the business of the firm. For example, in a financial firm, it is to provide guidelines for investment, marketing and speculative activities.

To conclude, a managerial economist is a thinker, a friend and a philosopher to the businessman. He should be both conceptual and a practical one.

1.9 Managerial Economics - Normative or Positive

According to **J.M.Keynes**, *"a positive science or positive scientific approach may be defined as a body of systematised knowledge concerning 'what is'* and *"a normative science or regulative science is a body of systematised knowledge relating to the criteria of 'what ought to be' and concerned with the ideals as distinguished from the actual."*

The objective of a positive science is the establishment of uniformities and of normative approach is determination of ideals.

The positive approach deals with things as they are. It explains the cause and effect, but it remains neutral as regards ends, hence it passes no value judgement. On the other hand, the normative approach deals with things *as they ought to be,* and does not hesitate in discussing moral judgement on it. For example, what determines the rate of interest in a community? An enquiry into these forces shall be considered as a positive enquiry, because here the things are to be discussed as they actually are. What constitutes a fair rate of interest? Such an enquiry would involve ethical consideration i.e., normative approach.

According to **Milton Friedman**, positive economics deals with how an economic problem is solved; normative economics deals with how an economic problem should be solved. A positive approach is based on *facts*; a normative approach involves *ethical values.* **Positive economics describes and normative economics prescribes.**

Thus, positive approach involves no value judgement which is present in normative approach.

Managerial economics is a blend of positive (pure) with normative (applied) science. It is positive when it is confined to statements about cause and effect and to functional relations of economic variables. And, it is normative when it involves norms and standards, mixing them with the cause and effect analysis.

A managerial function is to allocate given business resources possessed by the firm for achieving predetermined business goals. This is the positive aspect of managerial economics. But, one cannot disregard the normative functions of managerial economics. In other words, managerial economics is the logic of rational choice and a science for the betterment of business management but it should not refrain from essential value judgements. As an applied social science, managerial economics is firmly laced with social values and problems and hence, it cannot be made a pure value-free science. Cultural values and religious sentiments of the people coin the business ethics, which governs the managerial decision making in different economic activists. For example, a film producer while making a film cannot forget the thought of the social impact of his film. In industrial ventures, environmental abuses need to be minimised and ecological balance has to be maintained.

In short, business economists should seek to understand and examine not only what is happening in the business field; they should also seek to guide in formulating and choosing alternative policies that may influence the business activities for the betterment of the society at large.

1.10 The Basic Concepts

Economic theory provides a number of concepts and analytical tools which can be of considerable help to a manager in taking scientific decisions and business planning.

The basic concepts that form the basis of managerial economics can be understood as follows:

1. Incremental Principle

Incremental Reasoning: The most important concept in economics is the principle of incremental reasoning. It has a great impact on decision alternatives.

In real world, one is concerned not with 'unit' change but with 'chunk' change. Hence, it is difficult to apply the concept of "marginal principle" and it is to be replaced by "incremental principle".

The two basic concepts in incremental reasoning are – *incremental cost and incremental revenue.*

Incremental Cost is defined as "change in total cost resulting from a particular decision." Thus, Incremental cost is the change in total cost because of change in the level of output, investment, etc.

In symbolic terms, IC = $\dfrac{\Delta TC}{\Delta Q}$ Δ = change; Q = Quantity; TC= total cost.

Incremental Revenue is defined as "change in total revenue resulting from a particular decision." Thus, Incremental revenue is a change in total revenue, because of change in the level of output, price, etc.

Symbolic terms, IR = $\dfrac{\Delta TR}{\Delta Q}$ Δ = change; Q= quantity; TR = total revenue.

A manager determines the worthiness of a decision on the criterion of incremental revenue exceeding the incremental cost.

For example, if a bank goes in for computerisation of market information, the additional revenue (i.e. change in revenue) it earns, is incremental revenue and the incremental cost is the extra cost of setting up of computer facilities.

While making any decision on new investment, the manager's criteria of choice is that incremental revenue is greater than incremental cost (IR > IC).

The application or decision of incremental principle may be profitable by any manager, if:
- Revenue increases more than increase in costs;
- Total revenue given, costs is reduced from time-to-time;
- Percentage increase in costs to be greater than the falling percentage of revenue.

Example: Suppose a firm decides to increase its output. This may involve a rise in its total cost by 30% and with an increase in output by 10%. In such a case, the incremental cost (IC) is –

$$IC = \frac{30\%}{10\%} = 3\%.$$

And, now if the firm expects increase in total sales revenue by 40% (2nd basic component of Incremental principle) with the increase in 10% output, then incremental revenue (IR) is –

$$IR = \frac{40\%}{10\%} = 4\%.$$

In this case, IR = 4% and IC = 3%, i.e. IR > IC

It can be concluded that it is a profitable decision to undertake the new investment.

The firm may be interested to know the incremental reasoning as an increase or a change in the position of cost and revenue.

Taking the same illustration:

IR = Post decision total revenue – Pre decision total revenue.

IR = ₹ 300 cr. – ₹ 250 cr. = ₹ 50 crore.

Similarly, IC = Post decision total cost – Pre decision total cost.

Supposing Initial cost = ₹ 230 crores; new cost = ₹ 260 crore; then

IC= ₹ 260 cr.– ₹ 230 cr. = ₹ 30 crore.

Thus, Incremental profit = IR – IC, i.e. ₹ 50 cr.–₹ 30 cr. = ₹ 20 cr.

Or, profitable is the decision of the new investment.

When alternative options are available, then similar type of an exercise is to be carried out to arrive at the best option.

Suppose, option A investment profit = ₹ 3 cr.

Option B investment profit = ₹ 2.5 cr.

Option C investment profit = ₹ 3.2 cr. (Option C is chosen)

Some managers are of the view that to make an overall profit, the firm must make profit on each job. As a result they refuse orders that do not cover full costs, i.e. variable plus fixed cost plus profit. Incremental reasoning points out that this managerial rule may be inconsistent with profit maximisation in the short-run period. The manager refusing business below full cost means, losing a possibility of adding more revenue than to cost, because it is better to see covering the incremental cost than the full cost. At the same time incremental reasoning does not mean covering merely incremental cost. The acceptance of the job depends on the idle or excess capacity that would go unutilised in the absence of more profitable opportunities.

A manager can judge the worthiness of any decision based on two theories:

- A course of action can be pursued when at least *incremental benefits equal its incremental costs.* The acceptance or rejection of an order by a firm for its product depends on whether the resultant costs is lesser or greater than the resultant revenue. It will be profitable for the firm to take up the job when the execution of an order costs less to the firm than the revenue that it will bring in. And, if the firm has an idle capacity than execution of the order will not tend to raise the costs.

- Different courses of action can be pursued up to a point where all the courses provide equal marginal benefit per unit of cost. This is based on the equi-marginal principle, i.e. an input must be so allocated between various uses that the value added by the last unit of the input is the same in all its uses. Thus, various alternatives are gauged based on the marginal return from them. If the 'additional' (marginal) contribution of the inputs between different outputs is unequal, the firm would continue reallocating the input from low-productive use to high-productive use until its marginal/additional contribution to all outputs are equal.

The concept of incremental reasoning is of extreme importance. Many firms take this principle in consideration to maximise profits, as they must be able to make profit on *every unit of output.* Thus, the concept of incremental reasoning is quite helpful in optimal allocation of resources.

2. Opportunity Cost

Opportunity cost of a decision is the sacrifice of alternative required by that decision. Opportunity cost represents the benefits or revenue forgone by pursuing one course of action rather than another. When a choice is made *in* favour of a particular alternative that appears to be most desirable of all the given alternatives, it means that the next best alternative has not been chosen. The benefit of the next best alternative, which has been sacrificed due to the choice of the best alternative, is referred to as Opportunity Cost. If there is no sacrifice (monetary or real), then there is no opportunity cost. Monetary costs can be expressed as 'explicit' costs and real costs as 'implicit' costs. Explicit costs are recorded in the book of accounts, such as, the payment to labour, raw material, etc. Imputed or implicit costs are sacrifices, such as, cost of capital supplied by owner himself. The accounting costs include only explicit costs, while opportunity costs include both, the explicit and the implicit; therefore the opportunity cost of an alternative is generally higher than its accounting cost.

3. Principle of Time Perspective

Time Perspective: Economists often differentiate between the two time periods, i.e. the *short-run and the long-run.*

During the short-run, change in output can be achieved by using intensely the fixed inputs (as they cannot be altered), while during the long-run, all inputs can be changed and as such, change in output can be achieved by adjusting the scale of output.

However, managerial economists do not generally follow the theoretical time distinctions- short-run and long-run. To a managerial economist, short period is synonymous with immediate future and long period, to remote future.

From an operational point of view, a manager must make relevant distinction between the present and future implications of his policy.

A case mentioned by Haynes, Mote and Paul about a printing company which wanted to change the "image" that of an exploiter. The policy that it followed was that of never quoting price below full cost, (even when it had idle capacity). The reason was that the long-run consequences of pricing below full cost would offset the short-run gain. In addition, it did not want to present an impression, that the firm wanted to exploit the market when demand was favourable and reduce the price when adequate demand was not forthcoming.

A manager has to decide the time perspective of business options well in advance and execute them at an appropriate time. This will help any business to have success and follow just-in-time (JIT) strategy. Any businessman should avoid unwise decisions on time perspectives. For instance, a long-run preparation of bakery goods by a baker is not a very wise decision. Another example to highlight significance of 'time' factor can be quoted in education. The market demand for education on short-run perception by any University is not an intelligent decision. Here, it has to be long-term projection and long-term growth planning.

Generally, the basis for future actions in business is based on past observations. A foreseeable future action is mostly based on the results obtained in the relevant past period in the business trend analysis.

Short-term Perspectives are based on the short-run analysis of the business data and performance. For this, business cycles (i.e. seasonal fluctuations) are observed and accordingly the course of business is followed within a short period. For example, the advertisement costs are worth undertaking by Insurance Companies during the period of January to March, as it is an effective period of investment. Thus, the service industry (insurance companies) utilises this period for incurring "selling cost". Again, stocking fireworks or making more quantum of sweets during Diwali festival are examples of short-term perspective, as these examples depict short-term demand in the market.

Inventory management is most of the time based on short-term perspectives. For example, schools maintain stationery, answer sheets, guides, books based on the demand for the whole year. In other words, short-term business planning is to maintain business routine with the given business size.

When we think of short-term perspectives, we generally think in terms of circulating or working capital. The areas of business development, its growth, expansion are generally related to long-term perspectives.

It is to be noted that for short-term planning, it is generally the *internal factors* that influence the decision making. But, in the long-run, *external factors* are also considered. For example, a stadium for Pune Warriors India (PWI) built gives long-run perception to the hotel business for expansion and may be more growth in number of hotels around.

The significance of 'time' as a factor determining and influencing decision making cannot be understood lightly, because only an appropriate timely decision can be effective and rewarding.

4. Discounting Principle

The Discounting Principle: The word "discount" indicates something less than its full value. In economics, it is said that a rupee tomorrow is worth less than a rupee today. A *present* gain is valued more than a *future* gain. Even when the future income is certain, yet it must be discounted, as to wait for future, implies a sacrifice for the present. This concept is an extension of the concept of time perspective. The future is uncertain and incalculable and return in future is less attractive than the income in present, hence the future must be *discounted*, both for the elements of delay and risk of future. Thus, while deciding on investments, discounting of future value with the present one is very essential.

Illustration: A person is offered a choice of a gift of ₹ 100 at present or promises ₹ 100 next year. The person is surely going to opt for the present gift rather than promised ₹ 100 in future. The reasons are (a) future is uncertain, (b) even if he is assured of getting ₹ 100 in future, he knows that today's ₹ 100 will fetch him a rate of interest, say 5%. Hence he will prefer the first option as it allows him to earn more in future. In short, a rupee tomorrow is worth less than a rupee today. Now, by how much money today is equal to ₹ 100 one year hence? Suppose the rate of interest is 5%, then we shall discount ₹ 100 at 5% or (1/5) in order to ascertain how much money today will become ₹ 100 one year after. The formula is

$$V = \frac{A}{1 + i}$$

here, V = present value; A = returns expected during a year; i = current rate of interest.

To substitute the value,

$$V = \frac{₹\,100}{1 + i} = \frac{₹\,100}{1 + 0.05} = \frac{₹\,100}{1.05} = ₹\,95.23$$

The value of ₹ 100 in a year hence, after discounting principle, will be ₹ 95.23. And, if we multiply ₹ 95.23 by 1.05, we shall get the money which will accumulate at 5% after one year $95.23 \times 1.05 = 99.99$ (or ₹ 100).

Thus, the discounting principle, in the business decision making process, can be stated as, "If a decision affects costs and revenues at future dates, it is necessary to discount those costs and revenues to present values before a valid comparison of alternatives is possible."

5. Equi-Marginal Principle (Optimisation Technique)

This principle deals with the allocation of available resources among the alternative activities. According to Equi-Marginal principle, "an input should be so allocated that the value added by the last unit is the same in all cases." This 'general' statement is referred to as the optimisation technique or the equi-marginal principle.

"Now, if the value of the marginal product is greater in one activity than in another, then optimal allocation has not been achieved. Hence, it is profitable to shift labour from low marginal value activity to high marginal value activity. In this way, the tool of optimisation technique helps in increasing the total value of all products taken together. For example, if in activity 'A', the value of marginal product of labour ($VMPL_A$) is ₹ 30, while that in activity 'B', ($VMPL_B$) is ₹ 50, it is profitable to shift labour from activity 'A' to activity 'B'. It will reduce activity 'A' and expand activity 'B'.

Thus, Optimisation technique will be reached when $VMPL_A = VMPL_B = VMPL_C = VMPL_D$, i.e. when the value of the marginal product is equal in all four activities.

This principle is very significant in determining optimal condition in resource allocation.

In symbolic terms,

$$VMP_{LA} = VMP_{LB} = VMP_{LC} = VMP_{LD}.$$

Here,   VMPL = value of marginal product of labour; the subscripts $_{A, B, C, D}$ is labour in respective activities.

The application of equi-marginal principle in a business or managerial activity is illustrated in the table below:

Table 1.1: Application of Equi-Marginal Principle

• Multi-product firm (Profit maximisation)	$MPF_1 = MPF_2 = MPF_3$	MPF_n
• Multi-market seller (Sales revenue maximisation).	$MR_1 = MR_2 = MR_3$	MR_n
• Multi-plant firm (Cost minimisation)	$MC_1 = MC_2 = MC_3$	MC_n
• Multi-factor employer. (Marginal product of labour)	$MP_1 = MP_2 = MP_3$	MP_n

Here, MR = marginal revenue; MC = marginal cost; MP = marginal product; MPF = marginal profit earned in product 1, 2, 3 ....n (number product). Thus, n= n markets, plants, factors and products.

In practice, it may not always be possible to have data for each successive (marginal) unit. In such a case, equi-marginal principle will be replaced by the concept of equi-incrementalism.

6. Risks and Uncertainty

It is true that in the real world, uncertainty influences the estimation of costs and revenues and as a result, the decision of the firm. Management deals with decisions that have long-run bearing and since the future conditions are unpredictable largely, there is always a sense of risk and uncertainty about the outcome of such decisions.

In some cases, the risks are known as probability of occurrence, i.e. outcome is known. In such cases, the risks are covered through insurance or hedging. For example, fire insurance, theft insurance. But some risks are immeasurable and the outcomes are unknown. Gambling is one such risk. Again change in demand carries no insurance, this leads to business ups and downs.

Consumers, particularly, risk-averse consumers stick to a brand which they have used and would not like to easily switch over to another new brand. In other words, the consumers usually prefer the current and sure brand against the risky new brand.

Firms diversify to multi-products to minimise the market demand risk. Businesses usually involve risks and uncertainty influencing the mode of decision making. Though market demand may be predicted with some element of certainty, profits and success cannot be predicted with certainty. The decision taken by managers usually depends on scanty information available about the business conditions, thus increasing the uncertainties and risk element. The risk is reduced or averted by the managers by dividing the risks into known and unknown ones.

Thus, unexpected changes in the tastes and preferences of the consumers, environmental changes, changes in the policy of the government, competition from the rival firms in the industry, all these changes have to be accounted, if management wants to take a successful decision.

Economists have attempted to dilute the element of uncertainty with the help of subjective probability. It assumes that the profit expected by undertaking any action, may assume any value within a certain range of values, each value having an associated probability of being realised. The decision-maker assigns these subjective probabilities to the possible profits of each action or strategy and estimates its mathematical expectations. However, due to its practical and theoretical inadequacy, different firms with different time horizons and with different risk attitudes respond differently to even the same conditions of uncertainty.

7. Marginal Analysis

Since the resources are scarce with the manager, he has to utilise every unit of resource (inputs) in the best possible manner. In order to decide on the use of an additional man-hour or machine-hour, he needs to know what the additional output is expected therefrom. Thus, *marginal analysis means that the value of the marginal product of the labour should be equal to the value of the marginal product of capital.*

In terms of formula, we can say that,

$$\frac{MRP - A}{P - A} = \frac{MRP - B}{P - B} = \frac{MRP - C}{P - C} \text{ etc.}$$

Where, MRP = Marginal revenue productivity; A, B, C = factors of inputs; and

P-A, P-B, P-C = prices of factors A, B and C respectively.

8. Economic Model

A model refers to the theoretical environment assumed by an economist who wishes to work out the relationships between variables in precisely known conditions.

An economist has to study the relationships among economic variables in a world which is highly complex and complicated. There are thousands of economic forces at work in the economy and it poses a problem for the economist, to isolate the economic variables from those economic forces in which he is not interested. It means that, if the economist is to work out relationships among economic variables, in which he is interested, he will have to isolate these economic variables. For this purpose the economist builds models. A model is, thus, a simplification of reality.

For instance, an economist has to study the pricing of oranges. The prices of oranges are influenced by a number of factors. The analysis will be complex if all factors are taken into account. To simplify the analysis, the economist has to build a model of orange-pricing. It will include only the most essential factors, influencing the prices of oranges either from the demand side or supply side.

In short, in economics, a model is a theoretical construction that represents economic processes by a set of variables and a set of logical and quantitative relationship between them.

(9) Statics and Dynamics

Statics refers to that type of analysis where we establish the functional relations between two variables whose values relate to the *same point of time* or the same period of time. Thus, economic statics is the study of static relationship between relevant variables.

Dynamics refers to that analysis which considers the relationship between relevant variables whose values belong to *different points of time*. Thus, it can be said that economic statics is concerned with economic phenomenon *independently* of the time element. Economic dynamics is concerned with phenomenon which *varies with the element of time*.

The method of economic statics, depicts a 'still' picture of the national economy with all its inter-sectoral relationships at a particular moment of time. There is no attempt to present a glimpse of either the preceding or succeeding events of the economy.

The method of economic dynamics is a method which pictures the entire series of adjustments which take place between the break-up of the old equilibrium and the establishment of the new. Dynamics presents a continuous picture of the working of any national economy.

Thus, Statics excludes the time element; and Dynamics gives due consideration to the time element.

1.11 Basic Economic Problem

The main problem of an economy is of economising scarce resources. *Economics is the study of the allocation of scarce resources to alternative ends.*

The 'scarcity' problem arises due to the fact that human wants are numerous and the means to satisfy them are limited. This definitely involves the problem of '*choice*'. It is the choice of selecting alternative uses to which scarce resources can be put. The solution to this problem i.e. allocation of scarce resources lies in the '*pricing system*' which exists in every economic system- capitalist, socialist or mixed.

However, we first discuss the fundamental economic problems that every economy faces.

(a) What to produce and in what quantities?

(b) How to produce these goods?

(c) For whom are the goods produced?

(d) How efficiently are the resources being utilised?

(e) Is the economy growing?

(a) What to produce and in what quantities? (i.e. allocation of resources)

The first and the foremost problem is to decide what goods and services are to be produced and in what quantities. In other words, it is the problem of allocation of scarce resources.

As the resources are scarce, an economy has to decide about the goods to be produced like cloth, food grains, power, buildings, electronic items and so on. Once the society decides the nature of goods to be produced, it now has to take a decision regarding their quantities. How much of rice to be produced? How many KWS of power to be generated? Since the resources of the economy are scarce, the problem of as to what to produce and how much of it depends on the priorities of the society. If the economy gives preference to the production of more consumer goods now, it will have less in the future. On the other hand, more of capital goods mean less of consumer goods now. It is obvious the decision what the economy will decide will depend on the requirements of the country concerned. Every country has to decide what combinations of goods it shall produce in view of the limited economic resources at its disposal.

Let us explain the problem with the help of the production possibility curve.

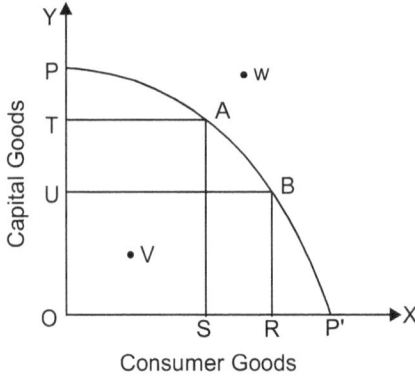

Fig. 1.1: Production Possibility Curve

The economy has to produce a combination of capital and consumer goods. It cannot choose the combination 'V' as it shows the inefficiency of the economy in employing its resources. 'V' lies inside the PP' curve.

It cannot choose 'W' as it is outside the current Production Possibility Curve i.e. in relation to its resources, the economy lacks the resources to produce this combination.

It will therefore, have to choose among the combinations A or B which gives the maximum level of satisfaction. If the economy goes for more capital goods it will choose combination 'A' and if it chooses consumer goods, it will choose the combination 'B'.

(b) How to produce these goods? (Alternate techniques exploitation of resources)

The second basic economic problem is to decide about the methods to be used to produce the required goods. This problem is mainly dependent upon the resources available within the economy. If there is surplus labour, it is a labour intensive technique. If land is abundant, extensive cultivation is possible.

The technique/method to be used also depends upon the type and quantity of goods to be produced. For instance, for producing capital goods and to have large output, complex and expensive machines and methods are required. On the other hand, simple consumer goods or smaller outputs need less expensive machines and simpler techniques.

It is also to be decided what goods and services are to be produced in the public sector and what in private sector.

On the whole it can be said that the methods adopted should bring about an efficient allocation of resources and that would increase the overall productivity in the economy.

Let us suppose the economy is producing certain quantities of capital and consumer goods at point X on PP_0. curve.

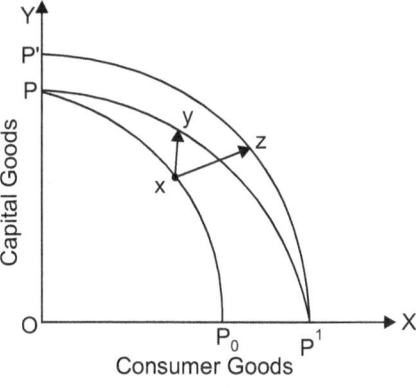

Fig. 1.2

When the economy adopts new techniques, with given factors, the productive efficiency rises, outwards to P'P'. As a result more can be produced of both the types of goods from point X (PP_0. curve) to point Z (on P^1P^1 curve).

If, suppose, the new techniques are used to produce only consumer goods, then PP' will be the new production possibility curve of the economy and the economy will move from point X to Y where more of both the goods are produced.

(c) For whom are the goods produced? (Distribution)

The third economic problem is the allocation of goods among the members of the society.

The allocation of basic consumer goods, necessaries, comforts, luxuries among the household takes place on the basis of among the distribution of national income. Now, whosoever possesses the means to buy goods may have them. For instance, a rich person may have a large share of the luxury goods while the poor person may have more quantities of the basic consumer goods.

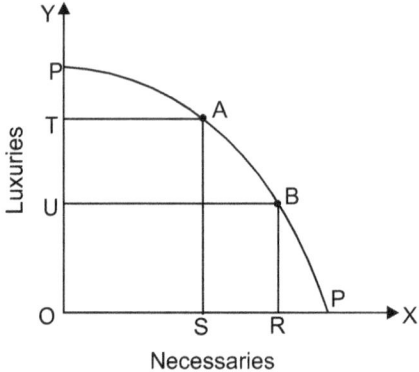

Fig. 1.3

The production possibility curve PP depicts the combinations of luxuries and necessaries. At point A, the economy produces more of luxuries (OT) and less of necessaries (OS) i.e. less for poor class and more production for rich class.

On the other hand, the situation is just the reverse at point 'B' more of necessaries (OR) and less of luxuries.

(d) How efficiently are the productive resources being utilised?

The society has to decide whether the resources it owns are being used efficiently. If any resource - land, capital, and human resource is left idle, then the society has to adopt such a policy (monetary, fiscal) whereby the resources are fully utilised.

An economy enjoys full employment or technical efficiency, when it fully utilises its resources.

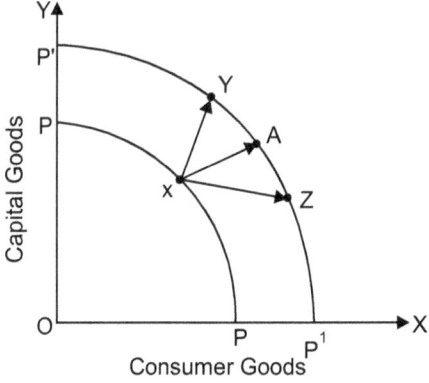

Fig. 1.4

PP, production possibility curve shows idleness of resources within the economy. On P'P' there is fuller uitlisation of resources (at point Y or Point Z).

The economy may choose Pt. Y for more capital goods or Pt. Z for more consumer goods or combination of both types of goods at Pt. A. All these 3 points on P'P' curve represent full employment of resources.

(e) Is the productive capacity of the economy increasing?

The last problem is to find out whether the economy is growing or is it stagnant through time.

Economic growth takes place through a higher rate of capital formation i.e. replacing the existing capital goods and also adding new and more capital goods by adopting innovative techniques.

Referring to the same Fig. 1.4, the outward shifting of the production possibility curve PP to P'P' represents growth in the economy. The economy now produces more from point X to Y or Z on P'P' curve. Point 'A' shows greater production of both the consumer and capital goods.

To sum up, all these basic economic problems are interrelated. *They arise from the fact that the resources are scarce and wants are multiple which leads to the problem of 'choice'.*

The solution to these five basic problems lies in the price mechanism.

1.11.1 Application of Managerial Economics in Managerial Decision Making

The prime function of any management executive in a business organisation is decision making. *Decision-making means the process of making a choice of one action from two or more alternative courses of action.*

The decision making function becomes one of making choices that will provide the most efficient means of attaining a desired end and profit maximisation. Once a decision is made about a particular goal to be achieved, then plans as to production, pricing, capital, raw materials, labour, etc., are prepared.

Why is decision making or selection of a choice so important?

- A manager has to take a number of decisions in conformity with the goals of the firm. That is, based on the goal of the firm, decisions have to be taken.

- Many business decisions are taken under the conditions of uncertainty and thus involve risk.

- Uncertainty and risk arise mainly because of changes in demand and supply conditions, changing business environment, government policy, social and political changes in the country.

- The degree of uncertainty and risk can be greatly reduced if market conditions could be predicted with a high degree of reliability. Equally important is to take appropriate business decisions and to formulate business strategy conforming to the goals of the firm. Thus, an appropriate decision becomes crucial to tide over the uncertainties of business.

The application of economics to business management, as put forward by Spencer and Siegelman is stated below:

(a) In economic theory, the technique of analysis is one of model building based on certain assumptions and on that basis conclusions such as to the behaviour of the firms are drawn. These assumptions make the theory of the firm unrealistic as it fails to provide a satisfactory explanation of what the firms actually do.

In actual business, certain terms like profits and costs have accounting concepts as different from economic concepts. In managerial economics, an attempt is made to reconcile the accounting concepts with the economic concepts so that financial data pertaining to profits and costs can be used more effectively to suit the needs of decision making and forward planning.

(b) **Decisions** in measurement of various types of elasticity of demand such as price elasticity, income elasticity, cross elasticity, cost-output relationships, etc.

(c) **Forecasting** relevant economic quantities, i.e., profit, demand, production, capital, etc., in numerical terms together with their probabilities. In the light of the predicted estimates, decision making and forward planning may be possible.

(d) **Using Economic Quantities** in decision making and forward planning. For any business manager there exists a quantified picture indicating the number of courses open, and their possible outcomes and also the quantified probability of each outcome. So he decides about the strategy to be chosen.

(e) A business manager has to **appraise the relevance and impact of external** forces, e.g., business cycles, government policies, international economics, government policies, foreign trade, labour relations, industrial licensing, price controls, monetary economics, etc., related to the particular business unit and its business policies.

In short, managerial economics shows how to apply economic concepts and theories of business, decision making and planning.

1.12 Circular Flow of Economic Activity (How Markets Solve the Economic Problems - Market Forces in Solving Economic Problems)

The basic economic problem of a society is of harnessing the scarce resources for the satisfaction of maximum wants.

An economic problem can be solved after taking decisions regarding production and distribution.

Production:

(a) What commodities and services to be produced?

(b) In what quantity are the commodities and services to be produced?

(c) Who is to produce?

(d) For production, which resources will be required and in what quantities?

(e) How are these resources to be mobilised?

(f) How are the resources to be allocated to the most productive activity?

(g) What techniques of production are to be used for efficient utilisation of resources?

Distribution:

(a) In what proportion are the goods produced to be distributed?

(b) What is to be the level of employment in the society and the level of income and consumption of goods and services for the people?

Every society, depending upon the economic and political ideology, will devise the essential institutions and will resort to mechanism to arrive at the decisions to solve the economic problems.

The institutional framework may be in the form of a capitalist economy, a socialist economy or a mixed economy.

The mechanisms evolved in the above mentioned institutional framework, to arrive at decisions are customs, command (central direction) and market mechanism within the chosen framework (capitalist, socialist or mixed economy), one or more of these mechanisms may be resorted to. For example, central planning authority or central direction mechanism is dominant in a socialist economy while market mechanism in a capitalist economy.

The different methods of mechanisms to solve the economic problem of resources adjustment are:

(i) Customs (or Traditions): Customs refer to old practices or traditions of a society. It is the most primitive method of solving economic problems. In a tradition bound economy, economic activities of production and distribution are governed by the procedures devised by customs, traditions and conventions (habits). These procedures become established through their long usage and become like unwritten laws. In earlier times, the wants were few, less complicated and villages were economically self sufficient. As such, the basic economic problems could be solved by custom through simple economic activities.

A tradition - dominant economy is static in nature. It operates automatically. It provides stability and security by taking care of the minimum needs of the people in a customary and traditional manner. Such an economy allows *no individual economic freedom*. For example, employment was mostly decided by castes in a caste ridden society. Such a rigid economy cannot adjust itself to the needs of a modern industrial economy and fails to solve its economic problems.

(ii) Central Direction (or Central Planning Authority): In many economies, central direction or command mechanism has been practiced since early times, to solve the basic economic problems. Under central control mechanism, production and distribution activity is organised by a delegated authority like a king, a director, or a central planning authority. Central direction implies a system of authoritarian economic organisation.

Some of the distinct characteristics of a modern command based economy are:

- Government intervention
- Economic security
- Planning and dynamism
- Purpose

(iii) Price-Mechanism (or Market Mechanism): Free price mechanism or *market mechanism is an important method of solving economic problems.* Such an economy, having market mechanism, is referred to as a market economy or free enterprise system or a capitalist economy.

In such a market oriented economy, the adjustment between the forces of demand and supply is brought about by the free movement of prices. It is the price-mechanism which reflects consumer's decisions of what to consume. Movement of prices also guides private individuals regarding major economic decisions as to what to produce, how much to produce and the distribution activity. In this way, *'prices'* in the market co-ordinate the decisions of the producers and the consumers and brings about the equilibrium between the two forces of the market i.e. the demand and the supply. It is the price mechanism that allocates the productive resources of the economy in the channels elected by consumers (through their demand) and distribution of national income.

The steering wheel of market mechanism is *'self-interest'* i.e. private profit and such a system is automatic in operation.

Market-mechanism's essential features are:

- Right to private property
- Freedom of enterprise
- Freedom of choice
- Pursuit of self-interest
- Perfect competition
- Limited role of government (or policy of laissez faire and non-intervention by the government).

According to **Adam Smith**, *it is the invisible hands of market mechanism that automatically brings optimum adjustments of resources.*

However, in practice, no economy is based purely on customs, central command or absolute market mechanism. Several elements of all these mechanisms are present in a lesser or greater degree in all the economies. In this way, *all modern economies are mixed economies* in a broad way. But, it can be said that an economy is described as capitalist, socialist or mixed by its predominant element. For example, it is price mechanism (or free market) dominantly deciding the economic activities, then it is referred as a capitalist economy.

The price mechanism works in a free market economy through demand and supply of goods in competitive markets. These, in turn, are determined by their prices. Prices determine production and distribution of goods and services.

(A) Allocation of Resources: One of the primary functions of the market mechanism is allocation of resources. Resources are scarce and have alternate uses; they must be used both wisely and economically.

The problem of allocating resources among various uses is nothing but answering the question 'what to produce?' An economy must produce the right combination of goods and services. Should it produce wheat and rice or colour TV sets or should the economy produce vegetables etc. Alongwith what to produce, the question 'how much' is also relevant in allocation of resources.

The market mechanism serves to establish prices of products and resources. *Producers are guided by the objective of profit maximisation*. They would, therefore, produce those goods which fetch profits and avoid production of goods which involve losses. Product prices provide the information necessary for calculating the total receipts the entrepreneurs can expect to receive. Resource prices (i.e. rent, wages interest and normal profits) furnish the data for calculating the total costs that the entrepreneurs will have to incur.

Since profits are the difference between total receipts and total cost, higher the receipts, more attractive will be the production of a commodity. The scarce resources will be transferred from less profitable units. *Profits, thus, cause an expansion of an industry and losses cause a decline of the concerned industry*. It also thus, decides the right combination of goods and services.

The right type of goods to be produced and in what quantities is decided by the consumers. When consumers enjoy a freedom of choice, they demand whatever they want. Every rupee that a consumer spends acts like a 'rupee vote' in favour of the product he demands. An increase in the rupee votes in favour of a product means a rise in its price and subsequent rise in profits of the firm producing that product. Some other product, getting fewer 'rupee votes' will involve losses to producers and thus gets rejected. This is how the rupee-votes of consumers play a key role in the determination of how resources will be allocated and what products will be produced. Thus, the consumer is said to be the king in a market economy.

In this way, the freedom enjoyed by firms is not unrestricted. Firms have to match their production choices to consumer choices. Those firms which do so get rewarded with profits.

Similarly, the freedom of households as resource-suppliers is also limited. The demand for resources (or factors) is a *'derived demand'*. It is derived from the demand for goods and services which the resource helps to produce. Guided by the price system, firms produce those goods which are preferred by the consumers and for productions of those goods they demand resources. Households, as resource-suppliers, are thus not free to sell their resources to the firms who produce goods which are not demanded by the consumers as such firms do not remain in the market.

In this way, producers and resource-suppliers (or factors) respond appropriately to the demand of the consumer. And, the demand of the consumer is communicated in the market through price-system. *Thus, the market mechanism with its price-system steers the resources to the industries whose products have a demand by the buyers and the firms make profits.* At the same time, scarce resources are withdrawn from those industries whose products consumers do not want.

The different prices which consumers pay for various commodities and services reflect the value of the goods to the producers i.e. which goods (capital or consumer) should be produced in larger supply.

With the change in consumer's tastes and preferences the prices change. The consumers register their preference towards commodities by paying more for them and show distaste by paying less for the others. E.g. typing when done on computers is paid more by the consumer than the work done on typewriters. It is a clear preference by the consumer.

Thus, a change in the price of a commodity acts like a warning signal for the producer or even the consumer. For instance, rise in the price warns the consumer to buy less but it guides the producer to produce more of it. The industry will show promising profits. Resource owners will shift their resources to a high-priced industry. Now, when more firms in the industry produce, supply increases more than the demand and price falls. While, on the other hand, when resources are withdrawn from the low priced commodity, it brings a fall in its output. But, in the long-run, due to shifting of consumer demand towards it, there is a rise in price. This will continue till both the commodities are equally priced and thus offer equal profit to the producers in the two industries.

On the other hand, if the price falls, it is a warning to the producers to produce less and an invitation to the buyers to buy more. The profits are low and induce the sellers to shift resources to high-priced industry. The tendency in the long-run will be that the supply will reduce in low priced commodity whereas the demand increases. As a result, price tends to rise. At the same time, in high-priced goods where resources were diverted, supply rises; demand is less and in the long-run price tends to fall.

In short, consumer is the sovereign. The more the producer produces, larger the profits they can earn and also the resource owners. But, if the consumer has no preference for his product, he has to set a low price. Thus, the producer reacts to the consumers' response and allocates his resources accordingly.

The next task of prices is to determine the techniques to be used for the production of commodities. For their services rendered, the factors receive rewards in the form of 'factor prices'. For instance, wage is the price for the services of labour, rent is the price for the service of land, interest to capital and profit to an entrepreneur. These altogether (rent, wages, interest, profit) make up the costs of production.

An economically efficient production process is one which produces goods with the minimum of costs. *The choice of production process depends upon the relative prices of the factor services and the quantity of goods to be produced.*

In order to reduce costs of production, the producer substitutes cheaper resources for the dearer ones. For instance, if labour is relatively cheaper than capital, labour-intensive production processes will be used. In developing economies where capital is scarce and labour is relatively cheap, techniques that involve more labour are least cost methods. And, in developed economies where labour is relatively expensive, it is labour saving and capital – using techniques are used, which prove efficient and least costs.

In a free market economy, single price rules, thus, those firms incapable of paying minimum rewards to resources close down or divert resources to production of some other commodity.

Technology is also influenced by the *type and quantity of goods to be produced.* For instance, for producing capital goods and larger outputs, the techniques will involve complicated and expensive machines. On the other hand, simple consumer goods and small outputs would need a comparatively simple technique.

(B) Income Distribution: Yet another function of *prices is to determine the distribution of income.* In a market economy, product distribution and income distribution are interdependent. The owners of factors sell their services for income and then spend that income to buy the goods produced by factor services. Producers sell goods and services to consumer for money and consumers receive income as owners of factor services. In this way, the income flows from consumers (as resource owners) to producers and back to consumers again. This is explained with the help of the circular flow of income.

Prices play an important role in this income flow.

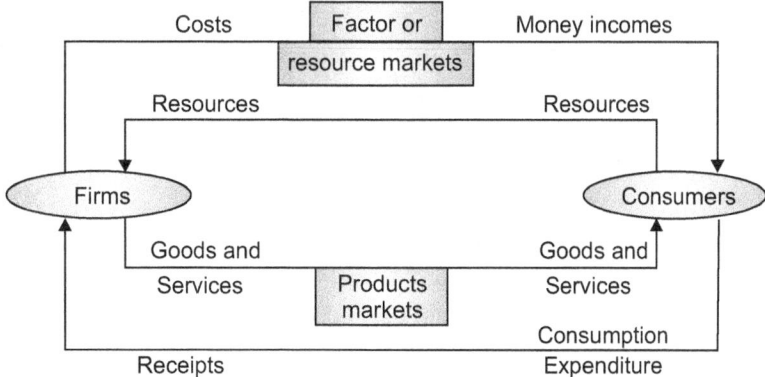

Fig. 1.5: Resource and Product Markets

When consumers purchase goods, it is their cost of living. When producers sell goods, it is their business receipts. What consumers receive as owners of factor-services, it is their personal income and it is producer's cost of production when producers pay for factor-services.

In other words, income of an individual depends upon the amount of resources owned by him. People owning large quantities of resources have high incomes and they contribute more to the production of goods which satisfy the consumers. And, people owning small quantities of resources have low incomes. They contribute little to the production of goods which satisfy the consumers.

Such differences in income are automatically corrected on its own. Since no individual would prefer to receive low income for long, the workers will move from low-income category to seek employment in an industry which pays higher wages. As a result, there is fall in the supply of workers in low-wages paid industry and increase in the supply of high-wages industry. Reduction in supply raises the price of the goods, increases the profits of the producer and worker's income. On the other hand, where the supply of workers has increased, the supply of goods will increase, price falls, and profits reduce and thus reduce the worker's income. This process continues till wage differences disappear.

Thus, prices not only determine income distribution but also bring its equality.

Efficient utilisation of Resources: The price mechanism also helps in fuller utilisation of the resources of an economy. Full employment of resources means fuller utilisation of resources.

In a growing economy saving and investment are equated by reduction in interest rates. When the economy is nearing the level of full employment by an efficient use of resources, income grows and so do the savings level. But, investment lags and to equate with savings, interest has to be reduced. Thus, the rate of interest acts as on equilibrating mechanism. However, in the economy, for full employment, only rate of interest cannot be relied upon and then needed are the monetary, fiscal and physical controls to influence the decisions of consumers and producers regarding saving and investment.

To provide an incentive to growth in the economy: Prices are an important factor in providing for economic growth. It is the price mechanism that encourages innovation and development.

Higher prices and profits encourage industries to spend more on research and develop better techniques.

The adaptation of the economic system to change in wants, techniques and so on takes place through prices. Larger profits in any industry lead to the adoption of modern technology which lowers the costs. The twin conditions - larger profits and low costs – attract new producers who provide new capital. This results in capital formation.

Economic growth depends upon a number of other factors, yet prices play an important role in providing for economic growth with stability.

To sum up, the price mechanism, working through demand and supply in a free economy acts as the principal organising force.

It is the *'price'* that determines what to produce and how much to produce, allocates the resources, brings about an equitable distribution of income.

1.13 Nature of the Firm (Rationale of a Firm)

It is significant to know the theory of firm behaviour as it is the centrepiece and central theme of managerial economics.

A Firm is an organisation that combines and organises the resources or factors of production with the aim of producing goods and/or services for sale.

There are a large number of firms in India. These include firms on proprietorship (i.e., firms owned by one individual), partnership firms (i.e., firms owned by two or more individuals) and Corporations (firms owned by stockholders). Firms produce more than two-thirds of all goods and services consumed in India. The balance is produced by the Government and not-for-profit organisations (hospitals, museums, foundations etc.).

The existence of firms is profit, as without it, it would be costly and inefficient for entrepreneurs to enter into and enforce contracts with workers and owners of factors like capital, land and other resources needed for each separate step of the production and distribution process. Entrepreneurs usually enter into longer term, broader contracts with labour to perform a number of tasks for specific wages and fringe benefits. Such a general contract (with the firm) is much less costly than many specific contracts and is highly beneficial, both to the entrepreneurs and to the workers and other resource owners. Thus, the firm exists to save on such transaction costs.

Further, by performing many functions within the firm, it saves on sales tax and avoids price controls and other government regulations that apply only to transactions among firms.

However, a firm, due to limitations on management's ability to effectively control and guide the operation of a 'large' firm, does not continue to grow larger and larger indefinitely. In other words, beyond a point, the large-size of the firm brings in diseconomies to that firm. It is true that up to a point, a firm can overcome these internal disadvantages of large-size or diseconomies of scale by decentralising the functions or setting up a number of semi-autonomous divisions. But, eventually the communication traffic, long distances between top management from the operation of each division, brings in diseconomies to the growth of a firm and thus limits its size to indefinite growth. The firm will reach a point where the cost of supplying additional (marginal) services within the firm *exceeds* the cost of purchasing these services from other firms.

Therefore, the function of firms is to purchase the inputs/factors of production like labour services, capital and raw materials to transform them into goods and services for sale. The owners of resources/factors of production (labour, capital-owners, landlords and raw materials) in turn use the goods and services produced by firms, thus completes *the circular flow of economic activity.*

The function of the firm highlights on the fact that in the process of supplying the goods and services and satisfying the demands of the society, the firm provides employment to workers and pay taxes, which the government utilises to provide various public services like education, health, infrastructure, national defence, etc. Such services cannot be provided at all or as efficiently as government units can.

1.14 Objective and Value of the Firm

The theory of the firm is the crux of the study of Managerial Economics, as it proves to be the base for analysing managerial decision making. Originally, the theory of the firm was based on the assumption that the objective of the firm was to maximise the short term or the present profits. Many managers complain of the pressure to report profits every year or every quarter that forces them to take actions that are not very conducive to the long-term profitability of the firm. Thus, it has been observed that firms sacrifice short-run profits for the increasing long-term or future profits. Expenditure on R & D, new capital equipment etc., are examples of the change in objectives of the firm (i.e. long-term profits). However, both short-term and long-term profits are significant, therefore, the theory of the firm emphasises that the primary objective of the firm is to maximise the wealth or value of the firm. This is given by the present value of all expected future profits of the firm. Future profits must be discounted to the present because a rupee of profit in the future is worth less than a rupee of profit today. Example, a ₹ 1 investment today at 10 percent interest will grow to ₹ 1.10 in one year. Thus, ₹ 1 can be defined as the current or present value of ₹ 1.10 due in 1 year.

Thus, the value (or wealth) of the firm is stated as --------

$$CV = \frac{\pi_1}{(1+r)^2} + \frac{\pi_2}{(1+r)^2} + \dots + \frac{\pi_n}{(1+r)^n} \qquad \dots (1)$$

$$= \sum_{t=1}^{n} \frac{\pi_t}{(1+r)^2} \qquad \dots (2)$$

Where,

CV = current (present) value of all expected future profits of the firm

$\pi_1, \pi_2, \pi_3, \dots \pi_n$ = expected profits in each of the considered n years

r = appropriate discount rate used to find the current value of future profits

$\sum$ = summation of

t = values from 1 up to the n years considered

Thus, in equation (2) $\sum_{t=1}^{n} \frac{\pi_t}{(1+r)^t}$ is a summation of $\frac{\pi_t}{(1+r)^t}$ terms resulting from substituting the values of 1 to n for t. In other words eq. 2 is equal to eq. 1 but in a abbreviated form.

The introduction of time dimension in equations 1 and 2 allows for the considerations of uncertainty. For e.g. if there is greater scope of uncertainty in the expected future profits, and the firm has used, as such, higher discounted rate, then smaller the present value of the firm.

As we know profit is obtained by deducting total cost (TC) from total revenue (TR), (P = TR – TC), thus eq. 2 can be rewritten as

$$\text{Value of the firm} = \sum_{t=1}^{n} \frac{TR_t - TC_t}{(1 + r)^t} \qquad \text{... (3)}$$

Thus, equation (3) provides a unified theme for the analysis of managerial decision making. Total revenue depends on the sales or on the demand for the firm's output and on the firm's pricing decisions.

The objective of the firm to maximise the value of the firm is the responsibility of –

- The marketing department
- The total cost that again depends on the technology of production and resource prices;
- On the production and personnel, i.e. human resource department;
- The discount rate (r) that depends on the perceived risk of the firm and on the cost of borrowing funds;
- Responsibility of the finance department.

The equation (as mentioned above 1 to 3) of calculating the current/present value of all expected future profits of the firm could be used to organise the discussion of how the various departments within the firm interact with one another. For instance, the marketing department can have cost reduction associated with a given output level by promoting off-season sales. The other department, say the HR department can stimulate sales by improvement in quality and by developing new products. The accounting department can, based on this equation, provide more timely information on sales and costs. All these activities increase the firm's efficiency and reduce its risk, thereby allowing the firm to use a lower discount rate (r) to determine the present value of its expected future profits that will increase the worth of the firm.

Limitations: However, the firm faces many limitations in attaining its objective of maximising the value (worth) of the firm. The constraints arise from limitations on the availability of essential inputs.

- A firm, in the short-run, might not be able to hire as many skilled workers as it wants;
- The firm may not be able to acquire all the specific raw materials as it needs;
- Limitations on factory and warehouse space;
- Limitations in the quantity of capital funds available for a given project;
- Besides resource constraints, the firm may also face many legal constraints. For example, minimum wage laws, health and safety standards, pollution emission standards, laws and regulations that prevents firms from employing unfair business practices.

The existence of these limitations restricts the range of possibilities of action of the firm and limits the value of the firm to a level that is lower. The absence of limitations would lead the firm to attain *unconstrained optimisation*. However, if it is within these constraints, the firm seeks to maximise its value. The Government and not-for-profit firms' goal may be other than wealth or value maximisation but they too face certain limitations in achieving their goals.

1.15 Maximising, Satisficing, Optimising

There are three styles or strategies of decision making.

Under a **maximising approach**, the decision maker chooses the action whose consequences are best for the case at hand. "Best" refers to some value, that the decision maker holds. The action chosen by the decision maker is 'best' in relation to the constraints, taking into account the direct costs and opportunity costs of decision making. This approach may be referred to as *optimising rather than maximising*. Because the maximiser focuses only on the case at hand, the optimiser acts to maximise value over an array of cases.

In contrast to both approaches, satisficing permits any decision whose results in the case at hand are good enough (although we will see that satisficing, like optimising, may itself represent an indirect strategy of maximisation).

The implication of these three different decision making strategies: maximising, means an effort to find the very best choice, all things considered, in the particular decision making context at hand; optimising, or maximisation that takes into account the direct costs and opportunity costs of acquiring information and making decisions.

Optimising and Satisficing are different ways of pursuing the same larger aim. Both strategies are based on an implicit recognition that to do what is 'best', overall, with respect to some particular decision in an array of decisions, is to do something that may not be globally best, or best from some larger perspective. In other words, both strategies are second-order (maximising) because the decision maker may do best to choose in a way that is *less than maximally* best with respect to the local decision at hand.

However, optimising and satisficing are different second-order decision strategies. The two strategies employ different stopping rules, or rules for constraining further search among possible options. For example, the optimiser stops searching when the marginal benefit of finding a better option, discounted by the probability of finding such an option, is equal to or less than the costs of further search. Moreover, the satisficer stops searching when he finds a good option.

Maximising is the ultimate standard: the maximiser does what is best, overall, taking into account the totality of the circumstances relevant to the local decision at hand. Optimising and Satisficing strategies both appeal to the higher-order virtues of rules, to the idea that a decision maker who takes into account less than the full set of considerations that bear on a particular decision may for a range of reasons do better, over a whole array of decisions, than does the simpleminded maximiser.

Illustration: Three decision theorists—M(Maximiser),O(Optimiser) and S(Satisficer)—enter the main university cafeteria, which holds twenty or above separate stations, each of which offers a different type of cuisine.

M is a simpleminded maximiser who seeks the most satisfying possible meal right now; M spends the next hour visiting each station, pondering possible choices, and so on. (By the time, M is done choosing his meal, O and S have finished eating and both are back in their offices working).

O is a second-order maximiser, who sees that maximising his satisfaction from this particular meal is suboptimal from an overall perspective. O thus adopts a stopping rule that is calculated to optimise his satisfaction, taking into account decision costs and opportunity costs. Calculating the *marginal costs and benefits*, O decides to visit five randomly selected stations out of the possible twenty, and then to choose from within this set the station whose offering maximises the satisfaction of O's tastes.

S is also a second-order maximiser, but he employs a different stopping rule: S proceeds along the stations until he finds an offering that is good enough, and then stops searching.

Although O and S may happen to light upon the same offering, and although it is true that both O and S manage to avoid the plight of the obsessive and self-defeating M, they have used different strategies to that end.

Of course, no maximiser really considers all things. M will eventually choose a meal, rather than spending an infinite amount of time evaluating micro-features of the alternatives. Yet M may spend far more time and effort on this local choice than would be justified from a second-order, globally maximising perspective.

1.16 Principal Agent Problem

Meaning: Principal-agent problem is a particular game-theoretic description of a situation.

In business, the decision taken of setting the price and output may not be realised where there is a divorce between ownership and control, as it can be difficult to monitor. How do the owners of a business know that managers making key day-to-day decisions are operating to maximise shareholder value?

This lack of information is known as the **principal-agent problem**. In other words, one person, the principal, hires an agent (e.g. a sales or finance manager) to perform tasks on his behalf but he cannot ensure that the agent performs them in precisely, the way the principal would like. The decisions and the performance of the agent are at times impossible and or expensive to monitor.

Examples of the principal-agent problem that have hit the financial headlines include the management of financial assets on behalf of investors (e.g. any cooperative bank or life insurance companies) and the management of companies on behalf of shareholders (e.g. during the turbulent years experienced by Marks and Spencer).

Another example drawn from the public sector might be the efficient and effective running of public services such as education, health, and transport in India, run by private firms under government regulation.

Thus, there is a player called a principal, and one or more other players called agents with utility functions that are in some sense different from that of the principal.

The principal can act more effectively through the agents than directly, and must construct incentive schemes to get them to behave at least partly according to the principal's interests. The principal-agent problem is that of designing the incentive scheme. The actions of the agents may not be observable, so it is not usually sufficient for the principal just to condition payment on the actions of the agents.

For example, if you (the principal) hire a gardener (your agent) to mow your lawn while you are away, all you can observe is how the lawn looks when you come back. He could have mowed it every ten days, as you agreed, or he could have waited until two days before you were due home and mowed it only once. By prevailing on a neighbour to monitor your employee's behaviour, you could find out what he actually did, although at some cost.

In another example, when one hires a solicitor, however, it is almost impossible for him to monitor the solicitor's efforts and diligence, he has not studied law, and much of what the solicitor does will be a mystery to him.

This latter situation is close to the relationship that exists between shareholders and managers. The managers have information and expertise that the shareholders do not have, indeed, that is why they are the managers. The shareholders can observe profits, but they cannot directly observe the managers' efforts. To complicate matters further, even when the managers' behaviour can be observed, the shareholders do not generally have the expertise to evaluate it. Everyone can see the firm's revenues, but it takes very detailed knowledge to estimate how large those revenues could have been, if the managers had acted differently. Boards of directors, who represent the firm's shareholders, can acquire some of the relevant expertise and monitor managerial behaviour, but again this is costly. These illustrations exhibit the principal-agent problem.

The principal-agent problem is the problem of *designing mechanisms that will induce agents to act in their principals' interests*. In general, it is observed that unless there is costly monitoring of agents' behaviour, the problem cannot be completely solved. Hired managers (like hired gardeners) will generally wish to pursue their own goals. They cannot ignore profits, however, because if they perform badly enough they will lose their jobs. Just how much latitude they have to pursue their own goals at the expense of profits depends on many things, including the degree of competition in the industry and the possibility of takeover by more profit-oriented management.

The principal-agent problem arises within the firm when ownership and control are separated and the self-interest of managers may lead them to act other than in the interest of the shareholders. The problem is to design monitoring or incentive systems that will make managers act in the best interest of the shareholders.

The way in which agents can be encouraged to act in the interest of principals is by the introduction of incentives to align the objectives of the two. There are at least three ways in which this is done in firms today. Thus, we discuss the strategies available for coping with the principal agent problem.

- The first way to align the interests of shareholders and managers is to ensure that managers themselves have an interest in the value of the shares. This can be done either by ensuring that managers buy (or are perhaps given) some shares or by giving them share options which will create wealth for the managers when the value of the firms' shares rises above some value. Some companies encourage a wide range of their employees to buy shares in the company through company savings schemes, in order to give these employees an interest in the profit of the company and not just in their own wage. Thus, there should be rapid expansion of employee share-ownership schemes. Ryan Air one of Europe's fastest growing low-cost airlines offered its pilots a share-scheme for the first time in January 2001. The deal entails a 15% rise in basic pay over five years for the more than 220 pilots as well as share options and a productivity agreement.

- A second way to give managers a shared interest in profit is by tying some part of their remuneration directly to the firm's profits. This could be an annual bonus that is linked to the previous year's profit of the company as a whole, or it could be some explicit share of the profit of the part of the company in which that manager works.

- A third way of achieving the alignment is to make promotion subject to the profits of the company as a whole or to the section in which the person is employed. Those who succeed in increasing profits in their divisions thus will get on well. Thus, in offsetting the principal agent problem there can be introduction of other variants of performance-related pay or long-term employment contracts for senior management.

1.17 Accounting Profit and Economic Profit

There are two ways of measuring profits: *Accounting profit* and *Economic profit.*

Profit is regarded as the revenue realised during the period minus the cost and expenses incurred in producing the revenue. This profit is known as 'residual concept'. Thus, Profits = TR − TC, where TR = Total Revenue; TC = Total Costs.

However, profit, the concept as used by the economists, is different from accounting profit.

The first way is to measure is based on what we actually receive (accounting profit) and the other is to trade off what we actually received with what we could have received (economic profit).

An accounting profit is the excess of business income over the business expenses, i.e., excess of revenue receipts over the costs incurred producing this revenue.

A business earns money after selling their goods or services. If the money they earn is more, than the money they spend for making/providing the goods or services, it is said that the business has made an *accounting profit*. Accounting expenses do not only include the tangible money that was spent by the business, but also includes any provision for losses or depreciation that the business makes over an accounting period. So, once all these costs are deducted from the total income earned by a business enterprise, if the balance amount is positive, it is an accounting profit. If the balance amount is negative, it is known as an accounting loss, which means that the business has spent beyond its earning capacity in the accounting period. *Thus, it can be said that an accounting profit is the excess of accounting income over accounting expenses.*

Accounting Profit = Total Income − Total Expenses

An Economic Profit is a slightly complicated concept. It is not just the excess of total accounting income over the total accounting expense. To the cost of an investment, it also adds the opportunity lost cost of another investment option. Thus, an economic profit means that not only did you make a profit on your investment, but you also made more profit than you would have made otherwise. Because, in accounting profit, the cost of business is only the paid-out costs while for an economist the costs are opportunity costs.

Economic Profit = Total income − Total Expenses − Opportunity Lost Cost

Opportunity costs are implicit costs that are ignored by an accountant. Implicit costs like wages, interest and rent on self-owned factors are deducted from the total revenue receipts. Thus, an economist's profits implies total revenue (TR) minus total costs (TC), where TC= Explicit + Implicit costs.

Thus, an economist does not agree with an accountant's approach to profit. An accountant would only deduct the explicit or actual costs from the revenue to determine profit, whereas an economist, along with explicit costs deducts implicit costs. Examples of implicit costs are: (a) rental income on self-owned land employed in business (which the owner could have earned by letting it on hire to market); (b) interest on self-owned capital (which could have been earned by investing it elsewhere). The profit, thus, arrived by deducting imputed costs from accounting profit is referred to as economic profit.

Illustration: A simple example will make the concept of opportunity cost clear. Let us suppose that a piece of land is being used to grow sugarcane. Is it the best use of that piece of land? What is the 'real' cost of growing sugarcane? The concept of opportunity cost can answer these questions. If sugarcane is not grown on that piece of land, what are the other alternatives? In order to earn expected income, let us say, the alternative crops that can be grown are wheat, cotton, etc. Whatever income wheat or cotton might have earned on that piece of land is forgone by using the land for sugarcane. Sugarcane growing is desirable so long as sugarcane fetches more earnings than wheat or cotton, only then sugarcane growing would be considered the best use of the land. Thus, opportunity cost of anything is just the next best alternative forgone in the use of the productive resources and not all alternative possible uses.

Numerical example: Suppose an individual faces two investment options. He invests the money in Option A and totally forgoes Option B. The opportunity cost lost, is the return he would get in case he had invested in Option B. Suppose both investment options cost ₹100,000. At the same time, he tracks the progress of option B, although he has not invested a penny in it. At the end his investment, option A, earns ₹ 150, 000 while Option B earns ₹ 120, 000. The accounting profit formula will tell him that by investing in Option A, he has made for himself, profit of ₹ 150,000 – ₹ 100,000 = ₹ 50,000. Had he invested in Option B, he would have made an accounting profit of ₹ 120, 000 – ₹ 100, 000= ₹ 20,000. He has made a larger profit by investing on Option A, of ₹ 30,000 more. This is accounting profit.

Therefore, he has earned some money, but he has forgone the option of investing in B. The ₹ 20,000 that he did not get is the opportunity lost cost or simply, opportunity cost of not investing in Option B. This explains what economic profit is. It is not just the excess of total accounting income over the total accounting expense. To the cost of an investment, it adds the opportunity lost cost of another investment option, like Option B in the above illustration.

Limitations of Accounting Profits: Accounting profits not only ignores opportunity costs but there are limitations in accounting techniques. Accounting figures are produced which are based upon arbitrary allocation of both revenues and costs to a given accounting period, say, one year period. The accountant must produce interim profit figures for shareholders (who need information on progress), for managers (to judge the past or provide basis for future decisions) and for tax authorities.

In economic sense, profit is the difference between the cash value of the firm today and its cash value at the end of its existence. In other words, the economists' look to the future when placing a value on today's assets.

Accountants define profits as *revenue minus cost over a given period*, say, one-year period. Both revenue and cost are calculated on an accrual basis. They are allocated to that time period in which they are earned (i.e. revenue) or incurred (i.e. costs). Thus, cost and revenue data used for calculation are not in anticipation (i.e. future costs and revenue). In short, in balance sheet terms, profits calculated is the difference between a firm's net worth (i.e. total assets minus reserves and liabilities) at the beginning and at the end of a year.

Thus, the economist is concerned with income expectations; the accountant aims at producing historical records or profits within the limitations of professional practices and company laws.

To sum up, Accountants measure profit as a difference between total receipt and total payments, while economists calculate profit as accountant's profit minus imputed costs.

The accounting calculation believes that true profit can be ascertained only after the business has been fully terminated, but in practice, the accountants arbitrarily allocate cost and revenue to each year to calculate profit.

Economists measure a firm's economic profit. Accountants measure the accounting profit.

Economic Cost = Total Revenue – Explicit Cost – Implicit cost.

Accounting Profit = Total Revenue - Explicit Cost.

1.18 Role of Profit in Market System

Markets' Coordination:

Any economy consists of thousands upon thousands of individual markets. There are markets for agricultural goods, for manufactured goods, and for consumers' services. There are markets for intermediate goods such as steel, which are outputs of some industries and inputs of others. There are markets for raw materials such as iron ore, and there are markets for land and for thousands of different types of labour. There are markets in which money is borrowed and in which securities are sold. An economy is not a series of markets functioning in isolation but an interlocking system in which an occurrence in one market affects many others.

Any change, such as an increase in demand for a product, requires many further changes and adjustments. Any change in the output of one product will generally require changes in other markets and will start a chain of adjustments.

The essential characteristic of the market system is that its coordination occurs in an unplanned, decentralised way. Millions of people make millions of independent decisions concerning production and consumption every day. Most of these decisions are not motivated by a desire to contribute to the social good or to make the whole economy work well but by considerations of self-interest. The price system coordinates these decentralised decisions, making the whole system fit together and respond to the wishes of individual consumers and producers.

Economists have long emphasised price as a signaling device. When a commodity becomes scarce, its free-market price rises. Firms and households that use the commodity are led to economise on it and to look for alternatives. Firms that produce it are led to produce more of it. When a shortage occurs in a market, price rises and profits develop; when a glut occurs, price falls and losses develop. These are signals, for all to see, that arise from the overall conditions of market supply and demand.

Although the free-market economy often is described as the *price system*, the basic engine that drives the economy is economic profits. Except when there is monopoly, economic profits and losses are symptoms of disequilibrium and they are the driving force in the adaptation of the economy to change.

A rise in demand or a fall in production costs creates profits for that commodity's producers. Profits make an industry attractive to new investment. They signal that there are too few resources devoted to that industry. In search of these profits, more resources enter the industry, increasing output and driving down price, until profits are driven to zero. A fall in demand or a rise in production costs creates losses. Losses signal the reverse and an excess of resources devoted to the industry. Resources will leave the industry until those left behind are no longer suffering losses.

The importance of profits is that they set in motion, forces that tend to move the economy toward a new equilibrium.

Individual households and firms respond to common signals according to their own best interests. There is nothing planned or intentionally coordinated about their actions, yet when, say, a shortage causes price to rise, individual buyers begin to reduce the quantities that they demand and individual firms begin to increase the quantities that they supply. As a result, the shortage begins to lessen. As it does, price begins to come back down, and profits reduce. Eventually, when the shortage eliminates, there are no profits to attract further increases in supply. The chain of adjustments to the original shortage is completed.

In the sequence of signal-response-signal-response, some firms respond to the signals for "more output" by increasing production, and they keep on increasing production until the signals get weaker and weaker and finally disappear. Some buyers withdraw from the market when they think that prices are too high, and perhaps they return gradually, as prices become "more reasonable." Households and firms, responding to market signals, not to the orders of government bureaucrats, "decide" who will increase production and who will limit consumption. Voluntary responses collectively produce the result.

Because the economy is adjusting to shocks continuously, a snapshot of the economy at any given moment reveals substantial positive profits in some industries and substantial losses in others. A snapshot at another moment also will reveal windfall profits and losses, but their locations will be different.

The price system, like an invisible hand (Adam Smith's famous phrase), coordinates the responses of individual decision makers who seek only their own self-interests. Because they respond to signals that reflect market conditions, their responses are coordinated without any conscious planning.

Profit serves the most important function in a free-enterprise economy. High profits serve as a clear signal that consumers want more of the output of that industry. It serves as incentive for firms to expand output and attracts new firms to that industry in the long-run. Further, lesser profits provide the incentive to the firms to increase their efficiency and/or produce less of the commodity and signal some firms to exit the industry for more profitable one. In short, profits provide the crucial signals for the reallocation of society's resources reflecting change in consumer's tastes and demand over time.

Case Study

Profits as a Signal in Personal Computer Industry

A classic example of the role, source and importance of profits in the U.S. economy is of Steven Jobs. His huge rewards from the setting up of Apple resulted from correctly anticipating, promoting and satisfying an important type of market demand.

A dropout from college, 20 years old Steven Jobs, with his friend developed a prototype desktop computer. The Apple Computer Company was born with the help of financing from private investors, and this company revolutionised the computer industry. In 1977, the sales of this company were $3 million that jumped to more than $ 1.9 billion in 1986, exhibiting profits of more than $150 million. The immense success of Apple attracted other competitors in the industry and by 1984; more than 75 companies had entered into the market.

Due to the increased competition, many of the early entrants, set up hurriedly, had dropped out by 1986 and there was a dip in the profits sharply. For instance, profit margins for the 11 largest U.S. computer companies that averaged to 11.5 percent from 1980 to 1985 dipped down to only 6.5 percent from 1986 to 1990. Since 1991, personal computer firms have been engaged in a severe price war. This has resulted in fall in profit margin as prices have dipped by as much as 20 to 40 percent per year. Personal Computers have now become practically a commodity and thus provide only a meagre operating margin of about 5 percent or so.

Job's huge rewards from the setting up of Apple resulted from correctly anticipating, promoting and satisfying an important type of market demand. Attracted by the huge profits, the competitors were quick to enter the industry of PCs and thus causing profits in this industry to fall sharply. In the process, more and more of society's resources were attracted to the computer industry, which supplied consumers with rapidly improving personal computers at sharply declining prices.

According to Drucker, profit serves three main purposes

(i)   It serves as an index of firm's performance. It measures the net effectiveness and soundness of a business effort. A higher profit is an indicator that the business is being run successfully and effectively. However, it is not a perfect indicator but the best indicator of the general efficiency of a firm. For the private firm, it is the most convenient method of judging the operational efficiency of business. Generally, profits are taken as an efficient measure of the use of economic resources by the firm.

(ii) Profit is a premium to cover cost of staying in business. Profit is regarded as a premium that covers the cost of staying in business. It guarantees the survival of the firm. The reason is that to stay or continue in business, the firm has to incur costs such as replacement cost, obsolescence cost and other costs that involve different degrees of risks. Thus, no firm can survive for long in the absence of at least a minimum rate of return on investment.

(iii) Profits ensure supply of re-investible capital. In other words, it can be looked upon not only as a source of financing future expansion of the firm but a part of profits can be ploughed back for future production. Thus, profits determine the future supply of capital to the firm. Even if the firm is not able to fully finance its activities of expansion and innovation out of its internal supply of capital, yet the rate of profits determine the firm's creditability in attracting external capital at minimum cost.

However, profits must be looked at from the point of view of sustained financial soundness of the firm and its contribution to the society's well-being rather than at the firm's short-term goal, i.e. yearly return on capital only. It implies that profit, as the sole objective to be achieved (short-term goal) is not the same thing, as the objective of rendering useful service to the social well being while earning profits in the process. All firms that aim to grow in a social set up, must learn to sacrifice short-term gains to build up image that will be useful and profitable in the long term.

The concept of 'profits' with time-perspective can also be understood with the help of distinction between "profit maximisation" and "profitability maximisation". Profit maximisation is a short-term objective, i.e. return on the capital invested, and while profitability maximisation is a broader concept, wherein the firm is treated as a social institution, rendering useful service to the society, rather than an individual entity. Naturally, profitability maximisation is socially superior in the terminology of profits.

Factors that determine the short-term and long-term goals of profit

Short-term goals of profit

1. **Environment for Business:** The general business conditions significantly influences the profits of a firm. For example, during recession firms are unable to make large profits over costs and may even incur losses.

2. **Consumer's tastes and preferences:** in a dynamic economy, changes in tastes, preferences, fashion etc., play a definite role in determining the quantum of profits of a firm.

3. **Life cycle of the product:** The age of the product is vital to influence the demand for the product. For example, in the growth stage of the product, it promises demand of the product while, when the product has passed the maturity stage, demand for these products will fall and shrinking profits occur to the firm.

4. **Fiscal policies:** government's taxation policy influences corporate profits.

5. **Degree of competition:** For instance, to monopoly firm, profits will be maximum and super normal and in competitive market, the competition is cutthroat and volume of profits is normal.

Long-term goals of profit

1. For long-term profitability, the growth of the firm assumes great importance. In addition, if the firm is able to generate regular and adequate supply of capital within the system then lesser will be dependence on external finance.

2. The firm must have an effective research and development department to remain update in the dynamic society, in production, technology and product line.

   The factors that give rise to clash between short-term and long-term profitability are-

   (i) If a firm thinks of labour welfare, i.e., by imparting skill to labour (long-term objective), it may reduce its volume of profit (short-term goal).

   (ii) On the other hand, short-term objective can override long-term objective when a firm ignores after-sales service and R & D activities and earn higher profits in that year.

   (iii) To establish its goodwill in the society, the firm has to ignore short-term interest of maximising profit.

Hence, factors that determine short-term and long-term goals of the firm have to be reconciled not only for the firm's survival but also for the well-being of the society.

1.19 Adam Smith and the Invisible Hand

Profit serves a crucial function in a free-enterprise economy. High profits provide the incentive for firms to expand output and for entry of new firms in that industry.

In his magnum opus 'Wealth of Nations'(over 1,000 pages), Adam Smith declared war on government intervention in the economy, and put on paper a universal formula for prosperity that would revolutionise economics and international trade. It promised a new world – a world of abundant wealth, and not just for the rich, but also for the common man and the poor.

Smith's solution was , giving people their freedom- "system of natural liberty". Adam Smith's symbol of free-market capitalism was a beautiful metaphor: *the invisible hand.* The idea is that when an individual is given the freedom to pursue his own interests, "he is led by an invisible hand to promote that of the society."

Adam Smith gave the principle of 'Invisible hand' in which he described that it is the natural force that by itself guides any free market economy, through competition for scarce resources.

According to Smith," in a free enterprise each participant will try to maximise self-interest, and the interaction of market participants, will lead to exchange of goods and services, enabling each participant to be better off, than when simply producing for himself/herself. He further said that in a free market, there would be no regulation of any type to ensure, the mutually beneficial exchange of goods and services took place. As this "invisible hand" would guide market participants to trade in the most mutually beneficial manner."

Adam Smith is often referred to as the father of economics. He believed that one of the most powerful forces promoting economic progress is self-interest directed by market prices. His theory of economics came to be known as the invisible hand principle. It suggested that market prices coordinate the actions of self-interested individuals and direct them toward activities that promote the general welfare.

Smith's book A*n Inquiry into the Nature and Causes of the Wealth of Nations* states:"Every individual is continually exerting himself to find out the most advantageous employment for whatever income he can command. It is his own advantage, indeed, and not that of the society, which he has in view. But the study of his own advantage naturally, or rather necessarily, leads him to prefer that employment which is most advantageous to society. He intends only his own gain, and he is in this, as in many other places, led by an invisible hand to promote an end which was not part of his intention. By pursuing his own interest he frequently promotes that of the society more effectually than when he really intends to promote it."

Adam Smith's philosophy makes a lot of sense. The market works 'automatically' as if an invisible hand were guiding it. With people pursuing what they think, will benefit them the most, **they actually end up benefiting not only their own interests but society as well.**

Moreover, it all occurs of free will of the economic players, consumers and producers. There is no central direction or control. It all happens naturally. For example, when shoppers line up to pay for the purchase, there is no authority telling them which counter they are assigned. They naturally just proceed to the counter that they believe will help them check out most quickly, and if one counter gets congested or held up for whatever reason, shoppers will relocate to other counters, smoothing the flow. So shoppers working toward their own self-interests result in working in the interest of everyone through social cooperation and, thereby, promoting the most efficient method for everyone.

Although people are initially motivated by self-interest, market prices direct their interests toward activities that promote economic progress and order.

Profits and losses are the primary indicators of favourable and unfavourable activities. Losses indicate that an economic activity is congested, and exit of firms could take place, whereas profits indicate that an activity offers potential and opportunity for new firms to enter. As producers pursue those activities that offer an opportunity for profit, they smooth out the flow of economic activities, promoting better efficient economic progress.

Thus, the invisible hand principle illustrates how self-interest of the individual and market prices work together to promote economic progress. Adam Smith's invisible hand principle is considered as the basic principle of economics.

1.20 Economics of Information

Both consumers and producers require complete information if they are to make efficient choices and decisions about what to buy and what to supply to the market. What happens when this information is missing or incomplete?

In the theory of competitive markets we assume that all "agents" in the market enjoy perfect information about the availability of goods and services and also have complete information about prices charged by suppliers. Consumers can make purchasing decisions on the basis of full and free information on the products that they are buying.

However, the reality is different. All of us, buyers and sellers, experience **information deficits** which can often lead to a misallocation of resources and hence the possibility of market failure. **Information failure** occurs when people have inaccurate, incomplete, uncertain or misunderstood data and so make potentially 'wrong' choices.

For example, demand for health or education services, where consumers may well underestimate the long term private benefits from investing time and money into extra education or buying a specific form of health treatment. There may well be a case for the government to intervene in the market in some way if information failures become serious.

Imperfect information can be caused by,
- **Misunderstanding the true costs or benefits of a product,** e.g. the private and social benefits from higher education when there are so many universities and courses to choose from.
- **Uncertainty about costs and benefits,** e.g. should younger workers be buying into pension schemes?

- **Complex information,** e.g. choosing between 'makes' of computers requires specialist knowledge of hardware. The problems of choosing a quality second hand car or deciding whether or not to buy a property.
- **Inaccurate or misleading information,** e.g. persuasive advertising may 'oversell' the benefits of a product leading to a higher demand and consumption than is optimal.
- **Addiction,** e.g. drug addicts may be unable to stop consumption of harmful substances.

To improve consumer information - Illustration

The food industry has made its first move towards issuing health warnings for snack foods. It marks a shift in the food industry's attitude towards consumers. Food companies have argued that consumer education is not their job. However, the threat of legislation to regulate the promotion of food to children has prompted the food and drink industry to become more proactive. Soft drink producers agreed to a voluntary ban on advertising to children in Europe. They also said they would provide better nutritional information on beverages and public education campaigns to promote healthy lifestyles.

Food and drink manufacturers have already made efforts to cut down on fats, salts and sugars, and provide more nutritional information. This week, Walkers crisps said it had made a multimillion pound investment in sun seed oil to reduce levels of saturated fats. Last month, Nestlé said it would put calorie information on the front of confectionery packets.

Source: Adapted from news reports, February 2006

Asymmetric Information

Many times in life, some people are better informed than others, and this difference in information can affect the choices they make and how they deal with one another. This topic of asymmetry information can shed light on many aspects of the world, from the market for used cars to the custom of gift giving.

Asymmetric information occurs when somebody knows more than somebody else in the market. Such asymmetric information can make it difficult for the two people to do business together

Examples: A worker knows more than his employer about how much effort he puts into his job. It is an example of *hidden action*. An employer is interested in hiring a new employee who is "skilled in learning." Of course, all prospective employees will claim to be "skilled at learning", but only they know if they really are. This is an information asymmetry. Skill in learning is malleable, and depends upon many factors, including diet, exercise and money.

A seller of a used car knows more than the buyer about the car's condition. This is an example of *hidden characteristics*.

There are two main problems that result from asymmetric information. These are: (1) adverse Selection; (2) Moral Hazard.

Asymmetric information can distort people's **incentives** to buy and sell goods and services at the right prices and as a result can lead to inefficiencies and market failure. Asymmetric information is so prevalent that economists have devoted much effort in recent decades to studying its effects. One of the classic examples of asymmetric information comes from research on the used car market by the Nobel Prize winning economist George Akerlof – in his theory of the **market for lemons**!

(A) Adverse Selection

Adverse selection is a problem that arises in markets where the seller knows more about the attributes of the good being sold than the buyer does. In such a situation, the buyer runs the risk of being sold a good of low quality. That is, the "selection" of goods sold may be "adverse" from the point of view of the uninformed buyer.

The classic example of adverse selection is the market for used cars. Sellers of used cars know their vehicles' defects while buyers often do not have the complete information. Many people avoid buying vehicles in the used car market because owners of the worst cars are more likely to sell them than are the owners of the best cars, buyers are apprehensive about getting a "lemon". This lemon problem can explain why a used car, just out of the showroom a week old, sells for thousand of rupees less than a new car of the same type.

Another example of adverse selection occurs in the labour market. According to the efficiency-wage theory, workers vary in their abilities, and they may know their own abilities better than do the firms that hire them. In such a case, when a firm cuts the wage it pays, the more talented workers are likely to quit, knowing that they may find better employment. On the other hand, a firm may choose to pay an above equilibrium wage to attract a better mix of workers in terms of abilities.

Let us take an example of insurance. The buyers of health insurance know more about their own health problems than do insurance companies. The reason is that people with greater hidden health problems are more likely to buy health insurance than are other people. The price of health insurance shows the costs of a sicker-than-average person. Thus, people in average health may be discouraged from buying health insurance by the high price.

When markets suffer from adverse selection, the invisible hand (government efforts) does not necessarily work its magic. Because:

- In the used car market, owners of good cars may choose to keep them rather than sell at low price that the sceptical buyer (buyer who doubts the seller) are willing to pay;
- In labour market, wages may be stuck above the level and raise unemployment;
- In insurance markets, buyers with low risk may choose to remain uninsured as the policies offered fail to reflect their true characteristics. This is why advocates of government-provided health insurance (e.g. L.I.C) point out to the problem of adverse selection as one reason not to trust the private market to provide the right amount of health insurance on its own.

(B) Moral Hazard

Moral hazard is a problem that arises when one person, called the *agent*, is performing some task on behalf of another person called the *principal*. Moral hazard refers to the risk, or "hazard", or immoral behaviour by the agent. In such a situation, the principal tries various ways to encourage the agent to act more responsibly.

For example, in employment relationship, the employer is the principal, and the worker is the agent. The moral hazard problem is the temptation of imperfectly monitored workers to shirk their responsibilities. Employers can respond to this hazard in many ways, such as:

- By better monitoring, for e.g. parents, when hire nanny, can use a hidden camera to record nanny's behaviour when parents are away.
- By high wages, for e.g. some employers may choose to pay their workers a wage above the level that equates supply and demand in the labour market. In such a case, a worker who earns an above-equilibrium wage is likely to be responsible because if he is caught and fired, he might not be able to find another high-paying wage.
- By delaying payments, for e.g. firms can delay part of a worker's compensation, so if the worker is caught and fired, he suffers a larger penalty.

Thus, an employer can use any one of them or a combination of the above said mechanism to reduce the problem of moral hazard.

Other example of moral hazard are a family may live near a river with a high risk of flooding because the family enjoys the scenic beauty, while the government bears the cost of disaster relief after a flood. Here, the government may reduce moral hazard by prohibiting building homes on land with high risk of flooding. But the hazard persists because the government does not have perfect information about the risk that families undertake when choosing where to live.

Market Signaling

Markets respond to problems of asymmetric information in many ways. One of them is signaling, which refers to actions taken by an informed party for the sole purpose of credibly revealing his private information. The firms may spend money on advertising to signal to potential customers that they have high-quality products. Again, students may earn college degrees, from high reputed colleges, to signal to potential employers that they are high-ability individuals. These two examples of signaling – advertising, education- may seem very different, but they are the same. In both cases, the informed party- the firm, the students- is using the signal to convince the uninformed party – the customer, the employer- that the informed party is offering something of high quality.

What is an effective signal? One it has to be costly, because if signals were free then everyone would use it, and it would convey no information. For this same reason, it is necessary that the signal should be less costly or more beneficial to the person with high-quality product. For instance, in the advertising case, a firm with a good product reaps a larger benefit from advertising, because customers who try the product once are more likely to become repeat customers. Hence, it is rational for the firm with a good product to pay for the advertising cost and rational for the customer to use signal as a piece of information about the product's quality. In the second case, i.e. education, it is rational for the talented person to pay for the cost of signal (education), and it is rational for the employer to use the signal as a piece of information about the person's talent. The world is filled with the instances of signaling- magazine ads, television etc. The firm is willing to pay for expensive signal i.e. spot on television, in the hope that the customer will infer that the product is of high-quality.

Case Study - (Gifts as Signals)

A man is thinking as to what to give to his girlfriend for her birthday. He feels that it would be better to gift cash which would allow the girl to buy things of her choice. But when he hands her the money, she is offended, as she is convinced that he really doesn't love her, she breaks off the relationship. In some ways, gift giving is a strange custom. Because people typically know their own preferences better than others do, so we might expect everyone to prefer cash (as the man in our example) to kind. Imagine if an employer substitute's merchandise of his choice to the pay-cheque, would it be accepted?

Here, gift giving reflects asymmetric information and signalling. The man in our example has private information that the girlfriend would like to know: Does he really love her? Choosing a good gift for her is a signal of his love. Certainly, the act of picking out a gift, rather than giving cash, has the right characteristics to be a signal.

The signalling theory of gift giving is consistent with another observation. People care most about the custom when the strength of affection is most in question. Thus, giving cash to a girlfriend or to a boyfriend is a bad move. But when college student receives cheque from their parents, it is less offending, as the cash gift is a signal of lack of affection is less in doubt, in this case.

Points to Remember

- **Definition -** Managerial economics refers to the application of economic theory and methods of decision sciences to arrive at the optimal solution to the various decision making problems faced by managers of business firms."
- **Micro & Macro economics -** "Micro" means individualistic and "Macro" means aggregative. When we analyse the problems of an economy as a *whole*, it is macro-economics. While an analysis of the behaviour of *any particular decision making unit*, such as a firm, an industry is micro economics.
- A managerial economist is an economic adviser to a firm or businessman
- **The Basic Concepts** for taking scientific decisions and business planning are:
  (a) Incremental principle
  (b) Opportunity cost
  (c) Principle of time perspective
  (d) Discounting principle
  (e) Equi-marginal principle (optimisation technique)
  (f) Risks and uncertainty
  (g) Marginal analysis
  (h) Economic model
  (i) Statics and dynamics
- The discounting principle, in business decision making process, can be stated as, "If a decision affects costs and revenues at future dates, it is necessary to discount those costs and revenues to present values before a valid comparison of alternatives is possible."

- **A Firm** is an organisation that combines and organizes the resources or factors of production with the aim of producing goods and/or services for sale
- *Principal-agent problem is a particular game-theoretic description of a situation.*
- *Profit is regarded as the revenue realised during the period minus the cost and expenses incurred in producing the revenue*
- **An accounting profit** is the excess of business income over the business expenses, i.e., excess of revenue receipts over the costs incurred producing this revenue
- *The importance of profits is that they set in motion, forces that tend to move the economy toward a new equilibrium*
- **Short-term goals of profit:**
  (a) Environment for Business
  (b) Consumer's tastes and preferences
  (c) Life cycle of the product
  (d) Fiscal policies
  (e) Degree of competition
- **Long-term goals of profit:**
  (a) The growth of the firm
  (b) An effective research and development department
- **Adam Smith and the Invisible Hand -** Adam Smith's solution was, giving people their freedom- "system of natural liberty". Adam Smith's symbol of free-market capitalism was a beautiful metaphor: *the invisible hand.* The idea is that when an individual is given the freedom to pursue his own interests, "he is led by an invisible hand to promote that of the society." Adam Smith's invisible hand principle is considered as the basic principle of economics.

Questions for Discussion

1. Explain the Nature and Significance of Managerial Economics. How is it related to Micro Economics?
2. What is meant by 'Managerial Economics'? Explain the scope of Managerial Economics in the present context.
3. How does the background of Managerial Economics assist in Business Decision Making.?
4. Explain the relationship of Micro Economics with Managerial Economics?
5. Give the practical significance and applications of Managerial Economics?
6. What is moral hazard? Give any three ways that an employer might do to reduce the severity of this problem.
7. What is adverse selection? Give an example of a market in which adverse selection might be a problem.
8. Write a note on asymmetry information?
9. Explain the significance of 'time' in economic activities?

10. Write short notes on – Equi-Marginal Analysis, Opportunity Costs, Incremental reasoning.

11. How is the concept of economic profit different from the concept of business profits that is generally used by the accountants? What role does the notion of normal profits play in this difference?

12. "The discounting principle and incremental cost concept are both special applications of opportunity cost reasoning." Explain.

Objective Questions

1. Indicate whether the following statements are true or false:
    (a) The opportunity cost of a machine which can produce only one product is high.
    (b) Risk and returns are directly related.
    (c) Discounting is an established technique of measuring opportunity cost of time preference.
    (Ans. (a) false; (b) true; (c) true)

2. The opportunity cost of a machine which can produce only one product is: (a) low; (b) Infinite.
    (Ans. (a) low)

3. Opportunity cost is a term which describes:
    (a) A bargain price for a factor of production;
    (b) Average variable cost;
    (c) Costs related to an optimum production level;
    (d) None of the above.
    (Ans. (d) none of the above)

4. What is the opportunity cost to you of each of the following:
    (a) Studying at weekends;
    (b) Doing charity work two evenings a week;
    (c) Working in paid employment during every vacation?

5. Given the prices of products X and Y equal to ₹ 10 and ₹ 20 respectively, compute the opportunity cost of one unit of X in terms of Y.

6. Johnson & Johnson, a MNC operating in India decide to enter the detergent market. Since the detergent market in India is competitive, Johnson & Johnson runs an expensive promotion campaign and offers its product at very competitive prices. This resulted in steep fall in profits of the company. But the management had the satiafaction of acquiring a significant part of the detergent market. Find out (a) the objectives of Johnson & Johnson and (b) if you were asked to oppose the move of the company to enter into detergent market of India, how it would be done?

■■■

Chapter 2...

Demand Analysis and Forecasting – Demand and Supply

Contents ...

Learning Objectives ...

- ➢ To equip the students of management with time tested tools and techniques of managerial economics to enable them to appreciate its relevance in decision-making.
- ➢ To know about the different market structures.
- ➢ To know the price determination under various market structures.
- ➢ To have knowledge about the oscillation that a market has to undergo before attaining equilibrium.
- ➢ To know about the Price-Output decisions taken in case of multi-plant and multi-product firms.
- ➢ To understand the behavior of commodity demand.
- ➢ To locate the sources of demand and identify the nature of demand.
- ➢ To learn the different methods of demand forecasting, its importance in demand analysis.
- ➢ To know about the various factors that determines demand at individual and market level.
- ➢ To know about the response of demand to change in its price, i.e. elasticity of demand.
- ➢ To learn the use of different methods for estimating demand.

Introduction

The knowledge of market structure within which a firm is to operate is very helpful in understanding the nature and extent of maneuverability that the firm has in deciding the price and quantity of the product. Many economic and legal factors combine to create the environment in which a firm must operate. The factors, such as, government policies towards growth of business, economies that may arise from large-scale production, potential buyers for output, etc., determine the pattern and nature of competition which prevails in the market. Therefore, economists classify industries or groups of firms into several categories on the basis of certain criteria, mainly the nature of competitive conditions and nature of product- homogenous or differentiated.

2.1 Meaning of Market

In common language, we always use the word 'market' as a place. We refer to it as wheat market, vegetable market, etc. However, in economics, 'market' has a different meaning.

According to **Cournet**, "Economists understand by the term market, not any particular market place in which things are bought and sold, but the whole of any region in which buyers and sellers are in such free interaction with one another that the prices of the same goods tend to equality easily and quickly."

According to **Jevons**, "The word (market) has been generalised, so as to mean anybody or persons who are intimate business relations and carry on extensive transactions in any commodity."

The modern view regarding market is, "The whole area over which buyers and sellers are in such contact with each other, directly or through middlemen, that the price of the commodity in one part influences it in the other parts of it."

Features of Market: The above definitions points out at the features of the term 'market'.

- By 'Market' in economics, we do not mean any particular place or any region.
- 'Market' is always of one single commodity. Every commodity has a separate market. Thus, as many markets as the commodities, may exist.
- To make a 'Market', a group of persons, i.e., buyers and sellers are to be present.
- The contact between the buyers and sellers can be direct or indirect, i.e., by correspondence, telephone, e-marketing, etc.
- There exists a 'commercial' relation between the buyers and sellers.
- The contact between the buyers and sellers should be free and close so as to allow one single price getting established easily throughout the market.

2.2 Determinants of Market Structure

Some of the main determinants of classification of market structure are:

1. **On the basis of 'Time':** Time element is one of the criteria of classification such as very short period, short period and long period. Shorter the period, greater is the

influence of demand on price, as supply is fixed. And, in cases where supply can be increased, lesser will be the impact of demand on price, with other things being equal.

2. **On the basis of 'status of sellers':** Markets are broadly classified into Primary market (wherein manufacturers who produce and are sellers of the product to the wholesalers); Secondary market (wherein the wholesalers are intermediaries between the manufacturers and retailers); and Terminal market (wherein the retailers who sell it to the ultimate consumer).

3. **On the basis of 'area':** The classification of market on basis of 'area' are local, regional, national and international markets. However, whether a market is local, regional, or national or international, depends on the nature of commodity- whether it is easily transferrable or not, on storage facility, on political stability at home and abroad.

4. **On the basis of the 'nature of transactions':** The markets can be classified as spot market (wherein goods are physically exchanged on the spot) and future market (wherein there is agreement of future exchange of goods) on the basis of the volume of business.

5. **On the basis of the 'volume of business':** The markets are wholesale and retail markets. Wholesale markets are a link between the producer and the retailer and the retail market is a link between wholesaler and the consumer.

6. **On basis of 'regulation':** When government stipulates certain conditions and regulations on transactions of some goods and services, it is a regulated market, and where transactions are left to market forces, those are unregulated markets.

7. **On the basis of market structure:** This is the most important basis of classification of market. The four components that decide the market structure are number of sellers, number of buyers, entry and exit of firms and nature of the product.

    (a) **Number of sellers:** Based on the number of sellers is the type of competition in the market. In perfect competition there are a large number of sellers and greater is the 'interdependence', i.e. the cross elasticity of quantity is near to infinity. In other words, the goods of different sellers in the same industry are close substitute to each other. On the other hand, a single seller is the feature of pure monopoly, two sellers under duopoly, few sellers under oligopoly and many sellers under monopolistic type of competition.

    (b) **Number of buyers:** A large number of small buyers is likely to pay almost the same price. As the number of buyers decrease or some of the buyers make relatively very big purchases, then the dominant buyers can have an impact on the price.

    (c) **Nature of the product:** Under perfect competition the product is homogenous and hence the buying decisions are based mainly on the price. The goods are homogenous and the sellers sell at the same price, hence buyers have no preference. Under imperfect competition, the products are generally 'differentiated' and the firm has an ability to influence the price. For e.g. Audi and Fiat both are automobiles, but the buyers pay a higher price for Audi as they perceive it as having additional desirable features.

(d) Entry and exit of firms: The market structure is determined by the entry and exit of firms in an industry. In perfect competition, there is freedom to firms, this influences the output behaviour. If entry is difficult or restricted, as under oligopoly or monopoly, the existing firms will have greater freedom in making pricing and output decisions.

2.3 Features of Perfect Competition

Though perfect competition is a rare, almost non-existent situation, we study this market situation as it furnishes us with a simple and logical starting point for economic analysis.

Perfect competition is an important type of market structure assumed by the Classical and Neoclassical economists as a theoretical model.

Perfect competition refers to the market structure where competition among the buyers and sellers is present in its most perfect form. In a perfectly competitive market, a 'uniform' price prevails for the commodity which is determined by the economic forces of total demand and total supply in the market. In this market, the buyers and sellers are 'price-takers'. Every buyer and seller has to accept the prevailing market price and neither the buyer nor the seller can individually influence the ruling market price.

The different features of Perfect Competition are as follows:

1. **Large Number of sellers**: A perfectly competitive market structure is basically formed by a large number of actual and potential firms or sellers. Their number is sufficiently large and as the size of each firm is relatively small, so an individual seller's or firm's supply is just a fraction of the total market supply. Consequently, any variation in individual supply has a negligible effect on the total supply. Thus, an individual firm or seller cannot exert any influence on the ruling market price.

2. **Large Number of Buyers**: There are a very large number of actual and potential buyers so that each individual buyer's demand constitutes just a fraction of the total market demand. Hence, no individual buyer is in a position to exert his influence on the prevailing price of the product.

3. **Product Homogeneity**: The commodity supplied by each firm in a perfectly competitive market is homogenous. Since each firm produces an identical product, their products can be readily substituted for each other. Hence, the buyer has no specific preference to buy from a particular seller only. His purchase from any particular seller is a matter of chance and not of choice, on account of the homogeneity of goods. The homogeneity of the products implies that they are perfect substitutes from the buyer's point of view.

The above features of perfect competition together ensure that the average revenue curve or price line of the firm shall be horizontal or parallel to the x-axis and no firm is in a position to influence the ruling price in the market. Further, due to homogenous product, the buyers do not consider one firm's product superior to another and hence no price difference in the market.

4. **Free Entry and Exit of Firms**: There is free entry of new firms into the market. There is no legal, technological, economic, financial or any other barrier to their entry. Similarly, existing firms are free to quit the market. Thus, the mobility of firms ensures that whenever there is scope in the business, new entry will take place and competition will always remain stiff. Due to the natural stiffness of competition, inefficient firms would have to eventually quit the industry.

5. **Perfect Knowledge of Market Conditions**: Perfect competition requires that all the buyers and sellers must possess perfect knowledge about the existing market conditions, especially regarding the market price, quantities and sources of supply. When there is such perfect knowledge, no buyer could be charged a price different from the market price. Similarly, no seller would unnecessarily lose by selling at a lower price than the prevailing market price. This way, perfect knowledge ensures transactions at a uniform price.

6. **Perfect Mobility of Factors of Production**: A necessary assumption of perfect competition is that factors of production are perfectly mobile. Perfect mobility of factors alone can ensure easy entry or exit of firms. Again it also ensures that the factor costs are the same for all firms.

7. **Government Non-intervention**: Perfect competition also implies that there is no government intervention in the working of market economy. That is, there are no tariffs, subsidies, rationing of goods, and control on supply of raw materials, licensing policy or other government interference. Government non-intervention is essential to permit free entry of firms and for automatic adjustment of demand and supply through the market mechanism.

8. **No Transport Cost:** A perfectly competitive market assumes the non-existence of transport costs. The assumption is on the basis of reasoning that the various firms are so close to each other that there are no transport costs. The assumption of no transport costs is because the goods are considered homogenous only when they happen to be in the same place. If goods are at different place, the two goods are not homogenous, as their price differs due to transport costs. And, since in perfect competition there is existence of uniform price hence there cannot exist transport costs.

9. **Absence of Selling Costs:** Under perfect competition, the costs of sales-promotion, advertisement, etc., does not arise because all firms produce a homogenous product.

To sum up,

- There are a great number of buyers and sellers of the product, and each seller and buyer is too small in relation to the market to be able to affect the price of the product by his or her own actions.
- The product of each competitive firm is homogenous, identical or perfectly standardised. This refers to not only the physical features of the product but also the 'environment', such as pleasantness of the seller and the selling location in which the purchase is made.
- There is perfect mobility of resources. There are no patents or copyrights, vast amounts of capital are not necessary to enter the market, and the already established firms do not have any lasting cost advantage over new entrants because of experience or size.
- Under perfect competition, consumers, resource owners and firms in the market have perfect knowledge as to present and future prices, costs and economic opportunities in general.

The features of perfect competition define this type of market, but it has never really existed. The nearest we might come to a perfectly competitive market is the stock market. In addition, (satisfying few assumptions and characteristics of this market) the market for agricultural commodities as wheat and corn or natural gas industry also approach perfect competition.

The usefulness of the perfectly competitive model is not diluted even though perfect competition in its pure form has never really existed in the real world. The perfectly competitive model does give us some useful explanations and predictions of many real-world economic phenomena. Moreover, this model assists us to evaluate and compare the efficiency with which resources are used under different forms of market organisation.

Pure and Perfect Competition: Sometimes a distinction is seen between pure competition and perfect competition. E. H. Chamberlin in his theory of pricing introduced the term 'pure competition' and the British economists used it as 'perfect competition'.

Is there really a difference between 'pure' and 'perfect' competition?

The fulfillment of conditions by the firms such as existence of large number of buyers and sellers, existence of homogenous product, absence of government intervention, free entry and exit makes for pure competition in the market. There is no element of monopoly in pure competition. Pure competition is a part and parcel of perfect competition.

For a market to be perfectly competitive, other conditions such as perfect knowledge on the part of buyers and sellers, perfect mobility of factors and absence of transport costs also exist. Thus, in perfect competition there is no imperfection either with regard to knowledge or of the mobility of factors of production.

Under perfect competition, the economy can adjust itself to any disturbances (on demand and supply side), almost immediately. But, under pure competition it takes longer time for adjustments due to imperfections in the market. In price theory, it is the term perfect competition that is used and not pure competition.

A single uniform price in the market is the most important criterion of perfect competition. This price is determined by the combined actions of all the buyers (total demand) and all sellers (total supply) taken together. No single seller can influence the price established by the market.

Theoretical Significance of Perfect Competition Market Model

Perfect competition is regarded as a very unrealistic phenomenon, however its theoretical importance is:

- It provides a clear insight into the working of an economy. It helps to give a clear perception of the basic principles governing the functioning of the market economy.
- It is a simple form of market structure to understand and to analyse.
- It is the first step in understanding the nature of more complex forms of market structures.
- It is a near abstraction of the market economy when capitalism reigned supreme.
- It is an ideal form of market regarding the norms.
- Competitive markets are not totally absent. Such markets are still found in some areas namely in food grain markets.

Though, a limiting and simplified model of market structure in theory, perfect competition, is a very useful concept for studying the laws of market and for understanding the mechanics of decision-making in practical life.

A competitive firm is a 'price-taker'. It accepts prevailing market price and determines equilibrium output.

CASE STUDY (Competition in Stock Market)

The market for stocks traded on major stock exchanges is closest to a perfectly competitive model. In the stock market, the price of a particular stock is determined by total demand and total supply of the stock. In other words, a single buyer or single seller of the stock has an insignificant impact on the price. Further, all stocks within each category are more or less homogenous. The resources are mobile as the stock is bought and sold frequently and as for perfect knowledge, information on prices and quantities is readily available.

Despite the fact that the stock market is close to perfectly competitive model, yet imperfections occur even in this market. For example, the sale of ₹ 20 crore worth of stocks by any large corporation will definitely depress, i.e. influence the price of its stocks. At times, when stock prices become grossly overvalued, it creates a *bubble market*, and thus requires steep corrections, equilibrium position is disturbed and fall in the prices is required. Stock market scams that were unearthed in 1992 and 2001 are some examples of this. The first scam, that was led by the then big bull Harshad Mehta and then the flamboyant (showy) Ketan Parekh scam that eroded the confidence of Indian markets leading to bearish periods are such examples.

On 16 October 2007, the stock markets regulator, SEBI, suggested that the foreign institutional investors should not be allowed to issue or renew offshore derivative instruments linked to futures and options leading to a sale of net $ 1.3 billion worth of Indian shares by foreign investors and bringing in a slump in the market.

During the last decade, the growth rates in Indian economy averaged at 6 to 7 per cent. There has been a huge inflow of funds, from foreign entities into the Indian markets and more and more Indians are trading in foreign stocks. This has become possible due to communication revolution that has linked stock markets around the world into a huge global market and it provides new earning possibilities. However, these factors also create the danger that a crisis in one market will quickly spread to other markets around the world.

Thus, global markets for securities, showing closeness to perfectly competitive model, with round the world, round-the-clock trading, could eclipse any single market's capitalising dominance in that country.

2.4 Conditions of Equilibrium

A firm is in equilibrium when it has no tendency to change its level of output, i.e. it needs neither any expansion nor contraction. Its objective is to earn maximum profits by equating its Marginal Cost with its Marginal Revenue (i.e. MR = MC).

The conditions of equilibrium of the firm are:

(a) *The MC curve must equate the MR curve.* This is the necessary and first order condition.

(b) *The MC curve must cut the MR curve form below* and after the point of equilibrium it must be above the MR. This is the second order condition.

Under conditions of competitive market, the MR curve of a firm coincides with the AR curve. The MR curve is horizontal to the X-axis. Thus, the firm is in equilibrium when MC = MR = AR (Price).

Diagrammatic Illustration:

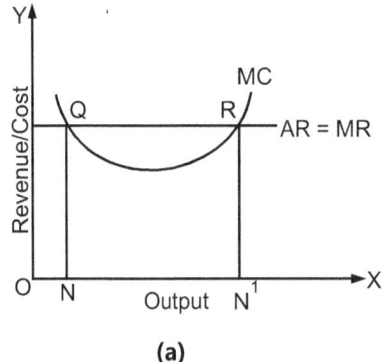

(a)

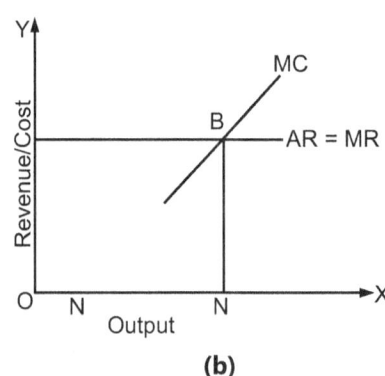

(b)

Fig. 2.1

In Fig. 2.1, the MC curve cuts the MR curve at point Q. At point Q, MR = MC i.e. it satisfies the first condition but it is not a point of maximum profits because at point Q, the MC curve is below the MR curve. Hence, it does not pay the firm to produce lesser output i.e. ON when it can make larger profits by producing beyond ON output.

At point R both the conditions of equilibrium are satisfied and the firm earns maximum profits. Between the two points Q and R, the firm can expand its output as MR > MC. However, the firm has to stop further production when it reaches the ON' level of output. Any plans of the firm to produce more than ON', will in turn incur losses as MC > MR beyond the equilibrium point 'R'. The same conclusions hold good in the case of a straight line MC curve as shown in Fig. 2.1 (b).

An industry is in equilibrium when –

(a) There is no tendency for firms in that industry to exit or any firm to enter that industry.

(b) When each firm in the industry is in equilibrium.

The first condition implies that the average cost curve coincides with the average revenue curves of all the firms in the industry. (AR = AC) and the firms are earning only normal profits. (Normal profits are included in the average cost of the firms).

The second condition refers to the equality of MR and MC.

Thus, under a perfectly competitive 'industry', these two conditions must be fulfilled at the point of equilibrium.

$$MR = MC \qquad \qquad \text{... (a)}$$
$$AR = AC \qquad \qquad \text{... (b)}$$

Since $\qquad\qquad AR = MR$

Thus, $\qquad MC = AC = AR$

Such a situation refers to full equilibrium of an industry.

2.4.1 Short-run Equilibrium of the Firm

In the short-run, a firm is in equilibrium when it has no tendency to expand or contract its output and the aim of the firm is to earn maximum profits or incur minimum losses.

The short period refers to that period during which the firm can adjust its output to the changing demand with the *existing* plant and machinery. If the demand for the product increases during the period, the firm will increase its output to meet this increased demand with intensive utilisation of the existing plant and machinery. The firm, thus, shall produce more only with the help of variable inputs along with the given fixed factors inputs. The number of firms in the industry is fixed as neither the existing firms can leave nor new firms enter it.

The assumptions when we analyse the short-run equilibrium of a firm are as follows:

(i)   All firms utilise homogenous factors of production.

(ii) Firms differ in efficiency.

(iii) Firms have different cost curves i.e. cost curves of firms vary from each other.

(iv) All firms sell their products at the uniform price determined by market forces of demand and supply curves of the industry.

As such, price of each firm P (Price) = AR = MR.

(v)   Firms produce and sell different quantities of output.

Explanation of Equilibrium

The short-run equilibrium of the firm can be explained with the help of marginal analysis and total cost and revenue analysis.

(A) Marginal Analysis (Marginal Cost and Marginal Revenue Analysis): In the short-run period, a firm will produce only if its price covers average variable cost or is higher than the average variable cost (AVC).

(i)   If the price is more than the average total costs (short-run average cost or ATC) i.e. Price = AR > SAC, the firm will earn *supernormal or abnormal profits*.

(ii) If price equals ATC i.e. P = AR = SAC, the firm will earn normal profits or will be at break-even point.

(iii) If price equals AVC, the firm will incur losses. And, if the price falls further below AVC, the firm will shut down. The reason, in order to produce the firm must cover at least its average variable cost (AVC) during the short-run.

Thus, in the short-run period, under perfect competition, a firm is in equilibrium in all the above cited situations.

Diagrammatic Illustration:

(i) **Supernormal Profits:** The firm will be earning supernormal profits in the short-run when price (AR) is higher than the short-run average cost (AC).

In Fig. 2.2 (i) the firm is in equilibrium at point E' where SMC = MR and SMC curve cuts MR curve form below, hence equilibrium output is OM' and equilibrium price is OP (or M'E').

M' B is the short-run average cost.

BE' (M' E' − M' B) is the profit per unit.

PC × CB = PCBE' as the supernormal profit.

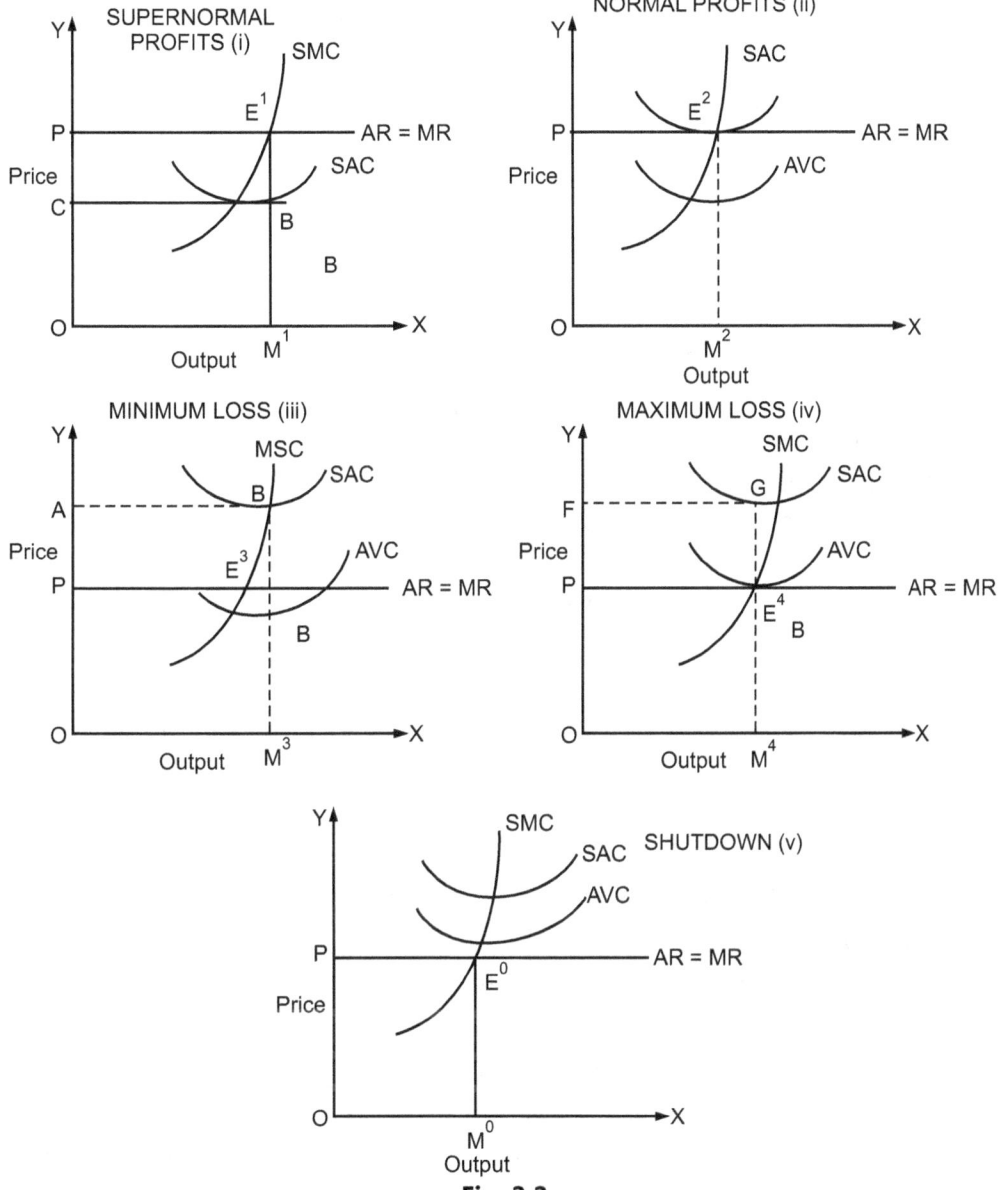

Fig. 2.2

(ii) Normal Profits: Normal profits are earned by a firm. Price equals the short run average cost as seen in Fig. 2.2 (ii). The firm is in equilibrium at point E^2 where SMC = MR and SMC cuts MR curve from below.

Equilibrium output is OM^2

Equilibrium price is OP (= $M^2 E^2$)

The firm is earning normal profits because,

Price = AR = MR = SMC = SAC at its minimum point E^2

(iii) Minimum Loss: In Fig. 2.2 (iii) we see that the firm is in equilibrium yet incurs loss when price (i.e. AR) is less than the short-run average costs.

Equilibrium of the firm is at point E^3, where SMC = MR and SMC curve cuts MR curve from below.

Equilibrium output is OM^3.

Equilibrium price is OP (= $M^3 E^3$)

Now, since the average costs $M^3 B$ are higher than the price $M^3 E^3$, thus $E^3 B$ is the ($M^3 B - M^3 E^3$).

Total loss is $PE^3 \times E^3 B = PE^3BA$

The firm will continue to produce OM^3 output as long the firm is covering its average variable costs (AVC) plus some of its fixed costs.

(iv) Maximum Loss: Now, when the price falls to the level to cover only AVC, the firm is indifferent whether to operate or close down as its losses are the maximum.

In Fig. 2.2 (iv) will pay such a firm to continue producing OM^4 output. It incurs PE^4 GF losses, but does not close down in the short-run.

OM^4 is the shutdown output because if the price falls below OP, the firm will stop production.

(v) Shutdown Stage: In Fig. 2.2 (v), shows a firm are not able to cover even its average variable cost (AVC) at OM^0 level of output. Price is below the AVC curve. Thus, the firm must shut down.

Therefore, in the short-run, there are firms which earn normal profits, supernormal profits and incur losses. To recapitulate,

(i)   When price (AR) > AC, there is excess profit.

(ii) When AR = AC, normal profits are yielded.

(iii) When AR < AC, firm incurs losses.

The analysis of firm's equilibrium in short run:

(i)   In the short-run, the firm has temporary equilibrium.

(ii) In the short-run, the firm is in equilibrium when SMC = MR at the given short-run equilibrium price (price determined by demand and supply).

(iii) Maximum profits to a firm is when price (AR) is higher to the firms ATC (average total costs).

(iv) A maximum loss is incurred by the firm when price is just equal to AVC. The loss is equal to the fixed costs. The loss is minimised when the price is less than ATC but above the variable cost.

(v)   The firm stops production, if the price is very low i.e. being less than the AVC.

(B) Explanation of Equilibrium of Firm in the Short-run by Total Cost and Total Revenue Analysis: We can understand the short-run equilibrium of the firm with the help of total cost and total revenue curves.

The firm's profits will be at its maximum when the positive difference is greatest between TR and TC.

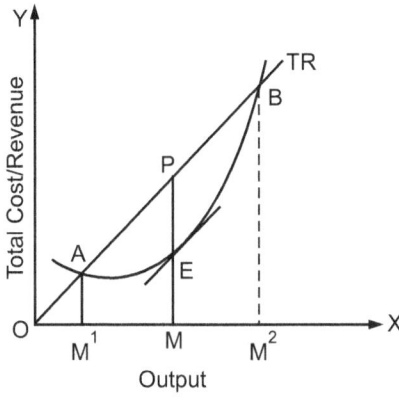

Fig. 2.3

In Fig. 2.3, TR is the total revenue curve and TC is the total cost curve.

TR curve is an upward sloping straight line curve starting form 'O' (Origin). TR has such a slope because the firm sells larger or small output at a constant price under perfect competition. If the firm produces nothing, TR will be zero. The more it produces, larger is the increase in TR. Thus, TR curve slopes upward and is linear.

The firm will earn maximum profits at that level of output where the gap is greatest between the TR and TC curve. It is that level at which the slope of a tangent drawn to the total cost curve equals the slope of the total revenue curve.

We see, in Fig. 2.3, the maximum profit is measured by EP at OM output. At output lesser or more than OM between A and B points, the firm's profits shrink.

If the firm produces OM' output, its losses are the maximum as the TC curve is above the TR curve. At M', its profits are zero. This is the break-even point of the firm (TR = TC). The firm will start earning profit when it produces beyond OM' output level. At OM^2 level, its profits are again zero. If it produces beyond this level, it incurs losses as TC > TR.

2.4.2 Short-run Equilibrium of the Industry

An industry is said to be in equilibrium in the short-run when there is no tendency for its total output to expand (by new firm's entry) or contract (by exit of firms). Thus, the following conditions must be satisfied for an industry to be in equilibrium in the short-run.

(i)   When each individual firm produces output at which it's MR = MC. Thus, all the existing firms must be producing an equilibrium level of output.

(ii)   It is not necessary that each firm in the industry should be earning normal profits in short-run. Because, some firms may be earning supernormal profits, some normal profits or some even incurring losses depending on their cost functions. In short, firms whether earning supernormal profits or maximum losses can coexist with the short-run equilibrium of the industry.

(iii) The short period demand and short-period supply are in equilibrium. When the total quantity demanded equals the total quantity supplied, at the short-run equilibrium price, the market is cleared and hence no reason to change the price in the short-run. Therefore, the market and all the firms in the industry attain short-run equilibrium at this price.

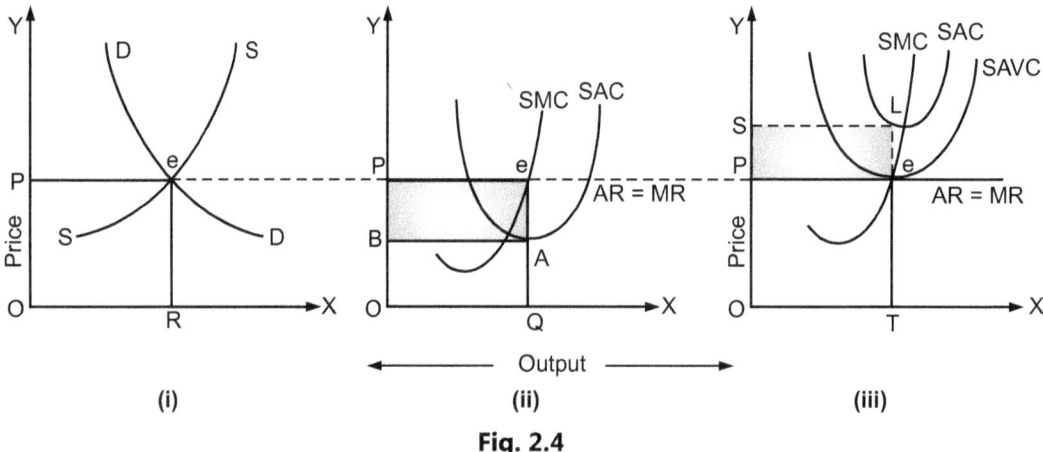

Fig. 2.4

In Fig. 2.4, SS is the short-run industry supply and DD is the short-run industry demand curve. Both curves intersect at point e. OP is the short-run equilibrium price at which OR is the quantity demanded equal to quantity supplied in the market.

At this determined price, industry is in equilibrium. The firms are also in equilibrium while equating MR with MC. However, in Fig. 2.4 (ii) the firm is making profits while in Fig. 2.4 (iii) the firm we see it is incurring losses.

2.4.3 Long-Run Equilibrium of the Firm

The long-run is a period of time in which the firm can change its plant and scale of operations to meet its changed demand. Thus, in the long-run all costs are variable and there are no fixed costs. In the long-run, under perfect competition, the firm is in equilibrium when it does not want to change its equilibrium output. *The firm is to earn only normal profits*.

If some firms are earning extra normal profits, new firms will enter the industry and these supernormal profits will be competed away.

If some firms are incurring losses, some firms will leave the industry till the existing firms earn normal profits.

Thus, there is no tendency for firms to enter or leave the industry because every firm must earn normal profits.

"In the long-run, firms are in equilibrium when they have adjusted their plant so as to produce at the minimum point of their LAC curve, which is tangent (at this lowest point) to the demand curve AR (which is the market price) to earn normal profits."

Long-run Equilibrium of the Firm Analysis is based on Certain Assumptions:
  (i)   There is free entry or exit of the firms.
  (ii) All firms are of equal efficiency.
  (iii) Cost functions of all firms are identical.
  (iv) The state of technology is same in all the firms.
  (v)   All factors are homogenous. They can be obtained at constant and uniform prices.
  (vi) All firms have perfect knowledge of price and output.

For attaining equilibrium, it is the same principle i.e. MR = MC, in the long-run.

In the long-run, since the firm can adjust its output by changing the scale of operations, the long-run average cost-curve is less 'U' pronounced (i.e. it is disc-shaped). The firms under perfect competition, demand curve being perfectly elastic at the given long-run market price, the LMR (= LAR) curve would be horizontal straight line. The equilibrium level of output would be when LMR = LMC and its profits are maximum.

Let us now graphically illustrate the process of long-run equilibrium adjustment in the output by a firm in response to different long-run market prices.

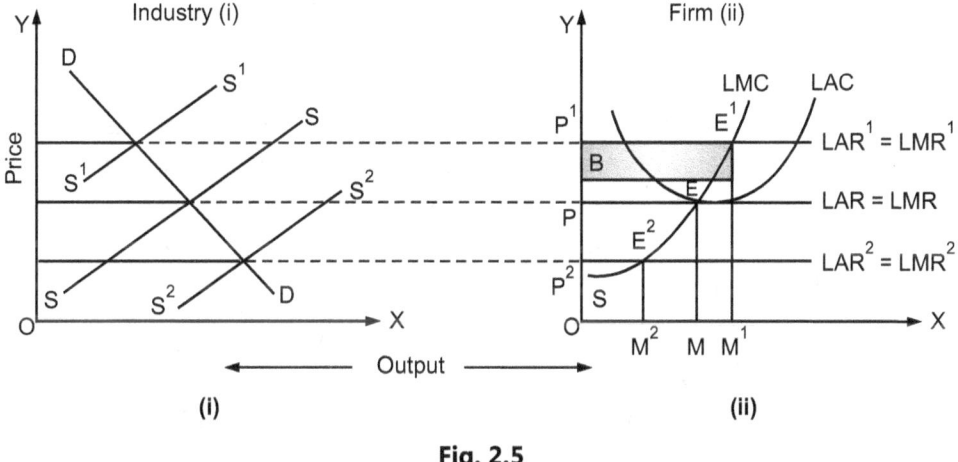

Fig. 2.5

In Fig. 2.5 (i) illustrates market demand and supply position of a given product, in the long-run.

Fig. 2.5 (ii) shows a typical firm's LAC and LMR at different price OP, OP^1, OP^2 etc.

The firm is a 'price-taker' and this market price (normal price) in the long-run is determined by equality between demand curve DD and supply curve SS of the industry.

OP^1 is the equilibrium price when S^1S^1 supply curve intersect DD demand curve.

At this price, the firm gets LMR' curve which intersects LMC curve at point E. The firm produces OM 'output'. The firm earns supernormal profits as LAR' > LAC. The amount of excess profit is the shaded area P^1E^1BA. These supernormal profits attract new firms in the industry. In the long-run ample time is available to the producers in other industry which shows more profits.

Under perfect competition there is mobility of firm from one industry to another. When the new firms enter the industry under consideration, the supply increases, the supply curve shifts to the right. The long-run equilibrium price falls, with demand remaining the same and supply increasing with price fall, the firm contracts its output and excess profits decline. It is possible that the firms may still yield some excess profits and it continues to attract entry of new firms to the industry. This shifts the supply curve to the right. Let's say, the new supply curve is SS. It intersects DD demand curve at a lower price OP. Now, the firm produces OM level of output, at which LMR = LMC. At this point LAC = Price or the firms get only normal profit.

If the supply curve would have shifted to $S^2 S^2$, the equilibrium price would have been OP^2. The firm would have attained a temporary equilibrium at point E^2. At this position the firm incurs losses. In the long-run, the firm must cover its full costs and should get normal profit. If it cannot then it has to quit the industry. With exit of some firms (which cannot earn normal profits) the supply curve shifts to the left, showing a decrease in supply – back to SS, equilibrium normal price OP is obtained. At OP price, the firm produces equilibrium output and earns normal profit.

Thus, under perfect competitions, long-run equilibrium is attained when the number of firms is so adjusted that any individual firm can get neither supernormal profits nor suffer any loss, but each firm earns only normal profit. This will be when LAR = LAC (at its minimum point).

Long-run equilibrium of a firm can be explained with the help of Fig. 2.6.

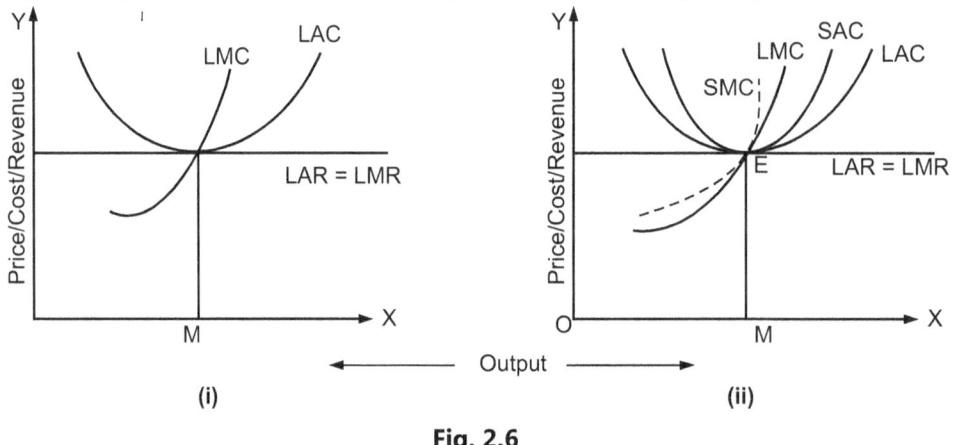

Fig. 2.6

Fig. 2.6 (i) the firm earns normal profits when the full equilibrium conditions in the long-run are fulfilled i.e.

P = LAR = LMR = LAC = LMC. Likewise, Fig. 2.6 (ii) depicts that

Long run Price = LMC = LMR = LAC = SAC = SMC.

In the long run, the firm has a single equilibrium point where:

Price = LMR = LMC = LAC

As the LMC curve intersects the LAC curve at the latter's minimum point, LMC = LMR = Price, will be possible only if the firm operates at the minimum point of the AC curve in the long-run. A firm in the long run must operate at this minimum point which is essential for its survival.

In the long run, thus, a firm's profit is just normal profits.

(a) Profit is maximised when LMC = LMR (at point E).

(b) Normal profits is yielded when price (AR) = LAC (at point - E).

(c) A firm a price - taker when we find LAR (Price) = LMR.

(d) The firm is operating at the minimum average cost when it equates LMC with LAC i.e. LMC = LAC.

The condition (d) indicates that all firms, under perfect competition, in the long-run must operate at their most efficient level of output, so that average cost is at the minimum (at point E in Fig. 2.6).

It is equally essential, for the firm that apart from long-run equilibrium condition, short-run equilibrium should also exist at the same time, because the long-run is composed of a series of short-run phases.

Hence, when a firm is in long-run equilibrium, it must be in short-run equilibrium too, but not vice versa. Short-run Marginal Cost (SMC) curve should intersect at the lowest point of the short-run average cost (SAC) curve, as seen in Fig. 2.6 (ii).

Therefore, when a firm is in long-run equilibrium, the position is:

Price = LMC = LMR = LAC = SAC = SMC.

Thus, industry, in the long-run automatically will attain equilibrium when all the firms attain equilibrium

In the long-run, thus, under perfectly competitive conditions, every firm in the industry and the industry as a whole, will be in full equilibrium when,

(i) Price i.e. AR = MR = MC = AC (short – run and long – run cost and revenue curves). i.e. SMC = LMC = MR = AR = P = SAC = LAC at its minimum point.

(ii) With given identical cost curves, under long-run full equilibrium, every firm will be producing the optimum output at the lowest average cost.

2.4.4 Long-run Equilibrium of the Industry

Certain conditions are to be fulfilled for equilibrium of a perfectly competitive industry. These are as follows:

(i) Industry is a collection of firms and hence for an industry to be in long-run equilibrium, all the existing firms in the industry must be producing an equilibrium level of output. This is attained when the long-run marginal cost is equal to long-run marginal revenue (LMR = LMC). Aggregate of their output comprises the total supply of the industry.

(ii) The number of firms in the industry must be stable. In other words, no new firms must enter; no firm should exit from the industry. This condition requires that all the existing firms must be earning normal profits. It is when all the firms have LAR = LAC.

If some firms are earning excess profits, it would encourage new firms in the industry which will change the industry supply and market prices in the long-run. Thus, it is essential that all the firms must earn normal profits in the long-run only then the industry enjoys an equilibrium position.

(iii) The long-run equilibrium price is determined in a way that in the long-run total quantities demanded is equal to the total quantities supplied and the market is cleared.

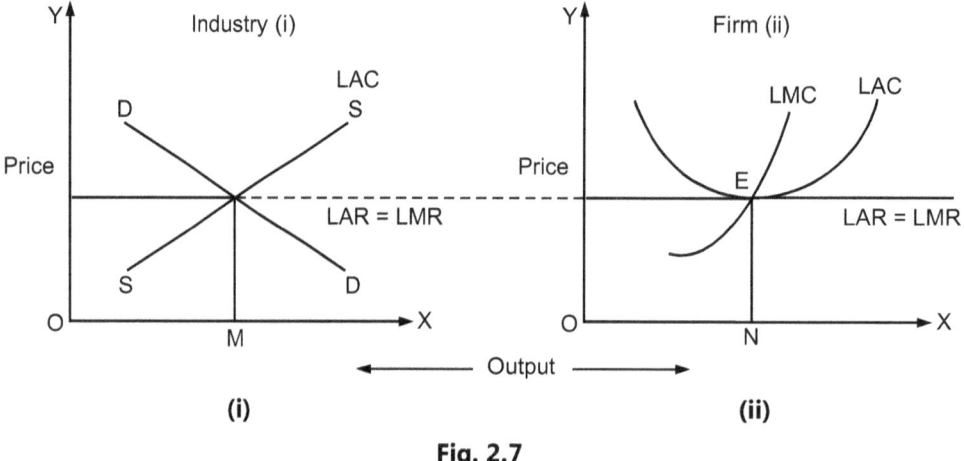

Fig. 2.7

In Fig. 2.7 (i) the long-run price OP is determined by the intersection of the long-run demand curve DD and long-run supply curves SS. At this price, the firm's equilibrium is determined by equating LMR = LMC. Equilibrium output of the firm in the long-run is ON. There is complete equilibrium position i.e. Price = LAR = LMR = LAC = LMC. As such the firm enjoys normal profits.

When all the firms are in equilibrium and all firms are earning normal profits.

In Fig. 2.7 (i) we observe OP as equilibrium price. It brings the industry in the long-run equilibrium. The firms under homogeneity (identical) conditions – i.e. all firms having identical cost functions hence they must operate at the minimum point of LAC (Fig. 2.7 (ii)).

The firms that are inefficient i.e. their cost functions are at a higher level (i.e. LAC) than the price, have to quit the industry in the long run as they fail to earn normal profits and losses are not sustainable by them.

Prof. Lipsey states that, "*a price-taking competing firm attains long-run equilibrium only when it is producing at the minimum point on its long-run average cost curve.*"

To conclude, industry and firms equilibrium conditions in the long-run are:

Long Equilibrium Price = LAR = LAC = LMR = LMC.

2.5 Pricing under Perfect Competition

Micro economics is also referred to as 'Price Theory' as price determines the allocation of resources, distribution of factor incomes, composition of production, variations in factor combinations etc. Most of the modern economies are market economies where the working of the entire economy is guided and regulated by price mechanism.

In perfect competition, market price is determined by the interaction of total demand and total supply. To obtain the average revenue curve (AR) or demand curve of an industry, i.e., total demand curve, we total the demand curves of all individual buyers. The demand curve for the industry slopes downwards depicting the law of demand, i.e., at higher price less demanded. The supply curve of an industry is summation of all the individual supply curves of individual firms. It slopes upwards indicating more is supplied at higher price.

Thus, the two economic forces- demand and supply- operate in opposite directions. Prof. Marshall has compared these two economic forces with the two blades of a pair of scissors. Just as to cut a piece of paper both the blades of the scissors are essential, similarly to determine the price in a competitive market, both the economic forces- total demand and total supply- are essential. The two forces are balanced or in equilibrium at the market price (market price = quantity demanded = quantity supplied). This price is also called as the 'Equilibrium Price'.

The term "equilibrium price" has no moral or ethical significance. It does not necessarily mean fair or just or in any way an equitable price. *The equilibrium price is the result of equilibrium between the demand and supply of the commodity.* That is, the quantity demanded in the market is equal to the quantity supplied at the price. It is not a normative concept. Equilibrium is said to be stable when any disturbance in it releases certain forces, which automatically call a return to the original situation.

To understand the mechanism of the equilibrium price (i.e. price determination) in competitive market, we illustrate it with the help of a schedule and diagram.

Table 2.1: Demand and Supply Schedule

Price of oranges (₹/Dozen)	Quantity Demanded Dozen/day	Quantity supplied Dozen/day	Price Movement
50	100	500	Downwards
40	200	400	Downwards
30	**300**	**300**	**Neutral**
20	400	200	Upwards
10	500	100	Upwards

In the above Table 2.1 we observe that when the price is high, say ₹ 50 per dozen of oranges, the total supply is 500 dozens per day but the total demand is 100 dozens per day. Hence, the goods remain unsold as the market supply exceeds the market demand. It puts pressure on the price to move downwards. As the price slides down, due to the feature of perfect competition- free entry and exit- some firms quit the market and the supply declines. But, with the price declining some new buyers enter the market and hence the market demand rises.

Now we analyse the price movement when the price is ₹ 10 per dozen of oranges. At this low price market demand exceeds the market supply, as there are many buyers but firms that cannot supply at this ruling price do not enter the market. Due to excess demand, the pressure on the price is to move upwards. As the price rises, some buyers exit the market but some new firms that find the ruling price attractive enter the market and the total supply rises.

It is only at ₹ 30 per dozen of oranges that we find the pressure on the price 'neutral' as at this ruling price buyers willing to buy equals the supply of the willing sellers. This is the 'market price' or the 'equilibrium price'. At this ruling price that has been established by the interaction of market demand and market supply the total demand for oranges is 300 dozens per day and the total supply is 300 dozens per day.

Diagrammatic Illustration

Fig. 2.8 illustrates price determination under perfect competition.

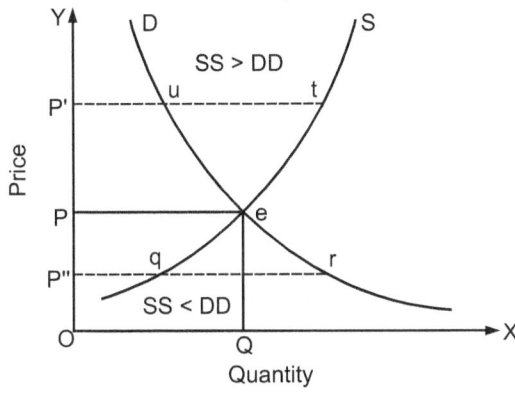

Fig. 2.8

OX – Axis measures quality demanded and supplied

OY – Axis measures price

DD – Demand Curve

SS – Supply Curve

SS is the supply curve which is lateral summation of all supply curves of individual firms in the industry. It slopes upwards from left to right indicating that more is supplied at higher price.

DD is the demand curve which is summation of all demand curves of all buyers in the market for that commodity. It slopes downwards from left to right indicating that more is demanded at lower price.

OP is the equilibrium price and at point e total demand (DD) is equal to total supply (SS) at quantity OQ. This is the market price.

At price OP' supply is P't and demand is P'u, i.e. supply is in excess of demand and the pressure on the price is to fall downwards to price OP (market price)

At price OP" supply is P"q and demand is P"r, i.e. supply is short of total demand. The pressure on the price is to move upwards to price OP (equilibrium price).

Effects

When price moves downwards:

- Firms exit from the market;
- Marginal buyers enter the market.

When price moves upwards:

- Firms enter the market;
- Marginal buyers exit the market.

Thus, any disturbance to the 'market price' OP (OP' or OP'') certain forces of the market will operate to establish the equilibrium price. Thus, the original equilibrium is a *stable equilibrium* till any change occurs on the demand or on the supply side. (e.g. any industrial strike causes the supply to reduce and keep the demand high which can disturb the market price but this is temporary as once the bottlenecks on supply side are cleared, then the market supply will equate market demand and settle at the old equilibrium).

2.6 Effect of Changes in Demand and Supply

(a) Change in Demand

Fig. 2.9 shows change in demand with supply remaining the same.

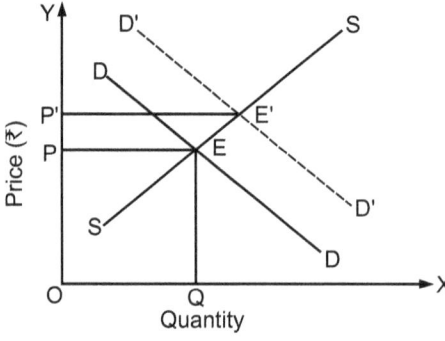

Fig. 2.9

Demand rises from DD to D'D', price rises from OP to OP'.

At equilibrium point E, demand OQ equals quantity supplied OQ, at price OP. When demand rises, depicted by rightward shift of demand curve DD to D^1D^1, the quantity demanded equals quantity supplied, now at new equilibrium position, i.e. E^1 at higher price OP^1. This change can be referred to as "a rise in demand price" or "an increase in demand".

(a) Change in Supply

Fig. 2.10 shows change in supply with demand remaining the same.

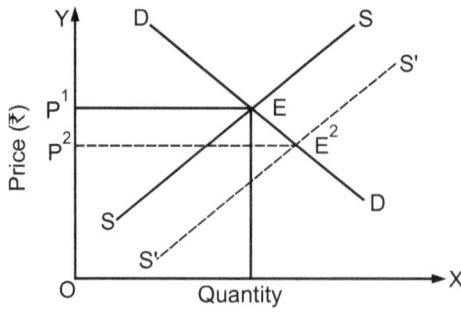

Fig. 2.10

At equilibrium E, quantity demanded OQ equals quantity supplied, at price OP. When supply rises, depicted by rightward shift of supply curve SS to S^1S^1, the quantity demanded equals quantity supplied, now at new equilibrium position, i.e. E^2 at lower price OP^2. As the supply has increased, the new equilibrium quantity demanded and quantity supplied is now OQ^2. This change can be referred to "as a fall in supply price" or "an increase in supply". At such a price, the sellers will supply a larger quantity of the commodity than before.

However, a given change in demand or supply conditions does not always cause the same change in price or sales.

2.7 Monopolistic Competition

Introduction

The model of monopolistic competition describes a common market structure in which firms have many competitors, but each one sells a slightly *different product*. Monopolistic competition as a market structure was first identified in the 1930s by American economist Edward Chamberlin, and English economist Joan Robinson.

2.8 Meaning of Imperfect Competition and Monopolistic Competition

In real life it is near to impossible to experience the two market situations – pure monopoly and perfect competition. Generally, the markets exhibit the features of both monopoly and competition. In some markets, an element of monopoly is noted more than competition while in others there is competition among the sellers. Thus, imperfect competition lies between the two extremes – pure monopoly and perfect competition.

Monopolistic competition is a market situation where there are many firms selling a 'differentiated' product and there is a keen competition (not perfect competition) amongst many firms.

Prior to 1933, Classical and many other economists believed that equilibrium in market was a normal situation and perfect competition was present, while monopoly was a rare situation. Any imperfections in the competition were not visualised. The publication of 'Economics of Imperfect Competition' by Mrs. Joan Robinson and 'Theory of Monopolistic Competition' by Prof. E.H.Chamberlin earmarked the beginning of the development of the theory of imperfect competition.

The characteristics of monopolistic competition were found to be more realistic, i.e. one could experience the presence of the features, such as sellers differentiate their products through various devices, engage in sales propaganda, etc. Thus, there is more imperfection in the market. It can be concluded that imperfect competition and monopolistic competition are not interchangeable terms. Imperfect competition is a comprehensive and wider term and monopolistic competition is one type of imperfect competition.

2.9 Characteristics of Monopolistic Competition

1. **Existence of a Large Number of Sellers:** There should be a large number of firms that are selling or supplying the product in the market. Even though there are many firms but none controls a major portion of the total output. Thus, there are many but small firms whose share in the market-sales does not exceed say more than 10%. Though the number of firms in the industry is less than that under perfect competition, but the number has to be large enough to allow a healthy competition amongst the firms. Under monopolistic competition, the supply of even the largest firm is small in relation to the market supply. Monopolistic competition is usually found in those fields of production where there are no special advantages of large scale production and where capital requirement is not very large and the decisions of one firm has no significant effect on the other firms.

2. **Product Differentiation:** This is a significant feature of monopolistic competition. Products of different firms are not homogenous as under perfect competition. On the contrary, every firm tries to impress the market with the 'differentness' and thereby proves its superiority of its own products. Basically, the product may be the same but even so, every firm attempts to differentiate its own product from the product of its rival firms. The situation is one in which there are many products in the market which are close substitutes of one another but apparently different from one another. Hence, there is competition amongst the various products that are similar but not the same and at the same time every firm enjoys monopoly in its own product. The markets for tooth-paste, shampoos, washing soaps, cosmetics, etc., are examples of monopolistic competition. There is competition among the producers but at the same time there is monopoly with regard to each 'brand'. Such a situation is referred to as monopolistic competition.

'Product differentiation' can be done by the following means:

- The firms may bring about product differentiation through differences in the quality of material used, durability, strength, workmanship or it can differentiate by bringing in differences in style and branding. Thus, it can be a host of many such devices to bring about artificial differences.

- The firms may differentiate their product by offering to their buyers supplementary and other after-sale services for the product. For instance, a firm may agree to provide life-long service after the sale of the product, credit facilities, free home delivery of goods, exchange offers, guarantee of repairs and servicing, acceptance of returned goods, etc.

- A firm may differentiate its product through advertisement, publicity and other sales propaganda. This is referred to as 'sales promotion'. If the sales promotion activity is effective, the buyers feel that the product of the given firm is superior to that being sold by other firms. Thus, sometimes monopolistic competition is called the case of 'differentiation' and 'large numbers'.

- The firm differentiates its product through difference in the 'location' of point of sale. A product sold in a boutique 'appears' to be different than the same product sold on the roadside.

According to E. H. Chamberlin, the theory of monopolistic competition is the most important contribution to economic thought in the 20th century.

3. Free Entry and Exit: The third important feature of monopolistic competition is that there is ease for new firms to enter into an existing industry or leave the industry. Since the firm's size is small, it makes it simple for the firm to enter or exit from the industry. The simplicity of production techniques and smallness of capital requirements place no serious obstacle to the entry of new firms or exit from the industry.

4. Absence of Firm's Interdependence: Under monopolistic competition the firms are not interdependent on one another. The reasons for absence of firm's interdependence are: (a) there are a large number of firms operating under monopolistic competition; (b) each firm's share is small enough in the total market. It may not exceed 10 per cent of the total market share; (c) each firm sells a 'differentiated' product; (d) due to product differentiation, each firm functions like a small monopolist in its segment of the market. The firm fixes the price-output independent of other firm's reactions.

Due to independent nature of firms, economists regard this market situation a mild and diluted form of monopoly, having competitive pressures from other firms in the market. Each firm is in a position to formulate its own price-output policy. Each firm has its own determinate demand curve for its product, assuming the prices of other firms as 'given'.

5. Nature of Revenue and Cost Curves under Monopolistic Competition:

Revenue curves: Average Revenue curve (AR) of the monopolistic firm is neither a horizontal straight line (parallel to x-axis) as seen in perfect competition, nor is it a downward steeply sloping line as under monopoly market.

The AR curve is not a horizontal straight line because the firm sells a 'differentiated' product (not homogenous product) having close substitutes (but not perfect substitutes) and there are also consumer preferences in relation to the product.

The AR curve of the firm is not a steeply downward-sloping as in monopolist market. The reason is that the monopoly firm produces a commodity which has no substitute, while the monopolistic firm has close substitutes available in the market. As a result, the demand for the product of the firm under monopolistic competition is much more sensitive even to a relatively small change in price. Hence, the AR (demand) curve of the firm is more 'elastic' than that of a monopoly firm. Graphically, the AR curve of the firm under monopolistic competition will have a lesser steepness that that of a monopoly firm.

However, to what extent is the demand curve elastic, depends on two factors:

- The extent of differentiation which exists between the product of one firm and that of the other firms, i.e., consumer's preferences for a particular 'brand' or 'make' of the product.
- The total number of firms operating in that group.

Fig. 2.11 shows the demand curve of a monopolistic firm.

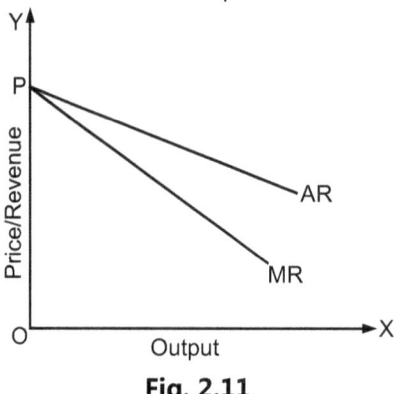

Fig. 2.11

In Fig. 2.11 we see the AR curve of a monopolistic firm which is downward-sloping elastic curve.

The AR curve has a continuous downward slope throughout its length, showing that the elasticity of a demand curve is the same both when price rises or it falls.

Thus, the revenue curve (AR curve) of the monopolistic firm is highly elastic though not perfectly elastic (as in perfect competition). The marginal curve (MR curve) lies below its AR curve. The slope of both the curves is gradual. The two curves (AR & MR) do not coincide, nor do they run parallel to the x-axis.

Cost Curves: In monopolistic competition there are many firms producing differentiated products. Although these various firms use similar factors of production and pay even similar factor prices, their cost curves are different from each other in view of internal economies enjoyed by these various firms and due to the product differentiation devices practised by them. Under monopolistic competition the cost curves pose a problem. There is no uniform price ruling in the market. The cost curves are not easy to be derived as for perfect competition cost curves that are derived from the 'industry' with the interaction of total demand and total supply. The products under monopolistic competition are not identical and are differentiated, hence considered as each one having their own market.

5. Selling Costs: Selling costs are a unique feature of monopolistic competition. Since products are differentiated and may be varied from time to time, for instance Dettol from soap cake to drop form in a bottle to change in colour when used for 10 seconds, hence advertising and other forms of sales propaganda form an integral part in marketing the goods. Selling costs are costs meant for sales promotion and thus distinguishes monopolistic competition from pure or perfect competition, in which products are homogenous and needs no costs of sales promotion. Under perfect competition, each firm experiences a perfectly elastic demand curve so that it can sell as much as it likes at the ruling price. However, under monopolistic competition, products are differentiated and these differences are made known to consumers through advertisement and other means of sales promotion. Moreover, monopolistic firms face demand curve which is downward sloping and hence selling efforts are needed to cause a shift in demand for the product and to capture a wider market. A firm through advertisement and sales promotion effort achieves the increase or rightward shift in the demand curve.

6. Two-dimensional Competition: Monopolistic competition has two faces: (i) price competition, and (ii) non-price competition, i.e. firms compete with each other on the price issue and on non-price issue to expand their sale. Non-price competition is in terms of product variation and selling costs incurred by each seller to capture his share in the market.

7. The Group: In the theory of price/value, Chamberlin introduced the concept of group in place of the traditional concept of industry. The term 'industry' is in perfect harmony with pure or perfect competition as 'industry' refers to a collection of firms producing a homogenous commodity. Monopolistic competition is characterised by product differentiation, i.e. not identical goods, as such, it is ridiculous to speak about the term 'industry'. For example, product groups like textiles, electronics, computers, soap, cosmetics, etc. Since there is no homogeneity of products sold by all the sellers in the monopolistic competitive market, we cannot think of industry as conceived by Prof. Marshall. *A 'group' is a cluster of firms producing very related but differentiated products.* Thus when there is product differentiation of products in the market, the collection of firms that produce similar varieties of product having quite a high negative cross elasticity of demand, it is referred to as a 'group' or 'product group'. It was based on the assumption that there is free entry of firms in the 'group' until it reaches complete equilibrium.

To sum up the features of Monopolistic competition:

1. Each firm makes independent decisions about price and output, based on its product, its market, and its *costs of production.*

2. Knowledge is widely spread between participants, but it is unlikely to be perfect. For example, diners can review all the menus available from restaurants in a town, before they make their choice. Once inside the restaurant, they can view the menu again, before ordering. However, they cannot fully appreciate the restaurant or the meal until after they have dined.

3. The entrepreneur has a more significant role than in firms that are perfectly competitive because of the increased risks associated with decision-making.

4. There is freedom to enter or leave the market, as there are no major barriers to entry or exit.

5. A central feature of monopolistic competition is that products are differentiated. There are four main types of differentiation:

   (a) *Physical product differentiation,* where firms use size, design, colour, shape, performance, and features to make their products different. For example, consumer electronics can easily be physically differentiated.

   (b) *Marketing differentiation,* where firms try to differentiate their product by distinctive packaging and other promotional techniques. For example, breakfast cereals can easily be differentiated through packaging.

(c) *Human capital differentiation*, where the firm creates differences through the skill of its employees, the level of training received, distinctive uniforms, and so on.

(d) *Differentiation through distribution*, including distribution via mail order or through internet shopping, such as Amazon.com, which differentiates itself from traditional bookstores by selling online.

6. Firms are price makers and are faced with a downward sloping demand curve. Because each firm makes a unique product, it can charge a higher or lower price than its rivals. The firm can set its own price and does not have to 'take' it from the industry as a whole, though the industry price may be a guideline, or may become a constraint. This also means that the demand curve will slope downwards.

7. Firms operating under monopolistic competition usually have to engage in advertising. Firms are often in fierce competition with other (local) firms offering a similar product or service, and may need to advertise on a local basis, to let customers know their differences. Common methods of advertising for these firms are through local press and radio, local cinema, posters, leaflets and special promotions.

8. Monopolistically competitive firms are assumed to have the sole objective of maximising profit.

9. There are usually large numbers of independent firms competing in the market.

Examples of monopolistic competition can be found in every high street.

Monopolistically competitive firms are most common in industries where differentiation is possible. Examples of Monopolistic competition are, the restaurant business; Hotels and pubs; General specialist retailing; Consumer services, such as hairdressing; etc.

2.10 Short-Period Equilibrium of the Firm under Monopolistic Competition

Short-run equilibrium of the firm under monopolistic competition can be more clearly understood when we make the following assumptions.

(i) There is a large number of sellers and they act independently of each other, i.e. each firm is a monopolist in his own product.

(ii) The product of each seller is 'differentiated' from the other product.

(iii) The firm has a determinate AR curve (i.e. determinate demand curve) which is elastic in nature.

(iv) The factor-services are in perfect elastic supply for the production of the 'given' product.

(v) Short-run cost curves of each firm differ from each other.

(vi) No new entrants are there in the industry.

Given these assumptions, we now explain the equilibrium of monopolistic competition in the short-period.

The short-run equilibrium of the firm, it is to be noted with regard to profits earned by the firm. If the firm earns abnormal profits by bringing out a new and popular product, it will have to be vigilant if it wants to continue profits. The reason is that the existence of excess profits will tempt other firms in the same group to bring out similar products and compete away the excess profits of the firm in question. Thus, in monopolistic competition, any excess profits earned by a firm will be competed away in the long period. However, in the short-period, the firm can earn abnormal profits as new firms do not enter during the short period. In the long-run, equilibrium position is only when individual firm earns only normal profits.

According to Prof. E. H. Chamberlin, the firms under monopolistic competition have many decisions to take than under perfect competition. It has to decide on variation of price, sales, output, quality of its product, sales tactics etc.

Similar to other market forms, the firm under monopolistic competition endeavours to maximise its profits. Hence, the firm will choose that price and output level which will secure its maximum profit.

The equilibrium position is indicated by equality of marginal revenue and marginal cost (MR = MC).

In the short-run, the monopolistic firm will have Average Fixed Cost (AFC), Average Variable Cost (AVC), Average Total Unit Cost (ATUC) and the Marginal Cost (MC). In the long-run, the firm has only ATUC and its corresponding MC curve.

To begin with, the equilibrium price and output is determined at a point where the short-run marginal cost (SMC) is equal to marginal revenue (MR) curve and SMC curve cuts the MR curve from below.

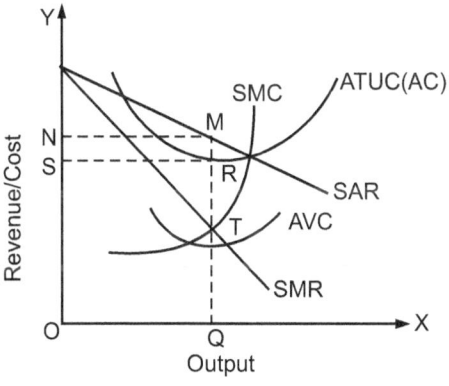

Fig. 2.12

In Fig. 2.12, SAR is the short-period average revenue curve, SMR is its corresponding short period marginal revenue curve, AVC is the average variable, and ATUC is average total unit cost. SMC is the short-run marginal cost curve.

The firm is in equilibrium at point T, as at this point MR = MC.

OQ is the equilibrium output, and

MQ (or ON) is the profit-maximising Price.

The firm is earning abnormal profits as shown by the shaded area NSRM. The firm under monopolistic competition can earn excess profit in the short-run, though in the long period such profits tend to disappear and only normal profits are earned by the firm.

In the above discussion, only one in hundred firms has been taken under consideration, i.e. the price charged and quality offered by this firm may not be identical with the prices and qualities of other firms.

As far as the price is concerned, well-established firms may charge a high price, while the new and young firms may charge a lower price.

Further, larger the firm, lower the average cost while the smaller firms' average cost may be higher. Thus, in the short-run some firms may earn abnormal profits, some to earn normal profits and some may even incur losses.

These three possibilities are depicted in:

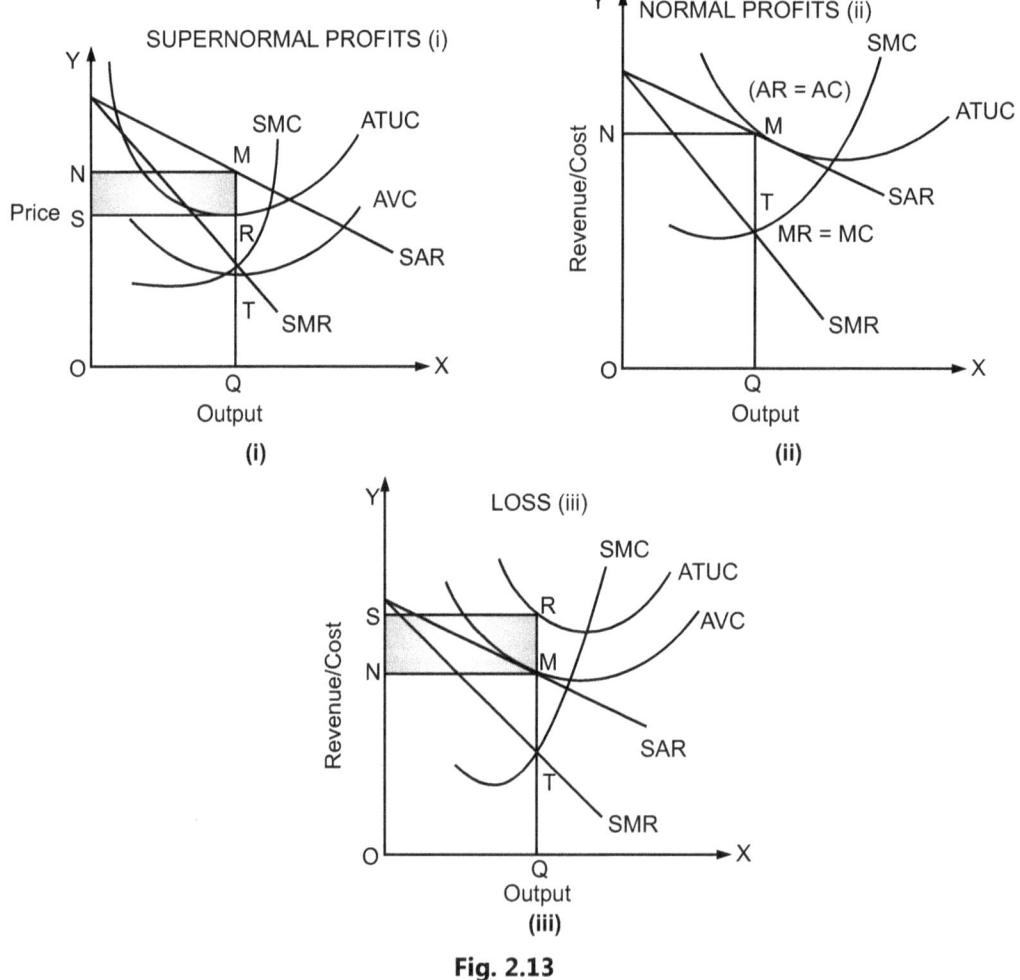

Fig. 2.13

(i) The firm earns supernormal profits shown by the shaded area NSRM.

At point T SMR = SMC.

Equilibrium output is OQ. Price is MQ (= ON)

The firm at this price not only covers its average variable cost (AVC) but also some of its fixed cost (ATUC).

(ii) In Fig. 2.13 at point T equilibrium output is OQ as at 'T' SMR = SMC.

Price MQ = AR and is also equal to AC as ATUC (AC) is tangent at point M.

The firm is earning only normal profit.

(MQ is not only the AR (or price), it is also the average cost).

(iii) The firm is incurring loss, shown by shaded area SNMR because the price MQ is lower than the average cost RQ. [Fig. 2.13 (iii)].

To sum up, in the short-run under monopolistic competition, the individual firm may attain its equilibrium (make maximum profits or incur losses), but the group as a whole is not in stable equilibrium due to the tendency of the firms to enter or exit the industry.

Full equilibrium is not possible under monopolistic competition in a short period.

2.11 Long-Period Equilibrium of the Firm under Monopolistic Competition

The firm can maximise its net revenue (i.e. profits) by equating marginal cost with its marginal revenue (MC = MR).

In the short-run, the individual firms are in equilibrium but the group is not in stable equilibrium, as there is a tendency for new firms to enter or exit the industry.

In the long-run, however, it is possible to attain 'full-equilibrium' i.e. the individual firm and the group to be in stable equilibrium.

To achieve this full equilibrium, two types of long-run adjustments will have to take place within the group of monopolistic competing firms. One adjustment is that at the established price the total sale (quantity offered by sale) must be equal to the total demand (quantity that the customers will take). The other adjustment is that of entry and exit of firms in response to the general position of the existing firms.

In the long-run there is entry and exit of firms in a monopolistic competitive industry as under perfect competition. The adjustment process will ultimately lead to the existence of only normal profits. This is a realistic assumption for in the long-run no firm can either excess profits or incur losses as each produces a similar product.

(a) If, under monopolistic competitive industry, firms are earning supernormal profits, new firms will be attracted into the group. When the new firms enter, the total market is divided among more sellers and each firm will sell lesser quantities of the product than before. Consequently, the demand curves faced by individual firms shift down to the left. It is also true that, entry of new firms will increase the demand and as a result the prices of factor-services will increase. It will shift the cost curves, e.g. for individual firms, upward.

These two-way adjustments, process-lowering the demand curve and raising the cost curves will reduce the super-normal profits. Therefore, each firm will earn only normal profits in the long run. (see Fig. 2.14).

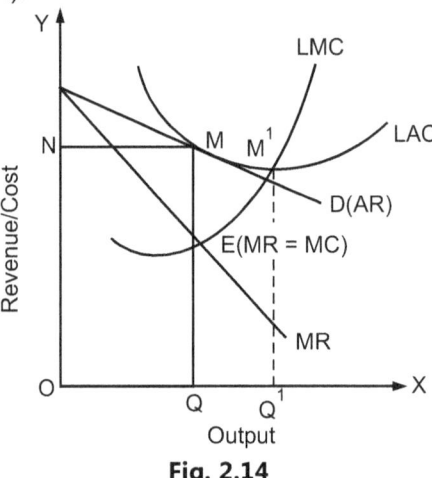

Fig. 2.14

In Fig. 2.14, all firms are in long-run equilibrium at point E as (a) LMC = MR and (b) LMC cuts MR curve from below. The LAC curve is tangent to the demand curve AR (D) at point M. Price is MQ = LAC at point M (i.e. AR = AC).

Each firm is thus, earning only normal profits and no firm has a tendency to enter or exit the industry.

Under monopolistic competition, this long-run equilibrium brings out one reality that each firm and the entire industry do not produce optimum output (i.e. it has excess and idle capacity). Thus, under monopolistic competition, there will always be 'excess capacity'. Hence, the firms do not enjoy the economies of large scale as they do not operate to their maximum capacity. In Fig. 2.14, we observe that LAC and AR (demand) curves are tangent at point M which is not at the lowest level. M' is the lowest point of LAC curve, which is to the right of point M. Thus, because the demand curve D = AR is not horizontal but slopes downwards to the right, each firm under monopolistic competition has unutilised capacity even in the long-run.

2.12 Group Equilibrium

Heterogeneous products cannot be added to form the market demand and market supply schedules. Therefore, Prof. Chamberlain replaced the term "industry" by "group".

"A group includes all those firms that produce closely related goods, that is, goods which are close technological and economic substitutes."

In the 'group', the demand for each product is highly elastic and is quite influenced by changes in the price of other products sold by the firms in the group.

The product differentiation helps each firm in charging a different price for its product. Further, due to product differentiation, the demand curve (**revenue curve**) for each firm, representing its share of the market, differs in elasticity and position. The firm's **cost curve** differs in the group due to efficiency difference among the firms. Given these conditions, there would be a cluster of equilibrium prices (because of each firm having their own demand and cost curve). Hence, Prof. Chamberlain assumes that both demand and cost curves for all 'products' are uniform throughout the group. The other assumptions of the 'Group' equilibrium are-

- The products of the firms in the group are 'differentiated' but are close substitute;
- The objective of the firm, in the short and long run, is profit-maximisation;
- Prices for factors of production and technology are given;
- There is free entry and exit of firms in the 'group'.

'Group' equilibrium can be discussed under two headings: (i) Short period unstable equilibrium and (ii) Long period stable equilibrium.

(i) Short-Period Unstable Equilibrium

Short period group equilibrium under monopolistic competition is similar to short-period equilibrium under perfect competition.

In group equilibrium, under monopolistic competition, each firm has its own demand or average revenue (AR) curve, showing different quantities which it can sell at different prices.

The height/slope of AR curve will be determined by the established 'general' market price. This general price has been determined by total group demand and total group supply. Each firm will adjust its own price and output to the 'general' established price at that level where Marginal Revenue equals Marginal Cost (MR = MC).

If the total supply of the product (i.e. adding all firms' individual output produced at its own MR=MC) is equal to the total amount demanded by the buyers at the existing general price, the 'group' is said to be in short-run provisional equilibrium (unstable equilibrium).

(i) If the total group supply is greater than the total demand for the product (supply > demand), the *general price will fall* and each firm will adjust its price and output to a lower general price.

(ii) If the total group supply is lesser than the total demand for the product (supply > demand), the *general price will rise* and each firm will adjust its price and output to a higher general price.

These adjustments will continue until the total group supply is equal to the total group demand, resulting in bringing about provisional equilibrium in the short-run.

It should be understood that the group brings about the equilibrium of individual firms, while the individual firms help the equilibrium of the group.

The short-run 'group equilibrium' can be with the existence of excess profits or losses in the case of some firms. But in the long period abnormal profits or losses disappear and all the firms earn only normal profits.

In the short period, the equality between total supply and total demand is brought about and this equilibrium is established through adjustments in the prices and output of individual firms.

(ii) Long Period Group Equilibrium.

In the long-run, 'group' equilibrium is established through the entry of new firms or the exit of existing firms and all firms earning normal profits.

Long-run group equilibrium can be understood by adopting the Chamberlin's assumption namely that each firm has identical demand or average revenue and cost curves. If the demand curves of all the firms are identical, it can be presumed that all the firms will have equal shares of the market.

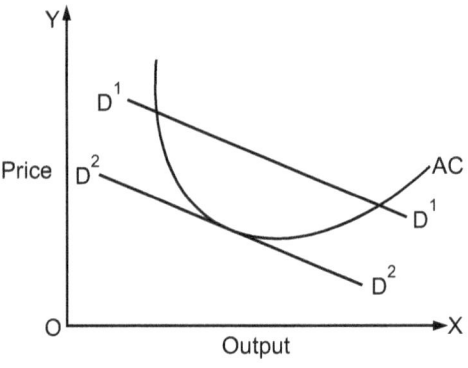

Fig. 2.15

The demand and cost curves are assumed to be common to all the firms. D'D' is the demand curve for each firm and AC is average cost of each firm. Each firm is earning abnormal profits with D'D' as (AR) demand curve and AC as cost curve.

In the long-period, new firms will enter the industry to take advantage of excess profits. This will increase new varieties of product in the market and thus reduce the sales of existing firms. The demand curve D'D' will shift downwards to the left – D^2D^2 and will be tangent to AC curve. Tangency between AR curve and AC curve implies normal profits to each firm. None of them would like to quit the group neither there will be any new entry. Thus, the 'group' is in long-run equilibrium. *In the long-run there is a tendency for prices to be pulled down to average cost.*

2.13 Effects of Monopolistic Competition

    (i)   Under monopolistic competition, the price of the product is higher and its output less than under perfect competition.

(ii) In monopolistic competition, the price (= AR) of the product equates the average cost of product, equates the average cost of production, in the long-run. The price will be equal to AC on the condition that new firms are not barred from entering into the industry.

(iii) Attempts on the part of an individual firm to expand its market may be offset by similar or greater attempts on the part of the other firms thus leading to wasteful expenditure on competitive advertisement.

(iv) With free entry into the industry, an individual firm will not be induced to produce at an optimum or ideal output level or produce at the minimum average cost. Thus, there is bound to be excess capacity under monopolistic competition.

(v) Monopolistic competition does provide to the consumer numerous varieties of a product form among which he makes a choice according to his tastes, fancies etc. However, the consumer finds himself unable to make a rational choice.

2.14 Distinction between Monopolistic and Perfect Competition

Let us first point out the similarities between the two types of competition:

(i)   There is freedom of entry and exit in both the markets.

(ii) The number of firms is quite large in both the type of competition.

(iii) There is keen competition between the firms.

(iv) The equilibrium is attained at the point where MC = MR.

(v)   In the short-run, firm may earn abnormal profits but in the long run period firms earn normal profits.

Differences

(i)   Under perfect competition, each firm produces homogenous product but there is product differentiation under monopolistic competition. Products are similar but not identical.

(ii) There in no need of incurring selling costs under perfect competition due to homogeneity of products. However, selling costs is an important component of monopolistic competition.

(iii) Under perfect competition, price is determined by forces of demand and supply for the entire industry. Under monopolistic competition every firm has its own price policy.

(iv) Under perfect competition the AR curve is perfectly elastic and is horizontal straight line. MR curve coincides with AR curve. But in monopolistic competition the demand (or AR) curve of a firm is downward sloping and MR curve lies below it. Further, it is not perfectly elastic but relatively elastic.

2.15 Concept of Excess Capacity

Mrs. Joan Robinson's and Prof. Chamberlin's discussion of imperfect competition reveal that monopolistic firms operate with unutilised (or excess) capacity.

A firm under monopolistic competition produces an output, in the long-period equilibrium, which is less than ideal (or optimum) output, i.e. firms do not produce that output level at which long-run average cost is at its minimum.

Under monopolistic competition, in the long-period equilibrium, a firm attains the optimum output when the AR curve (or demand curve) is tangent to the long-run average cost curve and thus earns normal profits. In such a case, the firms can reduce their average cost and (as a result price) by expanding their output to the minimum point of the AC curve. The firm will not do so as their profits has been maximised at point of output where MR = MC.

At this equality (MR = MC) the output is smaller than that at which long-run average cost is minimum.

Under perfect competition, the firm operates at the minimum point of long-run average cost curve. In short, the actual long-run output of the firm under monopolistic competition is lesser than what is produced under perfect competition and is considered as an ideal output level. This difference measures the extent of excess capacity under imperfect competition.

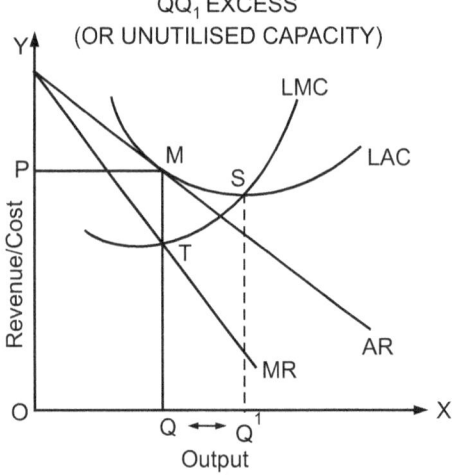

Fig. 2.16

Under monopolistic competition, a firm achieves long-run equilibrium at OQ output where MR = MC and price is equal to average cost.

AR is tangent to LAC at point M corresponding to output OQ. At this point (M), average cost is still falling and continues to fall till point 'S', where AC is at it's lowest. Hence, the firm produces QQ' quantity less than the ideal output (OQ'). Thus, QQ' is the excess capacity which emerges under monopolistic competition.

The concept of excess capacity refers only to the long-run. It emerges when there is free entry of firms but no price competition. The concept of excess capacity under monopolistic or imperfect competition has been criticised, particularly by **Harrod** and **Kaldor**. According to Kaldor, high degree of excess capacity under monopolistic competition exists due to the unrealistic assumptions made explicitly or implicitly by Prof. Chamberlin.

The firm in terms of allocation and productivity is inefficient in both the long and short run.

There is a tendency for excess capacity because firms can never fully exploit their fixed factors because mass production is difficult. This means they are productively inefficient in both the long and short run. However, this issue may be outweighed by the advantages of diversity and choice.

2.16 Product Differentiation

A unique feature of Monopolistic competition is product differentiation. What forms the basis and objectives of product differentiation? Product differentiation may range from strong to weak, which influences the consumer's psychology, preference or choice.

There are many ways of differentiating the product but the most common and essential feature that gives a unique identification of product is 'branding'.

"Branding" is a power-marketing concept. Producers of Pepsi, Coca Cola, Rado, Citizen, etc., use this timeless marketing concept, i.e. branding. A brand has characteristics like an identifiable product, service person or place, etc., to which the consumer perceives relevant unique value addition to the product. Branding is the creation of an integrated marketing communication programme or a mix of strategic marketing devices involving 7 p's- price, place, product, promotion, projection, physical evidence and prestige in today's competitive business environment.

Product differentiation may be classified into two types-

(a) Quality and characteristics of the product itself. The differentiation may be real or spurious and imaginary. The real differentiation can be related to the product's size, design, strength and durability, workmanship, etc. The imaginary or spurious differentiation relates to trade marks, brand names, colour and packaging, advertising claims and sales propaganda, which may influence the mind of buyers.

(b) Conditions relating to the sale of the product. In this regard, the prestige of the location of business, the firm's own business reputation, buyer's confidence, terms of trade like discount and credit facilities, after sales service and repairs, etc.

Product differentiation- real or spurious- identifies the seller and confers on the producer/seller a degree of monopoly power, which he can exploit to capture a segment of the market.

Objectives

- Product differentiation at a point of time aims at identifying the product of the seller from the product of rivals.

- Product differentiation as product development or quality variation over a period to time relates to adjusting the product more sensitively to the tastes and preferences of buyers, which would ensure their strong patronage. For example in electrical appliances, furniture, garments etc., material, design, size, style, and so on are varied for betterment of the product. By resorting to product improvement and giving new brand name to it, the producer hopes to have a more inelastic demand. This situation will allow the producer to charge a higher price, without losing patronage.

- Under monopolistic competition, the firms make constant attempts to convince the buyers that their products are virtually better than those of the rivals are.

- The competitors, in several businesses like Fast-Food restaurants, Toothpaste brands, etc., are out to resort to produce a variety of products to facilitate a wider choice for the consumers through product differentiation and undertake sales propaganda in a way to create a 'brand name'. The firm's strategy may also involve 'niche marketing'. It implies producing goods and services specifically for the customers in a particular market segment. In other words, the goods are 'tailored' to satisfy their specific needs. Again, 'green marketing' i.e., 'green product' or eco-friendly goods, for example, making of idols that are eco-friendly are meant to satisfy customers in a particular market segment. Such goods are produced to serve 'green marketing' strategy to satisfy the consumers who are conscious to environmental issues.

2.17 Sources of Product Differentiation

(i) **Branding:** For unique identification of their products, producers resort to 'branding', and brands are popularised through widespread advertising of the branded products. Branding is rewarding as strong and popular brands make the marketing task easy by providing a seal of approval for the quality of buyers.

(ii) **Product Prestige:** Producers can create product prestige of the firms in the market through material differences and brand variations. For example, in electronic goods, some companies like Sony, LG, Samsung have created its product prestige in the markets world over.

(iii) **Differences in Quality:** A producer may win over the buyers' choices by even notional difference of size, design, taste, colour, etc. The main point is to create a better image of the product.

(iv) **Differentiation by Location:** Businesses like hotel industry depends on site of the business. A hotel near the airport has a distinct advantage in gaining a better preference.

(v) **Additional Services:** Additional services with the main product play a significant role in the firm's product differentiation. For example, certain Airlines have earned a good reputation because of its service, better food, and safety norms. Further On road breakdown assistance provided by certain car manufacturers like Audi, Mercedes are other examples.

(vi) **After Sales Service:** In durable goods the firms provide after-sales service for repairing, replacement, etc. Warranty or guarantee period is also added to differentiate and compete in the market. The extended 5 year warranty provided by Hero Motors recently for its two wheelers is one such example.

2.18 Product Differentiation (Non-Price Competition)

The view that price is the only basis of competition is true in case of perfect competition. Under perfect competition, since the product is homogeneous, lowering the price is the only way of attracting customers. But under monopolistic competition, product is not homogeneous; and competition is possible in other ways, besides lowering the price. Non-price competition mainly takes the following three forms:

(a) Product Variation: Under monopolistic competition, as the products are differentiated, a firm faces competition in the form of product variation. A firm may make changes in its product by taking into account changes in consumer tastes and may attract new customers or snatch away the rival firms' customers. Thus, the basis of competition is not price but changes in the product or product variation. That is why; competition based on product variation becomes a type of non-price competition. The variation of the product may refer to an alteration in the quality of the product itself technical changes, a new design, better materials, it may mean a new package or container, it may mean more prompt or courteous service, a different way of doing business or perhaps a different location. In some cases, an alteration is specific and definite adoption of a new design for instance. In others, as a change in the quality of service, it may be gradual, perhaps not very obvious. This opinion of Chamberlin illustrates most lucidly the meaning of product variation and the various forms product variation can take. How far product variation is effective in increasing the sales of a firm depends upon how far the firm can impress upon the customers the superiority of its product. Where product differentiation exists, it is always possible to attract a group of customers by resorting to product variation.

By competition through product variation, Prof. Chamberlin means a quality competition. In this type of competition, the firm takes as 'given' the price that is established by custom or convention or tradition or any other reason. The firm, however, does have the freedom to change the quality of the product. By using this freedom, the firm effects some variations in the product. Such a variation may not necessarily be in the form of a change in intrinsic, quality or design of the product. It may well be in the form of a change in the packing or the cover. For example, an old novel with a new and attractive cover picture may attract a different group of buyers. This will increase the cost of production, but increase in sales will be more that compensate the increase in costs. Thus, the competitive strength of a firm can be increased with product variation and since price is unchanged, this competition is a kind of non-price competition.

(b) Advertising and Sales Promotion: Selling costs or costs incurred for sales promotion is another feature of monopolistic competition. Selling costs are an important element under monopolistic competition. A firm under monopolistic competition can so adjust its selling costs as to maximise its profits. Under perfect competition, because the firm can sell any amount of its product at the ruling price, selling costs are unnecessary. Under monopoly conditions, because there is no close substitute to the monopolist's product, advertising is unnecessary. But under monopolistic competition, because product differentiation is a basis of competition, a firm can increase its sales through advertising and sales promotion activities. Selling costs include all expenses on advertisements, salaries and allowances of sales representatives, show-rooms and so on. We have already noted two types of advertisement – informative and persuasive. Both these types serve to increase sales. So, advertising and all other types of sales promotion efforts are a kind of non-price competition. Once a preference for one's product is created in the minds of consumers, the consumers do not mind paying even a higher price for that particular brand. Thus, the basis of competition in this case is not lowering the price but creating a preference for one's brand through advertisement and other sales promotion devices.

(c) Market Research and Innovation: The third type of non-price competition can take the form of market research and innovation. Through market research a firm can sense the tastes and changes in the tastes of the consumers. This would enable the firm to make necessary changes in the product or the technique of production and prevail upon the rival firms in winning over a sizeable chunk of the market. Market research is, thus, useful for product variation. But it is also useful for introducing an innovation.

Innovation is probably the most important kind of business competition in the world. **Prof. Schumpeter** emphasises that the kind of competition which matters in the real capitalist world, as distinct from the text book model, is the competition from the new commodity, the new technology, the new source of supply the type of organisation - competition which demands a decisive cost or quality advantage and which strikes not at the margins of the profits and the outputs of existing firms but at their foundations and their very lives.

What Prof., Schumpeter means by innovation is clear from the above quotation and hardly needs any further explanation. In modern business, innovation has become an inseparable part of business pursuits. Innovation is different from product variation since it involves fundamental changes-though it includes product variation as well. Every slight variation in a product is in some sense an innovation. But innovation may be more fundamental like, introduction of man-made fibers, or plastic goods, or electronic instruments, products which are based on important and revolutionary inventions. **Savage** and **Small** have described innovation as consisting of some fundamental scientific discovery resulting in new technology, new goods and services usually for the mass market and wide consumer acceptance.

The above description of innovation underlines three stages in the process of innovation to make it successful:

(i)   In the first place, there must be some fundamental scientific discovery. Modern firms have well-equipped and properly manned research and development departments, laboratories, work-study sections etc.

(ii) Secondly, the commercial application of the new invention should be feasible. Innovations are not necessarily costly. But the change should be such as can be adjusted to various levels of production.

(iii) Finally, consumer acceptance is an important aspect of innovation. Consumer acceptance partly depends on sophistication and education of the consumers and partly on how far their expectations created by advertisements, are fulfilled by the product.

Innovation, therefore, acts as a substitute to price competition. However, innovations are not easy and are more advantageous in the long-run.

2.19 Non-Price Competition and Equilibrium

Price is not a very safe weapon to use for expanding sales as any price cut designed to increase sales may provoke retaliation from competitors. On the other hand, non-price competition (product variation and advertising) can provide effective competition in a much more subtle way. Non- price competition is an important feature of monopolistic competition.

In a monopolistic group, when a firm resorts to non-price competition, it undertakes **quality variations**. It means moulding a variant of the product item that makes a greater and wider appeal to the consumers. When a quality improvement of product is brought about with improved workmanship, service, material used, etc., the producer hopes to face a more inelastic demand for the product.

Due to quality variation, other things being constant, the producer finds demand curve for his product less elastic. In such a situation, he can charge a higher price than before for his product or alternatively at the same price he can increase his sale (due to product improvement), without experiencing any market contraction in the sale of his product.

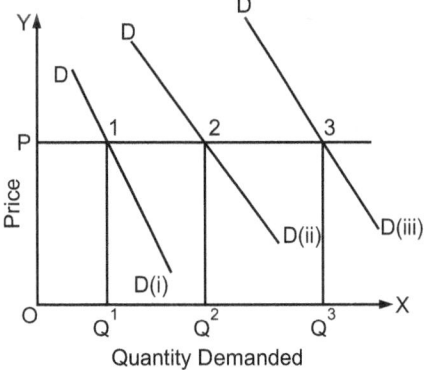

Fig. 2.17: Demand Curve with Product Variation

In Fig. 2.17, with different improved varieties 1, 2, 3, etc., of the product, the firm faces more and more inelastic demand, as such the demand curve keeps shifting to the right, say $D_{(i)}$, $D_{(ii)}$, $D_{(iii)}$, etc. It is to be noted that the shift of demand curve $D_{(i)}$ to $D_{(ii)}$ to $D_{(iii)}$ is not the same demand curve. These are different demand/sales curves for the three varieties of the product, namely 1, 2 and 3. At given price OP, we find points 1, 2, 3 etc., on each demand curve $D_{(i)}$, $D_{(ii)}$ $D_{(iii)}$, etc., showing their respective price-quantity relations.

Product variation also involves changes in the cost of production curve. That is, qualitative improvement in the product implies an increase in the cost of production and so the cost curve shifts. A series of product variations is difficult to be measured along an axis and displayed in a single diagram. As such, for each variety of products, a diagram is to be imagined with regard to its cost curve and the relative demand position.

In the product adjustment, a rational producer seeks to choose that variety of product at a given price, which yields the maximum total profit.

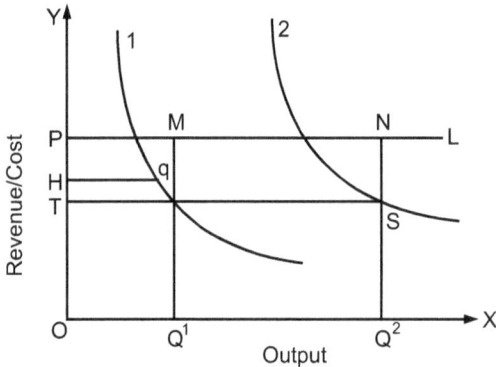

Fig. 2.18: Product Adjustment (Individual equilibrium)

Let us assume two variants of a product 1 and 2 at a given price OP. In Fig. 2.18, the curve 1 represents the cost curve for product 1 and the curve 2 represents the cost curve for product 2. At the given price OP, for both the varieties, OQ_1 quantity demanded for product 1 and OQ_2 demand for the product 2. PL represents a fixed price line but it is not a demand line.

At the same price, each variety of the product has its typical demand. In order to select a variety, the firm makes comparisons between costs and demands and the resulting profits for all possible varieties and chooses the most profitable one. In the above fig. 2.18 for product 1, the firm's total revenue at price OP is from OPM (MQ_1), while its total cost is $OHGQ_1$. Hence, the total profit is PMGH. For product 2, total revenue at OP Price is $OPNQ_2$ and total cost is for OQ_2 output is $OTSQ_2$. Hence, the total profit is PNST. Comparing the two it is observed that PNST > PMGH. It follows that a rational firm will choose product 2 and sell its OQ_2 amount of output at given price OP.

It is to be noted that the output OQ_2 may not be produced at the minimum point of average cost curve. Further, the product chosen may not necessarily be the one that is in demand. Suppose, we may take product 3 into consideration whose demand is high, but the cost is also relatively high. Then the relative profitability of product 3 may be less than that of product 2. In such a case, a rational firm will choose product 2 rather than product 3.

Variation in Price and Product (Individual Equilibrium).

Let us now consider both the factors- price and product, as variable. A rational producer will choose that variety of the product and price which yields him maximum total profits.

In our illustration, we assume three varieties- 1, 2, 3 of a product, demand curves as $D_{(i)}$, $D_{(ii)}$, $D_{(iii)}$ as shown in Fig. 2.19.

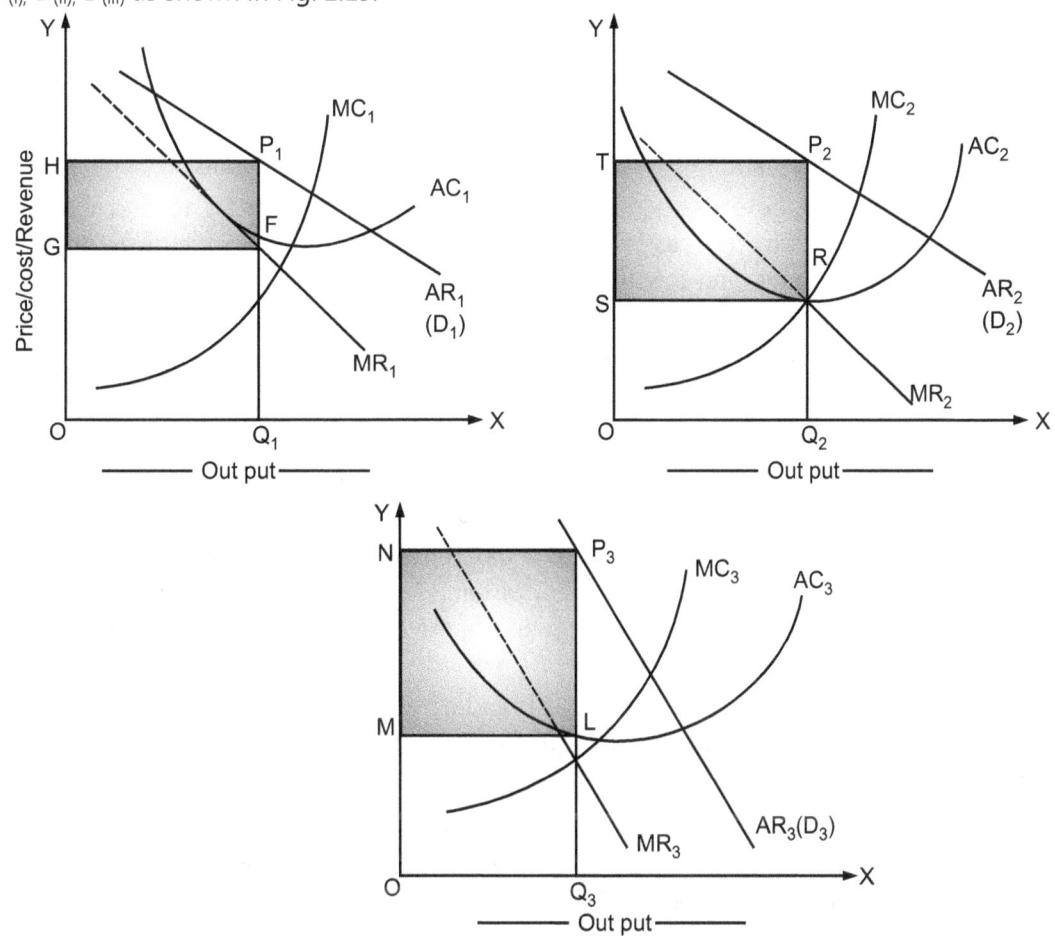

Fig. 2.19: Shows Price and Cost Variation (Individual Equilibrium)

For Product 1, equilibrium price and output conditions are P_1Q_1 and OQ_1 respectively. The profits are P_1FGH. Product 2 has its equilibrium condition with price-output as P_2Q_2 and OQ_2, with profit as P_2RST. For Product 3 the equilibrium condition of price and output is P_3Q_3 and OQ_3. This equilibrium condition yields profit level of P_3LMN. When compared $P_2RST > P_3LMN > P_3LMN$ (see shaded area). As Product 2 yields the highest profit, the producer will select product 2 and produce OQ_2 output at P_2Q_2 price.

Case Study (The Monopolistic competitive Restaurant Market)

In monopolistic market, since the firm is selling a 'differentiated' product and not a 'different' one, i.e. the product is almost a close substitute. In such a situation, in this market structure, advertisement is an important selling cost to be incurred. Further, a unique way of differentiating the product is through 'branding' and it is said that branding is rewarding.

What effect does advertising have on the price of a good or a place even like a hotel or restaurant?

On one hand, advertising might make consumers view products as being more different than they otherwise would. If it is so, it would make markets' less competitive and firms' demand curves less elastic and this would lead firms to charge higher prices.

On the other hand, advertising might make it easier for consumers to find the firms offering the best prices. In this case, it would make markets more competitive and firms' demand curves more elastic, and this would lead to lower prices.

The willingness of the firm to spend a large amount of money on advertising can itself be a signal to consumers about the quality of the product being offered.

This theory can explain why firms pay famous actors large amount of money to make advertisements that on the surface appear to convey no information at all. The information is not in the advertisement's content, but simply in its existence and expense.

Advertising is closely related to the existence of brand names.

Brand names cause consumers to perceive differences that do not really exist. In many cases, the generic good is almost indistinguishable from the brand-name good. The consumers' willingness to pay more for the brand-name is a form of irrationality fostered by advertising.

More recently, economists have defended brand names as a useful way for consumers to ensure that the goods they buy are of high quality. There are two related arguments.

First, brand names provide the consumers assurance about quality when quality cannot be easily judged in advance of purchase, like the quality of food items in a restaurant.

Second, brand names give firms an incentive to maintain high quality, because firms have a financial stake in maintaining the reputation of their brand names.

Example: *Restaurant Kamat*. Imagine that you are driving through an unfamiliar town and want to stop for a snack. You see Kamat and a local restaurant next to it. Which one would you choose? The local restaurant may in fact offer better food at lower prices, but you have no way of knowing that. By contrast, Kamat offers a consistent product across many cities. Its brand name is useful to you as a way of judging the quality of what you are about to buy.

The Kamat's brand name also ensures that the restaurant has an incentive to maintain quality. If some customers were to become ill from bad food sold at Kamat, the news would be disastrous for the company.

Kamat would lose much of the valuable reputation that it has built up with years of expensive advertising. As a result, it would lose sales and profit not just in the outlet that sold the bad food but also in its many outlets throughout the country.

Case Study (The Price of haircuts & the profits of hairdressers)

Suppose that there are many hairdressers and there is free entry into the industry. Assume that the prevalent price for women's haircuts is ₹ 200 and that at this price all hairdressers believe that their incomes are low and profit margin not lucrative.

With this common belief all hairdressers decide to form a trade association and the purpose is to impose a price of ₹ 300 for women's haircuts. Now, what is the result?

In the *short-run* the number of hairdressers is fixed and if the demand elasticity is less than one, i.e. number of hairdressers cannot be increased in the industry, then the total expenditure will rise and so will the incomes of hairdressers. But, if the demand elasticity increases more than one, i.e. number of hairdressers can be increased; the hairdresser's revenue will fall. Thus, knowledge of the elasticity of demand is essential. Assuming the elasticity of demand to be inelastic (less than 1), the hairdressers will be successful in earning more revenue with the change in price, *in the short run*.

In the long run, what is the effect of such an action, let us analyse the situation. Before the change in price, if the hairdressers were able to cover their costs and earn only normal profits (to keep them in the business), with increased price now they will be able to earn economic profits. Hairdressing will become an attractive trade in relation to other trades requiring equal skill and training. There will be new entrants into the industry. As the number of hairdressers rises, the business will be shared among more of them and earnings will decreases.

Profits may also be squeezed from another direction through non-price competition. When the number of firms increases in the industry, hairdressers may compete against one another for the limited number of customers. Their agreement does not allow them price-cuts but they may offer expensive magazines to their customers or may introduce welcome drinks suitable to the season to induce them. This type of non-price competition will raise the operating costs.

These changes will continue until hairdressers are just covering their opportunity costs, and the attraction for new entrants in the industry will vanish. The industry will be in equilibrium, in the long run, where each hairdresser is just able to earn normal profits – as before the price rise. In the industry there will be more hairdressers than they were in the original situation, but each one will be working for a smaller fraction of the day and will be idle for a large part of the day. The industry will have excess capacity. Customers will have to wait for lesser time even at peak period; they may enjoy more non-price competitive benefits of the firms at price of ₹ 300.

The trade association adopted the plan to raise the average income of the hairdressers, but it failed. But, with its plan it created more jobs for hairdressers, but not higher income for each.

In Monopolistic competition one cannot raise income by raising price above the competitive level unless one can prevent new entry or can otherwise reduce the quantity of the product or service provided.

2.20 Monopoly

Introduction

In classifying markets according to the degree of competition, perfect competition is an extreme case indicating maximum competition. The other extreme would therefore be a total absence of competition. Absence of competition means that there is only one producer. This is the state of monopoly.

The word 'Monopoly' is made up of two syllables 'Mono' and 'Poly'. Mono means single while Poly means selling. Hence, if there is only one single seller of a product in the market, such a situation will be referred to as monopoly.

In fact, *monopoly is a market situation in which there is only one seller or producer who controls the supply of single commodity which has no close substitutes.* This is only a literal meaning of the term Monopoly. In Economics, 'monopoly' is linked with the 'degree' of competition in the market.

2.21 Pure or Perfect (Absolute) Monopoly

Before going into the details of monopoly, it is necessary to have a clear idea of what we mean by monopoly. One possible variant of monopoly that can be conceived is 'pure monopoly.' If there is only one producer of a commodity, the situation is described as a monopoly. But for a pure monopoly, the following conditions must be satisfied.

(i)   There should be only one firm producing the commodity.

(ii) There should be no substitute for the commodity.

(iii) The above two conditions ensure that there is no direct competition. But as producers of all commodities are placing a claim on the limited income of the consumers, they are indirectly competing with one another. Absence of even this indirect competition is the essential condition for the monopoly to be 'pure'. Thus, it becomes the third condition of pure monopoly i.e. *even indirect competition is absent.*

In this way under pure monopoly, whatever the level of output of the monopolist firm, the firm is powerful enough to divert all the income of all the consumers to it. The Average Revenue (AR) curve also referred as demand curve faced by a firm under, pure monopoly is a 'rectangular hyperbola'.

Such a curve as seen in Fig. 2.20 indicates elastic demand and the elasticity is equal to one (unity). It implies that any point on curve DD1 indicates same elasticity of demand. With unit elasticity of demand, Total Revenue (TR) of the firm remains constant. Thus, under pure monopoly, even if there is a change in price and the quantity produced, the TR of the monopolist remains the same and is equal to the total expenditure of all the consumers.

Total expenditure of all the consumers, in turn, is equal to their total income. In other words, it means that all consumers in the market spend all their income to purchase the commodity produced by the monopolist.

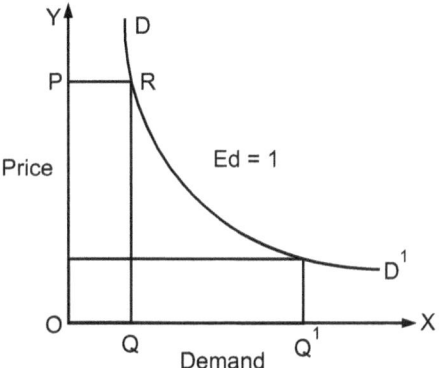

Fig. 2.20: Absolute Monopoly

From the above discussion it is clear, that pure monopoly can never exist in practice. In case of pure competition, though it cannot exist, there might be situations which come close to that of pure competition. Nevertheless pure monopoly is far off from reality and the concept is only of theoretical interest.

2.22 Simple or Limited Monopoly

Pure or perfect monopoly was mentioned merely as a possibility. However, an examination of the possibility revealed that we could not go any further in the analysis of monopoly price and monopoly equilibrium on the lines suggested by pure monopoly. It would therefore be desirable to build up some model of monopoly that may be useful in the study of the market. Such a concept of monopoly may refer to a limited or imperfect monopoly but it will have the advantage of being close to reality and of being theoretically plausible.

We can say that simple monopoly exists in the market of a commodity when there is only one producer, and there is no close substitute for the commodity he is producing. This monopolist is obviously less powerful than a 'pure monopolist' because there are substitutes to his product though they are not close ones. This is a fact the monopolist cannot afford to ignore. The supply of electricity by the Maharashtra State Electricity Board is an example of monopoly in this sense. There are substitutes for electricity; but they are no close substitutes. The board is the only supplier of electricity and as such, a monopolist in this sense.

Since there is only one firm producing a commodity, the distinction between the firm and the industry disappears. The assumptions of monopoly, in this limited sense, can be summarised as under.

(i) **Single Producer:** For a monopoly to exist, it is necessary that there be only one producer. The producer may be an individual, a partnership firm, a joint-stock company or a government corporation. Because of this condition, the distinction between a firm and an industry disappears.

(ii) Absence of Close Substitutes: To rule out the possibility of a rival to the monopolist, it is necessary that there be no close substitutes for the product of the monopolist. For example, a company may be the only one producing a particular brand of soap. But there are many other companies producing different brands of soap and each brand is a close substitute of every other brand. Such a situation cannot be called a monopolistic one. On the contrary, electric supply, where it is controlled wholly by a state electricity board, is an example of monopoly, as there are no close substitutes.

This condition of no close substitutes can be stated in terms of cross-elasticity of demand as well. Under monopoly, the cross-elasticity of demand for the monopolist's product is very low.

These two conditions together decide the power of the monopolist to determine the price. Control over price is the essence of monopoly. In perfect competition, a single firm has no control over prices. Under monopoly, the firm can control the price to a great extent. There are two courses open for the monopolist, either he can fix the price and adjust his supply to the market demand at that price, or alternatively, he can fix his supply and allow the price to be determined in accordance with the changes in market demand.

2.23 Emergence of Monopoly

An important feature of monopoly is the possibility of earning supernormal profits even in the long-run. The only condition is that there is no existing or potential rival to the monopolist. The possibility of a rival is eliminated because entry in the field is difficult. And because there is no rival, there is monopoly. The basis of monopoly is, thus, a barrier to the entry of new firms. This barrier can be of two types: (i) economic barrier and (ii) institutional or artificial barrier.

(i) Economic Barriers: A particular market may be so limited as to enable only a single firm to attain the optimum size. Until the optimum size is reached, costs go on decreasing and thus, the firm increases its output and supplies to the market. If any other firm tries to produce for the market, it will have to do so, on a small scale. This will deprive the rival firm of all the economies of large scale production and its costs will be higher. The firm thus will be unable to compete with the existing firm. The existing firm then becomes a monopolist.

(ii) Artificial Barriers: Control of vital raw materials, patent rights, keeping away rivals by waging a price-war (i.e. competitive price cutting) and creating various other types of artificial barriers are other ways of making entry in the field difficult. The monopolist may himself create such barriers or such barriers may exist due to institutional factors like patent laws. Such barriers then become the basis of monopoly.

2.24 Price-Output Determination under Monopoly (Assumptions)

'Monopoly' here means imperfect monopoly, because 'pure' monopoly is merely a theoretical limiting case. Imperfect monopoly here may be interpreted as a strong monopoly – a firm that is secure from potential rival firms or from government interference.

Now, how 'strong' the monopoly firm is will determine its price and output.

Below given assumptions are important, while studying the price-output policy of a monopolistic firm.

(i)   There are a large number of buyers in the market and there exists a perfect competition between them. No buyer can exert any influence on the price of the product through his own actions. Thus, the buyer is a 'price-taker.'

(ii)   It is also to be assumed that each buyer is rational and that he makes his purchases on a scale of preference which enables him to draw up his indifference map.

(iii)   The market demand curve of an industry under monopoly take the same shape as the market demand curve under perfect competition i.e. downward sloping from left to right.

(iv)   The monopoly firm does not differentiate between buyers and thus charge one single uniform price from all customers (not have price-discrimination).

(v)   It is also assumed that there are no close substitutes available for the product in the market. Not having close substitutes have a great impact on price-output determination.

(vi)   The monopolist does not charge discriminating price, in other words charges uniform price for his product.

(vii)   There are no restrictions on the power of the monopolist i.e. there is no institutional or governmental interference.

(viii)   Absence of close substitutes means there is no threat of entry of other firms in the market.

(xi)   It is assumed that the main objective of the monopolist firm is to earn maximum profits i.e. it seeks 'maximum, total profits' and not 'maximum unit profits'. Graphically, this position (of maximum total profits) would be when,

MR of the firm = MC

The demand curve (AR curve) for the product of the industry under monopoly, has a negative inclined slope as under perfect competition. But, as far as a *monopoly firm* is concerned, the AR curve has a different shape than the AR curve under perfect competition. In perfect competition the AR curve is a horizontal straight line as the firm is a 'price-taker'. The AR curve of the firm under monopoly slopes downwards from the left to the right throughout its length. Further, under perfect competition the AR and MR curve coincide. However, under monopoly, a firm has a downward sloping AR curve and hence MR curve lies below it.

Yet another difference between a competitive firm and firm under monopoly is that under the former the MR = MC = AR = AC when the firm is in equilibrium. But, under monopoly, MR = MC when the firm is in equilibrium but as MR is less than AR (as MR lies below AR), MC is also less than the AR. AR is the other name for price, thus MC has to be less than the price under monopoly. In pricing analysis, we consider the demand and supply conditions.

The demand curve (AR curve) for the product of the monopoly firm (or of industry) is negatively inclined i.e. slopes downwards same as in case of perfect competitive industry. But, one main difference between competitive firm and monopoly firm is that the monopoly firm is much better placed with regard to price and output determination. The monopoly firm has complete control over supply and thus is in a position to fix whatever price, it thinks, will maximise its profits. The demand curve of the monopoly firm slopes downwards indicating that the monopolist can sell more of the product only by reducing its price. *The demand curve of the monopoly firm is also its AR curve.* The AR curve has its corresponding MR curve lying below it.

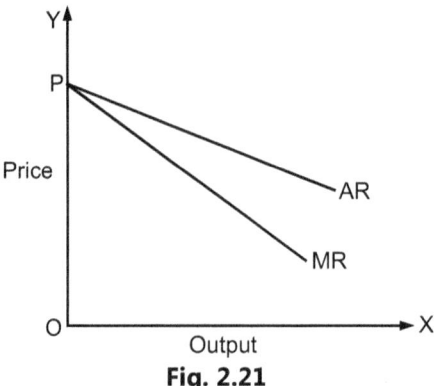

Fig. 2.21

In Fig. 2.21, the MR curve slopes downward right at a greater rate than the AR curve. Under perfect competition AR and MR curves coincide with each other. Under monopoly, the two curves are separate and the MR curve is steeper than the AR curve.

It is to be noted that *no monopolist can ever fix the output of his product at any level* where the elasticity of his demand curve (AR curve) is less than one. If he does so, his total revenue will fall as output increases and his marginal revenue will become negative.

A monopolist can earn larger profits by restricting his output, if he is producing an output at which the elasticity of demand for the product is *less than one*, provided his marginal costs (for producing additional output) is zero. Now, it is seldom that the MC is zero. Hence, no monopolist will ever fix the output at any level, where the elasticity of AR curve is less than one.

Another limiting case is, the monopoly firm will not fix the output at any level where the elasticity of the AR curve (demand curve) is equal to one. He will do so only if MC is zero.

Thus, the monopolist would be able to produce equilibrium output only at the level where the elasticity of demand for his product is *greater than one*.

Again, the MC curve of a perfectly competitive firm must always be rising at and near the output where the firm is in equilibrium. As AR and MR curves of a perfectly competitive firm coincide with each other, the firm can be in equilibrium only when the MC curve cuts the MR curve from below. Thus, a declining MC curve is not possible. Only possibility is that the marginal cost (MC) curve of a competitive firm *must* be rising at and near the equilibrium output.

However, this is not in the case in a monopolist firm. This type of firm can achieve equilibrium with all kinds of MC curves – rising, falling and constant. For equilibrium of a monopoly firm, conditions must be fulfilled i.e.

(a) The MR must be equal to MC. (MR = MC)

(b) MC curve must cut the MR curve from *below or left.*

Yet another difference relates to the size of profits. The competitive firm may be able to earn excess profits in the short-run as new firms may not enter the industry. But, in the long period supernormal profits disappear and only normal profits can be earned. In case of a monopoly firm, it can earn supernormal profits not only in the short-run but also in the long period, as free entry of new firms is not possible in a monopolistic situation.

It is to be pointed out that a monopoly firm does not always earn supernormal profits. A monopoly firm, under certain conditions, may earn only normal profits.

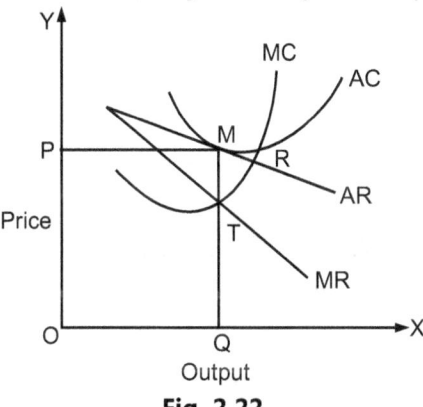

Fig. 2.22

In Fig. 2.22, AR is the average revenue curve; MR is the marginal revenue curve. OM is equilibrium output because the MC curve cuts the MR curve at T from below.

OP is the monopoly price. At OP price the firm earns only normal profits (as AR = AC). The average cost curve AC is tangent to AR curve at M. The firm earns only normal profits. But, it is to be noted that such a firm cannot produce optimum output (i.e. it cannot produce at the minimum average cost). As seen in Fig. 2.22, OM is not-optimum output. The lowest point is R on the AC curve and not 'M'. It should be remembered that a downward-sloping AR curve cannot be tangent to a U-shaped AC curve at or beyond its lowest point.

2.25 Monopoly Equilibrium in Short Period

Let us now analyse as to how the monopoly firm achieves equilibrium in the short period. In other words, how it determines price-output position.

The monopoly firm achieves equilibrium at that level of output where its marginal cost equates its marginal revenue (i.e. MC = MR). The firm either maximises its profits or minimises its losses at that output.

The short-period equilibrium of a monopoly firm is practically the same in nature as of a perfect competitive firm. During short-period, the time available to the firm is just enough to only increase or decrease its variable factors. It cannot alter the size of its fixed equipment, say plant.

Thus, if the demand for the product increases, its price goes up, the monopoly firm will only be able to increase the supply by increasing the variable factors. The fixed factors like machinery, plant, etc. will be overworked but the size of fixed factors cannot be increased. Similarly, if the demand falls, the monopoly firm will reduce the output by decreasing the variable factors and making a less intensive use of the existing fixed factors. However, the firm will not be in a position to reduce the size of the fixed factors in the short period.

It is to be noted that the monopoly price may be greater than, equal to or less than the average costs in the short period.

(a) If the monopoly price is greater than the average cost, the firm earns monopoly profits.

(b) If the price is less than average costs the firm suffers losses. But in that case, the firm will try to 'minimise' its losses by equating MC = MR. Thus, the monopoly firm will continue to operate in the short period even if the price does not fully cover its average costs.

(c) The price should not fall below the AVC. If the price falls so low that it does not cover even the AVC, then the monopoly firm will have no alternative but to close down the business.

In the short period, the monopoly firm can forego its fixed costs, but it cannot sacrifice its variable costs under any circumstances. But, in the long run, the monopoly firm must cover both fixed as well as variable costs-with its price.

Diagrammatic Illustration

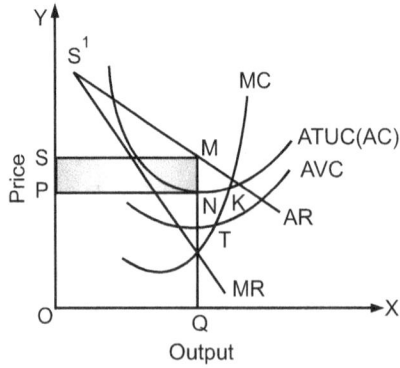

Fig. 2.23

In Fig. 2.23, the firm is in short period equilibrium at OQ output.

Thus, equilibrium output is OQ, equilibrium monopoly price is OS (= MQ) charged by the firm NQ is the ATUC (average total unit cost) SMNP (shaded area) is the monopoly profit. Theoretically, a monopolist can charge higher price say S'. But at this price, he cannot sell much of his output.

Since, maximisation of profits is the monopolist's interest, he will choose that particular output at which the MR = MC.

At OQ output and OS (= MQ) price, he yields maximum possible profit of SMNP. Any other combination of price and output will yield him less than the maximum possible profit. In short, he will stick to the OQ output and OS price.

However, it should be noted that the monopoly firm cannot achieve the short-run equilibrium at the optimum output or at an output level with the lowest average costs.

The OQ output, as seen in the diagram, is not being produced at the lowest average costs. NQ is not the lowest average cost. The lowest point on the ATUC curve is point K and not N. The monopoly price in the short period may even be less than the ATUC (AC).

In Fig. 2.24 equilibrium output is OQ.

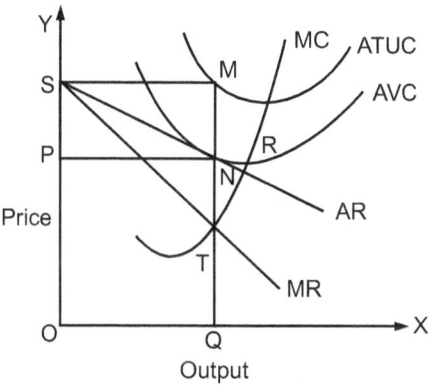

Fig. 2.24

Equilibrium output is OQ (as MR = MC at point T) NQ (or OP) is the price.

MQ is the ATUC (or average cost).

The price is lower than the ATUC at OQ output. But the price NQ covers only the AVC of the firm. The firm will continue its operations, even though this price does not cover the average total unit cost fully. The firm suffers a loss of MN per unit. The total loss is shown by the area SMNP.

In case the price falls below the AVC, the monopoly firm will stop its operations even in the short period.

Thus, it is misconception that a monopoly firm always makes profits.

2.26 Monopoly Equilibrium in Long Period

The monopoly firm will achieve equilibrium at that output level where the long period marginal cost equals the long period marginal revenue i.e. LPMC = LPMR.

Long period is a time period when there is sufficiently long time available to the firm to adjust its output to the changing demand. The firm can adjust its output to the changed demand by changing the fixed factors such as plant and machinery.

In the short period, output is adjusted with the help of changing variable factors and the fixed factors remain fixed. On the other hand in the long period both the factors-variable can be adjusted to match the changed demand. The demand for the product rises and as a result its price rises, the monopoly firm will try to increase the output by going in for a bigger-sized plant and also by increasing the size of the variable factors. In the same way, if the demand for the product falls, price of the product declines, the monopoly firm will reduce the output by not only decreasing the size of the variable factors but the firm will go in for a small-sized plant.

In short, in the long-period there is enough time for the firm to vary the size of its plant.

In the long period, the monopoly price could be *greater* than or *equal* to average total unit cost (ATUC). However, the price can never be lesser than ATUC. There is more possibility of the monopoly price to be higher than the ATUC, in the long period. It will enable the firm to earn excess (monopoly) profit. A competitive firm in the long-run can earn only normal profit. But, the monopoly firm could earn supernormal profits even in the long period, as there is no possibility of the entry of new firms into the industry. The entry of new firms is barred by technical, legal, natural reasons. Thus, the monopoly firm could go on earning supernormal profits in the long run undisturbed by the fear of new entrants into the field.

There is a possibility for the monopoly price to be equal to ATUC in the long period. The firm, in such a situation, would earn only normal profits. If a monopoly firm earns only normal profits in the long period, there would not be much point in continuing to remain in business.

In other words, there is greater possibility for the monopoly price to be greater than ATUC. On the other hand, there is no possibility of the monopoly price to be lesser than ATUC, in the long period. The firm would prefer to close down business rather than suffer losses.

In the short period, the firm may not be much concerned if the price is less than ATUC, but in the long-run, no monopoly firm would stay in business if it were to suffer financial loss.

Diagrammatic Illustration:

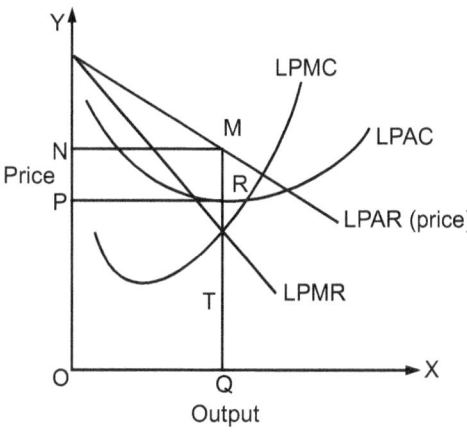

Fig. 2.25

In Fig. 2.25 we observe that the monopoly price ON (= MQ) is *higher* than the average cost RQ. The supernormal profit per unit is MR and the total monopoly supernormal profit is NMRP (shaded area).

Now, will the monopolist fix a high or low price for his product, in the long-run depends upon two conditions.

(a) Elasticity of the demand curve (AR curve).

(b) Behaviour of average cost as the output increases.

Let us analyse, taking these two factors in consideration.

If the elasticity of demand is low i.e. the product has inelastic or less elastic demand, *the monopolist can fix the higher price* and still have no fall in demand and output produced. In other words, the monopolist can increase his profit margin without any adverse effects on his sales. Thus, to yield maximum profit, the monopolist will fix a high price. But, if the elasticity of demand is high i.e. the demand for the product is elastic, the monopolist will fix a low price. Lower price will bring about an extension in demand and output and thus give him maximum profit.

Taking into consideration the second factor, viz. the behaviour of average costs, which is determined by the law of production, the output of the firm may be subject to increasing, constant or diminishing costs. For instance, if the output is subject to diminishing costs, that means, the average cost will go on diminishing as more output is produced. In such a situation, the firm should produce larger output and thus reduce its average cost. But, the dilemma is that if the demand is low, what he could do with larger output. The firm could increase the demand for its product by stepping up its output. The best way to increase the demand for the product is to fix *low price* for it. In short, it is in the monopolist's interest to fix lower price and produce larger supply, if his output is subject to diminishing costs. On the other hand, if the output is subject to increasing costs, then it is essential for the monopolist to produce smaller output but fix a higher price for his product and maximise his profits.

The case of constant costs does not influence the monopoly firm in either way.

To sum up, (a) the *elasticity of demand* is seen in the *marginal revenue curve and* (b) *behaviour of costs* in the *marginal cost curve.*

The monopolist takes into consideration both of these factors when he equalises MR = MC. These two factors, influencing the price output policy of the monopolist, are included in the principle of equality of MC with MR and are strictly followed by the monopolist in fixing price and output of his product.

2.27 Monopoly Equilibrium under Different Costs Conditions

We can explain this topic with the help of the diagrams given below.

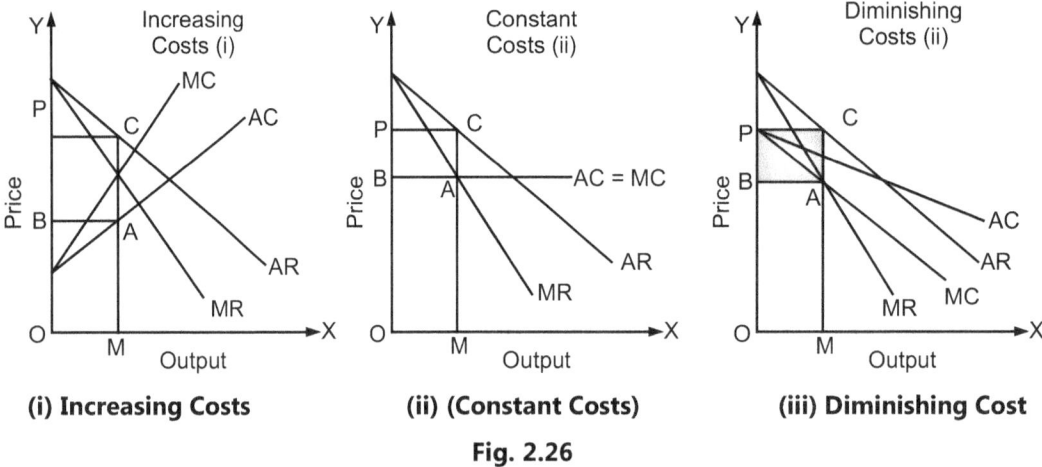

(i) Increasing Costs   (ii) (Constant Costs)   (iii) Diminishing Cost

Fig. 2.26

(i) **Increasing Costs:** Fig 2.26 (i) some industries experience increasing costs (or diminishing returns). The AC and MC cost curves are sloping upwards.

Equilibrium output is OM

CM (= OP) is the price.

PCAB show supernormal monopoly profit. The monopolists would not like to expand his output. By restricting output, he can charge high price and earn excess profits.

(ii) **Constant Costs:** Fig. 2.26 (ii) industries operating under constant costs have MC and AC as constant. MC and AC curves coincide and are parallel to X-axis.

Equilibrium price is OM

Monopoly profit is CM

Monopoly profit is PCAB

It is constant costs, level of output does not affect the average cost of production, hence monopolist is not concerned with size of production. He is more concerned with the position of demand i.e. AR curve.

(iii) Diminishing Costs: Fig. 2.26 (iii) it is a case of increasing returns or diminishing costs. The firm will increase its output to exploit fully the economies of large-scale production. The firm continues to expand and increase profits till it dominates the market.

Equilibrium output is OM

Monopoly profit is CM

Monopoly profit is PCAB

It must be noted that MC curve cuts the MR curve from below, yet at equilibrium output it continues to fall.

2.28 Difference between Monopoly Equilibrium and Perfect Competition Equilibrium

There are typical differences between the two types of market models and their equilibrium position.

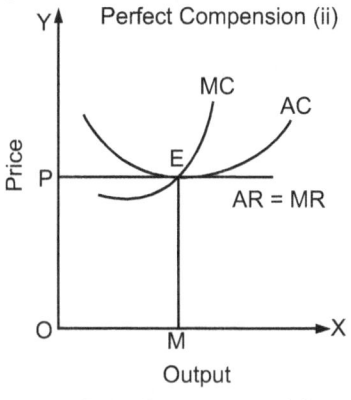
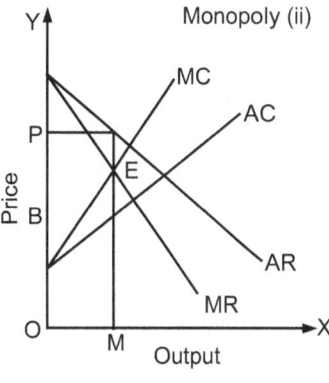

(i) Perfect competition   **(ii) Monopoly**

Fig. 2.27

AR = Average Revenue curve

MR = Marginal Revenue curve

MC = Marginal Cost curve

AC = Average Cost curve

E = Equilibrium Position

(i)   The demand curve (AR curve) for a competitive firm is a horizontal straight line. The firm can sell any level of output at the ruling market price. The AR curve of a monopolist firm is downward sloping. It means that he can sell more output only by lowering the price.

(ii) For a competitive firm, price is 'given' (i.e. firm is price-taker). At this price, AR and MR are the same and is horizontal straight line. Under monopoly, AR curve is downward sloping thus MR curve also slopes downwards and lies below AR curve. If it is linear, it lies half the distance between the price-axis and the demand curve.

(iii) Under perfect competition and monopoly, equilibrium is when MR = MC. A competitive firm achieves equilibrium when MC curve cuts MR curve from below i.e. MC must be *rising* at and near the equilibrium output. In fact, a competitive firm having MR curve horizontal straight line, it can never have *falling* Marginal Cost (i.e. returns increasing), equilibrium will not be achieved. Thus, increasing returns to scale or a continuously downward-sloping MC curve and perfect competition are incompatible.

Under monopoly, the MC curve of the firm must be rising at or near the equilibrium level of output is not essential. A monopoly firm can attain equilibrium under scale of rising, constant or falling cost conditions. The basic condition of monopoly equilibrium must be satisfied i.e. MR = MC and MC curve must cut the MR curve from below, but MC may not be rising at this point.

(iv) A competitive firm is a part of the whole industry while a monopoly firm is an industry itself. Thus, the monopoly price tends to be higher and output smaller than under perfect competition.

(v) The fundamental principle of profit maximisation is same in both the market forms i.e. MR = MC. The difference is - under competitive firm Price = AR = MR i.e. at equilibrium output MC = Price.

In monopoly, MR < AR (or price) at all levels of output and at equilibrium point MC = MR but MC < Price. Hence, under competition Price = MC but under monopoly Price > MC.

(vi) In a perfect normal equilibrium condition of a firm under competition in the long run, only normal profit is realised. In monopoly, excess monopoly profit can be earned in the long run.

(vii) In the long period, when competitive firm earns only normal profit, it operates at the minimum point of the LAC curve. The competitive firm is of optimum size.

A monopoly firm attains equilibrium at the falling path of the AC curve which means it has excess plant capacity and hence it operates at less than optimum size.

2.29 Monopoly Pricing and Profits

Some misconceptions about monopoly pricing and profits can now be discussed. It is generally believed that a monopolist can always charge a very high price and can thus earn higher profits, controls the market supply and is a 'price-maker'. This is not wholly true. A monopolist cannot determine price on the basis of his supply alone. He has to keep in consideration the demand aspect too. In short, monopoly price is determined by the relative strength of the forces of demand and supply.

While determining the equilibrium price and output, the objective of the monopolist is to maximise sale as he wants to maximise total profits and not unit profits. Now, if his demand is low, he has to set a low price corresponding to profit maximising condition of MR = MC. Again, it will be an error if the monopolist fix price of his product higher than the competitive price.

It depends on different considerations such as:

(i) If the demand is highly inelastic, with supply subject to increasing costs (i.e. output can be increased only at higher costs), the monopolist will restrict output to produce at lower cost and earn a higher profit. As such, the monopoly price will be very high compared to competitive price.

(ii) If the demand is highly inelastic, but the output is subject to decreasing costs (or increasing returns), the monopoly price would be nearer the competitive price. And, monopoly can be socially tolerated.

When there is a very limited market for a product, a monopolist can supply it at a lower price due to its low cost of production due to large scale economies than what is possible in a competitive market by a large number of firms producing goods on a small-scale.

Under competitive conditions, Price = AC, but the AC itself tends to be high due to lack of economies of scale and small-scale of production adopted by each firm. But, if there is monopoly which can cater the entire market, it will be on large-scale production and output will be produced on a lower cost due to economies of large-scale production. So, even if the monopolist sets a price higher than AC for higher profits, this price may relatively turn out to be lower than that of the competitive firm.

It is also not correct to say that the monopolist can always earn abnormal high profits due to his beneficial position in the market. It may be seen that at times demand and cost situations may not be very favourable to the monopolist and hence he cannot make profits. Further, in the long-run the monopolist may be under the threat of new entrants in his field of production, so that he may resort to price cut and earns lower profit and not maximum profit. If in the long-run the demand curve LAR is *tangent* to the long run average cost LAC, the monopoly firm earns only normal profits.

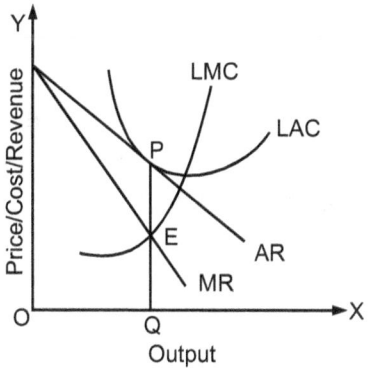

Fig. 2.28

If Fig. 2.28, the firm decides upon equilibrium output OQ and price charged is PQ.

Since the AR curve is tangent to LAC curve at point P, Price = AR = AC and the firm earns only a normal profit.

The only difference observed between normal profit under monopoly equilibrium and competitive equilibrium is that the monopolist is producing at less than optimum cost i.e. at a higher average cost's while a competitive firm when earns normal profit is producing at a minimum average cost (at optimum size). To put it differently, there is excess capacity of the plant under monopoly and capacity is fully utilised under perfect competition.

To sum up, the monopolist cannot always earn high monopoly profits. He should earn normal profits in the long run. He considers cost and demand situations in the long-run to determine price and output.

CASE STUDY (Monopoly in the Mumbai City Taxi Industry)

About 55,000 metered black-and-yellow taxis ply on the Mumbai roads. These taxis are an integral part of the city's heritage and ply throughout Mumbai. Auto rickshaws and taxis apart from public transport share the Mumbai roads. However, beyond Sion and Bandra, auto rickshaws are not allowed and one has to hire a taxi. Therefore the taxis enjoy the monopoly from Bandra to Chruchgate on the Western line and Sion to Chatrapati Shivaji Terminus on the Central line..

Taxi operators in Mumbai, as in most other municipalities in India, require a permit to operate a taxi. Since such permit holders are limited in number, this confers a monopoly power, i.e., the ability to earn economic/opportunity profit.

In 2006, the taxi operators launched a new scheme of modern, air-conditioned taxi service; the state government decided that no new permits would be issued to them because there is no room to put more taxis on the Mumbai's roads unless some of the old ones are pulled out. No new taxi permits have been issued in Mumbai for over a decade. Instead, the authorities felt that the new operator must negotiate with each permit-owner to acquire a permit. More than a year after the new scheme was launched, with two new taxi operators in business and a third service for women launched recently; there are fewer than 500 new taxis on Mumbai's roads.

Taxi Unions, such as Local taxi unions and associations, including the Mumbai Taxi Association, the Bombay Taxi Men's Union and the Mumbai Pune Taxi Association play a major role in the taxi industry. The local taxi unions have resisted the change, fearing that the new scheme would take away the taxi-owner's control of the trade turning them from self-employment into company employees. Recently, Mumbai's guardian minister had introduced the fleet taxi system as one of Mumbai's big 'makeover' projects. However, the taxi unions strongly opposed the swanky new taxis in a bid to protect their monopoly.

(This case study shows the barriers used to maintain monopoly status in the market. It is not a single firm but a particular trade that is being protected from entry of other types of transport in the market and it is 'area' monopoly).

2.30 OLIGOPOLY

Another form of imperfect competition is oligopoly or competition among a few. This type of market does not have only one producer as under monopoly nor does it have a very large number of sellers as under monopolistic competition. This is a market of a few or a limited number of sellers. The Word 'Oligopoly' is derived from two Greek words, 'oligoi' meaning 'a few' and 'pollen' meaning 'to sell'. Thus, the meaning of the word itself explains what an oligopolistic market is like.

2.30.1 Features of Oligopoly

The characteristics of an oligopolistic market are as under:

(i) Small Number of Sellers Producers: A small number of sellers or producers are a basic characteristic of oligopoly. Oligopoly comes into existence when a few firms dominate the market of a commodity. Generally speaking, when we refer to the big three or the big six producers we mean that a major portion of the market supply of the product concerned is under the control of these big producers. Such a market comes under the oligopolistic category of markets even if the remaining twenty or twenty-five per cent of the market supply is shared by a number of small firms.

When a number of firms producing for a market is small, every firm has a significant share of market supply. As such, the actions and policies of any firm will have repercussions on other firms. Hence, while trying to improve its own position in the market, every firm has to consider the probable reactions on and of its rivals.

The possible reactions of rival firms have to be taken into consideration while formulating policies regarding product price, advertising outlays, product quality and design and so on. This type of clear-cut mutual interdependence is a special feature of oligopoly. Such interdependence is absent in "perfect or monopolistic competition", because the number of firms is large. The monopolist on the other hand, has no rivals and so interdependence is ruled out, by definition. However, under oligopoly, because of the small number of firms, the actions of one firm exercise direct influence upon other firms. In all probability, it is possible to identify the firm that has caused such repercussions and it can be expected that the affected firms react accordingly.

(ii) Product Differentiation not a necessary condition: Product differentiation is possible under oligopoly, but it may not always be done. Generally, oligopolists produce more or less standardised products. Oligopolist firms producing raw materials or semifinished products offer almost uniform products to the buyers. For example, the production of iron and steel, copper or cement is dominated by a few firms and the products are more or less uniform. On the other hand, oligopolistic industries producing consumer goods offer differentiated products, for example, scooter tyres, cars, radio-sets and many other durable consumer goods products. Scooter tyres, cars, radio-sets and many other durable consumer goods in India are produced under oligopolistic conditions and the products are definitely differentiated.

(iii) Control over Price Circumscribed by Mutual Interdependence: Under oligopoly every firm is free to price its product; but this freedom is closely circumscribed by the mutual interdependence of firms which, as noted earlier, is a special feature of oligopoly. A firm can attract customers of rival firms to it by lowering the price of its product. But the rival firms losing their customers will retaliate by further lowering the prices of their products. This will result in competitive price cutting also known as price-war. Ultimately, all the firms in the industry will suffer losses. On the contrary, if a firm raises its price, it will lose its customers and the rival firms will gain by sticking to their existing prices. Price-raising would thus result in pricing oneself out of the market. Thus, under oligopoly, though every firm is free to fix its price, there is a general tendency to adhere to the existing prices.

(iv) Barriers to Entry: In oligopolistic industries, obstacles to entry are formidable. Entry of new firms is prevented by ownership of crucial patents or ownership of vital raw materials. Many times technological conditions are such that production is economic only on a large scale. A new firm therefore will have to start production on a large scale form the very outset. It is not possible to make a modest beginning and expanding gradually as the firm gets established. As such, the scale of production also may make entry of a new firm difficult. Also, distribution channels, goodwill of the customers etc., and any new firm desirous of entering the field will have to consider these factors which make entry difficult. However, entry of new firms is not impossible as under monopoly; it is only difficult.

(v) Advertising and Sales Promotion: Large amounts of money are usually spent on advertising and sales promotion under oligopoly. However, the nature of an advertisement and the expenditure on it depends on whether the products are differentiated or not. If products are differentiated, every firm would spend large sums of money on advertising. This would be done to convince the consumers that its product is superior to those of its rivals. This would be competitive advertising. On the other hand, when products are standardised, advertising is not competitive. Usually, some amount of expense is incurred on advertisements, but the purpose of advertising is to keep the firm in the public's eye. This is because the users of the products are themselves industrialists and skilled businessmen who know the quality of the product and who are not likely to be carried away by the claims of the advertisements. For instance, the users know the quality of steel produced by the Tata's, Mysore and Hindustan Steel Ltd. and consequently advertising for them is scarce. But there is great deal of competitive advertising for consumer products like toothpastes, hair oils and creams etc.

Quality competition attains great importance when products are differentiated under conditions of oligopoly. Therefore, oligopolist firms spend large sums of money on research and design as well as on packing, colour and so on.

The Basis of Oligopoly

Why does an oligopolistic market exist? The obvious answer is 'because entry of new firms is difficult'. Thus, the factors that makes entry of new firms' difficult act as the basis of oligopoly. These factors are as under.

(i) Patented techniques of production and control over the supply of raw material provide a cost advantage to the existing firm. This cost advantage acts as an obstacle to the entry of new firms.

(ii) If the products are differentiated, the buyers develop preferences and may have cultivated the habits of using a particular brand of product. This established habit of the buyers gives an advantage to the existing firms and acts as a deterrent to the new firms.

(iii) The production techniques, in some cases, are such as to take the optimum size of the firm to a very high level of production. Thus, if a commodity is to be produced at the lowest average cost, the scale of production is required to be large. This requires a large capital investment which new firms may not dare to risk.

(iv) Existing firms which enjoy one or more of the above mentioned advantages may themselves create artificial barriers to the entry of new firms.

(v) As a part of the industrial policy, the government may make it compulsory for new firms to obtain a license before starting production and the procedure of industrial licensing, if cumbersome and lengthy, may itself create an obstacle to the entry of new firms.

Classification of Oligopoly Situations

On the following basis, the oligopoly situations can be classified:-

(i) Product differentiation: Oligopoly may be *perfect*, i.e. pure or *imperfect*, i.e. differentiated. If the products in the industry are homogenous, the oligopoly is 'pure' or perfect. While if the products in the industry are differentiated, which are close substitutes but not perfect substitutes, we call this situation as imperfect or differentiated oligopoly. In practice one generally experiences differentiated oligopoly.

(ii) Entry of firms: Oligopoly is *open or closed* based on the entry conditions for new firms in an industry. When new firms are free to enter the industry, it is an open oligopoly and when few firms dominate the market and there is no free entry to new firms, it is closed oligopoly.

(iii) Price leadership: The oligopoly situation can be classified as *partial or full,* depending upon the presence or absence of a price leader. In a situation where one large firm dominates the industry (price leader) and the other firms follow the leader with respect to fixation of price, it is partial oligopoly. On the other hand, Full oligopoly exists where no firm is dominant enough to take on the role of a price leader.

(iv) **Agreement between firms:** The *collusive* oligopoly is a situation where the firms instead of competing with each other, follow a common price policy. The collusion may be in the form of an agreement (open collusion) or an understanding between the firms (tacit or secret collusion). In addition, when the firms are acting independently, i.e. no agreement or any understanding, it is *non-collusive oligopoly.*

2.31 Price – Output Determination Under Oligopoly

Under differentiated oligopoly, the number of firms is small and their products are differentiated. Here the price may be fixed by the firms of the 'monopoly' level or may come to be settled at the 'competitive' level. We can approach the price-output analysis via Duopoly. There are two firms in the market producing differentiated products. In this case, the two firms will not indulge into a price war by undercutting each other. The products being different it is not so certain that a change in price of one firm will attract retaliatory change.

Under duopoly with product differentiation, since the products are different it is possible for one firm to raise or lower its price without the fear of either a complete loss of all the customers or an immediate reaction by the other firm. Moreover, it is possible for the customers to be attached either to one or the other product.

There would be less likelihood of the monopoly solution of the price problem being adopted because the two firms deal with two products and not one. This analysis of duopoly with product differentiation can be applied as extended to cover the market situation represented by oligopoly with product differentiation. However it is possible that out of the two possibilities - price was monopoly - price war may take place between firms similar to that of monopolistic competition. This can be shown in the following Fig. 2.29.

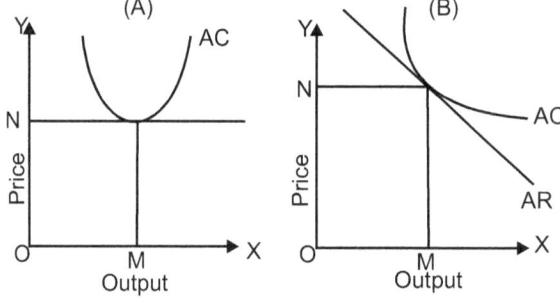

Fig. 2.29: Price Determination under Oligopoly

Fig. 2.29(B) shows the equilibrium of a single firm producing under condition of oligopoly 'without' product differentiation. Because of Price war the price has come down to   ON. The output becomes OM. The Firm is earning normal profits. If the firm raised its price beyond ON it will lose all its customers and if it lowers beyond ON it will go out of business. Fig. 2.29 (A) shows the equilibrium position of a firm producing under conditions of oligopoly with product differentiation. After a price war the price has come down to ON. The firm sells OM output and earns just normal profit. The output is less than optimum and it is similar to monopolistic competition. It is, therefore, likely that the final price under oligopoly with product differentiation will lie somewhere between the monopoly price and the cut throat competition price (or, price established by price -war). It will vary from case to case and will be governed by the conditions prevailing in the market. Various methods are employed by the firms to fix the actual price under conditions of oligopoly.

(A) Independent Pricing: In this case each firm under oligopoly may follow an independent price and output policy by calculating in an imperfect manner, of course, the reactions of the rivals. This price may be monopoly price. It is also possible that each firm may fix the price at the competitive level in case of price war between firms. Then there will be two limits - the upper limit laid down by the monopoly price and the lower limit determined by the competitive price, between which the actual price may be fixed under oligopolistic conditions. The actual price will be influenced by circumstances or conditions prevailing in the market. There are certain possibilities such as there might be complete instability due to price war, the price may itself come to settle at an indeterminate level as a result of the working of the market forces, the oligopolistic firm may accept the 'going price' and adjust itself to that price. The entrepreneur under differentiated oligopoly may like to prefer "a-live- and - let -live" or "a don't - rock - the - bottom" policy to the philosophy of profit maximisation. However the conclusion is that independent pricing under differentiated oligopoly, leads to uncertainty, insecurity and antagonism in the market. This type of pricing cannot last long.

(B) Concurrent Pricing or Pricing under Collusion or Centralized Cartel: This is known as collusive pricing or price fixation through collusion. Here we are referring to a Centralized Agency which determines the price and output of not only the industry but also the price and output of individual firms. A 'cartel' is formed. This cartel will be similar to monopoly. A price will be divided which will maximise the joint profits of the industry. This industry will be called 'strong Monopoly'. This can be illustrated by the following diagram 2.30

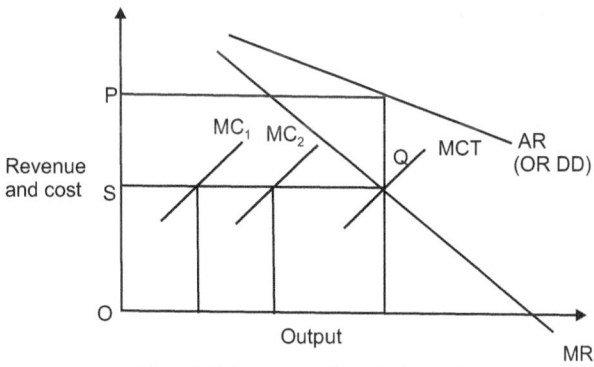

Fig. 2.30: Centralized Cartel

In this illustration AR (or DD) is the industry demand curve or its average revenue curve. MR is the Marginal revenue curve of the Industry. The next step for the agency is to calculate the marginal cost curve of the industry. In this case it is assumed that there are only two oligopolistic firm No. 1 and No. 2. The marginal cost curve of the entire industry therefore can be arrived at by adding together the marginal cost curves of the individual firms. The Marginal cost curves of the two industries are represented by MC_1 and MC_2 respectively. Firm No. 1 produces OM_1 output at marginal cost of OS. Firm No. 2 produces a larger output OM_2 at the same marginal cost OS. The two firms combined together to produce $OM_1 + OM_2$ output at a marginal cost of OS. By adding together the two outputs, we get the total output of the industry OM_3 at a marginal cost of OS. Q is therefore, a point on the marginal cost curve of the industry. The other points can be obtained in a similar manner by adding together the outputs of the two firms at each marginal cost. This then gives us the industry Marginal cost curve MCT. Firm No. 1 will produce OM_1 while firm No. 2 will produce OM_2 output. Both the firms will sell their outputs at OP price. Therefore the cartel will help in maximising profit for the firm. Each firm must get a share of the combined profits that will be greater than it could hope to secure in the absence of centralized pricing.

(C) Price Leadership: This is an important form of price-fixation, under oligopoly. This is the type of market situation in which price is determined by one firm in the industry, and then accepted by all the other firms in that industry. For example, this type of price fixation is found in industries like cement, cigarettes, petroleum, steel etc. Under price leadership one firm, usually the largest, initiates price changes and all the other firms more or less automatically follow the price change. Two types of price leadership are:

(i) Dominant firm type, (ii) Barometric type. In the dominant firm type, there is one large firm with large output and it sets the prices and the other firms accept it. The other type of price leadership is 'barometric' price leadership. The barometer price leader does not dominate the industry. It is not in a position to force other firms to follow its lead. But it fixes a price that is acceptable to the other firms in the industry. The dominant firm will obviously choose that price-output which maximises its profits. In the case of barometer price, any respectable firm makes an intelligent appraisal of the demand and supply conditions in the market and sets the price accordingly.

2.32 Price Discrimination

'Price Discrimination' is the art of selling the same commodity produced under a single control to different buyers at different prices. Price discrimination is possible and profitable only under the following conditions:

- **(a) Existence of two or more than two markets:** There must be two or more than two markets in which a monopolist can classify his customers and charge different prices for an identical product.
- **(b) Existence of different elasticities of demand in different markets:** In different markets, the elasticity of demand for a monopolist's product must be different. With the different elasticities, the monopolist will succeed in charging high price in the inelastic market and low price in the elastic market.

(c) No possibility of resale: It should neither be permissible nor possible to purchase commodity from a cheaper market and resell it in the costlier market.

If buyers themselves become sellers, it will prevent a discriminating monopoly firm from selling the commodity in the costlier or higher price market.

(d) Full control over supply: Existence of monopoly element is essential for the success of price discrimination. If there is keen competition among the sellers, the uniform price will prevail in the entire market.

2.33 Types/Forms of Price Discrimination

(a) Personal Discrimination: When the monopolist simultaneously charges different prices from different buyers, it is called personal discrimination. The following factors make the personal discrimination possible.

    (i) Ignorance of the Consumer: When the consumers are not aware of the prices at which goods are sold in the market, they may offer any price for the commodity due to ignorance.

    (ii) Irrationality of Consumers: The consumers suffer from this ill-conceived notion that if they offer high price for a commodity they will receive more satisfaction and the commodity they get will be of a better quality. This sort of imaginary classification (good or bad) makes personal discrimination possible.

    (iii) Nominal difference in price: Sometimes, the difference in the price is so nominal or insignificant that the consumers do not mind paying a little higher price.

    (iv) Nature of the commodity or service: Personal services are non- transferable. Therefore, a monopolist can resort to personal discrimination in the case of direct services. For example, a doctor in a locality may charge ₹ 50 as the visiting fee from a patient with low income and ₹ 200 from a patient with high income.

(b) Place Discrimination: When a monopolist charges different prices in different markets; it is referred to as place discrimination. In those markets where substitutes are available, the monopolist may charge a low price and in the markets, where the competition does not exist, he may charge a higher price. Thus, in the elastic market, the monopoly price will be low and in the market with inelastic demand, the price will be higher. Place discrimination may be extended to two countries. It is quite possible that a monopoly firm will charge high price for its product in the domestic market and a low price in the foreign market. Such a place discrimination is called 'dumping'.

(c) Trade Discrimination: When a monopolist charges different prices for different uses or for different occupations, it is 'trade discrimination'. For instance, an electricity company may charge a lower price for domestic consumption and may charge higher price for commercial purposes.

Can there be Oligopoly with Differentiated Products?

Under oligopoly firms generally produce goods that are close substitute to each other, i.e., are not homogenous. The firms often cannot act independently and the property of stickiness of prices forces oligopoly firms to stick to the prevailing prices. In such a situation the only way open for oligopoly firm is to push up their sales by concentrating on non-price competitive instruments, like advertisement, improvement in quality of the product, etc. Thus, the competition for increasing its market share is through non-price competition rather than by price war. If a firm has to obtain permanent increase in its market share, it must have to keep itself ahead of its rivals in non-price competition.

2.34 Price-Output Determination under Differentiated Oligopoly

Assume that there are two firms A and B producing differentiated products. Since the products are *not homogenous*, price change by any one of the firms will not be able to help the firm because it will not raise the price with the fear that it will lose its customers to its rival, and it will not cut the price, as it will invite retaliation from the rival firm. A firm can change its price, without losing their customer, to a certain extent, when there is possibility of customers are attached to the either of the firm. However, no firm fully wins over the customers of its rival by price-cut. It implies that under such a market with product differentiation, price cannot be a very effective instrument. Further, since the products are not homogenous, it would be difficult for the firm to come to an agreement or an understanding. Hence, in case of differentiated oligopoly (in our case duopoly as two firms are taken), firms generally operate under non-collusive conditions and mainly resort to non-price competition rather than price change to maintain and extend their market share.

2.35 Multi-Product Pricing

Most modern firms produce a variety of products rather than a single product. Thus, in modern business, a firm is a multi-product producer. The firm's pricing of multiple products has to see into the interdependence of demands, plant capacity utilisation and optimal product pricing of joint products produced in fixed or in variable proportions. The multiplicity of products by a firm creates four kinds of relationship:

1. **Demand relationships:** Due to cross elasticities, a price change in one product affects demand for the other, when the different products of the firm are either substitutes or complements of each other. The products sold by a firm may be interrelated as substitutes or complements. For example, A-Star and Estilo produced by Maruti are substitutes, while the various other options, such as music system, power windows, etc., produced by Maruti are complementary to its automobiles. Thus, in pricing of interrelated goods (substitutes or complements), the firm needs to consider the effect of a change in the price of one product on the demand for the other. Because, a fall in the price of Estilo may reduce the demand for a substitute

good A Star, sold by the same firm and may increase the demand for complementary products. For profit maximisation, thus, a firm needs to determine jointly and not independently the output levels and prices of its various products.

2. **Cost relationships:** Costs are variable and fixed in nature. When multiple products are produced with the help of the same production facilities, some costs (variable) remain directly chargeable to each product. In other words, labour and raw material are directly chargeable. However, the other costs (fixed- like rent, taxes, premium on insurance etc.) are common to all products.

3. **Production relationships:** When multiple products result from a single production process, it is found that usually there is one primary (or main) product with one or more by-products, which may be produced in either fixed or variable proportions.

4. **Capacity relationships:** When the firm has excess or idle capacity, the firm may use it to produce one or more additional products. As new products are added, i.e. the firm becomes multi-product, the fixed costs are shared on greater units and thus the firm enjoys greater efficiency with greater optimal output and price structure for all products.

A firm's number of products in its product line, classifies firms into single product firms, and multi product firms.

Multi-Product firm can be of the following kinds:

(i) **A joint product firm:** It is a firm, which produces a main product and a by-product, which is saleable, e.g. in the field of agriculture, dairying as the by-product.

(ii) **Related goods:** A firm may extend its product line to several related products. In each of the product, there are large numbers of varieties, sizes, shades, etc. For example, a hair colouring factory producing various kinds – quality, colour and size- of ladies and gents hair colour. Since the product is raised from the same plant and uses same labour and raw material, there is a degree of interdependence between different product-lines.

(iii) **Products unrelated to each other:** A firm may be engaged in a product – line whose products are unrelated to each other. For example, Godrej producing steel almirahs, refrigerators, locks, soaps, shaving cream, etc. These products use different production facilities, raw materials and labour. The firm diversifies in different unrelated product-lines mainly to take advantage of their goodwill and to make use of their existing sales network.

Pricing in Multi-Plant and Multi-Product Firm:

Multi-Plant Firm: Where a firm's output of the same product is produced on more than one site, the profit-maximising output rule states that marginal supply costs must be equal to marginal revenue. This rule remains unchanged. But in multi-plant firm the marginal costs is the sum of the separate plants marginal costs and production must be allocated between the plants so that the marginal supply cost at each plant is identical. Fig. 2.31 shows pricing in multi-plant firm.

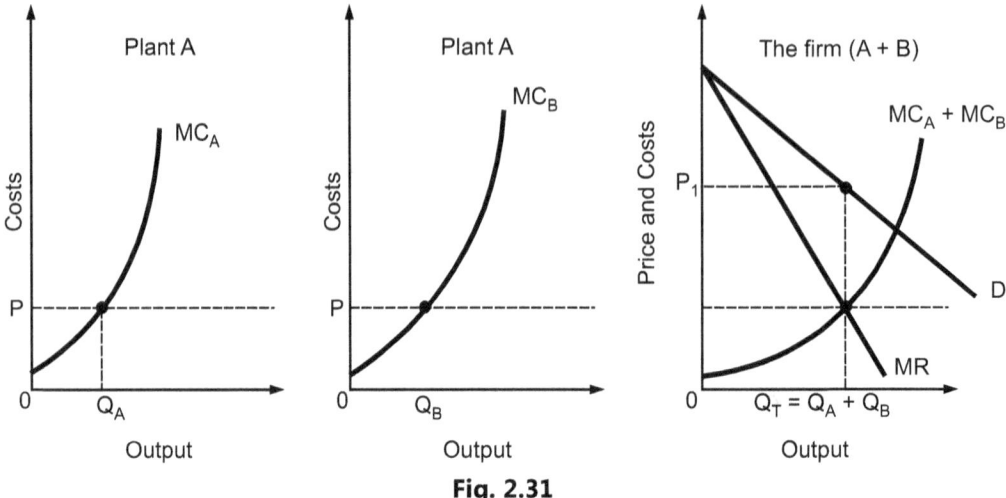

Fig. 2.31

Multi-Product Firm: When producing pricing a product, the multi-product firm has to take into consideration not only the impact on the demand for that product of a price change (its own price elasticities of demand) but the impact on the demand for other products in the firm's product range (the relevant cross price-elasticities). In other words, pricing involves obtaining maximum profits from the full product range rather than from the individual products.

2.36 Meaning of Demand

In ordinary dialect, demand means want or a desire. In economics 'demand' is a want backed up by the ability to pay for and willingness to pay. *Demand for a commodity refers to the quantity of the commodity which an individual consumer or a household is willing to purchase per unit of time at a particular price.*

Demand = Want (Desire) for a commodity (+) Willingness to buy the commodity (+) Sufficient purchasing power in his possession to pay for/buy the product.

In the absence of any of the elements, there is no demand. For example, a miser's want for a car may not become demand if he is *not willing* to part with the necessary purchasing power to pay for the car. A beggar's desire for a car is also not demand as he *does not have the capacity* to pay for the product. Thus, a desire does not become demand unless it is backed up by the ability and willingness to satisfy it.

Further, demand is a relative term. Demand for a product is related to 'time' and 'price'. Hence, demand is defined with reference to *per unit of time* and at a *particular price*.

The demand may arise from an individual, a household as well as a market. When demand arises from an individual, for example demand for cigarettes, books, etc., it is an *individual demand*. On the other hand when goods are demanded by households, for example demand for air-conditioners, refrigerators, etc., it is a *household demand*. When we consider the demand for a commodity by all the individuals or households in the market taken together, it is referred to as *market demand*.

2.36.1 Factors Determining Demand

Individual/Household Demand: In managerial economics, we are primarily interested in the demand for a commodity faced by the firm. This depends on the size of the total market or industry demand for the commodity, which in turn is the sum of the demands for the commodity from the individual consumers in the market. Consumer demand theory postulates that the quantity demanded is a function of various factors.

1. **Price:** Price is one of the most important factors influencing demand. Higher the price, lower the quantity demanded by an individual as it influences his capacity and willingness to pay for the product.

2. **Consumer's tastes habits and preferences:** The desire to purchase is revealed by tastes and preferences of the individuals/households. For e.g., preference for coffee will lead to greater demand for coffee from that individual.

3. **Consumer's income:** The capability to purchase depends upon his purchasing power which, in turn, depends upon his income.

4. **Prices of other goods:** Demand for a commodity is influenced by the prices of other related goods, i.e., by complementary goods and substitutes of that commodity.

Even the most unsophisticated managers have observed that when the firm increases the price of a commodity, sales generally decline. Besides, the price of the commodity, his income, his tastes, preferences and prices of other related goods, there are certain demand determinants that are specific to a specific category of goods. These determinants are called the *explanatory variables*, and the quantity demanded is called the *explained variable*. The relationship between these two kinds of variables is essential for successful management of business.

Individual Demand Schedule and Curve

The nature of demand will be more understood, if we construct a demand schedule for some commodity. Prof. Marshall, while explaining the price theory used 'demand schedule' as a technique.

"An individual demand schedule is a list of the various quantities of a commodity which an individual consumer purchases at various alternative prices in the market."

An individual demand schedule represents:

*   A tabular statement showing different quantities of a commodity demanded by an individual at different prices.

*   At each point, it indicates relationship between two variables viz., quantity demanded and price.

*   The schedule only shows the 'variation' in demand and not the 'change' in demand.

Illustration: Table Individual Demand Schedule.

Table 2.2: Individual Demand Schedule

Price of apples (₹ / Kg.)	Number of Units Demanded (Kg. / week)
50	10
40	20
30	30
20	40
10	50

The schedule shows a relationship between the two variables viz., as price rises, demand falls. It depicts an 'inverse' relationship between the price and the quantity demanded of the commodity per time period.

Individual Demand curve: The plot of data – price on the Y-axis and quantity demanded on the X-axis – gives the corresponding individual's demand curve.

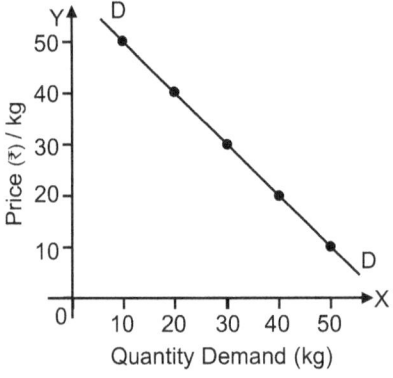

Fig. 2.32

The demand curve DD shows 'inverse' relationship between price and quantity demanded of apples. As the price rises, quantity demanded falls. Thus, demand curve DD slopes downwards from left to right, i.e., it has a *negative slope*. When price falls say from ₹ 50 per kg., to ₹ 40 per kg., the demand for the commodity increases because the individual substitutes in consumption X for other commodities (which are relatively expensive). This is 'substitution effect'. In addition, when the price of the commodity falls, a consumer can purchase more of the commodity with a 'given' money income (as his real income increases). This is called as the 'income effect'.

The demand curve depicted the relationship between the price and quantity demanded of the commodity. But, if other determinants held constant otherwise, change, then the demand curve shifts to the right (when demand increases) and to the left (when demand decreases).

When demand changes (increase or decrease) due to change in price (fall or rise), it is known as *'change in quantity demanded'*. It is depicted by *movement* on the *same* demand curve – upward movement is contraction of demand, downward movement is expansion of demand. When demand changes (increase or decrease) due to change in any other factor other than the price of that commodity, it is known as *'change in demand'*. It is depicted by *shift* in the demand curve – to the right of the original demand curve shows increase in demand, shift to the left of the original demand curve shows decrease in demand.

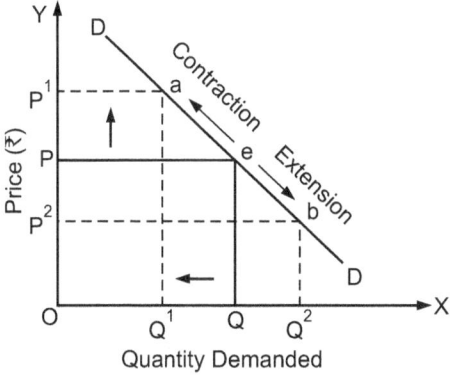

Fig. 2.33

In Fig. 2,33, we see that at price OP, quantity demanded is OQ, e is the equilibrium point. When price rises to OP^1, demand contracts to OQ^1 and the consumer moves upwards. When the price falls to OP^2, quantity demanded expands to OQ^2 and the buyer moves downwards from e to b.

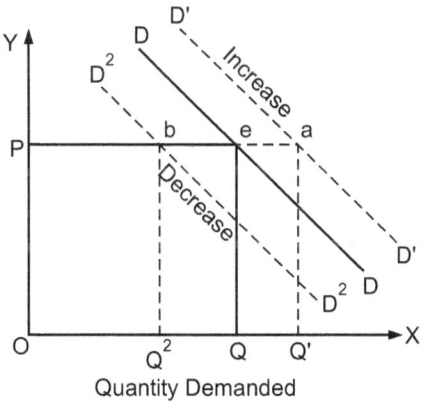

Fig. 2.34

In Fig. 2.34, we see that at price OP, OQ is quantity demanded. Increase in demand is shown by shift in the demand curve towards the right of the original- D^1D^1 right of DD at the same price OP. Decrease in demand is shown by shift in the demand curve towards the left of the original – D^2D^2 left of DD at the same price OP.

Market Demand: The transition from an individual demand schedule to a market demand schedule presents no difficulty in it. In a market, there are a number of buyers, each with his demand schedule. *"Market demand is the aggregate of all quantities purchased by all the buyers at a particular time and at a specific price."* The market demand schedule can be obtained by adding up all the individual demand schedules.

Table 2.3: Market Demand Schedule

Price of apples (₹ / Kg.)	Quantity Demanded of Apples kg./day			
	A's demand	B's demand	C's demand	Market Demand (A+B+C)
50	10	20	30	60
40	20	30	40	90
30	30	40	50	120
20	40	50	60	150
10	50	60	70	180

In the above hypothetical illustration of market demand schedule, we observe that:

- It is a tabular statement showing different quantities demanded by all the buyers at various prices at a particular period of time.
- Market demand schedule is obtained by horizontal summation of quantities demanded by all the buyers of a particular commodity.
- It shows 'inverse' relationship between price and quantity demanded.
- The schedule shows only 'variation' in demand.

Market Demand Curve: The graphical presentation of the market demand schedule gives us market demand curve. For convenience, in our illustration we have assumed three buyers: A, B, C. Market demand curve is summation A+B+C's individual demand curves.

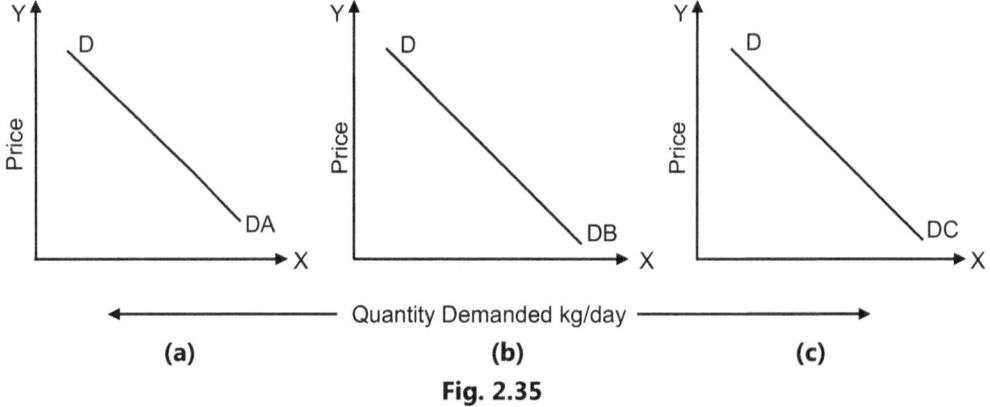

Fig. 2.35

Fig. 2.35 is the individual demand for a particular commodity of three buyers A, B, and C.

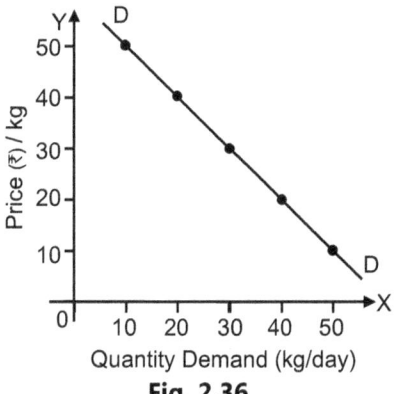

Fig. 2.36

Fig. 2.36 shows Market Demand curve. Technically, this market demand curve is the lateral sum of all individual demand curves of A, B and C buyers.

Nature of demand curves

If the commodity is *homogenous*, its market demands curves are *precise* and *definite*. But, in case of commodities with different varieties or brands, their market demand curves will not be precise and definite. In this case we have to prepare different demand schedules for each variety and have different demand curves based on the data.

Further, it is true that a market demand curve is simply horizontal summation of the individual demand curves *but only if* the consumption decisions of the individual consumers are independent. It is observed that people, some times, demand a commodity because others are purchasing it and in order to be with the 'happening' their consumption decisions are influenced by the fashion. The result is 'bandwagon effect' to *keep up with the Joneses*. The demand curve in such a case will be flatter than indicated in the above Fig. 2.37, based on horizontal summation of individual demand curves. At other times, in case of **snob effect**, consumers seek to have exclusive demand and be 'different' from others. This tends to make the market demand steeper than shown in Fig. 2.38, based on horizontal summation of individual demand curves. For convenience ignore the determinants of market demand – snob effect and bandwagon effect.

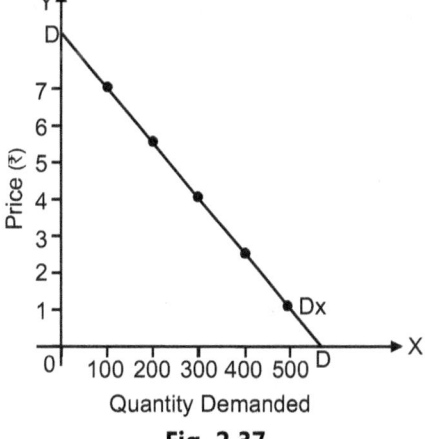

Fig. 2.37

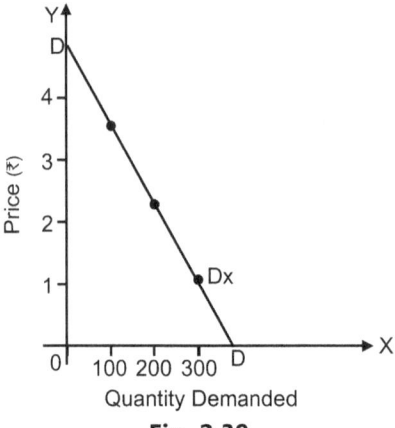

Fig. 2.38

2.36.2 Determinants of Market Demand

Price: Other things being equal, the demand for a good vary inversely with the price of it – more is demanded at a low price than at a higher price. We state this inverse relationship for a normal good. Other determinants remaining the same, a fall in the price of a normal good leads to rise in the consumer's purchasing power. He can, thus, buy more of it (due to substitution effect). Likewise, an increase in price will reduce his purchasing power or real income and thereby reducing the demand for the commodity (income effect).

Consumer's income: With an increase in income, a consumer/household buys an increased amount of most of the commodities in his consumption bundle though the extent of the increase may differ between commodities. For example, in certain commodities like foods, fruits, vegetables, etc., the amount demanded increases with the increase in income but up to a certain point. Beyond this point even when the income changes (increases) the quantity demanded remains unchanged. For certain commodities the quantity demanded falls with the increase in income, say for inferior goods. Here, inferior goods are not inferior in terms of quality but are exception to the law of demand. The relationship between income and quantity demanded was first explained by Engel. The relationship between income and quantity demanded is depicted in Fig. 2.39. The curves shown in the Fig. 2.39 are called as Engle's curves.

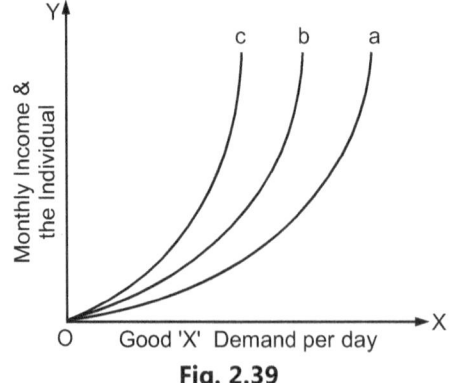

Fig. 2.39

Prices of other related goods: The two commodities are said to be related when the price of one influences the demand of the other commodity. These related commodities are of two kinds: substitutes and complements. 'Substitutes' are those goods when either of the commodities can satisfy the want, for example, tea and coffee, apple and pears, rail and road transport, etc. In case of substitutes the price of one commodity and the quantity demanded of the other commodity move in the *same* direction i.e., both increase together and decrease together. Fig. 2.40 (i).

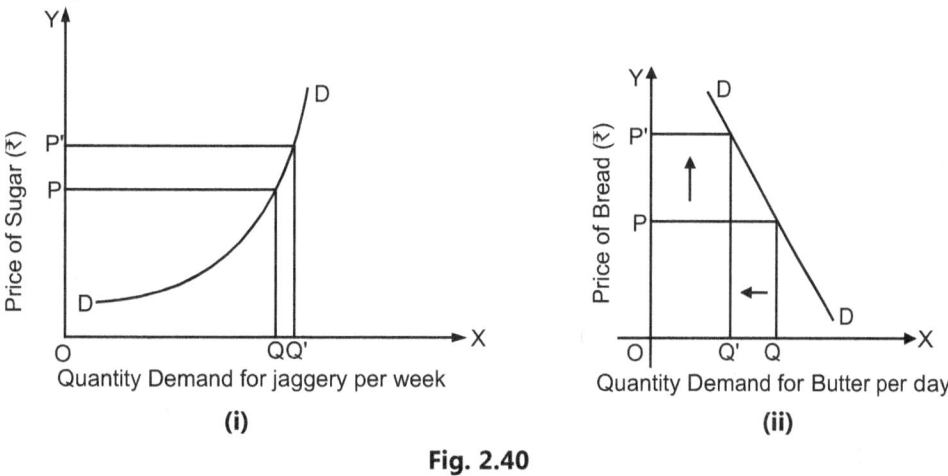

Fig. 2.40

Fig. 2.40 (ii) shows if the price of tea rises, with the price of coffee remaining the same, the demand for coffee rises, as in relation to coffee, price of tea is higher. 'Complementary goods' are when two or more goods are demanded at the same time to satisfy a single want. For example, pen and ink, car and petrol, bread and butter, etc. In case of complementary goods, when the price of one commodity rises, the demand for not only that commodity falls but also demand for the other good, in that group, falls. Thus, when price of one commodity and quantity demanded of the other commodity move in opposite direction, then the two commodities are said to be complementary to each other. Fig. 2.40 (ii) shows that when the price of bread rises then not only the demand for bread falls but the demand for butter also declines.

Consumer's tastes and preferences: Changes in the tastes and preferences of a consumer in favour of a commodity results in greater demand for the commodity and the change, if against the commodity, results in smaller demand for the commodity. For example, if a 'diet' drink catches the fancy of the consumers then the firms selling soft drinks will have greater demand for 'diet' drinks and other drinks may face a smaller demand. Modern business firms not only try to adjust to changes in market trends and fashions and fancies but in turn they also influence the market demand with their effective sales promotional activities.

Sales Propaganda/Advertisements: Producers spend a lot of money on advertising their products primarily because they can influence the tastes and preferences of the consumers in their favour and increase their sales.

Consumer's expectations: Generally the consumers have two kinds of expectations: (i) expectation related to their future income; (ii) expectation related to the future prices of the good and its related goods. In case the consumer expects a higher income in future, he spends more at present and thereby the demand for the commodity increases, even without any change in price of it. Likewise, if the consumer expects future price of a commodity to rise, he would increase his demand for that commodity because he would like to buy at present price rather than at higher price in future.

Taxes: Higher the direct taxes lower will be the market demand as the purchasing power of the individual is reduced.

Distribution of National Income: Demand for most products vary from consumer to consumer, thus distribution of consumers among appropriate categories exerts an influence on the market demand. If the income is equally distributed then there will be increased market demand for all types of goods. On the other hand, unequal income distribution will lead to relatively greater increase in the demand for luxuries.

Number of Buyers: Market demand for a commodity depends on the number of consumers. Other things remaining the same, larger the number of consumers, greater the size of the demand in the market. Thus, the demand for all products is increasing over time, partly because the population is increasing over time.

Demand Function

Demand function is *"a mathematical expression of the relationship between quantity demanded of the commodity and its determinants."* Individual demand function is when this relationship relates to the demand by an individual consumer, while if the relationship relates to market it is called market demand function.

Individual Demand Function:

$$Q_x = f(P_x, Y, P_c, T, S, E_y, E_p)$$

Where,

Q_x = Quantity demanded of commodity X, e.g. chocolate

P_x = Price of the commodity X

Y = Income of the consumer

T = Tastes and preferences of consumers

S = Sales propaganda or advertisement

P_c = Price of other related goods (complements and substitutes)

E_y = Consumer's expectations of future income

E_p = Consumer's expectations of future prices

Market Demand Function:

$$Q_x = f(P_x, Y, P_c, T, S, E_y, E_p, P, D)$$

P = Population or number of buyers in the market

D = Distribution of population/ income

The demand function – individual or market – is really just listing of the variables that influence demand. Managerial economists, of course, need a more explicit demand function.

Nature of Demand of a Firm and Industry

The focal point in managerial economics is the theory of the firm. Here, we are mainly interested in the demand for a commodity faced by a firm. The demand for a commodity faced by a particular firm depends upon many factors like: size of the market; industry demand for the commodity; the form in which the industry is organised and the number of firms in the industry, i.e., type of competition that the firm is facing.

- If it is a *monopolist firm* – sole producer of the product – and having no good substitutes, the firm represents the industry and it faces the market demand for the commodity. Such a situation, monopoly, is a rare phenomenon, and can be experienced in a government franchise, which is accompanied by government regulations. For example, public transportation, public utility companies.

- Under *perfect competition*, there are large numbers of firms producing a homogenous/identical product, and each firm is too small to influence the price of the commodity by its individual action, that is why the firm under perfect competition is a 'price-taker'. Since the firm is a price-taker, it faces a horizontal demand curve for the commodity and the firm can sell as many units it can at the 'given' price. Like monopoly this form of market is also not experienced in the real market.

- Many firms in industrial countries and even in India fall between the extremes of monopoly and perfect competition. These firms are in the forms of market organisation known as oligopoly and monopolistic competition. In oligopoly, there are a few firms in the industry, producing homogenous or standardised product, e.g., soft drinks, automobiles, etc. Under **oligopoly** the decision of the firms in the industry are interdependent. Since there are limited number of firms in the industry, the pricing, advertising, and other promotional activities of each firm influences other firms in the industry and evoke retaliation.

- In **monopolistic competition** there are many firms selling differentiated product. This market form has both the elements of competition and monopoly. The element of competition is seen because the number of firms is large in the industry. The monopoly element arises because each firm's product is somewhat different from the product of the other firm. Each firm enjoys some degree of monopoly in the market and *thus the firm faces downward sloping demand curve*. As far as the control over the price is concerned, the firm has limited control because many other firms are producing 'similar' products. Hence, though each firm faces downward-sloping demand curve but it *has fairly flat slope*, indicating expansion in demand with fall in price. This form of market organisation is common in the service sector of the economy – beauty parlours in a given area, each selling similar but not identical products or services.

- Under all forms of market organisation, except perfect competition, a firm faces a negatively sloped demand curve for the product it sells, and this demand curve (average revenue curve) shifts with changes in the number of consumers in the market, income of the consumers, price of other related goods, consumer's tastes and certain other specific forces that influence a firm's demand curve. Other factors may be future expectations of the prices, intensity of sales promotional activities on the part of the firm, pricing policy of other firms in the industry – like in oligopoly – availability of credit facility, and so on. A firm's sales can increase(at the current price) if the consumer's expect a rise in future price, or the firm introduces an innovation in its product and thus the firm faces a rightward shift in its demand curve. On the other hand, the demand curve of the firm may shift to the left if consumers expect prices to fall in the future or the competitors have reduced the price of their product.

- The demand curve faced by a firm also depends on the nature of the product that it sells. If the firm sells durable goods like home appliances, automobiles that require after-sale service not only during the year but also in subsequent years, the firm will generally face an unstable demand curve as compared to the firms selling non-durable goods. The reason for this is that a consumer can continue using the same unit of washing machine or car by putting in maintenance expenditure and buy a new unit of durable goods only when the consumer has received an incentive or a lucrative credit facility, etc. When the economy improves or credit incentives are introduced, the demand for durable goods can increase to a great extent and shift the demand curve rightwards.

- The demand faced by a firm will determine the type and quantity of inputs (producer's goods) that the firm will purchase or hire to meet the demand for goods and services that it sells. The demand of inputs that a firm uses depends on the demand for goods and services it sells, thus the firm's demand for inputs is known as *'derived demand'*. The greater the demand for the goods and services that the firm faces, greater will the demand for the resources that are required to produce those goods. All producers' goods have a derived demand. A firm's demand for capital equipments and other producer's goods/inputs is also unstable if producer's goods are durable goods.

2.37 Elasticity of Demand

Dr. Marshall has defined price elasticity of demand as: "the elasticity (or responsiveness) of demand in market is great or small according to the amount demanded increases much or little for a given rise in the price."

Thus, the responsiveness in the quantity demanded of a commodity to a change in its price is referred to as elasticity of demand or price elasticity of demand. It is not enough to know that a fall in price would lead to an extension of demand. The firm would like to know as to how much more it would be able to sell and change its total revenue. There is no quantitative unit relationship between price and quantity demanded. For example, a 10% fall in the price of a commodity may result in 10% increase in the quantity demanded; and at times may be 25% or even more. This response in quantity demanded of a commodity to a change in its price is very important to any firm. Sometimes lowering the price of the commodity increases the sales to such an extent that it brings about a change in the total revenue. But, sometimes lowering the prices of the commodity may actually reduce the firm's total revenue or there may be too marginal an increase that it gives the firm a feeling of worthlessness of reducing the prices. By affecting sales, the pricing policies of the firm also influence its cost of production and ultimately its profitability. Thus, to know the quantitative relationship between the change in the price of a commodity and the resultant change in quantity demanded, the concept of elasticity of demand was introduced by Caurnot and Mill; but was developed by Dr. Alfred Marshall.

Meaning/Definition

Elasticity of demand may be defined as *'the extent to which the quantity demanded of a commodity changes in response to a given change in price'*. It is the capacity of demand to expand or contract in response to given change in price.

The quantity demanded of a commodity in the market, during a given period of time, is determined by many factors such as price of that commodity, price of related goods, income, and so on. A change in any of these factors brings about a change in quantity demanded. Assuming all factors, except the price of that commodity, to be constant, we can relate the quantity demanded directly to the price. In case of elastic demand, quantity demanded responds in a greater degree to slight change in price and in case of inelastic demand; even a great change in price leaves the demand unaffected.

In the words of Stonier and Hague, "Elasticity of demand is a technical term used by the economists to describe the degree of responsiveness of the demand for a commodity to a fall in its price."

Dr. Marshall's analysis of the concept of elasticity was with reference to price changes, i.e. he referred to it as 'price-elasticity'. However, the modern economists have extended the application of this concept to several other determinants of demand.

Thus, we have basically, three kinds of elasticity of demand:

(i) **Price-elasticity of demand** referring to change in quantity demanded of a commodity in response to the change in its price.

(ii) **Income-elasticity of demand** referring to the change in quantity demanded in response to the change in an individual's income.

(iii) **Cross-elasticity** refers to change in the quantity demanded of 'X' commodity due to change in the price of 'Y' commodity.

Price elasticity of demand seeks to measure the exact responsiveness of demand to changes in its price. The elasticity of demand for commodity will be more or less depending upon a wide variety of factors influencing the elasticity of demand.

1. **Existence of Substitute:** The price elasticity of demand for a commodity depends primarily on the availability of substitutes for the commodity. The extent of the price elasticity of demand is larger when the substitutes are closer in nature to the commodity and there is greater number of substitutes available for the commodity in

question. For example, the demand for sugar is more elastic than the demand for salt. The reason is that sugar has more substitutes than salt. Thus, a given percentage increase in the price of sugar and salt will result in greater reduction in per time period in the quantity demanded of sugar than of salt. Generally, the substitutability of commodity ranges from zero to infinity. More closer to infinity is the substitution, it means that more narrowly is the commodity defined and will have many close substitutes. For example, if a producer of aspirin tries to increase the price above the normal range of market price for aspirins, then the producer will stand to lose a large part of his sales as buyers can easily and readily switch to its close substitute. In other words, price elasticity is large in case of goods having close substitutes.

2. **Degree of Necessity:** With the above example of salt, it needs to be mentioned that goods are classified as necessaries, comforts and luxuries. The greater the degree of necessity, the more likely is the demand for a commodity to be inelastic, such as salt. Other things remaining the same, the demand for necessities is less elastic than the demand for comforts and luxuries as such goods have no close substitute. Necessaries are goods which have to be bought at whatever price and so the demand is inelastic. On the other hand, if the price of luxury articles rises, the consumer can do either by buying less of it or not buying it at all.

3. **Time Period:** The price elasticity of demand is larger, i.e. demand is elastic, and when the time period is longer, as it allows the consumers to respond to the change in the commodity price. It usually takes some time for consumers to know about the availability of substitutes and also adjust to the changes in the price. Thus, for a given price change, the quantity response is likely to be much larger in the long run than in the short run.

4. **The Proportion of Consumer's Income spent on the Commodity:** The demand for a commodity on which the consumer spends only a small proportion of his income is inelastic. For example, the demand for match-boxes will not change even when its price rises by 100%. The reason for demand not responding to the change in price is that the proportion of an individual's income spent on match-boxes is insignificant.

5. **Habit:** The demand for a commodity to which a buyer is accustomed to is inelastic. For example, a person is habituated to a special brand of cigarette and when the price rises of it, the individual may not reduce the demand for it, as habits die hard. But, as cigarettes have substitute brands and if the price rise continues even in the long run of a particular brand, then the individual may switch to another brand or may buy less of the same brand. That is, demand responds to price change in the long run.

6. **Number of Uses of the Commodity:** A commodity which can be put to several uses has an elastic demand. For example, electricity. A fall in the price of electricity would

induce the consumer to use electricity for air-cooling, cooking, water-heating, besides using it as a source of energy for lighting, agriculture, industries etc. And, when the price rises, it will be used only for the essential purposes. Thus, demand can be adjusted to price changes.

7. **Deferred Consumption:** Commodities whose consumption can be postponed have elastic demand. In case of consumer durable goods, buyers generally wait for 'sale' or 'discount' in such commodities.

8. **Complementary Goods:** Certain commodities are jointly demanded, e.g. car and petrol, pen and ink, etc. If the demand for cars is less elastic, the demand for petrol will also be less elastic. Thus, the elasticity of demand for the goods demanded jointly is generally inelastic in nature.

9. **Range of Prices:** The range of prices also influences the elasticity of demand. The high-income group of people purchases high-priced goods. Thus, a small change in price of such goods does not cause any change in demand for these goods. In the same way, low-priced goods face inelastic demand. The reason is that those who purchased low-priced goods are already buying them and a fall in their price does not lead to any sizeable increase in the demand for them.

10. **Income Group:** Income level of an individual influences the elasticity of demand. The elasticity of demand for high-income group is inelastic, as they do not bother about small changes in price. Thus, they may demand practically the same quantities even though the price may undergo changes. On the other hand, the demand by the low-income group is elastic in nature as they are more sensitive to price changes.

11. **Effect of the Distribution of Wealth:** In the words of Prof. Taussig, " generally the demand becomes inelastic when there is irregular distribution of wealth in society and in case of equal distribution of wealth in the society the demand becomes elastic."

2.38 Types of Price-Elasticity of Demand

As has been mentioned earlier some commodities have greater elastic demand, while others have less elastic demand.

Demand is said to be *elastic* when the change in demand is *greater* than the change in price of that commodity. Demand is *inelastic* when the change in demand is *lesser* than the change in price of that commodity.

But the demand cannot be perfectly 'elastic' or perfectly 'inelastic'. Thus, let us now try to understand the different degrees of elasticity of demand.

1. **Unitary Elastic Demand:** *When the change in demand for a commodity is equal or same to the change in the price of that commodity, it is unitary elastic demand.* E.g. when price falls by 10% and the demand rises by 10%, it is unitary elastic demand.

$$Ed = \frac{\text{Relative Change in Quantity Demanded}}{\text{Relative Change in Price}} = 1$$

i.e. $\boxed{Ed = 1}$ Or $\boxed{Ed = \Delta Q = \Delta P}$

Here ΔQ = change in Quantity.

ΔP = change in price.

The demand curve, in this case, is a rectangular hyperbola.

When price falls from OP to OP_1, demand rises from OQ to OQ^1. Thus, OQ^1 to PP_1 or $\boxed{Ed = 1}$.

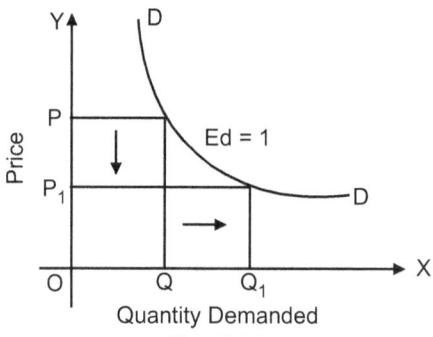

Fig. 2.41

2. **Relatively Elastic Demand:** When proportionate change in the quantity demanded is *greater than*, the proportionate change in price, it is a relatively elastic demand.

$$Ed = \frac{\text{Relative change in Quantity demanded}}{\text{Relative change in price}} > 1$$

i.e. $\Delta Q > \Delta P$ or $\boxed{Ed > 1}$

E.g. If the price falls by 10% and demand rises by 30%, it is Ed > 1.

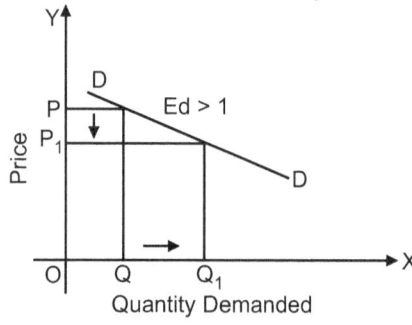

Fig. 2.42

The fall in price from OP to OP_1, leads to rise in demand from OQ to OQ^1.

$$\boxed{QQ^1 > PP_1} \text{ Or Ed > 1}$$

Generally, luxury goods have relatively elastic demand.

The demand curve in this case is flatter and has a gentle slope.

3. **Relatively Inelastic Demand:** When percentage in quantity demanded is *less* than the proportionate change in price, it is a case of relatively inelastic demand.

    If the price falls by 10% and demand rises by only 5%, it is Ed < 1.

    $$Ed = \frac{\text{Relative change in Quantity Demand}}{\text{Relative change in price}} < 1$$

    i.e. $\boxed{Ed < 1}$ or $\boxed{\Delta Q < \Delta P}$

    Demand curve in this case is steep and the curve declines speedily.

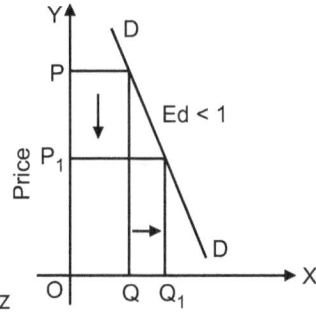

Fig. 2.43

Fall in the price OP to OP_1, is greater than the rise in demand OQ to OQ'.

i.e. $QQ' < PP_1$ or $\boxed{Ed < 1}$

Inelastic demand is in case of certain necessities.

4. **Perfectly Elastic Demand:** It is a situation when with the slightest change or no change in price of a commodity leads to *infinite* change in quantity demanded of that commodity.

    $$Ed = \frac{\text{Any change in Quantity Demanded}}{\text{No change in price}} \propto$$

    i.e. $\boxed{Ed = \propto}$

    Demand curve in this case, is horizontal and parallel to the OX – axis.

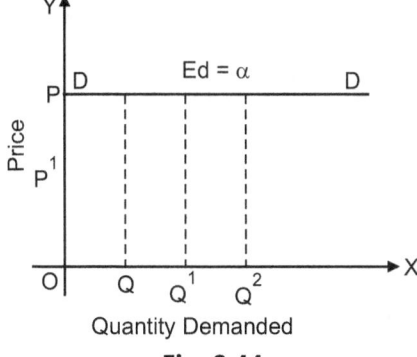

Fig. 2.44

Change in Quantity is any number i.e. OQ^1, OQ^2 etc.

Change in Price is zero (OP)   ∴ $\boxed{Ed = \infty}$

Perfectly elastic demand is an unrealistic situation; it has greater theoretical importance. Such a situation is assumed in a perfectly competitive market.

5. **Perfectly Inelastic Demand:** When any change in price of the commodity leads to *no change* in the demand of that commodity, it is perfectly inelastic demand.

$$Ed = \frac{\text{No change in Quantity Demanded}}{\text{Any or No Change in Price}} = 0$$

i.e. $\boxed{Ed = 0}$

Demand curve in this case, is vertical and parallel to the OY-axis.

Change in quantity is zero. It remains OQ. Change in price is any number.

In reality, there is no such commodity the demand for which may be absolutely inelastic. Some extension or contraction is bound to occur.

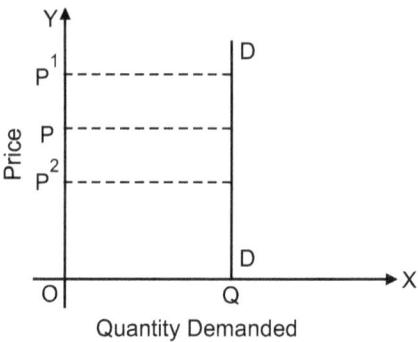

Fig. 2.45

To conclude, in reality the elasticity of demand for most of the goods and services lies between the two theoretical cases given above i.e. perfectly elastic and perfectly inelastic demand. That is, some goods have high elastic demand while others have less elastic demand but not perfectly elastic or inelastic.

2.39 Significance of Price – Elasticity of Demand

(a) **Finance Ministry:** The concept of elasticity assists the government in formulating its economic and tax policies. When the Finance Minister wants to tax certain product, he selects that product where demand is inelastic. Then he can collect more money from public by way of taxes. Yet, people demand more or less the same quantity of it. Similarly, government considers the elasticity of a product before imposing statutory control on it.

(b) Manufacturers and Businessmen: With a view to maximise its money profits, a firm has to decide upon the right type of price policy. At the time of fixing the price, the producer increases the prices of some goods for which the demand is inelastic, but people will continue to buy that product even if the price is high. This automatically increases the profitability of the businessman and producer. E.g. Even if the price of cooking gas goes up, its demand remains the same.

(c) Labour Leader: The concept is useful to trade union leaders in wage bargaining. If the demand for a particular type of labour is inelastic, the labour leader can force the employers to raise the wages of those workers, e.g. technicians, skilled workers etc. Same situation is not of unskilled labour because there are negligible chances for demand of unskilled labour to be inelastic. So the labour leader may not succeed to increase their wages.

(d) International Trade: That country will benefit most by the devaluation of its currency, if its demand for imports is very elastic and its demand for exports is highly elastic. Such a country will be able to export more and import less when devaluation takes place. The main aim of international trade is to earn maximum foreign exchange. This can be done by exporting commodities having inelastic demand; so that we can sell it at a higher price. On the other hand, we should import commodities having elastic demand. So that we can import at a cheaper rate or do not buy it, if it is costly.

(e) Price Discrimination: The producer knows the elasticity of demand for his product in each market. He can charge a higher price in the market where the demand for his product is relatively inelastic and a lower price in the market where the demand is elastic.

(f) Scope of Public Sector: The concept of elasticity is useful for deciding upon the scope of the public sector. Several commodities especially public utilities face an inelastic demand. The private producers under such circumstances are likely to exploit consumers. Such fields can preferably be taken by the government in the public sector.

The concept of price – elasticity of demand is useful in foreign trade as follows:

1. **Useful in gains from trade:** The gains from trade depend, among other factors, on the elasticity of demand. We will gain from international trade if we export goods with less elasticity of demand and import those goods for which our demand is elastic. In the first situation, we will be in a position to charge a high price for our commodities and in the second situation we will pay less for products obtained from the other nation. Thus, we gain both the ways and will be able to increase the volume of our exports and imports.

2. **Useful in determining terms of trade:** The terms of trade implies to the rate at which a country exchanges her exports for her imports from the other country. The exact rate, at which exchange will take place, will be determined by the relative elasticities and intensities of demand of the two countries for each others goods.

3. **Useful in tariff policy:** Tariffs, generally, tend to increase the prices of domestic goods. The extent, to which the internal prices will rise, depends on the elasticity of demand of the protected goods. If the demand for the goods having 'protection' is elastic, their sales will be reduced with the rise in prices. On the other hand, if the demand is less elastic, people will have to bear the burden of higher prices as a result of tariff policy.

4. **Useful in the policy of devaluation:** The concept of price elasticity of demand for imports and exports is important for a country, which is trying to correct its adverse balance of payments by devaluation.

    Devaluation leads to cheaper exports and dearer imports of the country. When a country resorts to devaluation of its currency, its first effect will be that the prices of its imports will rise and will lead to reduce its imports. However, it depends upon elasticity of demand for imports. Conversely, devaluation will make our exports cheaper and encourage exports. Again, by how much our export will increase will depend on the elasticity of demand of the foreigners for our goods.

    In short, to what extent we can bridge the gap between the receipts (from exports) and payments (for imports) of foreign exchange will depend upon the elasticities of demand for exports and imports.

5. **Useful in government policy:** The government considers the elasticity of demand of the products of those industries which apply for grant of a subsidy or protection. Protection is given only to those industries whose goods have an elastic demand. Thus, such industries are unable to face foreign competition, unless their prices are lowered through subsidy or by raising the prices of imported goods by imposing heavy tariffs on them.

2.40 Income Elasticity of Demand

Meaning

Elasticity is a '*general*' concept; it can be used wherever there is a functional relationship between variables.

We now discuss another determinant of demand viz. *income* and consider elasticity of demand by holding all other determinants, including price, constant income – elasticity of demand for a product shows the extent to which a consumer's demand for that product changes as a result of change in his income.

Income – elasticity of demand may be defined as '*the ratio of proportionate change in the quantity demanded of the commodity to a given proportionate change in the income of the consumer*'. The formula for measuring income – elasticity of demand can be stated, thus:

Formula 1:

$$Ey = \frac{\text{Proportionate change in quantity demanded}}{\text{Proportionate change in consumer's income}}$$

Here, Ey = Income elasticity of demand

E.g. A 20% rise in income causes a 30% increase in demand for a product 'X', what will be the income – elasticity of demand for 'X'?

Solution: Substituting the value in the above mentioned formula.

$$Ey = \frac{30}{20} = 1.5$$

Formula 2: A second formula which is mathematically more rational is suggested as under:

$$Ey = \frac{Q_2 - Q_1}{Q_2 + Q_1} \div \frac{Y_2 - Y_1}{Y_2 + Y_1}$$

In this formula, Q_1 is the initial consumer expenditure on any commodity 'X' (which represents the demand for the product 'X') and Q2 is the new expenditure on the same commodity after a change in income. Y_1 denotes initial income and Y_2 stands for changed (new) income.

Example: A consumer spends ₹ 60 per month on sugar when his income is ₹ 1500 per month. When his income increases to ₹ 1800 per month, he spends ₹ 84 on sugar. What will be the income elasticity of demand for sugar in this case?

Solution: According to the above formula:

$$Ey = \frac{84 - 60}{84 + 60} \div \frac{1800 - 1500}{1800 + 1500}$$

$$= \frac{24}{144} \div \frac{300}{3300}$$

$$= \frac{1}{6} \div \frac{1}{11}$$

$$= \frac{11}{6} \text{ or } 1.8$$

Income elasticity of demand in this case is 1.8.

∴ $Ey > 1$

2.41 Types of Income Elasticity of Demand

Like price elasticity we can classify income elasticity.

1. **Negative Income-Elasticity:** When a given increase in the consumer's money-income is followed by decrease in the quantity demanded of the commodity, it is negative income-elasticity.

   Symbolically, negative income elasticity of demand is represented as $E_y < 0$.

   Goods having negative income elasticity of demand are *inferior goods*.

2. **Zero Income-Elasticity:** It is a case where a given increase in consumers money-income does not result in any increase of the quantity demanded of the commodity. In other words, in spite of increase in the consumer's income, the quantity demanded remain the same.

   Symbolically, Ey = 0

3. **Unitary Income Elasticity of Demand:** It is a case where the proportion of the consumers income spent on the given product is *exactly* the same before and after the increase in income. Thus, income elasticity of demand is equal to unity.

    Symbolically, Ey = 1

    Unitary elasticity of demand is considered to be a dividing line between necessaries and comforts. In other words, the income elasticity of demand for necessaries will be less than unity; while the income elasticity of the demand for comforts will be more than unity. Both these cases are noted below.

4. **Income Elasticity Less than Unity:** It is a case where the consumer spends a smaller proportion of his money-income on the given product when he becomes richer.

    In case of necessaries, the income elasticity of demand is less than unity. In such cases, when the money-income goes up, the expenditure or demand increases in a smaller proportion.

    Symbolically, Ey < 1.

    In short, if the numerical value of *Ey is less than one, income elasticity of demand is low.*

5. **Income Elasticity of Demand Greater than Unity:** It is a case when, with the increase in the income of the consumer, the consumer spends (or demands) a greater proportion of his money-income on the 'given' product.

    Luxuries generally have income elasticity of demand greater than unity.

    Symbolically, Ey > 1.

    In short, if the numerical value of *Ey is more than one, income elasticity of demand is high.*

Diagram:

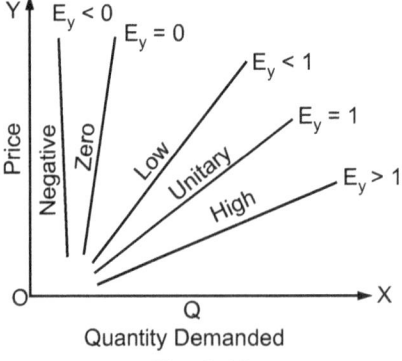

Fig. 2.46

The income elasticity for different products differs widely. Income elasticity of demand tends to be very high in respect of luxury articles like gold, precious stones, paintings, cars etc. As against this, income elasticity of demand is very low in respect of commodities like salt, vanaspati, match-box, kerosene, washing soap etc. Besides, the type of a commodity i.e. whether it is a necessary or comfort or luxury, the proportion of a consumer's income spent on the commodity is also a major factor influencing income elasticity of demand.

Types of Income Elasticity of Demand at a Glance

	Types of Income Elasticity of Demand	Description
(a)	Negative	Demand for a commodity falls as income rises (e.g. inferior goods)
(b)	Zero	Demand for a commodity does not change as income changes.
(c)	Greater than zero but less than one	Demand for a commodity rises less in proportion to a rise in income.
(d)	Unity	Demand for a commodity rises in the same proportion as rise in income.
(e)	Greater than Unity	Demand for a commodity rises in a larger proportion to rise in income.

2.42 Uses of the Concept of Income – Elasticity of Demand

(a) **Demand Forecasting**: With the help of statistical information regarding trends in growth of income as well as changes of distribution of income, the firm can forecast the demand for its product by using income elasticity of demand for that product as a guide.

(b) **Effect on the Economy**: The working of the economy is also affected by the nature of consumer demand, based on income of the consumer. It influences the total volume of goods and services produced in a particular country.

(c) **Economic Development**: When national income is increasing, we can find out how much will be the increase in the demand for a given product, by considering the income-elasticity of demand for that product. It also helps to understand the increase in demand for goods not in the country but also for imported goods.

(d) **Foreign Trade:** In the area of foreign trade, a country needs to take into account the income elasticity of demand for its imports as well as exports. A country exporting agricultural products and articles of necessity faces an income inelastic demand, compared to a country which is exporting articles of luxury. This difference influences terms of trade. Income-elasticity of demand serves as a guide in the matter of balance of payments disequilibrium also. For example, India has been an exporter of jute, tea, coffee and spices; but the demand for all these commodities is income-inelastic. The rate of growth of India's exports therefore has remained relatively low. As against this, India's demand for imports like electronics, machinery, consumer durable etc. is income-elastic. Consequently, the rate of growth of India's imports has remained high. Thus we have been facing the problem of an increasing trade deficit in India during the last few years.

2.43 Cross Elasticity of Demand

Meaning

In practice, commodities are seldom independent of one another. Among the wide range of products that we see at the market, we find that most of these goods are related. On the basis of the relationship, we can group these products either as *substitutes* or *complements* or as a third group of goods which are *neutral*.

In the context of these relationships, the concept of cross elasticity of demand may be defined as *'the ratio of proportionate change in the quantity demanded of commodity X to a given proportionate change in the price of the related commodity Y.*

Formula, $Ec = \dfrac{\text{Percentage change in quantity demaded of X}}{\text{Percentage change in the price of Y}}$

Here, Ec =   Cross elasticity of demand.

Assume that the two commodities X and Y are substitutes of each other. Further, suppose that the price of Y rises and that of X remains constant, the quantity demanded of X will increase because the consumers will now substitute X for Y, since Y has become costlier. On the other hand, if the price of Y falls leaving the price of X unchanged, the quantity demanded of X will decrease because the consumers will now substitute Y for X since Y has become cheaper than before.

If the goods are *no substitutes* at all i.e. are not related to each other, the cross elasticity of demand will be zero. It means, that a change in the price of one product will not influence the quantity demanded of the other.

The cross-elasticity of demand for 'substitute goods' ranges from infinity to zero.

If the substitutability does not exist, cross elasticity is zero.

And if goods are close substitutes then the cross elasticity is high.

If the two goods X and Y are complements to each other, the cross-elasticity in such a case will be *negative*. A rise in the price of Y, will not only bring a fall in the quantity demanded of Y, but also a fall in the quantity demanded of X as both the goods are demanded together. Thus, in case of joint demand, the cross-elasticity of joint demand goods is negative. For example, ball point pens and refills are complementary goods. When the price of refills rises, it causes a fall in the demand for refills as well as for ball-point pens, because both are demanded together.

Let us now illustrate the cross-elasticity of demand.

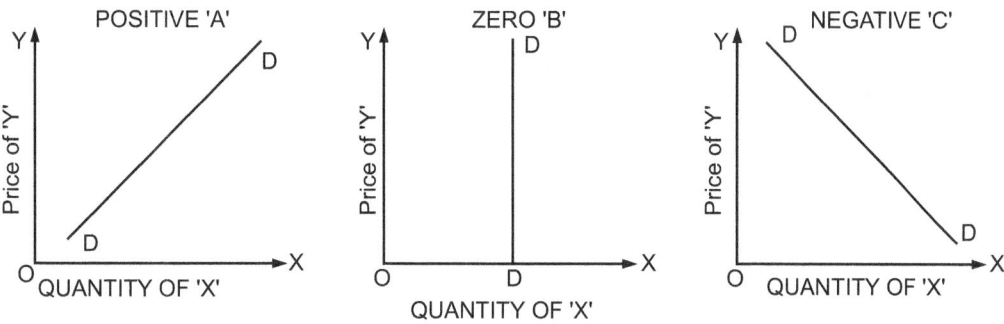

Fig. 2.47

The cross elasticity can be positive, zero and negative.

(i)   The cross elasticity of demand is *positive* when the two goods X and Y are good substitutes, e.g. tea and coffee.

(ii)   The cross elasticity is *zero* when the two goods are not related to each other or are perfectly independent of each other.

(iii) The cross elasticity is negative, e.g. ball-point pen and refill, when the two goods are complements.

In case of *substitutes*, a rise in the price of Y, assuming the price of X remaining the same, will cause a rise in the quantity demanded of X. The cross elasticity of demand is high in the case of close substitutes Fig. 2.47 (a).

In case, a rise or fall in the price of Y does not influence the quantity demanded of X at all, the cross elasticity is zero Fig. 2.47 (b).

In case, a rise in price of Y, with price of X remaining constant, will result in fall the quantity demanded of X, cross elasticity is negative Fig. 2.47 (c).

2.44 Use of Cross Elasticity of Demand

1.   **Control on International Monopoly:** The concept finds an important application in the enforcement of Anti-Trust Law.

     Thus, it helps the authorities concerned to define a monopolised good. A product is a monopolised product if the cross elasticity of its substitutes are low.

     Any business firm charged with violating Anit-Trust Laws will reflect that cross elasticity between its product and other similar ones are high i.e. are good substitutes. It also allows the consumers to exercise effective choice.

2.   **Price-Policy:** Perfect substitutes are seldom found in practice. Perfect complements are equally rare. But, broadly speaking, there are complementarities or competition

i.e. *substitutability* among several commodities. Under such circumstances, the entrepreneur can judge the effect of his pricing policy on the quantities demanded of the products of others and vice versa on the basis of the cross-elasticity of demand.

3. **Defines Industries:** The concept of cross elasticity of demand is used to define the frontiers of an industry. For instance, if the cross elasticity of demand between two commodities is very high, it means that the two commodities belong to the same industry. It is different industries, if the cross elasticity is low between the two goods.

   Thus, the concept of cross elasticity lays down the boundaries of industries in domestic and external sectors.

4. **Determination of terms of trade in external market:** It is possible to calculate the terms of trade between two countries only by taking into consideration the *mutual* elasticity of demand for each other's commodities. Terms of trade refers to the rate at which one unit of domestic good will exchange for units of a commodity of a foreign country. Thus, while calculating the terms of trade, we consider mutual elasticity of demand for the goods of the two countries.

2.45 Demand Forecasting

Introduction

Most business decisions are made in the face of risk or uncertainty, such as decisions regarding how much of each product to produce, what price to charge, how much to spend on advertising, plan the growth of the firm, etc. All these decisions are based on some forecast of the level of future economic activity in general and demand for the firm's products in particular. The objective of economic forecasting is to reduce the risk or uncertainty that the firm faces in its short-term operational decision making and in planning for its long-term growth.

Meaning of Demand Forecasting

The importance of demand or sales forecasting to business planning can hardly be over-emphasised. Good production and sales planning require forecasts of the business conditions and of their relationship to demand. Any demand forecasting requires managers to predict for the future which is unknown. In fact, it is to minimise the 'uncertainties' of the unknown future that these forecasts are needed.

A forecast is a prediction about a future event which is most likely to happen under given conditions. In a world full of uncertainties, formation of some view about the future is most essential. *Predictions of future demand for a firm's product or products are known as demand forecasts.* Thus, demand forecast refers to estimation of the demand for the given commodity in the forecast period. For example, if the good is a Ford car and the forecast period is the year 2015, then the forecasting problem is to estimate the demand for that model of Ford cars in 2015. Actually, the most important factor which goes into making an effective manager is his sense of predicting future events influencing the firm.

Demand forecasting is different from demand estimation in the sense that demand forecasting predicts about future trend of sales while the demand estimation tries to find out expected present sales level, given the present state of demand determinants. Forecasts can be both physical as well as financial in nature, and are used mostly for planning purposes.

When prediction about future is based on the assumption that the firm does not change the course of its action, it is referred to as *passive forecasts*.

When forecasting is done under the condition of likely future changes in the course of actions by the firm, it is referred to as *active forecasts*.

For example, if any car company thinks of bringing in an improvement in the quality of its car and at the same time is committed to go in for a vigorous advertising campaign, there will be changes influencing the demand. To estimate the changes in variables active demand forecasting is undertaken. Thus, active forecasts are more meaningful and realistic in assessing new policies in the market, as compared to passive forecasts.

Generally, business firms are interested in both passive and active forecasts. Often they predict sales after considering the changes in a host of policy variables, like prices of substitutes and complements, design, quality, advertisement expenditure, etc.

Purpose of Short-term Forecasts

(i) Product policy is one such immediate purpose. A firm has to prepare a short term plan for production which needs short-term forecasts so as to avoid either under-production or over-production.

(ii) For a realistic price policy the firm has to prepare short-term demand forecasts.

(iii) Cost-effectiveness is an important consideration in management. This can be introduced with the help of demand forecasts.

(iv) Securing short term credit on the basis of demand forecasts, the firm can tap various sources of credit in advance and thus save time and expenses which are likely to be wasted if the firm puts in efforts at the last minute when securing credit.

(v) Distribution channels can be arranged in anticipation of future demand if the forecasts of the demand are available.

Purpose of Long-term Forecasts

(i) *A plan of expansion* is usually prepared for a long-term by a firm. Such a plan involves expansion of existing plan, diversification of production and a training programme for workers.

(ii) *Raising of capital for future expansion* is another important purpose. Long-term demand forecasts spell out the capital needs of the firm and accordingly a plan of raising funds from various sources can be formulated.

(iii) Long-term forecasts can also assist the firm in *man-power planning*.

Steps involved in Forecasting

For an efficient demand forecast, the following steps are involved:

- **First Step: Identify the objective of forecast:** The purpose of the exercise may be estimation of one or more than one aspect – quantity and composition of demand, sales planning, price to be quoted, inventory control, etc. Thus, it is necessary to be clear about what does one want to get from the forecast.

- **Second Step: Determining the nature of goods under consideration:** Different groups of goods have their own distinctive demand patterns. Therefore, it is essential to classify them as capital goods, consumer durables and non-durables. This helps in identifying the approach of the forecasting exercise and in determining the variables to be taken into account in forecasting.
- **Third Step: Selection of an appropriate forecasting method:** Selection of an appropriate method depends on the objective of forecasting, type of data available, period for which the forecast is to be made, etc. For instance, if the data shows cyclical fluctuations then the use of linear trend will not be suitable.
- **Fourth Step: Interpretation of results:** Forecasts alone does not have much meaning to management, interpretation is equally important. Many-a-times, the forecast results are to be well-supported by the background factors like government policy, general business environment, etc., which have not been considered during the exercise of forecasting.

To conclude, forecasts are to be revised frequently in the light of changing circumstances because forecasts are made on the assumption of continuation of past events.

2.46 Necessity of Forecasting Demand

Demand forecasts are attempted by several organisations and individuals. For instance, the industrial organisations undertake demand forecasting for their corresponding industrial products and firms in their corresponding brands. Worldwide forecasts are carried out by international organisations like United Nations Organizations, the World Bank etc.

Thus, it means that forecasting of demand by some technique or the other is highly essential. An entrepreneur can forecast on the bases of intuition or personal judgement. But, forecast based on personal judgement is a game of guesswork. In fact, the significance of the forecasting studies can hardly be exaggerated. These studies are needed to plan future production and thereby future needs for arranging various resources like manpower, raw materials and funds. And, unless the future demand is known well in advance there may not be enough time to plan and execute the production to meet that demand. Accurate demand forecasts are essential to avoid shortages (production short of demand) of products (production more than demand) of in the market. As both, overproduction or underproduction influence the price structure of the various goods in the market.

There is no choice between forecasting and not forecasting. Because, not forecasting means that the firm assumes no change to take place in their product in this fast changing consumption habits of consumers. This is an unrealistic assumption on the part of the firm. Thus, the choice to make is in the various methods of demand forecasting rather than in the decision of whether to forecast or not to forecast.

An organised forecasting system may not be necessary as long as the concerned firms are small and their operations are simple. But as a business unit grows in size, in complexity and in diversity of its products and processes, forecasting becomes a specialised and a separate function of management.

Thus, we summarise the necessity of forecasting as follows:

1. **Achievement of Planned Objectives:** Every firm aims at certain pre-determined objectives. For attainment of these objectives, the firm needs a reasonably accurate forecast of trends in the economy in general and of its sales income in particular.

2. **Preparing a Budget:** Every firm has to prepare a well conceived budget incorporating cost of production and expected earnings. The expectations of earnings must be backed by a forecast of annual sales and prices. Such a budget enables the firm to control its costs and to reduce the area of avoidable risks. Such a systematic exercise to guide the business is better than guesswork on the part of the entrepreneur.

3. **Stabilisation of Production and Employment:** Due to seasonal, cyclical and erratic changes in the economy, market demand fluctuates. However, the level of production cannot be changed every now and then. If an annual forecast of demand is undertaken the firm can decide on the line of production planning for that coming year taking care of the seasonal variations. This policy would enable the firm to maintain a stable labour force. A stable labour force is essential as one cannot recruit or retrench work force at will, with variations in market conditions.

4. **Future Expansion:** Every firm has to think in terms of its plans of expansion in future. It is a long term plan that certainly is based on the demand forecast.

5. **Long-term Investment Programmes:** This plan of the firm of long-term investment is corollary to the earlier point (future expansion). Expansion plans for the future calls for long-term programme of investment and plan of future recruitment. Needless to say that investment plan is to be based on accurate demand forecasting.

6. **Sales Budgeting:** Demand forecasting is crucial for sales budgeting. It determines production and inventory plans, the level of costs and the level of employment. Sales budgets are also useful in computing standard costs, in establishing profit goals and in preparation of capital budgets, future cash flows and sources of funds. Sales forecasts and sales budget act as regulators of a firm's operations and serve to improve the quality of business decisions.

7. **Control of Inventories:** A satisfactory method of control of raw materials, semi-finished products, spare parts etc. must depend upon a satisfactory estimate of future requirements, their availability and their estimated prices.

Thus, forecasting can be of great help in introducing business discipline and scientific management.

Nature and Scope of Demand Forecasting

It is possible to use a demand forecast in a number of ways. Hence, it is necessary to outline the nature and scope of demand forecasting. The following factors have to be considered to outline the scope of demand forecasting:

1. **Time – frame**: A firm has to be certain about the time frame for which it needs to forecast. Every firm has to decide upon the period of time. The method to be chosen and accuracy of the method depends upon the time frame that the firm has chosen. Thus, the first step is to decide about the length of period for which the forecasting exercise is being taken up. The time – periods are usually divided into (a) short-term forecasts – a period up to 3 months; (b) medium-term forecasts – a period between 3 months and 1 year; (c) long-term forecasts – a period of more than 1 year.

   (a) **Short-term forecasts:** In the case of short-term forecasting, the factors considered are those which bring about fluctuations in the demand pattern in the market, like weather conditions, change in tastes, fashions, etc. These factors influence the demand for consumer goods and thus indirectly influence the demand for machinery, raw material required to produce these consumer goods etc. In short, *seasonal factors* are the main factors of short-term forecasting.

   (b) **Medium-term forecasts:** In the case of medium-term forecasting, experience and sound judgement are more important than statistical forecasting. Medium-term forecasts can assist in making the decision about timing of an activity, like advertising outlay. These forecasts contribute to revision of the decision based on long-term forecasts. The main feature of medium-term forecasts is the *trend*. The trends assist in employee recruitment and training etc.

   (c) **Long-term forecasts:** In the long-run, the validity of the trend itself must be made sure of. If the trend is likely to change for the worse, this would adversely affect the firm's entire long-term strategy. For example, the long-term forecasts could suggest diversification policy for the firm. For this forecast there is great dependence on statistical techniques, though judgement in identifying variables that are likely to influence future sales still remains important.

2. **Level of Forecasts**: Demand forecasts can be prepared at various levels:

   (a) **At Economy Level:** This forecasting is concerned with business conditions over the whole economy. These business conditions are measured with the help of various indices like those relating to national income, wholesale prices, etc. Thus, entrepreneurs can have their demand forecasts based on the Gross National Product (GNP) and the indices of various variables available. The growth of the economy and its influence on the demand for all goods and services can be taken into account.

   (b) **At the Industry(or market) Level:** Forecasts regarding prospects of an industry and future demand for the product of an industry can be formulated on the basis of market surveys, past trends in demand and other statistical methods. Such forecasts can give indications to a firm regarding the direction in which the whole industry will be moving. For example, Voltas will like to know the way air-conditioner industry is likely to behave in future, so as to decide about the way this firm should plan for future and in relation to rest of the industry, i.e., every firm can compare its own position in relation to the position of that industry.

    (c) At the Firm (or company) Level: It is this level of forecast which occupies an important place in micro economic analysis. This type of forecast is at an individual firm's level. A big firm will forecast for its own product, independent of the rest of the firms in the industry. Such forecasting shows whether or not the company is well placed to maintain or even improve its share in the market.

    (d) Product-line forecasting: This forecasting helps the firm to decide which of the product or products should have priority in the allocation of firm's limited resources. For example, Godrej may like to know whether it should produce more of store-well cupboards or locks or furniture, etc.

3. **For Established Products and for New Products**: For existing and established products, while forecasting demand, it is necessary to take into account the current level of the demand for these products and present competition in that field. For the established products, past sale trends and competitive conditions are considered. The statistical methods of demand forecasting can be of great importance in the case of established and existing products. However, this is not possible in the case of new products. Thus, for forecasting the demand for new products one has to use different methods.

4. **General and Specific Forecasts:** Many-a-times, demand forecasts are prepared in general for all the products of a firm. However, a firm may need more detailed information regarding the quantum of demand for each individual product. This requires specific forecast. Too many details may overshadow the overall picture based on a general forecast.

5. **Classification of Products:** Economists broadly classify goods into capital goods, consumer durables and non-durable goods. While preparing demand forecasts it is essential to classify the products. For example, the demand for durable consumer goods can be postponed and generally the demand declines during depression. The demand for capital goods is a derived demand and thus faces severe fluctuations. The demand for consumer goods is related to the income of the community. Increase in income can result in higher demand for consumer goods. Thus, for each of these categories of goods there would be distinctive patterns of demand.

6. **Special Factors:** While forecasting, decision has to be made regarding the extent of sociological and psychological factors that influence the exercise of forecasting. For example, the nature of competition, the extent of uncertainty, the unforeseen risks and possibilities of forecasts going wrong are some of the special factors to be looked into. Likewise there are product-wise differences in the combinations of such special factors entering into demand forecasts. For example, change in fashion is a special factor that enters into demand forecast for readymade garments and weather forecasts are significant to the producers of air coolers, rain coats, etc.

2.47 Criteria for a Good Method of Demand Forecasting

There are various methods of demand forecasting. Out of these alternative methods available to a firm, it has to choose the best method. Which method would be the best? For answering the question we can outline the following criteria, which would serve as parameters for testing the various methods of demand forecasting:

1. **Plausibility:** The method of demand forecasting should be intelligent to the executives who are going to use it. At the same time, they should feel confident that the technique used by following any certain method will be helpful to them in formulating a particular demand forecast.

2. **Simplicity:** Various mathematical and economic models can be used with an advantage; however they are highly sophisticated and complex. Majority of these models thus, are not acceptable to small and medium-sized firms. Such models are more used by national and multi-national corporations because they can afford to have special cells for demand forecasting. Majority of the managements however require a method which is simple and easy to understand.

3. **Economical:** Techniques of demand-forecasting involve costs. These costs must be weighed against returns. A method yielding high level of benefits but involving huge amount of costs may not be acceptable. In areas where accuracy is likely to bring in huge profits, the high costs of forecasting may prove to be worthwhile. Thus, economies suggest a balance of costs involved and benefits expected of the method of demand-forecasting.

4. **Accuracy:** Every firm expects its forecasting to be as accurate as possible. By accuracy, we mean closeness to reality. Some check of accuracy of past performance against the present happening and the forecast against future predictions is highly desirable. Accuracy can be increased by finding out deviations after every forecast. We must, however, remember the fact that precision would involve higher costs and would go against the criterion of economy.

5. **Availability:** The criterion of availability refers to the timely availability of the forecast as well as availability of adequate and up to date statistical data for the preparation of the forecast. To what extent is a forecast meaningful depends upon the statistical date used by the forecaster. At the same time, if the forecaster tries to collect too much of data and spends a lot of time in arriving at the forecasts, the forecasts are likely to be meaningless for decision making. They would reach the management too late and the purpose will be defeated of forming demand on the basis of forecast.

6. **Durability:** The criterion of durability is important because a forecast prepared by incurring sizeable costs must last over a reasonable period of time. Forecasts which are based on stability of the underlying variables measured in the past and which are simple in nature are likely to be more durable.

7. **Flexibility:** A forecast should be flexible and not rigid because an element of uncertainty is always associated with business plans. A set of variables whose coefficients can be adjusted from time to time for meeting the changing conditions can prove to be a more practical way of imparting flexibility to a method of demand forecasting.

8. **Consistency:** Consistency implies that a firm's forecasts should be consistent with the forecasts at the level of the industry or on the national level. For example, forecast indicating buoyant demand for one's product would be inconsistent if the national level forecast is that of imminent depression and unemployment.

Determinants for Demand Forecast
(A) For Consumer Durables

The demand for consumer durables falls into two categories: replacement demand and new demand. The special peculiarities in forecasting for consumer durables are:

(i) **Changes in demographic factors:** Demand for consumer durables is closely related to the size and characteristics of population- growth rate, age and sex composition. For example, demand for toys is dependent on the birth rate in the recent past. Similarly, the number and size of households determines the demand for goods such as refrigerators, television sets, etc.

(ii) **Limit of the market:** The potential market for additional units of goods such as cars, furniture becomes very limited and this demand is only replacement demand.

(iii) **Availability of the goods:** Larger the stock, greater will be the amount of replacement, shorter the life of the good, earlier will be the replacement.

(iv) **Replacement and new demand:** Since replacement demand comes from those who already own the good while new demand results from the coming forward of new customers, each of these demands are determined by separate factors.

(v) **Consumers' level of income:** Larger the possibility of increase in GNP or disposable personal income, greater will be the possibility of increase in demand. There is a close relationship between the discretionary income and demand for consumer durables.

(vi) **Tastes and preferences:** The knowledge of changes in consumer's tastes and preferences indicates future trends in market demands.

(vii) **Consumer's purchasing power:** Higher the amount of credit offered to the consumers, higher will be the demand for a good. But, since the customer has to pay back the debt in future, it may lead to a cut in the future discretionary power and reduce the demand. Hence, the forecaster tries to find out the status of consumer debt outstanding before estimating the demand for a durable consumer good.

The forecaster of consumer durables uses different techniques to determine his future level of sales. For finding out changes in consumer attitudes and credit outstanding, the forecaster has to resort to a survey of the consumer plans. And, once these future changes are known, these can be fed into a regression model to get the level of future sales.

(B) For Non-durable Consumer Goods

These are consumer goods which can be used only once, e.g., food, beverages, and so on. Demand for such goods is influenced by factors such as – purchasing power of the consumer, price of the commodity, population and its characteristics.

(i) **Disposable income (purchasing power):** Disposable income refers to personal income minus direct taxes. Economists are of the view that instead of purchasing power it is better to use discretionary income, particularly for demand for forecasts of luxuries.

(ii) **Price of the commodity:** Demand for a good depends upon its own price in relation to the price of its substitutes and complements. For estimating and forecasting demand for non-durable consumer goods price elasticity and cross elasticity concepts can be used. Those non-durable consumer goods which can be stored and are independent of fashion changes, are more price elastic.

(iii) **Characteristics of population:** Demand for non-durable consumer goods are influenced by factors like total population, income groups, rural and urban ratios, level of education, etc. With the help of demographic variables, demand for each market segment can be estimated as distinct from total market demand.

(C) Capital Goods

Capital/Producer goods – factory buildings, machinery - are those goods which help in further production of goods. Capital goods have derived demand, which will depend upon the profitability, capacity utilisation and wage rates in the industry using the capital good. Further, demand for capital good is of two types – replacement demand and new demand. The forecaster can forecast the demand for any capital good in question by collecting data on factors such as – the rate of obsolescence of capital goods, the existing stock of capital goods, availability of funds with the firm for capital goods, growth of industries using the capital goods, etc.

Methods of Demand Forecasting

Forecasts, by its definition, involve future predictions, which are inherently uncertain. The paradoxical situation is that forecasts are essential but there is no way to generate absolutely accurate forecasts.

Over the past few years various techniques of forecasting demand, with respect to either economy as a whole, or an industry or an individual firm has been evolved. A forecaster has to choose one or more techniques by testing them against the criteria. There is perhaps no unique method, as methodology is always plural.

For short term forecasts, when quantitative data are not available, Surveys and Opinion polls are often used. To supplement quantitative techniques, qualitative methods are used and assist in anticipating changes in consumer tastes or future expectations about economic conditions.

(A) Survey Techniques (Buyer's Interviews or Survey of Buyer's Intentions)

The most direct method of estimating demand in the short run is to ask buyers what they plan to buy for the forthcoming time period – usually a year. The logic for forecasting based on surveys of buyer's intentions is that many economic decisions are made well in advance of actual expenditures. For example, consumers' decisions to buy television sets, automobiles, mobiles, to go on vacation, or plan education, etc., are made months or years in advance of actual expenditure incurred on them. Likewise, business firms plan to grow or expand or buy equipments long before expenditures are actually done. Government agencies prepare budgets and anticipate expenditures a year or more in advance. Surveys of buyer's intentions can be used as a basis for forecasting future purchases of consumer goods, capital goods and inventory changes etc.

Some of the surveys used to forecast economic activity in general are:

- Surveys of business executives' plant and equipment expenditure plans are periodically conducted by Ministry of Commerce, the Ministry of Statistics, SEBI, CII, FICCI, and CMIE. For example, the Ministry of Commerce survey is very comprehensive and it is conducted annually. It is published in the Annual Economic Survey and Annual Report.

- Surveys of Consumers' expenditure plans are periodically conducted by the Directorate of Economics and Statistics, CSO and CMIE. These surveys project buyer's intentions to purchase specific products, including automobiles, consumer appliances, houses, etc. The results of these surveys are of immense importance to forecasters in general and they give an idea of consumer confidence in the economy.

- Surveys of plans for inventory changes and sales expectations are periodically conducted by the Ministry of Commerce, CII, FICCI, etc. They report on business executives' plans for inventory changes and expectations about future sales.

These agencies have generally been reporting well in forecasting actual expenditures. These surveys when used in addition with other quantitative methods prove very useful in forecasting economic activity in specific sectors of the economy and for the whole of the economy in general.

Each year firms in India spend a significant amount of money to interview and ask more than 500 lakh consumers for their opinion on a large variety of products or services. However, a growing number of consumers are refusing to answer and participate in market surveys. The reasons may be – time involved, loss of privacy, refusing to part with personal information, pressure from salesperson operating under the cover of market research. These problems have led to difficulties in obtaining representative samples and also in forming a trend to be used in observational research.

(B) Opinion Polling: (Sales Force Polling/ Collective Opinion)

Although the reports of Surveys published on the expected expenditures of consumers, government agencies, business firms are very useful, the firms need to know specific forecasts for their own product, as surveys only give a general opinion. It is true that the sales of any firm depend on the general level of economic activity and sales for the industry as a whole, but they also depend on the policies adopted by the firm. For this the firm involves itself in opinion polling – inside and outside the firm- , i.e., sales force polling and collective polling.

- **Sales force polling:** This is a forecast of the firm's sales in each region and for each product line. The sales force is closest to the market and hence their opinion of future sales can provide valuable information to the management department of the firm.

- **Consumer's intentions polling:** Companies selling furniture, automobiles and other consumer goods carry on polling by conducting on a sample of potential buyers on their purchasing intentions. These results are used by the firm to forecast its national sales for different levels of consumer's future disposable income.

- **Executive polling:** This method is 'collective polling' as it involves, while examining the forecasts, the wisdom of experts such as sales manager, marketing manager, finance manager, etc. Thus, it is polling opinion from top management for their views on the sales outlook for the firm during the next quarter or a year. However, this method is highly subjective and is likely to carry biases of the salesmen into the estimation of their reports. This polling is useful for short-term forecasts and the salesmen may not be aware of the broader economic changes likely to influence the future demand. Outside market experts could be polled and to avoid a bandwagon effect (opinions of salesmen may be overshadowed by some dominant personality and they all give same opinion) the *Delphi method* can be used. In this method, the experts are polled separately, and their feedback is provided without identifying the expert responsible for a particular opinion. This feedback procedure may give the experts some commonly agreed upon forecasts.

(C) Soliciting a Foreign Perspective

Many Indian firms deal in exports, i.e., sell an increasing share of their output abroad and face competition at home and abroad from foreign firms. It is essential for such firms to forecast changes in markets and products abroad as these changes influence not only the firm's exports but its competitiveness at home. To have an insight in international markets, an increasing number of firms in India are forming councils of distinguished foreign dignitaries and business people, especially in Europe. The rationale is that there is no better way to forecast and figure out what is going to happen in Europe than to solicit (ask for) the ideas of government and business leaders who live there. For example, IBM calls on its advisory councils in Europe, Asia, and Latin America to help develop strategic plans. The advantage of such foreign councils is that they do not have to spend time in reviewing budgets or handling other duties but can devote their full attention to international issues that can have deep impact on the firm's future as a global competitor. The impact of such foreign councils becomes an invaluable tool to get a global perspective and plan long-term domestic and foreign strategies.

Case Study (Fortune Forecasting McDonald's Abroad)

Increased competition and lower profit margins at home have driven McDonald's and other large U.S. fast-food chains to expand abroad, where competition is weaker and profit margins are higher.

By 2005, there were more McDonald's restaurants abroad – 17,500- than in the U.S.- 13,100. McDonald's operated in 122 countries and the statistics showed that 4 out of 5 of its new restaurants were abroad.

Based on each country's population and per capita income, *Fortune* magazine estimated the potential number of restaurants that McDonald's could build in each country if tastes were similar to U.S. tastes. *Fortune* came up with a total worldwide number of 42,000 restaurants. When Fortune estimated in 1993, the number of McDonald's abroad was 3,597. By 2005, there were 30,600. In this way McDonald's is reaching the estimated minimum market potential abroad.

Even in countries in which McDonald's is hardly present are estimated to sustain a large number of its restaurants. For instance, *Fortune* estimated minimum market potential in India as 489 restaurants and numbers of McDonald's in 2007 were 135.

Fortune's estimates were based on the assumption that tastes in the rest of the world were the same as in the U.S. However, convergence of tastes is unlikely to ever become the same.

In 2005, McDonald's forecasts that it would reach 50,000 restaurants abroad (worldwide) during this decade. During this prediction time it had 600 outlets in China and planned 400 more.

(Source: Fortune- October 17, 1994 – page 104 "McDonald's Conquers the World", www.mcdonalds.com)

(D) Time-Series Analysis (Projecting Past Experience)

Statistical Methods

Time-series analysis is based on the assumption that the time series will continue to move as in the past, i.e., it forecasts future values of the time series by examining past observations of the data. When we take 'time' as an explanatory variable in a forecasting exercise, we assume that factors influencing sales in the past will behave exactly in the same manner in future too. This may not be true all the time. The reason is that factors like advertising, one's own price, competitor's price, etc., might have undergone a change and 'time' will not be able to explain the movement in sales. In such cases, statistical tools are used to construct estimating equations, and tests can be carried out to see observed association between past sales and another variable that is statistically significant. Statistical methods are also known as 'economic methods'. These methods are based on the past sales pattern. They are used when the available sales data relates to different time periods. Therefore, it is known as Time Series Analysis or Trend Projection Method.

- **Naive Models:** These models are as effective as the sophisticated other models. These models are cheaper and easier to use. They are generally useful where situation shows a gradual change or conditions are stable. So long as their results are fairly accurate they will be quite helpful. For example, the firm may use the ratio/percentage of advertising expenditure and the resultant sales of the past to forecast for future sales with the advertising expenditure.

- **Correlation and Regression Method:** It is the most popular method of forecasting. This method does not use 'time' as an independent variable and the method realises that sales depend upon other factors too. A set of variables influencing sales is identified through a correlation and a regression equation is then specified to study changes in sales.

Correlation Analysis: It is correlation analysis when two series vary together, e.g. income and expenditure of households. It is *positive correlation* when the two series vary in the *same* direction (R > 0), while it is *negative correlation* when the two series vary in the *opposite* direction (R < 0).

Correlation analysis can be of two types: simple/partial correlation and multiple correlations. It is simple correlation when only one independent variable, say income, is taken to explain variations in the dependent variable, say sales. It is multiple correlations when there are more than one independent variable, say price, advertisement is taken to explain variations in dependent variable, say sales.

The main objective of this analysis is to identify the most appropriate set of variables influencing the dependent variable and this depends on the closeness of the dependent and independent variables. The coefficient of correlation helps to find out the relationship between the dependent and independent variables.

Coefficient of Correlation: To know the closeness, assuming two variables – A and B, we can find the correlation coefficient (R) by using the formula:

$$R = \frac{N \, \Sigma AB - \Sigma A \, \Sigma B}{\sqrt{[N\Sigma A^2 - (\Sigma A)^2] \, [N\Sigma B^2 - (\Sigma B)^2]}}$$

The above formula can be restated as

$$R = \frac{\Sigma ab}{\sqrt{\Sigma a^2 \cdot \Sigma b^2}}$$

Where,   a = deviation of A from its assumed mean

     b = deviation of B from its assumed mean

     Σ = sign of summation

     N = number of items in each set of variables

Higher the value of R, greater is the closeness of the variables A and B. Finding such values of R for each of the independent variables with the dependent variable and comparing them, we can identify a set of independent variables which vary closely with the dependent variable.

Example: Calculate coefficient correlation from the following given data:

Year	2000	2001	2002	2003	2004
Sales/ Output ('000 tonnes)	100	102	104	107	112
Advertising Outlay ('000 rupees)	30	24	26	22	20

Calculation of Coefficients

Year	Sales (A)	(A – A') = a	a^2	Advt. Exp (B)	(B – B') = b	b^2	ab
2000	100	-5	25	30	5.6	31.36	-28
2001	102	-3	9	24	-0.4	0.16	1.2
2002	104	-1	1	26	1.6	2.56	-1.6
2003	107	2	4	22	-2.4	5.76	-4.8
2004	112	7	49	20	-4.4	19.36	-30.8
	$\sum A = 525$	$\sum a = 0$	$\sum a^2 = 88$	$\sum B = 122$	$\sum b = 0$	$\sum b^2 = 59.2$	$\sum ab = -64$

$$A' = \frac{\sum A}{N} = \frac{525}{5} = 105 \quad B' = \frac{\sum B}{N} = \frac{122}{5} = 24.4$$

Solution:

$$R = \frac{\sum ab}{\sqrt{\sum a^2 \cdot \sum b^2}} = \frac{-64}{\sqrt{88 \times 59.2}} = \frac{-64}{72.17} = -0.8867$$

The coefficient shows negative correlation (R < 0) i.e. the sales and advertisement expenditure move in opposite direction. As sales increases, the advertisement outlay is spread on greater number of units of outputs. Hence, the average will be less.

Regression Equation Method: After the variables are identified that are to be included in the forecasting exercise, we may express them in an equation form for undertaking regression analysis. Now, we have to find the nature of the equation form representing the relationship between the dependent and independent variables. It is a *linear equation* when the trend of the dependent variable is linear, e.g.,

Export of Good A = a (National Income) + b (Domestic Price of A) + c (International Price of A) + d (Weather).

If the trend of the dependent variable is non-linear then it is a *non-linear regression equation* for forecasting. The non-linear regression equation can take any one of the forms – parabolic, logarithmic, and exponential, etc.

The various regression equations which can be used for forecasting exercise:

Simple Linear Regression: In this case a straight line is fitted to the data containing one dependent variable and only one independent variable, e.g.

Sales = a +b. (price)

Fitting of the linear regression equation can be done either graphically or by Least Square Method.

Graphical Method: In this method the two variables are plotted on the two axes – dependent variable on x-axis and independent variable on y-axis. The regression line is then approximated by sketching it freehand in a manner that the line passes through the middle of the scatter of points.

Fig. 2.48 shows Graphical Method (Scatter Diagram).

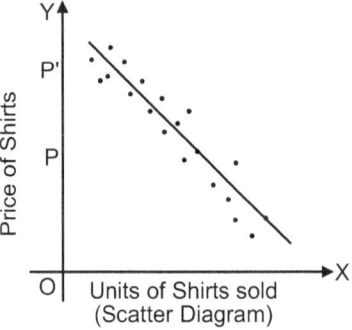

Fig. 2.48

Least Square Method:

Least Square method is a powerful tool to estimate the coefficient of a linear function. It is based on the minimisation of squared deviations between the best fitting lines of the original observations given. The task of the Least Square Method is to find out the coefficients of the best fitting line.

The equation showing a linear trend is given by

$$Y = m + nX$$

m = intercept of the demand curve

n = slope of the curve

X = deviation from the mean of the independent variables

Equation of this model can be formulated as:

$$\Sigma Y = nm + n\Sigma X$$
$$\Sigma XY = m\Sigma X + n\Sigma X^2$$

Solving the above equation simultaneously, we can find the coefficients m and n.

$$m = \frac{\Sigma y}{n} \quad n = \frac{\Sigma XY}{\Sigma X^2}$$

Using these coefficients we can easily estimate the best fitting curve and estimate the future values.

Example:

Forecasting the trend for cellular phones manufactured by Alltime mobiles Pvt Ltd. We will consider a data set of 5 years.

Year	Demand (in lakhs)
2000	120
2001	140
2002	120
2003	150
2004	180

Year	Demand (in lakhs) (Y)	Deviation from 2002 (X)	X^2	XY
2000	120	−2	4	−240
2001	140	−1	1	−140
2002	120	0	0	0
2003	150	1	1	150
2004	180	2	4	360
n = 5	$\sum Y = 710$	$\sum X = 0$	$\sum X^2 = 10$	$\sum XY = 130$

The linear trend equation is Y = m + nX

$$m = \frac{\sum y}{n} = 142$$

$$n = \frac{\sum XY}{\sum X^2} = 13$$

Therefore, the linear equation formulates as

$$Y = 142 + 13.X$$

Based on this equation we can calculate the trend in the next years as follows

Year	Y = 142 + 13.X	Y
2005	142 + 13.(3)	181
2006	142 + 13.(4)	194
2007	142 + 13.(5)	207
2008	142 + 13.(6)	220

For Non-linear Regression Equation

There are two popular methods:

Logarithmic Method: If we consider the example explained above and plot a free hand curve to fit maximum points, a logarithmic method would be more appropriate to fit it. The logarithmic linear format can be represented as follows:

$$\log Y = m + nX$$

$$\log Y = \text{logarithm of the sales}, X = \text{price}$$

Parabolic Method: In some cases, a curve needs to be used for the data set and when by change of variables it cannot be reduced to a linear form. In such cases the curved line may be 2nd degree or a 3rd degree polynomial etc. Assuming a 2nd degree polynomial

$$Y = l + mX + nX^2$$

The l, m, n can be calculated as

$$\Sigma Y = Nl + m\Sigma X + n\Sigma X^2$$

$$\Sigma XY = l\Sigma X + m\Sigma X^2 + n\Sigma X^3$$

Similar polynomial equations of higher degree can be formulated.

Multiple Regression Analysis

Generally, for demand forecasting purposes, the parameters of the demand function are estimated with regression analysis.

When more than one independent variable is taken in the regression model, we are referring to multiple regression coefficients and equations.

In demand regression equations, relevant variables have to be included with practical considerations and relevant data have to be obtained. To explain this point, we may cite a few examples:

(a) Personal disposable income (PDI) towards demand for consumer goods,

(b) Agricultural income towards demand for agricultural goods such as farm equipments, fertilizers, etc.

(c) Construction contracts for demand towards building material like cement, sand, steel, tiles, etc., and

(d) Registration of automobile over a period towards demand for automobile spare parts, petrol, etc.

After collecting such information, demand parameters may be computed with the help of regression analysis.

A multiple regression model, say for sales, may be stated as:

Sales = (a) price + (b) advertising + (c) visits to retailers by salesmen + (d) rivals' price levels + (e) personal disposable income + u

Where, (a), (b), (c), (d) and (e) are the partial regression, which reflect the effect of corresponding variable on sales. For instance, (a) price represents the percentage change in sales due to 1% change in price, other things remaining the same. In the same way, (b) advertising, it shows the percentage change in sales due to 1% change in advertising expenditure. The constant u represents the effect of all the variables, which have been left out in the equation but have an influence on sales.

In the equation, the left-hand side, i.e. the sales is the *dependent variable* and all the variables on the right-hand side of the equation are *independent variables*. Thus, sales (dependent variable) is function of independent variables. If the expected values of the independent variables are substituted in the equation, the sales will be forecasted.

The regression equation can also be written in a multiplicative form, such as-

Sales = (a) price x (b) advertising x (c) visits to retailers by salesmen x (d) rivals' price levels x (e) personal disposable income x u

The advantage of this model is that the effect of a large number of variables can be taken into consideration. Further, this type of model enables the businessperson to experiment with what might happen under extreme or uncertain conditions. For instance, the businessperson would like to know the effect on total sales, when he reduces his outlay on advertising. With this model, he can simply inject these values into the model and get the required results.

However, this model suffers from certain limitations. The regression method forecasts are based on past data. To the extent the future is not a reflection of the past, such forecasts based on this method would be inaccurate to that extent. Secondly, the accuracy of measurement of independent variables determines the degree to which the confidence that can be placed in the forecasted values of the dependent variable.

Smoothing Techniques

Smoothing techniques are useful when the time series exhibit little trend or seasonal variations but a great deal of irregular or random variation. The irregular variation is then smoothed, and future values are forecast based on some average of past observations. We discuss below two smoothing techniques – moving average and exponential smoothing.

Moving Average Method can be sub-categorised into two types:

Moving (Simple) average: In this method all the values in the data set are assigned equal weights. This method forecasts on the basis of values during the recent past. This method is mainly applicable in cases where the time series does not have a ear cut pattern of fluctuations.

$$D_n = \frac{\sum_{i=1}^{n} D_i}{n}$$

where D_i = demand in the ith period

n = number of periods in the moving average

Example: Dello supplies laptops to various companies and institutes in the NCR region. The manager of the company has been given the task of ensuring that there are no failures in the future as they had happened in the past in the company. Thus the manager wants to forecast the number of orders that will occur in the next month. For this he takes the data base from the sales department of the company and with 3 and 5 months moving average he forecasts demand for the month of December.

Month	Jan	Feb	Mar	Apr	May	June	July	Aug	Sept	Oct	Nov
Order	120	180	200	100	110	60	70	110	120	100	110

Calculating moving average for the month of December with 3 or 5 months data.

For 3 months:
$$D = \frac{\sum_{i=1}^{3} D_i}{n} = \frac{(110 + 100 + 120)}{3} = 110$$

For 5 months:
$$D = \frac{\sum_{i=1}^{5} D_i}{n} = \frac{(110 + 100 + 120 + 110 + 70)}{5} = 102$$

Weighted Moving Average: This is an improved version of the Moving Average (Simple) method. According to this method, each data is given a particular weight as per observations.

$$D_n = \frac{\sum_{i=1}^{n} w_i D_i}{n}$$

Where, D_i = demand in the ith period

n = number of periods in the moving average

w_i = weight assigned as per observation

Example: Considering the same data set given in the example above of Moving Average method.

Considering 3 month weighted average using weights equal to 0.5, 0.3, 0.2

$$D = (0.5 \times 110 + 0.3 \times 100 + 0.2 \times 120)$$
$$= (55 + 30 + 24) = 109$$

Exponential Smoothing Technique: To have more realistic estimates of the fluctuations, greater weights are given to the most recent data assigned by this method. The weights range in between 0 and 1 and if we approach to an infinitely large number of observations, the weights would sum up to 1. The equation of this technique is as follows:

$$F_{t+1} = w \times D_t + (1 - w) \times F_t$$

Where D_{t+1} is forecast for the next period and D_t is the actual demand at present period. F_t =previously determined forecast for the present period. w= weight factor termed as smoothing constant.

$$F_{t+1} = w \times Dt + (1-w)(w \times D_{t-1} + (1-w) \times F_{t-1})$$
$$= w \times Dt + (1-w) \times w \times D_{t-1} + (1-w)^2 \times F_{t-1}$$

Continuing the substitution, we get

$$F_{t+1} = w \times D_t + (1-w) \times w \times D_{t-1} + (1-w)^2 \times F_{t-1} \ldots\ldots\ldots w \times (1-w) \times F_1$$

New forecast = previous forecast + error adjustment occurred in previous forecast

This method is particularly applicable in time series in which recent changes in the data are due to actual change (seasonal pattern) rather than any random fluctuation.

The moving average method awards equal importance to each observation included in the average and none to the observations preceding the oldest included data. But Exponential method assigns higher weights to the recent observation and decreasing importance to the more distance pasts. In other words, older the data smaller is the weight. Closer the weight is to 0, the lesser would be the sensitivity of the forecast to the difference between actual and forecasted demand.

Example: Using the above example, compute Exponential Smoothing forecast using smoothing constant = 0.30

Period	1	2	3	4	5	6	7	8	9	10	11	12
Month	Jan	Feb	Mar	Apr	May	Jun	Jul	Aug	Sept	Oct	Nov	Dec
Order	120	180	200	100	110	60	70	110	120	100	110	-
Forecasted order	-	117.45	136.2	155.3	138.7	130.1	109.08	97.3	101.1	106.8	104.7	106.3

$$F_2 = 0.3 \times 120 + 0.7 \times 116.3$$
$$= 117.45 \text{ (as this is the first calculation, } F_1 = \text{avg of all values)}$$
$$F_3 = 0.3 \times 180 + 0.7 \times 117.45 = 136.2$$

Causes for fluctuations in Time-Series Data: If the time series is plotted on a graph, it will show fluctuations and wave-like patterns over time. This variation is usually caused by secular rends (T), cyclical changes (C), seasonal variations(S) and irregular or random movements (I).

(i)   **Secular trend:** It refers to a long-run increase or decrease in the data series (see Fig. 2.49). For example, the trend in operating revenues of Indian Railways from 1977 to 1998. Long-term trends generally exist as some of the important underlying factors like population, national income, competitive conditions, etc., move steadily and thus produce only a gradual change over time. The sales of typewriters follow a declining trend as more and more consumers switch to personal computers.

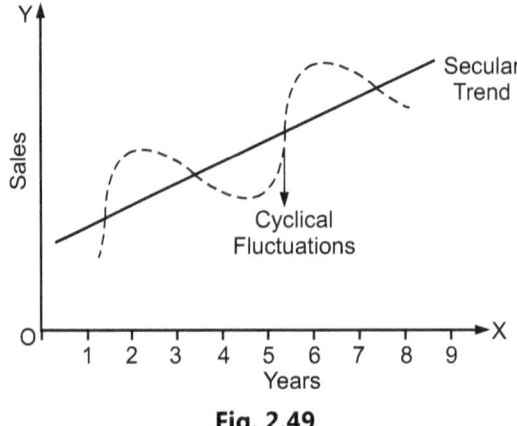

Fig. 2.49

(ii) **Cyclical fluctuations:** The cycle component of a time series is a wave-like, major expansion and contraction in most economic time series that seem to recur every several years. For example, the housing construction industry follows long cyclical swings lasting 15 to 20 years. On the other hand, the automobile industry follows much shorter cycles.

(iii) **Seasonal fluctuations:** These are regularly recurring fluctuations in economic activity during each year (see Fig. 2.50) due to weather and social customs changes. For example, retail sales are greatest during the festive time, or sale of woollen wear is high during month of November due to winter weather. Seasonal fluctuations are measured by seasonal indices and enable managers to carry on with short-term forecasts.

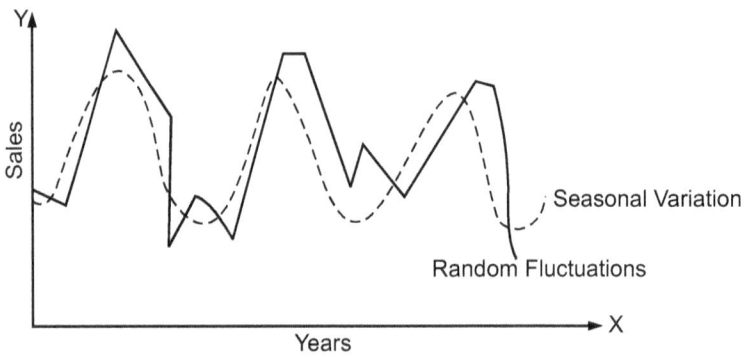

Fig. 2.50

(iv) **Irregular influences:** These are those variations that are left over after isolating the other components. For example, sudden onset of epidemics like swine flu pushed up the sale of medical masks and sanitisers. Such irregular variations do not lend much to predictions.

The total variation in the time series of sales is the result of all four factors operating together. These four components T, C, S and I may be related to each other in an additive or in multiplicative form.

Symbolically, in additive form, O = T + S + C + I (where, O= original data)

In multiplicative form, O = T × S × C × I

Most of the series relating to business and economics are of multiplicative nature.

ARIMA Method (or Box-Jenkin Method): Box and Jenkin developed a technique of forecasting using ARIMA (Auto-regressive Integrated Moving Averages). This technique is suitable in situations when the underlying series is highly complicated or difficult to understand. It can be used for short-term forecasting.

5 stages of analysis are involved in the method:

(a) **Removal of the Trend:** In case of stationary time series the method becomes very useful. Stationary time series is time series that do not have a long-term trend component. The method of *differencing* (the difference between values at adjacent period of time) is used to remove the underlying trend, if any, in the time series. The analysis is performed on the first differences of successive observations.

(b) **Model Identification:** Box-Jenkin model involves the following combinations:

• The order of involvement of auto-regressive terms;

• Number of differences of the original series necessary to remove any inherent trend;

• The order of moving average terms.

Out of the various possible combinations of this model, those combinations are selected that give an adequate fit to the underlying time series and it is done by matching *computed* auto-correlations with the *theoretical* auto-correlation functions given by the combination.

(c) **Parameter Estimation:** Once a particular combination of the three elements (mentioned above in point two the various combinations) is identified, the method of least squares is used to fit this model to the time series and coefficients are obtained for the model.

(d) **Verification:** How "good" is the adequate fit to the underlying time series of the model is checked by analysing the residuals it generates? If these residuals do not show any specific pattern, then it is a 'good' fit of the estimated model. If not, then the process has to be restarted by trying to develop a new group of combinations/model.

(e) **Forecasting:** Once we arrive at a model which is a 'good' fit, we can use its coefficients to generate forecasts of future values.

Box-Jenkin model is a complex one and is based on search method, therefore, forecast handling through this method is done with the help of computers. Some computer software are now available for using this technique. But this creates three types of problems:

- Computer programmes designed to handle this model (Box-Jenkin technique) are often very expensive. And, since this technique is used primarily for short-term forecasts, cost of computation becomes a deterrent factor.

- The users of forecast find it difficult to comprehend the analysis and results and thus operation of this model reduces its popularity.

Barometric or Leading Indicator Technique

Barometric technique is based on the presumption that a relationship can exist among various economic time series. For example, industrial production overtime and industrial loans by commercial banks overtime may move in the same direction. Among economic time series there are 3 types of relationships: (i) Leading series; (ii) Coincident series; and (iii) Lagging series.

A leading series consists of the data that *move ahead of the series* being compared, e.g., applications for the amount of housing loan overtime are a leading series for the demand of construction material. When data in series moves up and down along with some other series, it is known as coincident series. For example, a series of data on national income is often coincident with the series of employment in an economy. Lagging series is where data moves up and down *behind the series* being compared, e.g., data on industrial wages over time is a lagging series when compared with a series of price index for industrial workers.

All the three types of series – leading, coincident and lagging – can be used to forecast change in an economic variable. The barometric technique is based on the idea that future can be predicted from certain events occurring in the present. Formally, the barometric technique involves statistical indicators, usually time series, which when combined in certain ways provide indication of the *direction of change* in an economy or in the specific industries. *A study of all barometric techniques shows that these methods can at best serve as a complement to the other forecasting techniques.*

The following stages are involved in forecasting through barometric techniques:

- To locate the leading indicator for the variable whose forecast is being undertaken;

- To estimate a mathematical or statistical relationship of leading indicator with the variable under forecast;

- To find out the forecasted values of the variable;

- To verify the validity of the forecast with the help of coincident and/or lagging indicators.

2.48 Forecasting the Demand for New Products

New products naturally call for different methods of forecasting. When the product is new, the buyers may not be able to give their opinion or the firm will not be in a position to project its past experience in the future since it has no past experience at all. Hence, Joel Dean has suggested the following six approaches:

1. **Evolutionary Approach:** The demand for a new product can be projected as an outgrowth and evolution of an existing old product. This method is applicable to those cases only where the new product is so close to the old one that it can be treated as the potential development of the existing product. For example, the demand for acrylic emulsion paints can be projected as an outgrowth of oil-bound paints; or the demand for colour T. V. sets can be based on the assumption that colour television picks up where black and white television left off.

   Limitations:
   (i) The new product should be capable of being treated as an outgrowth of an established product.
   (ii) The basic problem is to estimate how the demand for the new product will differ from that of the old one.

2. **Substitute Approach:** The new product can be treated as a substitute for some existing product. If used scientifically this can be a useful approach. Since most of the new products are generally substitutes for some old products this method can be widely used. For example, steel door frames and doors are substitutes for wooden frames and doors.

   New products are mostly improvements over old ones (i.e. innovated goods). Therefore the demand for an old product can be considered to be a limit which can be crossed for new products.

   Limitations:
   (i) When a new product has many uses, each use has a different substitutability. This creates problems in forecasting.
   (ii) The effects of price differentials and policies of rival firms remain uncertain.

3. **Growth Curve Approach:** This approach estimates the rate of growth and the ultimate level of demand for the new product on the basis of the pattern of growth of established products. For example, the firm can analyse growth curve of established cosmetics and then try to establish an empirical law of market development applicable to the new cosmetics. Growth pattern of an established product serves as the basis for potential demand estimation in case of the new product.

   Limitation:
   (i) This approach has limited application because tracing the growth curve for the new product on the basis of actual rate of growth of a similar product is a tedious job.

4. **Opinion - Polling Approach:** Under this approach, demand is estimated by direct enquiries from the ultimate purchasers on a sample basis and then the sample is blown up to full scale for finding the estimate of future demand. This technique of surveying the intentions of buyers as revealed by personal interviews has been successfully used by

many concerns for exploring the potential demand for a new product. The demand for a new chemical, for instance, can be forecast by sending a description of properties of the chemical to prospective buyers along with its probable price. The demand for a new drug can thus, be explored through medical representatives by distributing samples and personal interviews with medical practitioners and owners of drugstores.

Limitation:

All the limitations of sales force polling we discussed earlier are applicable in this case also.

5. **Sales Experience Approach:** In this approach, a new product is offered for sale in a sample market and on the basis of experience gained in the sample market, the total demand is estimated for a fully developed market.

Limitations:

(i) This is similar to controlled experiment. Therefore, market differentials regarding tastes etc. make the job difficult.

(ii) The sample market should be representative of the whole market, another difficult problem of choice.

6. **Vicarious Approach:** This approach consists of surveying consumer's reactions to a new product indirectly through the eyes of specialised dealers who are supposed to be well informed about the needs of the consumers. This method is cheap, easy and quick. But its success depends upon the experience and foresight of the dealers.

Limitations:

(i) The specialised dealer's judgment should be objective and unbiased which is very difficult.

(ii) The experience of the dealer itself limits the area of operation of this method.

Points to Remember

- According to Cournet, "Economists understand by the term market, not any particular market place in which things are bought and sold, but the whole of any region in which buyers and sellers are in such free interaction with one another that the prices of the same goods tend to equality easily and quickly."

- **Determinants of Market Structure:** Number of sellers, Number of buyers, Nature of the product, entry and exit of firms.

- **Features of Perfect Competition:** Large number of buyers and sellers, homogenous products, free entry and exit of firms, perfect knowledge of market conditions, no transport costs, no government interference, perfect mobility of factors.

- Since there are large numbers of buyers and sellers of a product in a perfectly competitive market, each firm is a 'price taker', as a result MR = price. The perfectly competitive firms only need to determine what quantity to produce so that market price matches with marginal cost of the output.

- In pure monopoly, there is a single seller of a product. This product has no close substitutes. Monopoly may exist because of the firm's control over technology, strategic raw material, patent rights, etc. There are high barriers to entry i monopoly. Since the threat of entry is very low for a monopolist, he is free to optimize profit at the output level for which MR = MC.

- In monopolistic competition, firms take independent decisions and compete by selling differentiated products which are highly substitutable. Firms generate their monopoly power by product differentiation and such firms earn supernormal profits in the short run as in the long run entry of new firms takes place and profits may be driven to zero.

- In order to enhance his revenue, a monopolist may decide to discriminate between buyers. He may charge the maximum price each buyer can pay or subdivide the market and charge different price for each sub-group.

- Price discrimination is possible only when each sub-group of the market has different elasticity.

- The quantity demanded is inversely related to price. Other factors determining demand are – income of consumers, prices of related product, tastes and preferences, number of buyers.

- A change in quantity demanded refers to a movement along a particular demand curve caused by a change in the price of the good ad it is known as extension ad contraction of demand.

- A change in demand refers to a shift of demand curve resulting from a change in consumer preferences, income or prices of related goods.

- Market demand is the sum total of individual demands at each price.

- Price elasticity is defined as the percentage change in quantity demanded that results from a change in its own price.

- Demand is more elastic - if more close substitutes are available, consumers have got enough time to adjust fully to change in price, expenditure on the goods accounts for a significant proportion of total expenditure.

- Income elasticity of demand is the percentage change in demand for a percentage change in income.

- Cross elasticity is the percentage change in quantity demanded of good X for a percentage change in the price of good Y.

- There are three basic methods of demand forecasting, viz., market experimentation, survey of consumers' intention and regression analysis.

- Survey of consumer intentions is done by contacting consumers personally either by sample or census method.

- Market experimentation consist of actual market method, market simulation method.

- Regression analysis is a statistical technique in which changes in independent variables like income, advertisement expenditure, etc., are used to estimate demand.

QUESTIONS FOR DISCUSSION

1. Explain the characteristics of Perfect Competition.
2. What is the theoretical significance of a Perfectly Competitive market?
3. Discuss the conditions of equilibrium under perfect competition.
4. How does a competitive firm attain equilibrium under short period?
5. Mention the features of monopolistic competition.
6. 'Full-equilibrium' is only achieved in the long-term under monopolistic competition. Explain.
7. Discuss the effects of monopolistic competition.
8. Differentiate between monopolistic and perfect competition.
9. Which are the different ways in which 'product differentiation' is done?
10. How does a monopoly firm attain equilibrium in the short period?
11. Analyse equilibrium of monopoly firm under different cost situations.
12. Define Price elasticity of demand and explain different types of price elasticity of demand.
13. With the help of diagrams, explain the different types of income elasticity of demand.
14. Explain the practical importance of the cross-elasticity of demand.
15. Define cross elasticity of demand. Show the nature of elasticity of demand for (a) substitutes; (b) complementary goods; and (c) independent goods.
16. Explain the concept of elasticity of demand.
17. What is income elasticity of demand? Explain its types.
18. Discuss the different types of demand forecasting.
19. Mention the scope of demand forecasting.
20. What are the different methods of forecasting the demand for new products?
21. Write a short note on regression analysis.

Objective Questions

1. State whether the following statements are true or false:
   (a) If more is demanded at the same price, the fact is known as increase of demand.
   (b) Demand curve is always negatively sloping.
   (c) Change in demand means an increase in demand or a decrease in demand.
   (d) A decrease in the price of the complementary product shall increase the demand for the given product.
   (e) Downwards shift in demand is known as decrease in demand.
   [Ans.: (a) True, (b) False, (c) True, (d) True, (e) False]

2. Choose the correct alternative:
    (a) In the typical demand schedule, quantity demanded:
        (i)   Varies indirectly with price;
        (ii) Varies directly with price;
        (iii) Varies inversely with price;
        (iv) Is independent of price.
    (b) We can say with certainty that when the demand for mobiles increases in the long run, prices:
        (i)   Will go up;
        (ii) Settle at the original level;
        (iii) Will go down;
        (iv) Cannot be predicted without the knowledge of elasticity of demand.
    (c) By increase in demand we mean:
        (i)   Movement upwards of a demand curve;
        (ii) Movement upwards on a demand curve;
        (iii) Movement downwards of a demand curve
        (iv) None of the above.
    (d) On a linear demand curve two points X(Q=2500, P= 10) ad Y (Q=1500, P=20) have been identified. The demand function is:
        (i)   Q = 2000 – 100P
        (ii) Q = 500 – 40P
        (iii) Q = 1000 – 20P
        (iv) None of the above.
    (e) The demand for a commodity is said to be elastic if the total amount spent on it is:
        (i)   More when the price is low than when the price is high;
        (ii) Less when the price is low than when the price is high;
        (iii) The same whether the price is high or low;
        (iv) None of the above.
    (f) Demand for electricity is elastic because:
        (i)   It is cheap;
        (ii) It has alternative uses;
        (iii) It has a number of substitutes;
        (iv) None of the above.
    (g) If demand is inelastic and price increases:
        (i)   Total revenue will fall;
        (ii) Total revenue will rise;
        (iii) Total revenue will remain the same;
        (iv) None of the above.
    [Ans.: (a) (iii), (b) (iv), (c) (i), (d) (iii), (e) (iv), (f) (ii), (g) (ii)]

Chapter 3...

Cost Concepts

Contents ...

Learning Objectives ...

➢ To understand the various cost concepts and its relevance in managerial decision-making.

➢ To understand the difference between certain costs concepts like opportunity costs and accounting costs.

➢ To develop understanding of the break-even point, i.e., learn about the cost-volume-profit analysis.

➢ To understand about management of risk in business activity.

➢ To have knowledge about the various ways of managing risks, such as through insurance, diversification, hedging.

➢ To be aware of how managers make decisions having different outcomes and striking on the best probable strategy, through decision tree analysis.

Introduction

Cost analysis has a key role to play in business economics as every aspect of business economics virtually involves a comparison between costs and returns.

Cost is not a unique single-valued concept. In fact, there are various types of costs and it is important to distinguish amongst them and know the use of each one of them too.

The term cost has different meanings for different people. Accountants view costs differently than the economists. The accountants tend to focus on the explicit and historical costs. Economists believe that for efficient decision-making by the firm it is the opportunity cost rather than the explicit and historical costs that must be considered.

Prof. Joel Dean mentions the following purposes of taking into account various cost concepts and cost distinctions:

1. **Clearing the Fallacies in the Traditional Outlook:** In traditional thinking, actual costs or costs recorded in the account books of a firm are believed to be the only important costs. In fact, they are no more than the recorded history of moneys expended by the firm. They are useful for legal as well as auditing purposes, but for decision-making, more logical and appropriate cost concepts must be taken into account.

2. **To provide a Proper Perspective to Cost:** The cost concepts and distinctions enable us to examine the practical problems in their correct perspective.

3. **Analysis of Accounting Costs:** Manyatimes it is necessary to analyse accounting cost into proper classes for a better understanding of a given problem. This can be done with the help of different cost concepts.

4. **Forecasting and Policy Making:** For forecasting and taking policy decisions regarding the size of the plant, the level of output, the nature of advertising etc., it is essential to consider various cost distinctions.

3.1 Opportunity Cost (Economic Cost)

A cost concept which has become popular in recent years is that of Opportunity Costs, also known as Alternative Costs, or Economic Costs.

The concept of opportunity cost is a basic concept of cost in economics. Here we look at costs from another angle. One of the cardinal tenets of economics is that resources are scarce. That means every time we choose to use a resource one way, we have given up the opportunity to utilise it another way. The cost of something is what you give up to get it. Thus, *the opportunity cost of a product is the value of the next best alternative product that is forgone so as to release resources for greater production of the former.* As the resources of the society are scarce, we cannot produce all goods that the people may desire. Thus, when more resources are allocated to one product, some other product has to be foregone or sacrificed. In other words, making a choice in effect costs us the opportunity to do something else. *The best alternative forgone is called the opportunity cost.*

In our own lives we constantly keep taking decisions about what to do with our limited income and time. The immediate rupee cost of going to a movie instead of studying is the price of a ticket, but the opportunity cost also includes the possibility· of getting higher grades in the exam. *The opportunity costs of a decision include all its consequences, whether they reflect monetary transactions or not.*

Decisions have opportunity costs because choosing one thing in a world of scarcity means giving up something else. *The opportunity cost is the value of the most valuable good or service forgone.*

The concept of opportunity cost can be explained with a simple illustration. If you went to a public university in 2012, the total costs of books, tuition, and travel averaged about ₹ 60,000. Does this mean that ₹ 60, 000 was your opportunity cost of going to school? It is definitely not. In opportunity you must include the time spent studying and going to classes. A full-time job for a college-age high school graduate paid ₹ 80,000 in 2012. If we add up both the actual expenses and the earnings forgone, we would find that the opportunity cost of college was ₹ 80,000 + ₹ 60,000 = ₹ 1, 40,000, rather than just ₹ 60,000 per year.

Business decisions have opportunity costs too. As a manager is faced with the problem of constrained optimisation, the knowledge of opportunity cost is necessary for managerial decision-making. A manager works within a budget constraint. Whenever more resources are allocated by him to one department of the firm, they have to be withdrawn from another and thus the opportunity cost is involved. For example, if some resources are to be allocated to Quality Control department, it may result in withdrawal of resources from Production Department which means reduction in the current output of the product, though allocation of more resources to Quality control Department may result in better products in future yielding more profits to the firm in future. Such a decision is taken only if the management is sure of greater profits in future.

All opportunity costs, however, do not show up on the profit-and-loss statement. In general, business accounts include only transactions in which money actually changes hands. On the other hand, the economist always tries to uncover the real consequences that lie behind the money flows and to measure the true resource costs of an activity. *Economists therefore include all costs – whether they reflect monetary transactions or non-monetary transactions.*

There are several important opportunity costs that do not show up on income statements. For example, in many small family run businesses, the family may put in many unpaid hours, which are not included in accounting costs. Accounting costs may also not include the capital charges for the owner's financial contributions. It may not include the cost of the environmental damage that occurs when a business dumps toxic wastes into a stream. But, from an economic point of view, each of these is a genuine cost to the economy.

To take another example, a farmer who is producing wheat, can also produce sugarcane with the same factors. Thus, the opportunity cost of a quintal of wheat is the amount of output of sugarcane given up. Thus, the opportunity cost of anything is the next best alternative that could be produced instead by the same resources having the same monetary value.

It may be noted that *market prices of goods do not always reflect their true social opportunity costs*. The resources will remain employed in the production of a particular good when they are being paid at least the money rewards that are sufficient to induce them to stay in the industry. In other words, a collection of factors employed in the production of a good must be paid equal to their opportunity costs. The greater the opportunity cost of the collection of factors used in the production of goods, the greater must be the price of the goods. For example, if the same collection of factors can produce either 1 tractor or 2 scooters, then the price of 1 tractor will be twice that of 1 scooter.

Market prices of goods do not always reflect their true social opportunity costs. This is because the market prices of factors or resources used for the production of goods may fail to reflect their opportunity costs from the social point of view – their true scarcity value or the true cost of diverting resources from alternative uses in the economy as a whole. For example, labour in India is surplus and a there is high level of unemployment that prevails in the Indian economy and therefore its scarcity value is zero, that is, from the social point of view, opportunity cost of labour is zero. But due to several social and institutional factors, labour commands a price in the market which the entrepreneurs will have to include in their private costs of production. Similarly, in India due to cheap credit policy, liberal depreciation allowance on investment granted to the business entrepreneurs in corporate taxation policy has kept the effective price of capital lower than that warranted by its scarcity in the Indian economy. Thus, higher labour cost and lower price of capital than their social opportunity costs have encouraged the choice of capital-intensive techniques and production processes in the Indian industries.

The concept of opportunity cost is particularly crucial when you are analysing transactions that take place outside markets. How do you measure the value of a road or a park or allocation of student time? The notion of opportunity cost explains why students watch more television the week after exams than the week before exams. Watching television right before an exam has a high opportunity cost, because the alternative use of *time* (studying) *has high value* in improving grade performance and getting a better job. After exam, *time* has a *lower opportunity cost.*

To conclude,

- Opportunity cost is a measure of what has been given up when we make a decision.
- Economic costs include, in addition to explicit money outlays, those opportunity costs incurred because resources could have been used in alternative ways. Thus, it includes not only the obvious out-of-pocket purchases or monetary transactions but also more subtle opportunity costs, such as return to labour supplied by the owner of a firm.
- These opportunity costs are tightly constrained by the bids and offers in competitive markets, so price is close to opportunity cost for marketed goods and services.
- The most important application of opportunity cost arises for non-market goods – those like clean air or health or recreation – which may be highly valuable even though they are not bought and sold in markets.

3.2 Incremental Costs
(or Differential, or Avoidable or Escapable Costs)

The incremental costs are the additions to costs resulting from a change in the nature and level of business activity. The incremental or differential costs can be due to change in product line or output level, adding or replacing a machine with a more efficient one, changing distribution channels, or expansion into additional markets, etc. Incremental costs are referred to as *avoidable* or *escapable* costs as these costs can be avoided by not bringing about any change in the activity. Moreover, since incremental costs may also be regarded as the difference in total costs resulting from a contemplated change, these are also called as *differential* costs. In short, the question of incremental or differential cost would arise only when a change is thought about in the existing business.

3.3 Sunk Costs (Non-avoidable or Non-escapable Costs)

Sunk costs are those costs that do not change by varying the nature or the level of business activity. That is, sunk costs remain the same whatever the level of activity. One of the most important sunk costs is the amortization of past expenses, e.g. depreciation.

The sunk and incremental costs bear difference in importance when evaluating the alternatives. Sunk costs are not relevant for decision-making, as they do not change with the changes contemplated for future by the management. For decision-making, it is the incremental costs which are important as they result in additions to the costs.

3.4 Cost Concepts (Types of Costs) and Classification

1. **Explicit Costs vs. Implicit Costs:** Explicit costs are paid-out costs, i.e. are those expenses which are actually paid by the firm. These costs appear in the book of accounts for records of the firm. While, implicit (imputed) costs are earnings of those employed resources which belong to the owner himself. Implicit costs are theoretical costs as they go unrecognised by the accounting system. Explicit costs include those payments which are made by the employer to those factors of production which are not owned by the employer himself. The explicit costs are in the form of 'contractual payments'. For example, the interest payment on borrowed funds is an explicit cost and enters the accounting system, but the amount of interest which the employer could have earned (and which he forgoes when he uses his own capital in the firm) is his implicit cost. The explicit costs are important for calculation of profit and loss account, but for economic decision-making the firm takes into account both the explicit and implicit costs.

2. **Sunk Costs vs. Outlay Costs:** Outlay costs refers to the actual expenditure incurred for producing or acquiring a good or a service. These costs are also known as actual costs or absolute costs. These actual expenditures are recorded in the accounts book

of the business unit, example, the wage bill. Sunk costs are costs that do not change by change in quantity and cannot be recovered, for example, depreciation. Sunk costs are a part of the outlay costs. However, for most managerial decisions, cost estimates that are incremental and not sunk in nature, are important.

3. **Shutdown Costs vs. Abandonment Costs:** Shutdown Costs are those which the firm incurs if it temporarily stops its operations. These costs would not be incurred if the operations are allowed to continue. Shutdown costs, besides fixed costs, include the cost of sheltering plant and equipment, lay-off expenses, etc. Abandonment Costs are the costs of retiring altogether a fixed asset from use. For instance, the plant installed during war time may be so improvised that it may not be needed during the peace time. Thus, it is the disposal of assets that results in abandonment cost.

4. **Direct Costs vs. Indirect Costs:** The direct (traceable or assignable) costs are the ones that have direct relationship with a unit of operation like a product, a process or a department of the firm. Thus, the costs which are directly and definitely identifiable are called the direct costs. While, the indirect (non-traceable or common or non-assignable) costs are costs whose course cannot be easily and definitely traced to a plant, a product, a process or a department. For instance, in operating railway services the cost of station, tracks, etc., cannot be assigned to either passenger or goods transportation, as these are common costs. Whether a specific cost is direct or indirect depends upon the costing under consideration.

Since all the direct costs are linked to a particular product/process they vary with changes in them and as such all direct costs are variable. While, indirect costs may or may not be variable, they can be fixed costs too. For example, the cost of a factory building is a fixed indirect cost, while those of machines, labour services, etc. (which are common) can be classified under variable indirect costs. The importance is of variable indirect costs and attempt should be made to allocate these costs to products, processes, etc.

It is important to differentiate between the direct costs and indirect costs. Modern firms are often multiple product ones. Any decision to expand output or to change the output-mix affects the total costs in complex ways. Any rational producer will like to know about the amount of change in costs which can be brought about by changing the amount or the mix of the output. Given this information he can minimise cost, maximise output or maximise profits. Thus, the traceability of costs is quite important in decision involving addition or subtraction from the product line, product marketing, changes in processes, etc. Traceability of costs is also important where the multiple products that incurred common costs differ considerably in production or marketing processes.

5. **Controllable Costs Vs. Non-Controllable Costs:** Controllable *costs* are those which are capable of being controlled or regulated by executive vigilance, and therefore, can be used for assessing executive efficiency. Thus, a controllable cost may be

defined as one which is reasonably subject to regulation by the executive with whose responsibility that cost is being identified. The controllability of a certain cost may be shared by two or more executives. For instance, materials cost, where price paid is the responsibility of the purchasing department and the usage is the responsibility of the production supervisor. Direct material and direct labour costs are usually controllable. As regards overheads, some costs are controllable and others are not. Non-controllable costs are those which cannot be subject to administrative control and supervision. Most of the costs are controllable, except, of course, those due to obsolescence and depreciation. However, the level at which such control can be exercised differs. For instance, some costs like capital costs, are not controllable at factory's shop level, but inventory costs can be controlled at the shop level.

6. **Urgent Costs Vs Postponable Costs:** Costs that must be incurred so that the operations of the firm continue are urgent costs, such as the costs on material, labour, fuel, etc. Costs whose postponement does not affect, at least for some time, the operational efficiency of the firm, are known as postponable costs, such as maintenance of the building, machinery, etc.

   This classification of the costs becomes obvious during the period of war or inflation or any economic upheaval when firms want to produce the maximum and postpone the maintenance of the plant, or machinery, building, etc.

7. **Business Costs vs Full Costs:** Business costs are account's costs which are relevant for the firm's profit and loss accounts and for legal and tax purposes. These costs include all the payments and contractual obligations made by the firm. It also includes the book cost of depreciation on plant and equipment. Full costs is the sum total of opportunity costs and normal profit. Opportunity cost is the expected earnings from the next best alternative use of the firm's resources like capital, land, building and entrepreneur's time and energy. Again for any firm to remain in business, it must earn a minimum return on all its investment, i.e. normal profits.

8. **Book Costs vs Out-of-pocket Costs:** Out-of-pocket costs are those expenses which are current cash payments to outsiders. All the explicit costs like payment of rent, interest, salaries, wages, transport charges, etc., belong to this category of costs. While, the book costs are those business costs which do not involve any cash payments but for them a provision is made in the books of account to include them in the profit and loss accounts and take tax advantages, such as provisions for depreciation and for unpaid amount of the interest on the owner's capital employed in the firm (implicit costs). Thus, it can be said that book costs are the implicit/imputed costs or the payments by a firm to itself. Book costs can be converted into out-of-pocket costs by selling the assets and having them on hire. Rent would then replace depreciation and interest.

9. **Accounting Costs vs Economic Costs:** This classification of costs relates to time period as to when they occur. Accounting costs are the actual or outlay costs. These

costs point out how much expenditure has already been incurred on a particular process or on production. Since these costs relate to the past, these are generally sunk costs. On the other hand, economic costs relate to future. They are in the nature of incremental costs, both the imputed and explicit costs as well as the opportunity costs. Economic costs have great significance in managerial decision-making as the only costs that matter for business decisions are the future costs.

10. **Incremental Costs vs Sunk Costs:** The incremental costs can also be referred to as the avoidable or escapable or differential costs. These costs are the additions to costs resulting from a change in the nature and level of business activity. For example, change in product line or output level, adding or replacing a machine, changing distribution channels, etc. Since these costs can be avoided by not bringing about any change in the activity, the incremental costs are also called as avoidable costs or escapable costs. Further, incremental costs are also called differential costs, as incremental costs are the difference in total costs resulting from a contemplated change. Sunk costs are those that do not change by varying the nature or the level of business activity. For example, all the past costs are sunk costs as any change in the activity and the resulting incremental costs will have to take into account the preceding costs as given. Depreciation costs, i.e. amortisation of past expenses are an example of sunk costs. It is incremental cost and not sunk costs that are relevant for decision-making as they change with the changes contemplated for future by the management.

Although variable costs are generally incremental but all incremental costs are not variable costs and can include fixed costs, such as a new proposal may involve some expenditure of a fixed nature. Further, whether a particular cost belongs to the category of sunk or incremental cost depends upon the conditions of each business activity as a particular cost may be sunk cost in one case and incremental cost in the other case.

11. **Replacement Costs vs Original (Historical) Costs:** Historical costs of an asset comprise the cost of plant, equipment and materials at the price paid originally for them. On the other hand, replacement cost indicates the cost that the firm would have to incur if it wants to replace or acquire the same assets now. Thus, the difference between the historical and replacement costs results from price changes over time. For example, a machine was acquired for ₹ 20,000 in 1990 and the same machine can be acquired for ₹ 24,000 in 2010. Here, ₹ 20,000 is the historical or original cost of the machine and ₹ 24,000 is its replacement cost. The difference of ₹ 4, 000 between the two costs has resulted due to price change over time. In the book of accounts the value of assets is shown as historical costs, but for decision-making, firms should try to adjust historical costs to reflect price level changes. It can

be said that the basis of classification between historical and replacement costs is the way in which the assets are carried on in the balance sheet and the manner in which the amount of cost is determined.

12. **Private Costs vs Social Costs:** Economic costs can be calculated at two levels: micro-level and macro-level. The micro-level economic costs relate to functioning of a firm as a production unit, while the macro-level economic costs are the ones that are generated by the decisions of the firm but are paid by the society and not the firm. Private costs are the opportunity costs of resources that are borne by the owners of an enterprise. Social costs are the opportunity costs borne by the whole society. For example, if the decision of a firm to expand its output leads to increase in the costs, this is private costs. Whereas, if it also leads to certain costs to the society like greater pollution, greater congestion, or any disutility generated by the project, etc., these costs are external to the firm and are termed as social costs from society's point of view. Thus, private costs are those which are actually incurred by an individual or a firm for its business activity (includes both explicit and implicit costs). Social costs are the total costs to the society on account of production of a good. In this way, *the economic costs include both the private and social costs but net social cost is the total social cost minus the private cost.*

13. **Accounting Costs:** To understand this concept of cost, we first distinguish between opportunity cost and accounting cost. This difference also makes clear the meaning of economic profits. The accounting costs are called *explicit costs* which include wages to hire labour, prices of raw materials, rental price of capital equipment and buildings. When an entrepreneur undertakes an act of production, he has to pay prices for the factors which he employs for production. For example, he pays wages to the labour employed, price for the raw materials, rent for the building he hires for the production work and the rate of interest on the money borrowed for doing business. All these are included in the cost of production and an accountant will take into account only the expenditure incurred on buying or hiring various inputs for use in production.

An economist's view of cost is different from an accountant's view. It generally happens that the entrepreneur invests a certain amount of his own money capital into his business. If the money capital invested by the entrepreneur in his own business had been invested elsewhere, it would have earned a certain amount of interest. The economists, therefore, also include in his cost of production the opportunity costs of the self-owned factors. Thus, in calculation of costs the economists will include – (i) the normal return on capital invested by the entrepreneur himself in his own business, which he could have earned if invested elsewhere; (ii) the wages or salary he could have earned if he sold his services to others as a manager. The accountants do not include these two items in cost of production but economists will include them.

The accountants consider only those costs which involve actual cash payments by the entrepreneur of the firm to others, whereas the economists consider all of these accounting costs and in addition also consider the amount of money the entrepreneur could have earned if he had invested the money capital and sold his services and other factors in the next best alternative use.

Economic Costs = Accounting costs (explicit costs) + Implicit costs.

The concept of opportunity cost applies not only to implicit costs but also to explicit costs. For example, when a firm buys raw materials, it foregoes the opportunity of purchasing something else with the same amount of money that it has spent on the raw materials. Thus, the explicit costs are also the private opportunity costs.

A firm will earn *economic profits only if it is making revenue in* **excess** *of the total of explicit and implicit costs.* Thus, when the firm is in no profit and no loss position, it means that the firm is making revenue *equal* to the sum of explicit and implicit costs and no more.

Thus, **Economic profit = Total Revenue – Economic Costs**

Or, **Economic profits = Total Revenue – (Explicit costs + Implicit costs)**

14. **Total, Average and Marginal Costs:** The three types of costs- total, average and marginal costs on the supply side are the counterparts of the total, average and marginal revenue on the demand side.

Total Costs is the total money costs of producing a commodity. Thus, it is the aggregate of expenditure incurred by the firm in producing a given level of output. If the production function is : $Q = f (a, b, c, ...n)$, then total cost is **TC = f(Q).** The total cost is dependent upon the level of output. Total costs include all kinds of money costs (explicit costs and implicit costs).

Marginal Costs is the cost of producing the 'final' or the 'marginal' or 'additional' unit of the commodity. It can also be expressed as the total cost of units of output minus the total cost of n-1 units.

MC = TC$_n$ – TC$_{n-1}$ which gives us the cost of producing an additional unit of the commodity. *Marginal cost is the cost of producing an extra unit of output.*

Marginal cost may also be defined as "the change in total cost associated with one unit change in output." It is incremental cost or 'extra unit cost'. It can be measured by dividing the change in total cost by one unit change in output.

MC $= \dfrac{\Delta TC}{\Delta Q}$, where Δ = change in output by 1 unit only in the quantity.

Marginal costs consist of variable costs only. The change in the total variable costs for producing an additional unit of output determines the marginal costs.

Average Costs: Average cost is the cost per unit of output, assuming that production of each unit of output incurs the same cost. That is,

AC = TC ÷ Number of Units

Table 3.1: Illustrate the relationship between TC, AC, MC

Units of good produced (Q) (1)	Total Cost (TC) (2) (₹)	Average Cost (AC) = TC/Q (3) (₹)	Marginal Cost (MC) = $TC_n - TC_{n-1}$ (4) (₹)
10	2,000	200.00	-
11	2,150	195.5	150
12	2,250	187.5	100
13	2,300	177.0	50
14	2,400	171.4	100
15	2,600	173.3	200
16	2,900	181.3	300

It can be observed that – (i) total cost increases through all the units at different rate; (ii) Average costs and marginal costs at first decline and then rise- MC rising earlier than AC.

15. **Short-run Costs & Long-run Costs:** The element of 'time' exercises great influence on cost. The costs in the short period may be different from the long period. The 'short period' may be defined as that period of time within which the firm can increase its output only by engaging more workers and buying large supplies of raw materials. The period is not long enough to allow any increase in the capital equipment or machinery of the firm. Thus, in short period, there are certain factors of production whose supply is fixed and cannot be increased even if the employer wishes to do so. The costs corresponding to these factors are called *fixed costs*. The factors like raw material, labour engaged that can be changed to change the output in the short period are variable factors and costs corresponding to them are called *variable costs*. Thus, in the *short-run*, by definition, some inputs are fixed while the others are variable. Therefore, in the short-run there are two types of costs, fixed costs and variable costs. The fixed costs remain unchanged, while the variable costs fluctuate with the output. Long-run is a period long enough to effect changes in the scale of operations or to introduce other adjustments in the organisational set-up of the firm. The firm in the long run can build any desired scale of plant. *All factors are variable, none is fixed.* Hence, *all costs are variable.*

16. **Incremental Cost and Marginal Cost:** These two costs are closely related. In some applications the marginal cost is more efficient while in others it is the incremental cost that is more suitable.
   - Marginal cost (MC) deals with unit-by-unit changes in output, whereas Incremental cost (IC) is not restricted to a unit change. Thus, MC is the amount added to the total cost by a unit increase in output. IC is related to change in any number of units of output or cost related even to a change in quality.

- MC as a concept is particularly superior to IC in decision-making for the following reasons: (a) in selection of *optimum level of inputs*, when the input-output relationship reveals diminishing returns, i.e should there be any more additional increase in input. (b) in selection of *optimum cost combination of inputs*, where the products substitute at decreasing rates; (c) in selection of *optimum maturity of productive assets*, where assets gain value at decreasing rates over time.
- Though MC as a concept is superior to IC but IC gains mileage over MC in following situations: For example, it is the IC that can allow the comparisons between the two technical processes (giving same level of output) and not the MC. IC is mainly useful in case of linear cost functions, as in such functions only the end points of a range need to be compared and not each additional unit.

3.5 Break-Even Point (Cost-Volume-Profit) Analysis

Break-even point is the point where the total cost just equals the total revenue; it is no loss, no profit point.

Cost-volume-profit or break-even analysis examines the relationship among the total revenue, total costs and total profits of the firm at various levels of output. The break-even analysis is often used by business executives to determine the sales volume required for the firm to break even and the total profits and losses at other sales levels. Thus, break- even analysis is about determining profit at different projected levels of sales, identifying the breakeven point, and making a managerial decision regarding the relationship between likely sales and the breakeven point.

There are several approaches to breakeven analysis. These are discussed below:

1. **Graphical Method:** In Fig. 3.1 TR and TC are total revenue and total costs curves, represented by straight lines. On x-axis we measure the total costs and total revenue and on the y-axis we measure output or sale per time period.

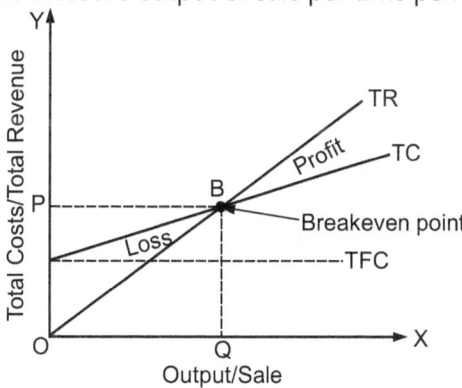

Fig. 3.1: Break-even Analysis

- Under the assumption that price of the commodity is not affected by its quantity sold total revenue is proportional to output and hence the TR curve is a straight line through the origin.

- The TC curve indicates total fixed costs (TFC) and constant Average Variable Cost (AVC) for a given range of output; hence a firm's total cost function is given as a straight line.
- The firm breaks even with TR = TC at Q per time period with TR equating TC at point B.
- The firm incurs losses at smaller outputs and earns profits at higher output levels.
- The cost-volume-profit or breakeven chart is a flexible tool to quickly analyse the effect of changing conditions on the firm.

2. **Algebraic Method:** Cost-volume-profit analysis can also be performed algebraically.
- Let P = Price of a commodity per unit; Q = Quantity of output or sales.

$$TR = P.Q \qquad \qquad \text{... (i)}$$

- TC = TFC + TVC and since TVC is equal to average (per unit) variable costs (AVC) multiplied by the quantity of output.
- Now substituting TVC, we have

$$TC = TFC + AVC.Q \qquad \qquad \text{... (ii)}$$

- Setting TR = TC and substituting Q_B (the breakeven output) for Q, we have

$$TR = TC \qquad \qquad \text{... (iii)}$$
$$P.Q_B = TFC + AVC.Q_B \qquad \qquad \text{... (iv)}$$

Solving Equation (iv) for the breakeven output Q_B , we get

$$P.Q_B - AVC\,Q_B = TFC$$
$$Q_B.(P - AVC) = TFC$$
$$Q_B = \frac{TFC}{P - AVC} \qquad \qquad \text{... (v)}$$

Suppose TFC = ₹ 200, P = ₹ 10 and AVC = ₹ 5,

Thus, $\qquad Q_B = \dfrac{₹\,200}{₹\,10 - ₹\,5} = 40$

This is relatively easily computable by firms, because data on TFC and AVC are more readily available than MC (marginal costs).

Contribution Margin Per Unit

- This is the breakeven output (Q) shown on the cost-volume-profit chart in **Fig. 3.1.** The denominator in Equation in (v) (P – AVC) is called the contribution margin per unit because it represents the portion of the selling price that can be applied to cover fixed costs of the firm and to provide for profits.
- Suppose the firm wishes to earn a specific profit and wants to estimate the quantity that it must sell to earn that profit, then the cost-volume-profit or breakeven analysis can be used in determining the target output (Q_r) at which a target profit (P_r) can be achieved.
- For this we simply add (P_r) to the numerator to the Equation (v) and we have,

$$Q_r = \frac{TFC + P_r}{P - AVC} \qquad \qquad \text{... (vi)}$$

- **Illustration:** If the firm wishes to earn a target profit of ₹ 100, the target output would be :

$$Q_r = \frac{₹\,200 + ₹\,100}{₹\,10 - ₹\,5} = \frac{₹\,300}{₹\,5} = 60$$

- With the Output of Q = 60 that led to the target profit (P_r) of ₹ 100

$$TR = P.Q = (₹\,10) \times (60) = ₹\,600$$

$$TC = TFC + (AVC) \times (Q) = ₹\,200 + (₹\,5) \times (60) = ₹\,500$$

And,
$$P_r = TR - TC = ₹\,600 - ₹\,500 = ₹\,100.$$

Certain limitations of this analysis:

- While linear breakeven analysis is frequently used by business executives, government agencies, and not-for-profit organisations, care must be taken to apply it only when constant prices exist and AVC are held constant.
- The breakeven analysis also assumes that the firm produces a single product or a constant mix of products.
- With time, the product mix changes, and it may be difficult to allocate the fixed costs among the various products.
- Despite these limitations, cost-volume-profit analysis can be very useful in managerial decision-making.

Japanese Cost-Management Systems

Japanese firms turn cost-volume-profit analysis on its head, i.e. they start in reverse. Instead of designing a new product and then estimating the cost of producing it, Japanese firms sometimes start with a target cost based on the market price at which the firm believes buyers will buy the product and then strive to produce the product at the specified targeted cost.

Under such Japanese cost-management systems, the firm subtracts the desired profit from the expected selling price and then allocates targeted costs to each part, component, and process required to produce the product in such a way as to keep costs within the targeted level.

3.6 Risk Analysis and Decision Making

Until now we have examined managerial decision making under conditions of certainty. In such cases, the manager knows exactly the outcome of each possible course of action. Many managerial decisions are, indeed, made under conditions of certainty, especially in the short run. For example, it has been assumed that the consumer knows with certainty about the present and future prices of goods and the managers of firms know with certainty the present and future demand and cost conditions facing them. Even though the assumption of certainty about the outcomes is not entirely correct it is good enough to make reasonably correct predictions about the outcomes of the decisions made.

However, the real world is full of uncertainty and due to this, choices or decisions made by individuals and firms involve risk. Thus, in managerial decisions, the manager often does not know the exact outcome of each possible course of action. For example, the return on a long-run investment depends on economic conditions in future, the political climate, degree of future competition, consumer's tastes, technological advances, and other such factors about which the firm has only imperfect knowledge. In such cases, we can say that the firm faces "risk" or "uncertainty", and most strategic decisions of the firm are of this kind.

In this section we thus first explain the concept of risk and how to measure it. Risk is considered to be undesirable. Many individuals are risk averse and like to avoid risks, but some others are willing to bear risk, if it yields them sufficient return. It is through diversification, insurance and gathering of information that risk can be reduced.

3.7 Concept of Risk

Managerial decisions are made under conditions of certainty, risk or uncertainty.

Certainty refers to the situation where there is only one possible outcome to a decision and this outcome is known precisely. For example, investing in Treasury bills leads to only one outcome, the amount of returns, and this is known with certainty. The reason is that there is virtually no chance that the government will fail to redeem these securities at maturity or that it will default on interest payments.

Risk refers to a situation in which there is more than one possible outcome to a decision and the probability of each specific outcome is known or can be estimated. The analysis of risk requires that the decision maker knows all the possible outcomes of the decision and has some idea of the probability of each outcome's occurrence. For example, in tossing a coin, we can get either a head or a tail, and each possibility has 50-50 chance of occurring. Likewise, introducing a new product can lead one to a set of possible outcomes, and the probability of each possible outcome can be estimated from past experience or from market studies. In general, the greater the variability of possible outcomes, the greater is the risk associated with the decision or action.

Uncertainty refers to the situation when there is more than one possible outcome to a decision and where the probability of each specific outcome occurring is not known or even meaningful or cannot be estimated. This may be due to insufficient information or there may be instability in the structure of the variables. In some extreme cases of uncertainty, outcomes themselves are not known. For example, drilling for oil in unproven field carries uncertainty with it if the investor does not know either the possible oil output or even the probability of its occurrence.

In decision making involving risk or uncertainty the three terms often used are: (i) strategy; (ii) state of nature ; (iii) outcome.

A **Strategy** refers to one of several alternative courses of action that a decision maker can take to achieve a goal. For example, to maximise the profits a manager may have to decide on the strategy of building a new technologically more efficient plant to reduce the cost of production; launching a new marketing campaign to increase sales etc. The course of action chosen is the strategy.

States of Nature refers to conditions in the future that will have a significant impact on the degree of success or failure of any strategy, but over which the decision maker has little or no control. For example, in case of building a plant that is technologically superior, the different states of nature that may exist in some future years are – boom, recession or normal conditions. The decision maker has no control over the states of nature in future but the future states of nature will certainly influence the outcome of any strategy that he may adopt. Thus, the particular decision taken will depend on the decision maker's knowledge or estimation of how a particular future state of nature will influence the outcome of each particular strategy.

Outcome refers to the results which are usually in the form of profit that results due to implementation of a strategy. And, a payoff matrix is a table that shows the possible outcomes or results of each strategy under each state of nature. For example, a payoff matrix may show the level of profit that would result if the firm introduces a technologically more efficient plant or new marketing campaign along with a combination of each of the states of nature that is whether the economy will be booming, normal or recessionary in the future.

Case Study ("Old Coke Coming Back After Outcry by Faithful")

Coke is the leading soft drink in the world, and the company took an unusual risk in tampering with its highly successful product. On April 23, 1985, the Coca-Cola Company announced that it was changing its 70-year-old recipe for Coke. The company thought that this strategy would ward off the challenge from Pepsi-Cola, its biggest competitor and which was eroding coke's market. The new coke was a little sweeter and less fizzy in taste and it was aiming at reversing Pepsi's market gains. It conducted taste tests on more than 190,000 consumers over a 3-year period. The test revealed that consumers preferred the new Coke over the old one by 61 percent to 39 percent. Coca-Cola's advertising outlay for its new product was more than $10 million. When the new Coke was finally introduced in May 1985, there was nearly a revolt by the consumers against the new Coke and the company was forced to bring back the old Coke under the brand name Coca-Cola Classic. The irony is that with the Classic and new Coke sold side by side, Coca-Cola regained some of the market share that it had lost to Pepsi.

Most marketing experts are convinced that Coca-Cola had underestimated consumers'loyalty to the old coke. This did not come up in the extensive taste test that was conducted by Coca-Cola because the consumers who were tested were not informed that the company intended to replace the old Coke with the new Coke rather than sell alongwith the old one. This example illustrates that even a well-conceived strategy is full of risks and can lead to outcomes estimated to have a small probability of occurrence. It was lucky that Coca-Cola company could withstand this risk,most companies are not lucky.

(Source: "Old Coke Coming Back After Outcry by Faithful", Pg. 13,The New York Times, July 11, 1985; "A Better Mode? Diversified Pepsi Steals Some of the Coke's Sparkle", Financial Times-February 28, 2005,pg. 15.)

3.8 Expected Value

When outcomes are risky, one of the measures of incorporating risk in the decision-making is 'The Expected Value'.

Risk refers to the situation when there is more than one possible outcome of a decision and the probability of each outcome is either known or can be estimated. Individuals and firms face situations where a number of outcomes can occur each of which results in a certain payoff or cash flow, that is, monetary gain or loss. If the probability of each outcome is known, then one can find out the expected monetary value in this uncertain situation.

Thus, in a situation of certainty, any investment gives only one possible cash flow, but in a risky situation several cash flows are possible, each with a given probability. By finding average of all such possible outcomes (X), weighted by their respective probabilities (P), we can get a single value for the cash flows. This value is known as expected value E(X), whose generalised expression is

$$E(X) = \sum_{i=1}^{n} X_i P_i$$

The expected monetary value is the weighted average of payoffs of all possible outcomes with the probability of each outcome used as weights. Hence, the expected value of an uncertain income is the average payoff of the various outcomes. For example, if there are two possible outcomes in an illustration of offshore oil exploration – success of the project yielding cash flow of ₹ 40 per share with a probability of 0.30 and the failure yielding a payoff/cash flow ₹ 10 per share with a probability of 0.70.

Thus, in this case, expected value of investment per share

= 0.30 × 40 + 0.70 × 10

= 12 + 7.0

= 19

The expected value is simply the average of all possible outcomes.

Hypothetical Illustration 1: Consider a production unit which has tabulated its daily production over a period of 200 days as follows:

Production (Nos.) per day	No. of days
200	20
300	50
400	90
500	30
600	10

The next step is to calculate the probability of a particular level of output and the expected value of production.

Probability at each Level of Output

Production per day (Nos.)	Number of Days	No. of Days ÷ 200	Equals to	Probability
200	20	20 ÷ 200	=	0.10
300	50	50 ÷ 200	=	0.25
400	90	90 ÷ 200	=	0.45
500	30	30 ÷ 200	=	0.15
600	10	10 ÷ 200	=	0.05
	200			**1.00**

(The sum of probability must be equal to unity).

Expected Value of Production

Production per day (Nos.)	Probability	Expected Value = (Production x Probability)
200	0.10	20
300	0.25	75
400	0.45	180
500	0.15	75
600	0.05	30
		380

Thus for this production unit, the expected output is 380 units per day.

Now, based on the computation given above, we implement in decisions to be taken using expected value method.

Hypothetical Illustration 2: Consider two production plans 1 and 2, which generate output flow over time with associated probabilities as follows:

Production Plan 1		Production Plan 2	
Output flow (₹)	Probability	Output flow (₹)	Probability
20,000	0.4	10,000	0.5
40,000	0.4	30,000	0.3
30,000	0.3	80,000	0.2

The decision to be taken is regarding which production plan is preferable?

To compute:

Expected Value of production plan 1 (EX_1)

= $(20{,}000 \times 0.4) + (40{,}000 \times 0.4) + (30{,}000 \times 0.3)$

= $8{,}000 + 16{,}000 + 9{,}000 = $ **₹ 33,000**

Expected Value of production plan 2 (EX$_2$)

$= (10,000 \times 0.5) + (30,000 \times 0.3) + (80,000 \times 0.2)$

$= 5,000 + 9,000 + 16,000 = ₹$ **30,000**

By incorporating risk into calculation, production plan 1 is preferable to production plan 2.

3.9 Risk Management Through Diversification

Diversification is about reducing the correlation between your investments.

Chances are that when you consider a stock, your question is, "How much money can I make with this?" However, money managers claim that the key to financial success is managing risk. So, your question really should be, "How much can I lose?"

Effective market participants are aware of risk's meaning and hence define risk as potential loss, i.e., Risk = Potential for Loss.

Risk is not necessarily a bad thing. Indeed, the relationship between risk and reward has long been recognised. The real problem though is that either through ignorance or emotional impediments, people often take on more risk than they should. It is true that capital must be preserved if wealth is to be accumulated. In other words, if you lose all your money, it's hard to stay in the game.

There are many strategies for managing risk, such as (i) reducing correlation between investments or (ii) actively controlling the degree of loss.

Reducing Correlation between Assets (Diversification)

There is a well-known saying, "Don't put all your eggs in one basket." The concept applies towards managing financial market risk. A classic example can be experienced in the Enron Story. **Enron** - What began as a natural gas distribution company grew into a firm that ranked near the top of the fortune 500. By the late 1990's many Enron employees *allocated* with much enthusiasm large amounts of their net worth, even the bulk of their retirement account assets, towards the company stock. Enron's stock price climbed higher and many shareholders saw their net worth (though on paper) doubled and tripled in short period of time. However, by late 2000, the rocket ride was over, the trip to cloud nine was over and the company's stock left many employees with little or negative net worth.

The question that can be asked here is that, is this an isolated incident of Enron where employees have allocated and concentrated their bet on company's share price? The answer is negative, because employees at many companies have similarly allocated large amounts of their wealth towards their company's stock. The difference between the concentrated bets of Enron employees and those of employees elsewhere is that the risk reflected in Enron employee bets was actually realised. A risk, when realised, becomes a loss.

One way to reduce risk is to diversify, i.e., 'spread the eggs around'. However, a portfolio of financial assets is not well diversified if prices of the holdings are highly correlated- prices of many stocks may move up and down together. Assets that are less positively correlated, or perhaps even negatively correlated, are desirable from a diversification point of view. Effective diversification is often achieved by acquiring assets from different market groups. Thus, asset allocation is spreading capital among different asset categories and studies suggest that asset allocation is perhaps the most important determinant of long term investment returns.

Though it is useful to observe portfolios of other investors and their asset allocation choices it is not advisable to copy the decisions of others. Risk management strategy differs for each individual and there are many factors that have to be kept in mind, such as – financial goals, risk tolerance, time horizon, portfolio value and capacity for monitoring the financial environment among many others.

Diversification requires careful thought because too much diversification can dilute returns, while too little diversification can be disastrous. The key is finding a level of diversification that reflects 'risk profile' that works for the individual.

To sum up, to forecast the degree of diversification that a particular portfolio would provide, investors usually examine historical correlations between financial assets. The assumption is that historical correlations are likely to continue in the future. This assumption is not always accurate, because correlations between assets can change from one period to the next depending on a variety of factors. It implies that investors need to monitor actual correlations between their portfolio holdings to determine whether they are actually achieving the desired level of diversification or not.

Diversification is one way to prudently manage risk.

3.10 Risk Management Through Insurance

One of the oldest and most established ways of protecting against risk is to buy insurance to cover specific event risk. Just as a home owner buys insurance on his or her house to protect against the eventuality of fire or storm damage, companies can buy insurance to protect their assets against possible loss. In fact, it can be argued that, inspite of the attention given to the use of derivatives in risk management, traditional insurance remains the primary vehicle for managing risk.

Insurance does not eliminate risk. Rather, it shifts the risk from the firm buying the insurance to the insurance firm selling it.

Thus, another method of management of risk is through insurance. Most people buy insurance when they are faced with risky and uncertain situations. Thus, to avoid risk individuals are willing to give up some income. *The price which an individual is willing to forego or pay for insurance is called risk premium.* Hence, if the cost of insurance is equal to the amount of risk premium which they are ready to forego to assure them a certain income in a risky and uncertain situation; they will buy the insurance policy. For example, if an individual owns a furniture shop worth ₹ 20 lakhs and faces a probability of 0.01 (1 per cent) chance of his shop getting burnt down, then the expected value of loss is

$\dfrac{1}{100} \times 20,000,00 = ₹\ 20,000$. If a fire insurance policy is offered to the shop owner for ₹ 20,000, he will definitely buy it. Such an insurance premium is fairly priced as it is equal to the expected loss that may accrue to the individual in case his shop is burnt down due to fire and considering the probability of it actually happening. In fact, to avoid risk, an individual may be willing to pay more than this depending on the degree of his risk-aversion as measured by the risk premium he is prepared to pay.

Generally, individuals buy insurance from the companies which specialise in the insurance business. These insurance companies operate on the basis of the law of large numbers. For example, the insurance companies, from part information, know that 1 per cent shops will catch fire. To provide insurance cover they pool a large number of policies. It insures 100 policy holders against the expected loss, whereas they will actually pay just one policy holder if the probability of shops catching fire is one per cent. The premium fixed by the company would also be an amount such that they are able to earn profits after compensating the loss to the individuals. In other words, the insurance companies not only insure against the loss suffered by the individuals but also earn profits in their business.

Smith and Mayer argued that this risk shifting from the firm to the insurance company may provide a benefit to both sides, for a number of reasons. (i) The insurance company may be able to create a portfolio of risks, thereby gaining diversification benefits that the self-insured firm itself cannot obtain. (ii) The insurance company might acquire the expertise to evaluate risk and process claims more efficiently as a consequence of its repeated exposure to that risk. (iii) Insurance companies might provide other services, such as inspection and safety services that benefit both sides.

From the standpoint of the insured, the rationale for insurance is simple. In return for paying a premium, they are protected against risks that have a low probability of occurrence but have a large impact if they do. The cost of buying insurance becomes part of the operating expenses of the business, reducing the earnings of the company. The benefit is implicit and shows up as more stable earnings over time.

The insurer offers to protect multiple risk takers against specific risks in return for premiums and hopes to use the collective income from these premiums to cover the losses incurred by a few.

Consequently, we can draw the following conclusions about the effectiveness of insurance:

(a) It is more effective against individual or firm-specific risks that affect a few and leave the majority untouched and less effective against market-wide or systematic risks.

(b) It is more effective against large risks than against small risks.

(c) It is more effective against event risks, where the probabilities of occurrence and expected losses can be estimated from past history, than against continuous risk.

An earthquake, hurricane or terrorist event would be an example of the former whereas exchange rate risk would be an example of the latter.

Reviewing the conditions, it is easy to see why insurance is most often used to hedge against "acts of god" – events that often have catastrophic effects on specific localities but leave the rest of the population relatively untouched.

3.11 Risk Management Through Hedging

What risks are most commonly hedged? While a significant proportion of firms hedge against risk, some risks seem to be hedged more often than others. The two most widely hedged risks are exchange risk and commodity price risk.

Exchange Rate Risk

Surveys consistently indicate that the most widely hedged risk remains currency risk. There are three simple reasons for this phenomenon.

(a) **It is ubiquitous:** It is not just large multi-national firms that are exposed to exchange rate risk. Even small firms that derive almost all of their revenues domestically are often dependent upon inputs that come from foreign markets and are thus exposed to exchange rate risk. An entertainment software firm that gets its software written in India for sale in the United States is exposed to variations in the U.S. dollar/ Indian Rupee exchange rate.

(b) **It affects earnings:** Accounting conventions also force firms to reflect the effects of exchange rate movements on earnings in the periods in which they occur. Thus, the earnings per share of firms that do not hedge exchange rate risk will be more volatile than firms that do. As a consequence, firms are much more aware of the effects of the exchange rate risk, which may provide a motivation for managing it.

(c) **It is easy to hedge:** Exchange rate risk can be managed both easily and cheaply. Firms can use an array of market-traded instruments including options and futures contracts to reduce or even eliminate the effects of exchange rate risk.

Investing in foreign securities gives rise to a foreign-exchange risk because the foreign currency can depreciate or decrease in value during the time of investment.

Hedging refers to the covering of a foreign-exchange risk. Hedging is usually accomplished with a *forward contract.*

Hedging is an agreement to purchase or sell a specific amount of a foreign currency at a rate specified today for delivery at a specific future date.

For example, suppose that a U.S. exporter expects to receive £ 1 million in 3 months. At today's exchange rate of $1/ £1, the exporter expects to receive £1million in 3 months. To avoid the risk of large dollar depreciation by the time the exporter is to receive payment (and thus receive much fewer Dollars than anticipated),the exporter hedges his foreign-exchange risk. He does so by selling £1million forward at today's forward rate for delivery in 3 months, so as to coincide with the receipt of the £1 million from his exports. Even if today's forward rate is $0.99/£1, the exporter willingly "pays" 1 cent per Pound to avoid the foreign-exchange risk. In 3 months, when the U.S. exporter receives the £1 million, he will be able to immediately exchange it for $990,000 by fulfilling the forward contract. This would avoid a possible large foreign-exchange loss. An importer avoids the foreign-exchange risk by doing the opposite.

Hedging can also be accomplished with a ***future contract.*** This is a standardised forward contract for *predetermined quantities* of the currency and *selected calendar dates*, for example, £25,000 for March 20 delivery.

Future contracts are more liquid than forward contracts. There is a *forward market in many currencies* and a *future market in the world's most important currencies*, such as, U.S. Dollar, Euro, British Pound, Japanese Yen, Canadian Dollar, Swiss Franc.

Future markets exist not only in currencies but also in many other financial instruments or derivatives –a broad class of transactions whose value is derived from a financial market like stocks or interest rates and currencies- and commodities like oats, soybeans, wheat, cotton; cocoa, coffee, orange juice; cattle, pork bellies; copper, gold, silver and platinum.

Hedging in forward or future markets reduces transaction costs and risks and increases the volume of domestic and foreign trade in the commodity, currency, or other financial instruments.

Forward and future contracts can also be used for speculation, where they can lead to very large gains or huge losses.

To conclude, Hedging involves reducing risk in a particular position by making an offsetting or counterbalancing bet. Hedging seems similar to diversification. Hedging is associated with managing risk over a shorter time horizon. Traders commonly employ hedging, often by comparing long and short positions, as a means for managing risk in ups and down of daily market price movement. Hedging helps manage risk – particularly with respect to extreme losses.

3.12 Decision Trees

Most real-world managerial decisions are very complex. There are two methods of organising and analysing these more complex, real-world situations that involve risk – decision trees and simulation.

Managerial decisions involving risk are often made in stages, with subsequent decisions and events depending on the outcome of earlier decisions and events. *A decision tree shows the sequence of possible managerial decisions and their expected outcomes under a set of circumstances or states of nature.*

This technique is referred to as *decision tree* because the sequence of decisions and events is represented diagrammatically/graphically as the branches of a tree.

Steps involved in representing managerial decisions through the technique of decision tree:

- The construction of decision trees starts with the earliest decision and then moves forward in time through a series of subsequent events and decisions.

- At every point that a decision must be made or a different event can take place, the tree branches out until all the possible outcomes have been depicted.
- In the construction of decision trees, normally boxes are used to depict decision points and circles show states of nature.
- Branches coming out of the boxes show the alternative strategies and ways of courses of action thatare open to the firm.
- Branches coming out of the circles depict the different states of nature – and their possibility of occurrence – that affect the outcome.

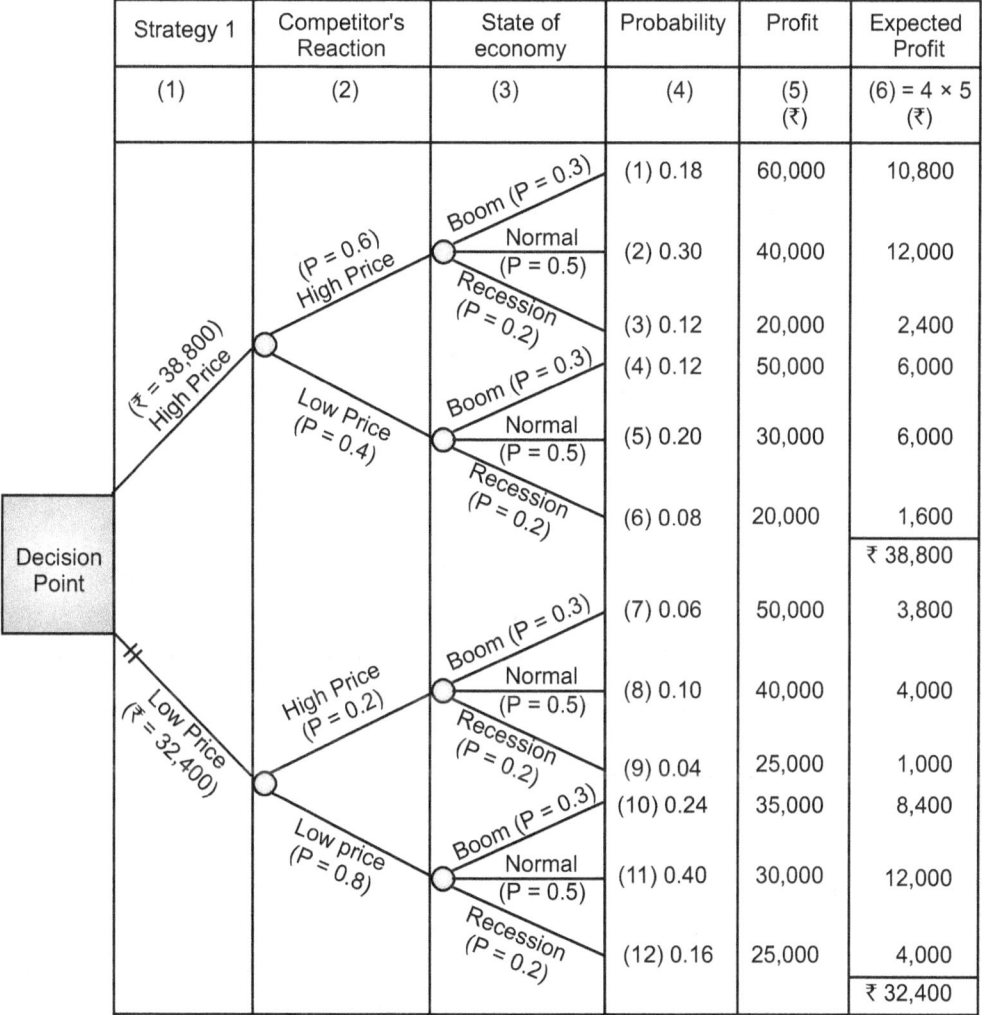

Strategy 1	Competitor's Reaction	State of economy	Probability	Profit	Expected Profit
(1)	(2)	(3)	(4)	(5) (₹)	(6) = 4 × 5 (₹)
	(P = 0.6) High Price	Boom (P = 0.3)	(1) 0.18	60,000	10,800
		Normal (P = 0.5)	(2) 0.30	40,000	12,000
		Recession (P = 0.2)	(3) 0.12	20,000	2,400
(₹ = 38,800) High Price	Low Price (P = 0.4)	Boom (P = 0.3)	(4) 0.12	50,000	6,000
		Normal (P = 0.5)	(5) 0.20	30,000	6,000
		Recession (P = 0.2)	(6) 0.08	20,000	1,600
					₹ 38,800
	High Price (P = 0.2)	Boom (P = 0.3)	(7) 0.06	50,000	3,800
		Normal (P = 0.5)	(8) 0.10	40,000	4,000
		Recession (P = 0.2)	(9) 0.04	25,000	1,000
Low Price (₹ = 32,400)	Low price (P = 0.8)	Boom (P = 0.3)	(10) 0.24	35,000	8,400
		Normal (P = 0.5)	(11) 0.40	30,000	12,000
		Recession (P = 0.2)	(12) 0.16	25,000	4,000
					₹ 32,400

Fig. 3.2: Assuming that the firm has considered the difference in risk in estimating the net present value of profits of the two strategies, it will choose the high-price strategy and the low price strategy is slashed of (//) as suboptimal

Fig 3.2 represents a decision tree that a firm can use to determine the pricing policy – whether to adopt a high price or a low price strategy. (see the box – Decision point).

Since the firm has control over this strategy of charging high or low price, no probabilities are attached to these branches.

Thus, starting at the left of the Fig. 3.2 we see that the firm can adopt either a high or a low price strategy (₹ 38,800 High price strategy or ₹ 32,400 low price strategy).

Each of these strategies can lead to either a high or low price response by competitors, each with a particular probability of occurrence. (See competitor's reactions).

The firm estimates that if it adopts a high-price strategy, there is 60 per cent (P = 0.6) that rivals will retaliate with a high price of their own, and 40 per cent (P = 0.4) that they will respond with a low price.

Now, see lower part in section of strategy of adopting low price. If the firm adopts a low-price strategy there is 20% probability (P = 0.2) that competitive firms will respond with a high price and 80% (P = 0.8) with a low price.

The sum of probabilities of competitor's response to each pricing strategy of the firm adds up to 1.00 or 100 percent. For example, 0.6 + 0.4 when strategy is high-price and 0.2 + 0.8 at low price strategy.

Each pricing strategy on the part of the firm and the competitor's price response or reaction can occur under 3 states of the economy – boom, normal and recession – with specific probabilities of occurrence, (see section state of economy). At high price strategy the probabilities of occurrence under 3 states of the economy are – Boom (p = 0.3), Normal (p = 0.5), recession (p = 0.2), i.e. 30, 50 and 20 percent respectively. In this way we have 12 possible outcomes, 6 for the high-price strategy of the firm (top branch) and 6 for low-price strategy (bottom branch).

The probability of each joint outcome or conditional probability is obtained by multiplying the probability of each state of the economy. That is, multiply boom (0.3) times by the probability of each competitor's price response (high price = 0.6). Thus, the probability of both boom and high price by competitors (outcome 1) is 0.18 (0.3 × 0.6 = 0.18) or 18 percent. Likewise probability for normal conditions in the economy and a high competitor's price (outcome 2) is given by 0.5 times × 0.6 = 0.30 or 30 percent. In this way, there are 12 outcomes (see serial number given in probability section).

Section 5 shows the estimated net present value of the profits of the firm associated with each of the 12 possible outcomes.

Section 6 is the expected profit which is obtained by multiplying section 4 and section 5, i.e., probability of occurrence of each possible outcome by the profit associated with that particular outcome.

Assuming that the firm already considered the difference in risk in estimating the net present value of profits of the two strategies, it will choose the high-price strategy. On the decision tree the low price strategy is slashed off.

There are certain things to be pointed out with respect to the decision tree.

Though the decision tree starts at the left and moves forward to the right through a series of subsequent events and decisions, but the analysis of the decision tree begins at the right (at the end of the sequence) and moves backwards to the left.

In section 4, the sum of joint probabilities of the 6 possible outcomes (outcome 1 to 6 i.e., 0.18 + 0.30 +0.12 + 0.12 + 0.20) resulting from the firm's high-price strategy is equal to 1 and so is from the firm's low-price strategy (outcomes 7 to 12 i.e., 0.6 +0.10 + 0.04 + 0.24 + 0.40 + 0.16) is equal to 1.

While in the decision tree the firm has to take only one decision, i.e., the decision point box seen in Fig. 3.2 on the left, there can be several decision points in between several states of nature. Thus, for many real-world business decisions, decision trees can become much more complex.

Case Study on Decision Tree Technique

A decision tree is an outcome and probability map of the scenario. Most business problems may potentially have more than one solution. Each choice can lead to varying outcomes, some more likely than others.

To illustrate this point, we consider the decision faced by Property company for property development business.

The company owns a town centre building site. This could be sold now for an estimated ₹ 1.6 m. Alternatively the site could be developed with shops and a restaurant at a cost of ₹ 1.5 m. The property could then be sold for ₹ 4m - provided that a bypass proposal is rejected by the local council. The odds of the bypass being rejected are judged at about 75:25 due to environmental objections. If, however, the bypass were to be built, much tourist trade would be lost and the value of the development would only be ₹ 2m. Which choice should Property Company make? A decision tree is a useful tool when analysing choices of this kind.

Possible Outcomes

There are three possible outcomes to this scenario, each of which can be given a financial value.

Outcome	Probability	Estimated Value.
Outcome 1 – the site is developed and the bypass is rejected.	The development value is ₹ 4m. However, there is only a 75% chance of this occurring.	A 75% chance of receiving ₹ 4m is 'worth' ₹ 4m × 0.75 = ₹ 3m.
Outcome 2 – the site is developed and the bypass goes ahead.	There is 25% chance of receiving only ₹ 2m.	If the bypass goes ahead it is 'worth' ₹ 2m x 0.25 = ₹ 0.5m.
Outcome 3 – the site is sold undeveloped.		Undeveloped, the sale is worth ₹ 1.6m.

- To calculate the possible yield of developing the site, the values of outcomes 1 and 2 are combined. The cost of development is then subtracted: ₹ 3m + ₹ 0.5m – ₹ 1.5m = ₹ 2m.
- This compares to the value of selling the undeveloped site at only ₹ 1.6m. On this basis, depending on its attitude to risk and the likely timescales, the company is likely to build the shops and restaurant.
- Decision trees encourage managers to look at a range of options rather than relying on *'gut feeling'*. However, they are only as accurate as the data on which they are based. This data is usually based on estimates. They do also run the risk of over-simplifying a problem particularly where human or other external factors are involved. Other analysing tools can supplement the decision making process in such cases.

To sum up, the difference between a good decision and a bad one can be the difference between success and disaster, profit and loss, or even life and death. Decision analysis software can help decision-makers identify factors that influence the decision at hand and choose a path to desirable outcomes.

Fig. 3.3 shows the possible outcomes diagrammatically.

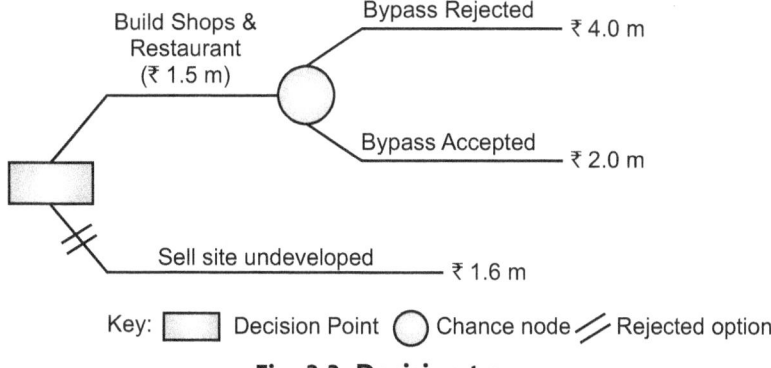

Fig. 3.3: Decision tree

Case Study on Marginal Costs

Marginal cost is an estimate of how economic cost would change if the output changed. Marginal means a first derivative, but in practice, because of indivisibilities in plant sizes, we are often interested in the **_per unit change in cost_** that will be caused by a substantial change in a future output, not of a one unit change. Furthermore, investment and capacity are not continuously variable, they are lumpy. For e.g., Transco builds 900 mm pipelines but has never considered building 901 mm ones. The result is that even when the concept of marginal cost is completely agreed in principle, its estimation involves far more than calculations founded upon a set of rules.

There is a difference between marginal private costs and marginal social costs as understood in this example: Road use – The private marginal cost to a car owner of driving a mile is the petrol cost per litre divided by miles per litre, plus some extra depreciation in the value of the car and an allowance for the driver of his skill and time. Now, marginal social cost will differ because it values petrol only at factor cost; by adding to congestion, if the mile is driven on a busy road, a time cost is imposed upon other drivers and their passengers; and this inconvenience caused to other passengers is the marginal social cost and cannot be valued in money terms. A second example relates to buses. Putting one more or one less bus on a route adds or subtracts from the bus operator's costs. However, by increasing or decreasing the frequency of the service, it reduces or increases the average waiting time of passengers. Since time has a value – though it is difficult to estimate – marginal social cost is less than marginal private cost.

Points to Remember

- The opportunity cost (or alternative cost) is the return from the second-best use of a resource, which the firm foregoes when taking up the opportunity of its best use.
- The costs which do not change with the nature or level of production are sunk costs, while the costs which change with output are incremental costs (also known as avoidable or escapable costs).

- The implicit costs are the earnings of the resources which belong to the owner himself. For decision-making both explicit (or paid-out) and the implicit costs are important.
- Decision tree is a graphic device that shows a sequence of strategic decisions ad expected consequences under each possible situation.
- Risk refers to a situation in which there are several possible outcomes, each outcome occurring with a probability to the decision-maker.
- Uncertainty refers to a situation in which there are several possible outcomes of an action whose probabilities are either not known or are not meaningful.
- Diversification is about reducing the correlation between your investments.
- Hedging is an agreement to purchase or sell a specific amount of a foreign currency at a rate specified today for delivery at a specific future date.
- When outcomes are risky, one of the measures of incorporating risk in the decision-making is 'The Expected Value'.

Questions for Discussion

1. Explain the term 'Cost' as understood in Economics.
2. Write a note on 'Opportunity Cost'.
3. How do you explain 'Incremental Cost'?
4. Explain the different types of costs.
5. Classify the different cost concepts.
6. Explain the importance of difference between Economic costs and Accounting costs.
7. With the help of diagram and illustrations explain the cost-volume-profit (Breakeven) Analysis.
8. Differentiate between certainty, risk and uncertainty.
9. Give the different components of risk management.
10. Illustrate any case study on 'Risk Management'
11. What do you mean by 'Expected Value'?
12. Explain risk management through (a) Insurance; (b) Hedging; (c) Diversification.
13. Illustrate with example the concept of 'Decision tree'.
14. Why does an exporter face a foreign exchange risk? How can the exporter hedge its foreign exchange risk?

Objective Questions

1. A U.S. firm imports £100,000 worth of goods from the European Monetary Union and agrees to pay in 3 months. The exchange rate is $1/£1 and the 3-month forward rate is $1.01/£1. Explain how the importer can hedge his foreign exchange risk.

2. Opportunity cost is a term which describes:
   (i) Cost related to an optimum level of production.
   (ii) Variable cost.
   (iii) Short-run cost.
   (iv) Cost of one product in terms of production of others forgone.
   [Ans. (iv)]

3. Which of the following is an implicit cost:
   (i) Wages paid to its employees.
   (ii) Rent paid for hired equipment.
   (iii) Depreciation charged on company-owned equipment.
   (iv) Taxes on property owned by the company.
   [Ans. (iii)]

4. Indicate whether the following statements are True/False:
   (i) Depreciation is an out-of-pocket cost.
   (ii) All out-of-pocket costs are variable costs.
   (iii) All direct costs are variable and all indirect costs are fixed.
   [Ans.: (i) False; (ii) False; (iii) False]

■■■

Chapter 4...

Money and Capital Markets in India

Contents ...

Learning Objectives ...

➢ To understand the organised and unorganised money markets in India.

➢ To understand the importance of money markets in India.

➢ To learn about the various instruments transacted in the money markets.

➢ To learn about the role/functions of the apex bank of the country-Reserve Bank of India.

➢ To understand the role of RBI with reference to currency, credit and balance of payment, and open market operations.

➢ To have knowledge on the working and significance of the capital market in India.

➢ To understand the working of the stock exchanges in India.

➢ To understand the role/function of SEBI.

Introduction

A money market comprises a well-organised banking system. The money market is a market for lending and borrowing of short-term funds. Various financial instruments are used for transactions in a money market having a maturity period of one day to one year. Money market is not a place (like the stock market). It is in fact, a mechanism undertaken through telephone. There is perfect mobility of funds in a money market. The instruments in the money market are close substitutes for money as they are of short-term and highly liquid. It is a collection of markets for several financial instruments such as call money market, commercial bill market, etc.

4.1 Money Market – Concept and Meaning

The Indian money market comprises of organised sector and unorganised sector. While the organised sector comes under the direct regulation of RBI, the unorganised sector comprises of indigenous bankers, money lenders and unregulated non-banking financial institutions. There are two types of financial markets viz., the money market and the capital market. The money market is that part of a financial market which deals in the borrowing and lending of short-term loans generally for a period of one day to one year. It is a mechanism to clear short-term monetary transactions in an economy.

Thus, the money market is a market for lending and borrowing of short-term funds. It deals in highly liquid financial instruments like call money, treasury bills, commercial bills, commercial paper, etc. The RBI, Government, commercial banks, financial institutions, corporate firms, money lenders, etc are the important players in the Indian Money Market. In spite of the various measures taken by the RBI to strengthen and deepen the money market, it still remains comparatively underdeveloped.

4.2 Definitions of Money Market

These definitions help us identify the basic characteristics of a money market.

According to **Crowther**, "The money market is a name given to the various firms and institutions that deal in the various grades of near money."

According to the **RBI**, "The money market is the centre for dealing mainly of short character, in monetary assets; it meets the short-term requirements of borrowers and provides liquidity or cash to the lenders. It is a place where short-term surplus investible funds at the disposal of financial and other institutions and individuals are bid by borrowers, again comprising institutions and individuals and also by the government."

According to **Nadler and Shipman**, "A money market is a mechanical device through which short-term funds are loaned and borrowed through which a large part of the financial transactions of a particular country or world are dealt with A money market is distinct from but supplementary to the commercial banking system."

4.3 Participants in the Money Market

The transactions in the money market are of high volume involving large amounts. So, money market is dominated by a small number of large capacity players. Some of the important players in the money market are: (i) Government; (ii) Reserve Bank of India; (iii) Discount and Finance House of India; (iv) Banks; (v) Financial Institutions; (vi) Corporate Firms; (vii) Mutual funds; (viii) Non-Banking Finance Companies; (ix) Primary Dealers; (x) Securities Trading Corporation of India; (xi) Provident Funds; (xii) Public Sector Undertakings.

4.4 Structure of Indian Money Market

    (a) Organised market;

    (b) Unorganised market.

Organised Sector:

- The RBI is the apex institution that controls and monitors all the organisations in the organised sector of the money market.

- The organised money market is composed of various components or instruments that are highly liquid in nature.

- The various instruments traded are call money, treasury bills, commercial bills, certificates of deposits, commercial papers, repos etc.

- The organised money market is further diversified with the establishment of the Discount and Finance House of India (DFHI) and Money Market Mutual Funds (MMMFs).

Unorganised Sector:

- The unorganised Indian money market mainly comprises of indigenous bankers, money lenders and unregulated non-banking financial intermediaries.

- Though they may exist in urban centres, their activities are mainly concentrated in rural areas. In fact, 36% of rural households depend on these for their financial requirement.

- The main components of unorganised money market are: indigenous bankers, money lenders, unregulated non banking financial intermediaries.

4.5 Importance and Functions of Money Market

Money market is an important part of the economy. It plays very significant functions. Basically it is a market for short-term monetary transactions. Thus it has to provide facility for adjusting liquidity to the banks, business corporations, non-banking financial institutions (NBFs) and other financial institutions along with investors.

The importance and major functions of money market are given below:

1. **Financing Trade:** Money Market plays crucial role in financing both internal as well as international trade. Commercial finance is made available to the traders through bills of exchange, which are discounted by the bill market. The acceptance houses and discount markets help in financing foreign trade.

2. **Financing Industry:** Money market contributes to the growth of industries in two ways:

   (a) Money market helps the industries in securing short-term loans to meet their working capital requirements through the system of finance bills, commercial papers, etc.

   (b) Industries generally need long-term loans, which are available in the capital market. However, capital market depends upon the nature of and the conditions in the money market. The short-term interest rates of the money market influence the long-term interest rates of the capital market. Thus, money market indirectly helps the industries through its link with and influence on long-term capital market.

3. **Profitable Investment:** Money market enables commercial banks to use their excess reserves in profitable investments. The main objective of the commercial banks is to earn income from its reserves as well as maintain liquidity to meet the uncertain cash demand of the depositors. In the money market, the excess reserves of the commercial banks are invested in near-money assets (*e.g.* short-term bills of exchange) which are highly liquid and can be easily converted into cash. Thus, the commercial banks earn profits without losing liquidity.

4. **Self-Sufficiency of Commercial Bank:** A developed money market helps the commercial banks to become self-sufficient. In a situation of emergency, when commercial banks have scarcity of funds, they need not approach the central bank and borrow at a higher interest rate. Instead, they can meet their requirements by recalling their old short-run loans from the money market.

5. **Help to Central Bank:** Though the Central bank can function and influence the banking system in the absence of a money market, the existence of a developed money market smoothens the functioning and increases the efficiency of the Central bank.

Money market helps the Central bank in two ways:

   (a) The short-run interest rate of the money market serves as an indicator of the monetary and banking conditions in the country and, in this way, guides the central bank to adopt an appropriate banking policy,

   (b) The sensitive and integrated money market helps the central bank to secure quick and widespread influence on the sub-markets, and thus achieve effective implementation of its policy.

To sum up, the functions of money market that reveal its importance as under:

- **To maintain monetary equilibrium:.** Money market provides a mechanism to achieve the EQUILIBRIUM between DEMAND and SUPPLY of short-term monetary transaction funds.

- **To promote economic growth:** Money market can promote economic development by making short-term funds available to various units in the economy such as agriculture, small scale industries, etc.

- **To provide help to Trade and Industry:** Money market provides adequate finance to trade and industry. Similarly it also provides facility of discounting bills of exchange for trade and industry.

- **To help in implementing Monetary Policy:** It provides a mechanism for an effective implementation of the RBI's monetary policy.

- **To help in Capital Formation:** Money market makes available investment avenues for short-term period with fair returns to investors. Thus, it helps in generating savings and investments in the economy.

- **Employment:** Money market helps in employment generation.

- **To meet deficits:** Money market provides non-inflationary sources of finance to government. It is possible to raise short loans by issuing treasury bills. However, this does not lead to increase in the prices. In this way, it provides funds to government to meet its deficits.

- **Commercial banks:** It instils financial discipline in commercial banks.

A well-developed money market is essential for a modern economy. Though, historically, money market has developed as a result of industrial and commercial progress, it also had an important role to play in the process of industrialisation and economic development of a country.

4.6 Instruments of Money Market

The instruments of the Organised money Market are:

(a) Call Money and Notice Money Market

- The **call money market** is the most important segment of the Indian money market. It is also called as *inter-bank call money market*.

- Under call money market, funds are transacted for an over-night. Generally, banks rely on call money market where they raise funds for a single day.

- The rate at which funds are borrowed / lent in this market is called the call money rate. The call money rate (that depends on demand for and supply of funds) is highly variable from day to day and from centre to centre.

- The main participants in the call money market are commercial banks (excluding RRBs), co-operative banks and primary dealers.

- The Discount and Finance House of India and non-banking financial institutions like LIC, GIC, UTI, NABARD, etc, also participate in the call money market.
- Call money markets are generally concentrated in large commercial centres like Mumbai, Delhi, Chennai, Kolkata and Ahmedabad.
- The RBI intervenes in the call money market because it is highly sensitive and it is the indicator of liquidity position in the organised money market.
- The **notice money market** funds are transacted for a period of 2 to 14 days. The loans are to be repaid at the option of either the lender or the borrower.

(b) Treasury Bills Market

- Treasury bills are short-term securities issued by the RBI on behalf of the Government of India.
- Treasury bills are of three types: 91 day treasury bills, 182 days treasury bills and 364 day treasury bills.
- Since these bills are issued through auctions, interest rates on all types of treasury bills are determined by market forces of demand and supply.
- Treasury bills are highly liquid and are readily available. They give assured yields at a low transaction cost.
- Treasury Bills are eligible for inclusion in the SLR. Moreover, they have negligible capital depreciation.
- Treasury Bills are available for a minimum amount of ₹ 25000 and in multiples of ₹ 25000.
- Treasury Bills are traded in the secondary market. Commercial banks, Primary Dealers, Mutual Funds, Corporate, and Financial Institutions, Provident / Pension funds and Insurance companies participate in the treasury Bills Market.
- However Treasury Bills Market in India is very narrow and undeveloped.

(c) Commercial Bills

- A commercial bill is a short-term, negotiable, self-liquidating instrument drawn by the seller on the buyer for the value of goods delivered by him. Such bills are called trade bills / bills of exchange and when they are accepted by banks, they are called *commercial bills.*
- Generally the bill is payable at a future date (mostly, the maturity period is up to 90 days).
- During this period, the seller may discount the bill with the banks. The commercial banks may rediscount these bills with Financial Institutions like EXIM bank, SIDBI, IDBI, etc. Thus, commercial bills are very important for providing short-term credit to trade and commerce.

(d) Certificates of Deposits (CDs)

- CDs are unsecured, negotiable promissory notes issued by commercial banks and development financial institutions. Thus, CDs are marketable receipts of funds deposited in a bank for a fixed period at a specified rate of interest.
- They are highly liquid and riskless money market instruments.
- CDs were originally introduced in India to enable commercial banks to raise funds from the market.
- The RBI has modified its original scheme for CDs. The following are the recent guidelines for the issue of CDs:

In terms of Eligibility: CDs can be issued by commercial banks (except Regional Rural Banks and Local Area Banks) and financial institutions that have been permitted to raise short-term loans by RBI.

In terms of Amount: Banks can issue CDs depending on their requirements; financial institutions can issue CDs within the limit fixed by the RBI.

In terms of Size: The minimum size of an issue for a single investor is ₹ 1 lakh and it can be increased in multiples of ₹ 1 lakh.

In terms of Discount Rate: Banks / Financial institutions are free to determine discount rates on floating rate basis.

In terms of Investors: CDs are issued to Individuals, Corporations, Companies, Trusts, etc.

In terms of Transferability: CDs are freely transferable by endorsements / delivery. However DEMAT CDs have to transferred as per specified procedures. There is no lock-in period for CDs.

In terms of Maturity: Commercial banks can issue CDs with a maturity period between 7 days to 1 year. Financial institutions can issue CDs with a maturity period ranging from 1 year to 3 years.

In terms of reserve Requirements: CDs are subject to CRR and SLR since banks have to report CDs to RBI.

In terms of Loans/Buy-Back: Commercial banks / Financial Institutions (FIs) cannot give loans against CDs. Similarly, they cannot buy-back their own CDs before maturity period.

In terms of Format: Banks / FIs should issue CDs only in the dematerialised form. However, investors have the option to seek CDs in physical form.

However, due to absence of a well-developed secondary market in CDs, the size of CD market in India is quite small.

(e) Commercial Papers

- Commercial paper is an unsecured, highly liquid money market instrument in the form of a promissory note / a dematerialised form through any of the depositories registered with SEBI.

- It has a fixed maturity whereby the purchaser is promised a fixed amount at a future date.
- Commercial paper is issued by leading nationally reputed manufacturing and finance companies (public / private sector).
- They are issued on discount to face value.
- Commercial papers are issued (by corporates/ primary dealers / all India financial institutions) on the following conditions:
  - (i) The tangible net worth of the issuing company should not be less than ₹ 4 crores.
  - (ii) The working capital limit of the company has been sanctioned by banks / financial institution.
  - (iii) The borrowable account of the company is rated as a standard asset by banks / financial institutions.
  - (iv) All eligible participants should have a minimum rating P2 from CRISIL.
  - (v) Commercial Papers have maturity period between 7 days and 1 year from the date of issue.
  - (vi) CP is issued in denominations of ₹ 5 lakhs (minimum) or multiples of ₹ 5 lakhs.
  - (vii) Individuals, banks, corporate bodies, NRIs and FIIs can invest in commercial papers.
  - (viii) Every issuer must appoint an IPA (Issuing and Paying Agent) for issuance of commercial papers. Only a scheduled commercial bank can act as an IPA.

(f) Repos and Reverse Repos

- The RBI achieves the function of maintaining liquidity in the money market through REPOS and REVERSE REPOS.
- The repo and reverse repo is a very important money market instrument to facilitate short-term liquidity adjustment among banks, financial institutions and other money market players.
- A repo and reverse repo is a transaction in which two parties agree to sell and repurchase the same security at a mutually decided future date and price.
- *Repo* is a transaction from the *seller's* point of view, whereby the seller gets immediate funds by selling the securities with an agreement to repurchase the same at a future date. *Reverse repo* is transaction from the *buyer's* point of view, whereby the buyer buys the securities with an agreement to resell the same at a future date.
- The participants in the repos and reverse repo transactions are the RBI, commercial banks and primary dealers.
- The financial institutions can deal only in the reverse repo transactions i.e. they are allowed only to lend money through reverse repos to the RBI, other banks and Primary dealers. The maturity date varies from 1 day to 14 days.

- The two types of repos are: (a) Inter-bank repos (transaction between banks and DFHI); (b) RBI repos (transaction between banks and the RBI to stabilise and maintain liquidity in the market).

- Repos and Reverse Repos are used for following purposes: (a) for injection or absorption of liquidity; (b) to create an equilibrium between the demand for and supply of short-term funds; (c) to borrow securities to meet SLR requirements; (d) to increase returns on funds; (e) to meet deficit in cash positions.

(g) Discount and Finance House of India (DFHI)

- The DFHI is jointly owned by the RBI, the public sector banks and all India financial institutions.

- The DFHI helps in developing and stabilising the money market by stimulating activity in the money market instruments and developing secondary market in those instruments.

- The DFHI deals in treasury bills, commercial bills certificates of deposits, commercial papers, short-term deposits, call money market and govt. securities. It also participates in repo operations.

- Thus, the DFHI has helped corporate firms, banks and financial institutions to invest their short-term surpluses in money market instruments.

(h) Money Market Mutual Funds (MMMFs)

- The RBI introduced Money Market Mutual Funds to enable small investors to participate in the money market. Thus, MMMFs mobilise saving of mutual funds and invest them in such money market instruments that mature in less than one year.

- The following are the important features of MMMFs:
  (a) MMMFs can be set by scheduled commercial banks and public finance institutions.
  (b) Individuals, Corporates, etc can invest in MMMFs.
  (c) The lock-in period has been reduced to 15 days.
  (d) MMMFs are under the regulation of SEBI.
  (e) NRIs and Overseas Corporate Bodies can invest in MMMFs (on a non-repatriation basis) floated by commercial banks / public sector financial institutions / private sector financial institutions. However, they do not need separate permission from the RBI.
  (f) MMMFs are ideal for investors seeking low-risk investment for short-term surpluses.

The instruments of Unorganised Sector

The unorganised Indian money market mainly comprises of indigenous bankers, money lenders and unregulated non-banking financial intermediaries.

Though they may exist in urban centres, their activities are mainly concentrated in rural areas. In fact, 36% of rural households depend on these for their financial requirements.

The main components of unorganised money market are:

(a) Indigenous Bankers

- These financial intermediaries operate as banks by receiving deposits, giving loans and dealing in *'Hundies'*. The *Hundi* is a short-term indigenous bill of exchange.
- The rate of interest varies from market to market / bank to bank.
- They do not solely depend on deposits, they may also use their own funds.
- They are called by different names like *'Kathawals'*, *'Saraf'*, *'Shroffs'*,*'Chettis'*,etc.
- They provide loans to trade and industry and agriculture.
- The main advantages of indigenous bankers are simple and flexible operations, informal approach, personal contact, quick services and availability of timely funds.
- However, they suffer from drawbacks like a very high rate of interest (18% to 36%), combining banking with trade, interest in non-banking activities like general merchants, brokers, etc.

(b) Money Lenders

- Money lenders predominate in villages and they deal in the business of lending money.
- Their interest rates are very exorbitant.
- Loans are given to agricultural labourers, marginal and small farmers, artisans, factory workers, etc for productive and unproductive purposes.
- Their services are prompt, informal and flexible.

(c) Unregulated Non-Bank Financial Intermediaries

(i) Chit funds:

- They are saving institutions wherein members make regular contribution to the fund.
- The fund is given to some member by bids or draws.
- Chit funds are famous in Kerala and Tamil Nadu.

(ii) Nidhis:

- They are mutual benefit funds given as loan to members (from the deposits made by members themselves) at a reasonable rate of interest.
- The loans are generally given for purposes like house construction / repairs.
- Nidhis are prevalent in South India.

(iii) Loan Companies

- Loan Companies (also known as finance companies) have capital in the form of borrowings, deposits or owned funds.
- They attract deposits by offering high rate of interest and other incentives. Loans are also given at a very high rate of interest, say 36% to 48% per annum.
- The main participants are traders, small-scale industries and self-employed people.

(iv) Finance Brokers

- They are found in all major urban markets, especially in cloth markets, commodity markets and grain markets.
- They are intermediaries between lenders and borrowers.

4.7 Drawbacks of Indian Money Market

The following are some of the drawbacks of the Indian Money Market:-

(A) Dichotomy

1. Dichotomy i.e. existence of two markets (organised money market and unorganised money market) is itself a major defect of the Indian Money Market.
2. The unorganised money market comprises of indigenous bankers, money lenders, chit funds, nidhis, loan companies and finance brokers that do not come under the control and supervision of the RBI.
3. This unorganised sector is mainly concentrated in the rural areas and it does not differentiate between short-term and long-term finance and between the purposes of finance. This puts a limit on the RBI's control over the money market.

(B) Lack of Integration

1. The RBI finds it difficult to integrate the organised and the unorganised money market. While the RBI can control and supervise the working of the organised sector effectively, the heterogeneous unorganised sector is out of RBI's control.
2. There is no uniformity in the practices and operations of the unorganised money market.
3. Moreover, the interest rates in both the markets are also different.

Thus there is a lack of integration in the Indian money market.

(C) Multiplicity in Interest Rates

1. There is diversity in rates of interest in the Indian money market. This multiplicity in the interest rates is due to lack of mobility of funds from one section of the money market to another.
2. The rates differ from institution to institution even for funds of the same duration. Although the wide differences are being narrowed down, the existing differences do hamper the efficiency of the money market.

(D) Absence of Organised Bill Market

1. The existence of a well-organised bill market is essential for effective linking up of various credit agencies. It refers to a mechanism wherein bills of exchange are purchased and discounted by commercial banks / financial institutions.
2. The bill market is not yet developed in India due to the following reasons:
   - Banks keeping large amount of cash.
   - Preference for borrowing rather than discounting bills.
   - Overdependence on cash / cheque transactions.

(E) Shortage of Funds

1. The Indian money market is characterised by shortage of funds.
2. Various factors like inadequate banking facilities, low savings, lack of banking habits, existence of parallel economy, etc lead to shortage of funds.
3. The demand for short-term funds far exceeds the supply. This results in high interest rate.

However, now banks are flushed with funds especially in urban area as people prefer to invest their money with banks rather than keeping them as deposits in the unorganised sector.

(F) Seasonal Stringency of Money

1. Since agriculture continues to play a major role in the Indian economy, farm operations do influence the demand for and supply of money. Thus seasonal stringency of money and high interest rates during the busy season (November to June) is a striking feature of the Indian money market.
2. Also, there are wide fluctuations in the interest rates from one reason to another.

However, the RBI makes attempt to reduce the fluctuations by adding money into the money market during the busy season and withdrawing the funds during the slack season.

(G) Inadequate Credit Instruments

1. The Indian money market lacked adequate short-term paper instruments till 1985-86, only call money market and bill market existed.
2. Also there were no specialised dealers / brokers in the money market.

After 1985-86 the RBI Introduced new credit instruments in the market like certificate of deposits, commercial papers, MMMF, etc, but they have not yet fully developed in India.

(H) Absence of a well-organised Banking Sector in Rural Area

1. The banking system in the rural area remains poor due to the problems of overheads and maintenance of branches.
2. The commercial bank branches in rural area are only 40% of the total bank branches. This also hampers the development of money market in India.

(I) Inefficient and Corrupt Management

1. Faulty selection, lack of training, poor performance appraisal and faulty promotions result in inefficiency and corruption in the banking sector. This adversely affects the success and performance of money market.

To conclude,

- The Indian money market is relatively less developed.
- It has yet to acquire sufficient depth and width.
- It cannot be compared with the developed money markets in London and New York.

4.8 Reforms in the Indian Money Market

Money market is a market for lending and borrowing of short-term funds and it deals in highly liquid financial instruments. Indian Money Market comprises of unorganised and organised sectors that suffer from various drawbacks. To overcome these drawbacks and to strengthen the market, the RBI has taken certain measures.

The following are the measures taken by the RBI to reform the Indian Money Market:-

1. **Deregulation of Interest Rates**
   - The RBI has deregulated interest rates on deposits (except saving deposits) as well as on advances (except on export credit for a period of 180days before shipment).
   - The ceiling on the call money market, inter-bank short-term deposits, bill rediscounting and inter-bank participation has been removed and the rates are decided on market forces. This ensures healthy competition and improves efficiency.

2. **Introduction of New Money Market Instruments**
   - To diversify the Indian money market and to make it more effective RBI has introduced new money market instruments.
   - These include instruments such as 182-day treasury bill, 364-day treasury bill, commercial papers (CPs) and certificates of deposits (CDs).
   - Government, commercial banks, financial institutions and corporates can raise funds through these instruments.
   - The RBI has also reduced the minimum investment amount and the minimum maturity period to expand the investor base for CDs and CPs.

3. **Reduction in CRR and SLR**
   - The RBI has brought about considerable reduction in the Cash Reserve Ratio (CRR) and the Statutory Liquidity Ratio. This reduction improves the liquidity of banks and they can lend more money in the market.

4. **Remittance of Stamp Duty**
   - The RBI has remitted the stamp duty on bills to make the bill market more popular in India.
   - In fact the bill market is not developed in India due to: high discount rates, over dependence on cash/cheque transactions and greater chances of dishonour.

5. **Repos and Reverse Repos**
   - The RBI introduced Repos in Dec. 1992 and Reverse Repos in November 1996.
   - Repos and Reverse Repos bring about a balance in the short-term fluctuations in the liquidity existing in the money market. They also provide a short-term avenue to the banks to park their surplus funds in the money market.

6. **Liquidity Adjustment Facility (LAF)**
   - The RBI introduced LAF as an important tool for adjusting liquidity through REPOS and REVERSE REPOS. This stabilises the short-term interest rates / call rates in the money market.

7. **Money Market Mutual Funds**
   - The RBI introduced Money Market Mutual Funds to enable small investors to participate in the money market. Thus, MMMFs mobilise the savings of the mutual funds and invest them in such money market instruments that mature in less than one year.
   - The following are the important features of MMMFs:
     (i) MMMFs can be set by scheduled commercial banks and public finance institutions.
     (ii) Individuals, corporates, etc can invest in MMMFs.
     (iii) The lock-in period has been reduced to 15 days.
     (iv) MMMFs are under the regulation of SEBI.
     (v) NRIs and Overseas Corporate Bodies can invest in MMMFs (on a non-repatriation basis) floated by commercial banks / public sector financial institutions / private sector financial institutions. However, they do not need separate permission from the RBI.
     (vi) MMMFs are ideal for investors seeking low-risk investment for short-term surpluses.
     (vii) Resources mobilised through this scheme can be invested in money market instruments as well as in rated corporate bonds / debentures with a maturity period up to 1 year.

8. **Discount and Finance House of India-(DFHI)**
   - In 1988, DFHI was set up jointly by the RBI, public sector banks and financial institutions. The main reason for setting up DFHI was to impart liquidity to money market instruments and the development of active secondary market in these instruments.

9. **Development of Inter-Bank Call and Notice Money Market**
   - The call and notice money market is an inter-bank market all over the world. So, the Narshimam Committee recommended adopting the same policy in India. However, the RBI had permitted the non-banking institutions to participate in the call and notice money market as lenders. The RBI is now taking steps to gradually reduce the role of non-banking institutions and transform the call and notice money market into a pure interbank money market.

10. **Regulation of Non-Banking Financial Corporations**
    - RBI regulates the Non-Banking financial Corporations.
    - A non-banking financial corporation (NBFC) cannot carry on any business of a financial institution (including acceptance of Public Deposit) without a Certificate of Registration (COR) from the RBI.

- Companies accepting public deposits are required to comply with all the directions on public deposits, prudential norms and liquid assets. They are obliged to submit regular returns to the RBI.

11. Clearing Corporation of India Limited - (CCIL)

- The CCIL was registered under the Companies Act 1956, with the State Bank of India as the chief promoter.
- The CCIL clears all transactions in government securities and repos reported on the NDS (Negotiated Dealing System) of the RBI.
- It also clears rupee / US Dollar foreign exchange spot and forward deals.
- All trades in government securities below ₹ 20 crores have to be settled through the CCIL. Trades in government securities above ₹ 20 crores can be settled through the CCIL or the RBI.

12. Recovery of Debts

- For speedy recovery of debts, the RBI has set up Special Recovery Tribunals in 1993. These provide legal assistance to banks to recover their dues.

13. Minimum Lock-in-period

- In October 2004, the RBI reduced the minimum lock-in period for term deposits (below ₹ 15 lakhs) from 15 days to 7 days. Thus, the depositor can deposit money for 7 days and earn interest. This increases the term-deposits with the banks.

4.9 Reserve Bank of India

The Reserve Bank of India was established on April 1, 1935 in accordance with the provisions of the Reserve Bank of India Act, 1934.

Initially, the Central Office of the Reserve Bank was established in Calcutta (now Kolkata) but was permanently moved to Mumbai in 1937. The Central Office is the seat of the Governor and where policies are formulated. Originally it was privately-owned but since Nationalisation in 1949, the Reserve Bank is fully owned by the Government of India.

The Preamble of the Reserve Bank of India describes the basic functions of the Reserve Bank as : "......to regulate the issue of Bank Notes and keeping of reserves with a view to securing monetary stability in India and generally to operate the currency and credit system of the country to its advantage."

Central Board: The affairs of the Reserve Bank are governed by a Central Board of Directors. The board is appointed by the Government of India in accordance with the Reserve Bank of India Act.

The Board is appointed/nominated for a period of four years. Its Constitution is as follows:

Official Directors: Full time – Governor and Deputy Governors (Deputy Governors not more than four).

Non-Official Directors: They are nominated by Government. These are 10 Directors from various fields and Government Officials. In Others- four Directors- one each from four local boards.

The *functions* of Central Board are General Superintendence and direction of the Bank's affairs.

Local Boards: Local Board consists of one each for the four regions of the country in Mumbai, Kolkata, Chennai and New Delhi.

Membership: Local Board membership consists of 5 members each. They are appointed by the Central Government for a term of four years.

Functions of Local Boards:

(i)   to advise the Central Bank on local matters;

(ii) to represent territorial and economic interests' of local cooperative and indigenous banks;

(iii) to perform such other functions as delegated by Central Board from time to time.

Central Board of Directors – Governor –Deputy Governors –Executive Directors – Principal Chief General Manager – Chief General Manager – General Manager – Deputy General Manager – Assistant General Manager – Managers – Assistant Managers – Support Staff.

4.10 Functions of the Reserve Bank of India

The Reserve Bank of India performs various traditional central banking functions and also undertakes different promotional and developmental methods to meet the dynamic requirements of the country.

The broad objectives of the Reserve Bank of India are:

- Regulating the issue of currency in India;
- Keeping the foreign exchange reserves of the country;
- Establishing the monetary stability in the country; and
- Developing the financial structure of the country on sound lines in tune with the national socio-economic objectives and policies.

We discuss below the main functions of the RBI:

1. Note Issue:

The Reserve Bank has the monopoly of note issue in the country. It has the sole right to issue currency notes of all denominations except one-rupee notes. One-rupee notes are issued by the Ministry of Finance of the Government of India.

The Reserve Bank acts as the only source of legal tender money because even the one-rupee notes are circulated through RBI.

Under the original Act, there was a provision for issuing currency notes according to the *proportional reserve system*, but this system was less elastic and was found not suitable to the requirements of development planning. Thus, the original Act was amended and replaced by the *minimum reserve system*. Thus, the Reserve Bank has a separate Issue Department, which is entrusted with the job of issuing currency notes and the **Reserve Bank has adopted minimum reserve system of note issue.** Since 1957, it maintains gold and foreign exchange reserves of ₹ 200 crore, of which at least ₹ 115 crore should be in gold.

There is a division of work between the Issue and the Banking Departments of the RBI in respect of note issue. Currency notes are being issued by the Issue Department and on the basis of demand are made by the Banking Department for which the Department has to transfer government or other approved securities to the Issue Department.

2. **Banker to Government:**

   The Reserve Bank acts as the banker, agent and advisor to the Government of India:

   - It maintains and operates government deposits;
   - It has the obligation to transact the banking business of the Central and State governments. Thus, it collects and makes payments on behalf of the government.
   - It helps the government to float new loans and manages the public debt. For ensuring the success of the loan operations it actively operates in the gilt-edged market.
   - It sells for the Central Government treasury bills of 91 days duration.
   - It makes 'Ways and Means' advances to the Central and State Governments for periods not exceeding three months.
   - It provides development finance to the government for carrying out five year plans.
   - It undertakes foreign exchange transactions on behalf of the Central Government.
   - It acts as the agent of the Government of India in the latter's dealings with the International Monetary Fund (IMF), the World Bank, and other international financial institutions.
   - The need for co-ordination between the monetary and fiscal policies is now being universally recognised. As such, central bank's function as the advisor to the government has assumed new significance. It advises the government on all financial matters such as loan operations, investments, agricultural and industrial finance, banking, planning, economic development, etc.

3. **RBI is Banker's Bank**

   RBI acts as banker's bank in the following ways:

   (i) Every Bank is under the statutory obligation to keep a certain minimum of cash reserves (CRR) with the RBI. The objective of cash reserves is to enable the RBI to extend financial assistance to the Scheduled Banks in times of emergency and act as the lender of the last resort.

   According to the Banking Regulation Act, 1949, all Scheduled Banks are required to maintain with the Reserve Bank minimum cash reserves of 5% of the demand liabilities and 2% of their time liabilities.

The Reserve Bank (Amendment) Act, 1956 empowered the Reserve Bank to raise the cash reserve ratio to 20% in the case of demand deposits and to 8% in case of time deposits. However, there was difficulty in classifying deposits into demand and time categories hence the amendment to the Banking Regulation Act in September 1972 changed the provision of reserves to 3% of aggregate deposit liabilities, which can be raised to 15% if the Reserve Bank considers it necessary.

(ii) The Reserve Bank provides financial assistance to the Scheduled banks by discounting their eligible bills and through loans and advances against approved securities. The RBI has the power to deny rediscounting facility to any bank without assigning any reason for it.

(iii) Under the Banking Regulation Act, 1949 and its various amendments, the Reserve Bank has been given extensive powers of supervision and control over the banking system. These regulatory powers relate to the licensing of banks and their branch expansion; liquidity of assets of the banks; management and methods of working of the banks; amalgamation, reconstruction and liquidation of banks; inspection of banks; etc.

(iv) For exercising its control over the commercial banks, the RBI conducts their inspection by its own staff and also calls for returns and other necessary information. In case banking operations of any one of them are found unsatisfactory, it suggests remedial measures.

4. Custodian of Exchange Reserves

- The Reserve Bank is the *custodian* of India's foreign exchange reserves as it maintains and stabilises the external value of the rupee. It is obligatory for the RBI to buy and sell currencies of all the members of the IMF. The RBI administers direct methods of exchange controls and other restrictions imposed by the government, and manage the foreign exchange reserves. The direct methods have become a permanent instrument of economic management.

- Initially, the stability of exchange rate was maintained through selling and purchasing sterling at fixed rates. But after India became a member of the international Monetary Fund (IMF) in 1947, the rupee was delinked from Sterling and became a multilaterally convertible currency. Therefore the Reserve Bank now sells and buys foreign currencies, and not Sterling alone, in order to achieve the objective of exchange stability. The Reserve Bank fixes the selling and buying rates of foreign currencies.

- All Indian remittances to foreign countries and foreign remittances to India are made through the Reserve Bank.

- In 1947, the Foreign Exchange Regulation Act (FERA) was passed and with it foreign exchange management and control became a distinct function of the RBI. The Act empowered the RBI to exercise control over foreign securities, foreign payments and transfer of currency, bullion and securities to foreign nationals. Over the years, FERA was amended a number of times and has been replaced by Foreign Exchange Management Act (FEMA).

5. **Controller of Credit**

   - The Reserve Bank is the central bank of the country and hence undertakes the responsibility of controlling credit in order to ensure internal price stability and promote economic growth. The objective of RBI is to achieve price stability in the country and avoid inflationary and deflationary tendencies in the country.

   - Price stability is essential for economic development.

   - The Reserve Bank regulates the money supply in accordance with the changing requirements of the economy.

   - The Reserve Bank makes extensive use of various quantitative and qualitative techniques to effectively control and regulate credit in the country.

6. **Collection and Promotional Functions**

   - The RBI has been entrusted with the task of collection and compilation of statistical information relating to banking and other financial sectors of the economy.

   - The two most important publications of RBI are *The RBI Bulletin* which is a monthly publication and the other is *The Report on Currency and Finance* which is an annual publication.

7. **Agricultural Finance**

   - Pointing to the importance of RBI's role in agricultural finance B. Rama Rao, a former Governor of the RBI, has stated: *"The RBI could not have justified its existence in India if it confined its activities to the industrial sector and completely ignored agricultural sector, on the prosperity of which industrial development to a large extent depended."*

   - For RBI to fulfil its role, it has laid down for setting up of a special Agricultural Credit Department.

   - With the setting up of the National Bank for Agricultural and Rural Development (NABARD) on July 12, 1982 the major functions of the Agricultural Credit Department of the RBI were taken over by the former.

8. **Ordinary Banking Functions**

   Various banking functions performed by the Reserve Bank of India are:

   - It accepts deposits from the central government, state governments and even private individuals, without interest.

   - It buys and sells and rediscounts the bills of exchange and promissory notes of the Scheduled banks without restrictions.

   - It grants loans and advances to the central government, state governments, local authorities, scheduled banks and state cooperative banks, repayable within 90 days.

   - It buys and sells securities of the Government of India and foreign securities.

   - It buys from and sells to the scheduled banks foreign exchange for a minimum amount of ₹ 1 lakh.

   - It can borrow from any scheduled bank in India or from any foreign bank.

- It can open an account in the World Bank or in some foreign central bank.
- It accepts valuables, securities, etc., for keeping them in safe custody.
- It buys and sells gold and silver.

9. Other Functions

Certain other miscellaneous functions are:

(a) RBI has set up College for Banker's training, i.e., to extend training facilities to supervisory staff of commercial banks. Arrangements have also been made to impart training to people who run cooperatives..

(b) The Reserve Bank collects and publishes statistical information relating to banking, finance, credit, currency, agricultural and industrial production, etc. It also publishes the results of various studies and review of economic situation of the country in its monthly bulletins and periodicals.

10. Forbidden Business

The Reserve Bank is the central bank of the country, hence (a) it should not compete with member banks; and (b) it should keep its assets in liquid form to meet any situation of economic crisis. RBI is forbidden to do certain other types of business, such as:

- It can neither participate in, nor directly provide financial assistance to any business, trade or industry.
- It can neither buy its own shares nor those of other banks or of commercial and industrial undertakings.
- It cannot grant unsecured loans and advances.
- It cannot give loans against mortgage security.
- It cannot give interest on deposits.
- It cannot purchase immovable property except for its own offices.
- It cannot draw or accept bills payable on demand.

11. Promotional and Developmental Functions

The promotional and developmental functions of the RBI are:

(a) From the beginning, the Reserve Bank has been making efforts to promote institutional agricultural credit by developing cooperative credit institutions.

(b) The RBI helps to promote the process of industrialisation in the country by setting up specialised institutions for industrial finance.

(c) The RBI helps to mobilise savings in the country through the institutions like Unit Trust of India.

(d) It undertakes measures for developing bill market in the country.

(e) The RBI encourages the commercial banks to expand their branches in the semi-urban and rural areas. In this way, the RBI helps – to reduce the dependence of the people in these areas on the unorganised sector of indigenous bankers and money lenders, and to develop the banking habits of the people.

(f) By establishing the Deposit Insurance Corporation, the RBI helps to develop the banking system of the country, instils confidence of the depositors and thus avoids bank failures.

12. Detection of Fake Currency

In order to curb fake currency menace, the Reserve Bank has launched a website to raise awareness among masses about fake notes in the market and provides information about identifying fake currency.(*www.paisaboltahai.rbi.org.in*)

RBI – Monetary Management. (RBI w.r.t. currency, credit control, balance of payment)

One of the most important functions of central banks is formulation and execution of monetary policy. In the Indian context, the basic functions of the Reserve Bank of India as enunciated in the Preamble to the RBI Act, 1934 are: "to regulate the issue of Bank notes and the keeping of reserves with a view to securing monetary stability in India and generally to operate the currency and credit system of the country to its advantage." Thus, the Reserve Bank's mandate for monetary policy flows from its monetary stability objective.

Essentially, monetary policy deals with the use of various policy instruments for influencing the cost and availability of money in the economy.

As macroeconomic conditions change, a central bank may change the choice of instruments in its monetary policy. The overall goal is to promote economic growth and ensure price stability.

The Reserve Bank's regulatory and supervisory domain extends not only to the Indian banking system but also to the development financial institutions (DFIs), non-banking financial companies (NBFCs), primary dealers, credit information companies and to select segments of the financial markets. In respect of banks, the Reserve Bank derives its powers from the provisions of the Banking Regulation Act, 1949, while the other entities and markets are regulated and supervised under the provisions of the Reserve Bank of India Act, 1934.

Control of Currency by the RBI

Control of currency generally implies the control over the supply of currency and coins. Coins constitute a very small part of money supply in the country and special measures are not needed to regulate its quantity. However, regulation of the quantity of currency notes is very important and the RBI enjoys monopoly authority to issue currency notes.

There is a separate Issue Department in the RBI for issuing currency notes.

The RBI can issue any amount of notes on the basis of reserves maintained in the form of gold bullion, foreign securities, Rupee coins, Rupee securities and Treasury bills. The condition is that it maintains gold and foreign exchange reserves of ₹ 200 crore, of which at least ₹ 115 crore should be in gold.

Under the original Act, there was provision for issuing currency note according to the *proportional reserve system.* This system did not carry within the seed of inflation. But this system being relatively inelastic was found less suitable to the growing requirements of the development planning. The Act was amended and the proportional reserve system gave place to the *minimum reserve system*, i.e. gold and foreign exchange reserves of ₹ 200 crore, of which at least ₹ 115 crore should be in gold. This system of note issue inherently suffers from inflationary tendency.

Mechanics of note-issue

- When the RBI wants to issue currency notes, it generally transfers either foreign securities or rupee securities or both from the Banking Department to the Issue Department.

- It is to be mentioned that the amount of note issue will be equal to the amount of securities received by the Issue Department from the Banking Department.

- The RBI is empowered to issue notes also on the basis of reserves maintained in the form of treasury bills.

- In case RBI has to follow contractionary policy, it reverses the above process. That is the securities are transferred from the Issue Department to the Banking Department, and the currency notes of an equal amount are withdrawn from circulation.

- The role of RBI in successfully regulating the supply of currency is under question as the rampant inflation over the years clearly indicates its failure.

- Some other economists hold the government responsible for the inflation and they hold the view that the RBI is completely passive and obedient to the government. It could not pursue an independent policy when the government recklessly indulged in deficit financing under various Plans.

- In USA, the Federal Reserve System (i.e. the central bank) is an autonomous institution and thus has the sole monetary authority.

- In India there is a difference. The RBI (central bank) is not a completely autonomous monetary institution. It is undera statutory obligation to lend any amount of money that the Central Government decides to borrow from it.

- The state governments are not empowered to borrow from the RBI but they draw unauthorised overdraft from the RBI with impunity.

- It can be said that the role of the RBI has been undermined by the government. In practice, there are two monetary authorities in this country- the Central Government and the RBI, of which the Central Government is more powerful.

Control of Credit by the Reserve Bank of India

In India, the legal framework of the RBI's control over the credit structure has been provided under the RBI Act, 1934 and the Banking Regulation Act, 1949. The RBI has been empowered to use almost all the traditional instruments of credit control under the RBI Act, 1934 and the Banking Regulation Act, 1949 has given RBI additional powers to use some other direct methods of credit regulation.

Like any other central bank, the RBI resorts to bank rate manipulation, direct action, rationing of credit and moral suasion. Apart from this, it directly influences commercial banks' lending policy, rates of interest, form of securities against loans and portfolio distribution.

However, inspite of RBI having authoritative powers that it enjoys, its control over the supply of credit is rather weak. The reason for this is the underdeveloped character of the Indian money market. The traditional sector which includes moneylenders and indigenous bankers as its components, is quite outside the control of RBI, i.e., RBI has little control over the traditional sector. Whatever limited success that RBI has achieved in the past is mainly due to its control over the modern sector of the money market.

The RBI uses Quantitative and Qualitative methods to control credit supply in the country.

The Bank Rate Policy: The RBI is empowered to use bank rate as an instrument of credit control. How effective will be the bank rate policy depends mainly on the conditions: (a) that the commercial banks in the country should not hesitant to availing rediscounting facility from the central bank; (b) that these banks do not maintain any excess cash reserve against deposits; (c) that banks must hold adequate quantity of such credit instruments which will be rediscounted by the central bank as per the legislation. The ineffectiveness of the instrument is due to absence of the last two conditions. In India, the commercial banks are not much dependent on the RBI for financial assistance and due to an underdeveloped bill market these banks lack adequate quantity of eligible bills which can be rediscounted from the RBI.

The bank rate was 10 per cent during the 1980s and was raised to 12 per cent from October 8, 1991 to counteract inflationary pressures in the country. However, the changes in the bank rate were not a very effective method to regulate the supply of credit and money.

On the effects of the RBI's bank rate changes on the Indian money market, B. Rama Rao had stated, "The increase in the bank rate was intended to be a warning signal, for apart from its psychological effect, I doubt if under Indian conditions a slight increase of the rate can have any appreciable influence on inflationary situation."

The bank rate has been reduced in the post 1991 period as a part of economic reforms. It was reduced to 6 per cent on April 30, 2003 and currently it is around 9.0 per cent.

In its Monetary Policy for the year 2011-12 announced by the Reserve Bank on May 3, 2011, it has decided to shift to a single policy rate regime- i.e., repo rate.

Open Market Operations: (RBI with reference to Open Market Operations): The need for open market operations was felt only when the bank rate policy turned out to be a weak instrument of monetary control. Some monetary economists assert that bank rate policy and open market operations are complementary methods of monetary management.

The importance of open market operations has been recognised as the government securities market is fairly well developed in the country and the environment for open market operations is quite favourable.

The RBI Act authorises the RBI to conduct purchase and sale operations in the government securities, treasury bills and other approved securities.

RBI is also empowered to buy and sell short-term commercial bills. But, due to absence of organised bill market in the country, it has served little purpose. In India, since government securities are mainly held by institutional investors, like banks and insurance companies, dealings of the RBI regarding open market operations are mostly confined to them.

In theory, the method of open market operations is superior to bank rate measure. The reason is that for the success of open market operations, the RBI does not have to depend on the cooperation of the commercial banks as it is needed in the success of bank rate policy. With the technique of open market operations, RBI can influence the reserve position of the commercial banks and thereby reduce their capacity to advance credit.

Cash Reserve Ratio (CRR): CRR is an effective instrument of credit control. According to the RBI (Amendment) Act 1962, the RBI is empowered to determine CRR for the commercial banks in the range of 3 percent to 15 percent for the total demand and time liabilities. This method of credit control was used quite often during the 1970s and 1980s for controlling inflation. Since in the late 1980s, there was rapid growth of liquidity the CRR was raised from 10 per cent to 15 per cent and for four years it remained unchanged at 15 per cent.

To fight inflationary pressures the use of CRR was not favoured by the Narsimham Committee through its report in November 1991. The reason was that a high CRR adversely affected profitability of the bank and banks were compelled to charge high interest rates on their commercial sector advances, which would in turn lead to lower investments by the commercial sector. Hence the CRR was brought down from its peak of 15 per cent in 1994-95 to 8.0 per cent in 2000-01 and further reduced to 4.5 per cent effective from June 14, 2003. These reductions resulted in greater lendable resources at the disposal of commercial banks.

However, to control inflationary pressures in the economy, the CRR was subsequently raised in stages to 9.0 percent in August 2008, again reduced to 5.0 per cent on January 17, 2009, and raised again to 6.0 per cent on April 24, 2010 to control inflationary tendencies. But, with the slowdown in economic growth in the 4th quarter of 2011-12, the CRR was reduced to 5.5 per cent on January 24, 2012 to pump in permanent liquidity into the system and the CRR was reduced to 4.75 per cent on March 12, 2012. Currently it is at 4%. Thus, with the stroke of the pen RBI can control the availability of the cash reserves with the banks and in adjust the money supply in the economy.

The Statutory Liquidity Ratio: (SLR): Apart from the CRR, banks are also required to maintain liquid assets in the form of gold, cash and approved securities. Higher liquidity ratio forces commercial banks to maintain a larger proportion of their resources in liquid form and thus reduces their capacity to grant loans and advances, thus it is an anti-inflationary impact. A higher liquidity ratio diverts the bank funds from loans and advances to investment in government and approved securities.

In well-developed economies, central banks use open market operations—buying and selling of eligible securities by central bank in the money market—to influence the volume of cash reserves with commercial banks and thus influence the volume of loans and advances they can make to the commercial and industrial sectors. In the open money market, government securities are traded at market related rates of interest. The RBI is resorting more to open market operations in the recent years.

The Banking Regulation (Amendment) Act 1962 provides for maintaining a minimum statutory liquidity ratio (SLR) of 25 per cent by the banks against their net demand and time liabilities. If necessary to control liquidity, the Act also empowers the RBI to raise the SLR upto 40 per cent. Thus, the RBI is vested with the power to determine SLR for commercial banks.

During 1970s and 1980s, RBI used this power to raise SLR quite often. The SLR was made as high as 38.5 per cent of the commercial banks' net demand and time liabilities, effective from September 22, 1990 and remained high upto March 31, 1992. RBI raised the SLR for banks for two reasons – (a) it reduced commercial banks' ability to create credit and thus eased the inflationary pressures; (b) it made larger resources available to the State.

The Narsimham Committee did not favour maintenance of a high SLR as it had become an instrument in the hands of the government to mobilise resources in support of the Central and State budgets. As suggested by the Committee, the government decided to reduce SLR in stages from 38.5 per cent to 25 per cent. On November 8, 2008, SLR was reduced to 24.0 per cent, raised to 25.0 per cent on November 7, 2009 but reduced again to 24.0 per cent on December 18, 2010. Current SLR is at 23%.

Selective Credit Control (Qualitative Credit Controls)

The qualitative credit controls are generally meant to regulate credit for specific purposes. In any developing economy frequent use of General/ Quantitative techniques may jeopardise development efforts. *The RBI, like many other central banks in various countries, has been empowered to use selective credit controls to regulate credit to specific branches of economic activities, prevent speculative hoardings of essential goods and undue rise in prices.*

Generally RBI uses three kinds of selective credit controls:

1. Minimum margins for lending against specific securities.
2. Ceiling on the amounts of credit for certain purposes.
3. Discriminatory rate of interest charged on certain types of advances.

Apart from these measures the RBI may give directions to banks in general or even some particular bank as to the purpose for which loans may or may not be given.

The main thrust of selective controls is against speculative hoarding of essential commodities by traders. For 40 years, the RBI had extensively relied on the technique of margin requirements to check the hoarding of essential commodities.

In 1996-97 the selective credit controls were liberalised on bank advances against a large number of price sensitive commodities.

4.11 Meaning and Concept of Capital Market

Capital Market is one of the significant aspects of every financial market. In broad terms, the capital market is a market for financial assets which have a long or indefinite maturity. Unlike money market instruments, the capital market instruments become mature for the period above one year. Capital market consists of financial institutions like IDBI, ICICI, UTI, LIC, etc. In the capital market, these institutions play the role of lenders and this market is involved in various instruments which can be used for financial transactions. Capital market provides long-term debt and equity finance for the government and the corporate sector. Capital market institutions provide rupee loans, foreign exchange loans, consultancy services and underwriting.

Capital market can be classified into – Primary and Secondary markets. Primary market is a market for new shares, whereas in the secondary market the existing securities are traded.

4.12 Role and Functions of Capital Market

Capital market plays a significant role in the national economy. A developed, dynamic and vibrant capital market can immensely contribute for speedy economic growth and development.

Let us understand as to what do you mean by a Capital Market?

The Indian financial system, like any other economy, consists of financial institutions, financial instruments, financial markets, and financial services.

There are two types of financial institutions– banking and non-banking. Financial markets are divided into two categories – money market and capital market.

Capital market is further divided into three categories namely- corporate securities, government securities and derivatives.

Capital markets in India form an essential part of the financial system. All the entrepreneurs need capital to start up a business of any kind. However, the size of the capital may vary depending upon the nature of the business. Generally the entrepreneurs do not have sufficient capital, and have to borrow money from banks or financial institutions to initiate the business. Borrowing of money is obviously not free of cost. The entrepreneurs have to pay interest on the borrowed amount of capital. Interest can put a severe burden on the profits of the business especially if the undertaken project has a long gestation period. On the other hand, interest can be beneficial to a certain extent because it comes with a tax advantage.

After taking into consideration various cost aspects of the business the promoters have to decide upon how they will bring in the capital for the business. When the entrepreneurs apply for loans they have to provide the banks with some collateral securities. Many times it is not possible for them to secure loans even against security. Then the entrepreneurs have to collect capital by way of public offering by issuing certain financial instruments such as equity shares, bonds, debentures and so on, for which they have to follow all the rules and regulations laid down by SEBI. The financial requirement raised by the entrepreneurs in a market is known as the 'Capital Market'.

Thus, Capital Market is a market which consists of long-term debt instruments and equity shares. Capital funds are raised by the entrepreneurs in the form of debt and equity instruments only. The instruments are traded in the capital market to raise the money. The financial instruments traded here also includes private placement of debt and equity sources as well as instruments from organized markets like all the stock exchanges. Money market and capital market play a significant role for the economy. A progressive capital market can speed up a country's economic growth to a great extent.

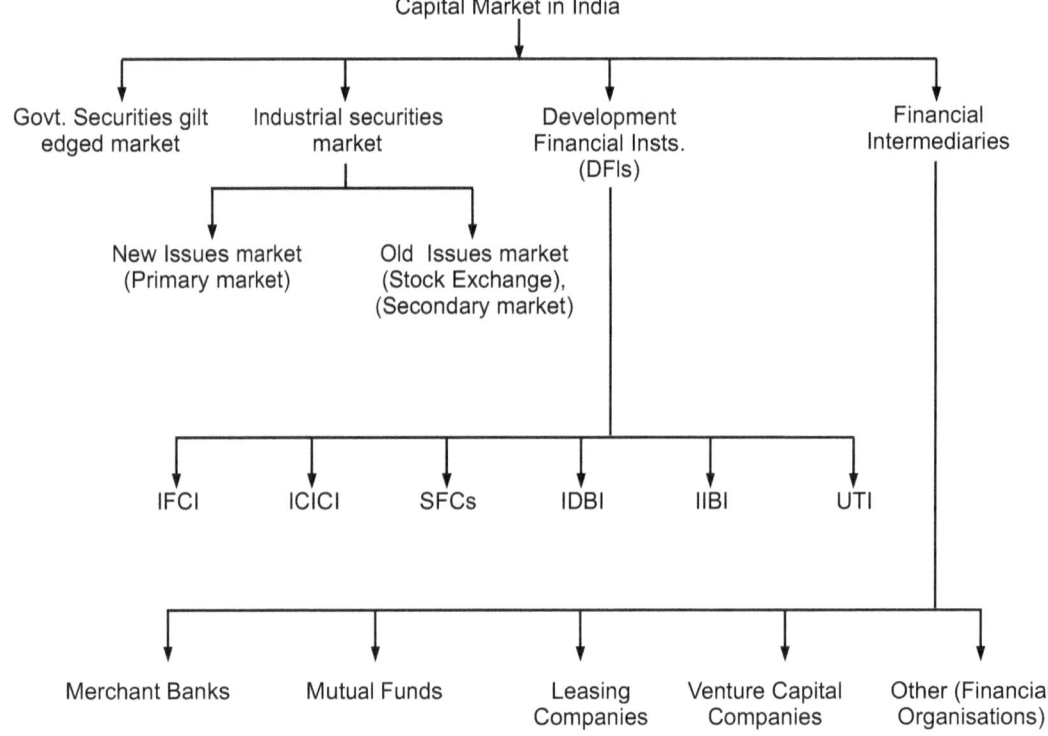

Fig. 4.1: The Structure of Indian Capital Market

On basis of the nature of the instrument brought in the market, the Capital Market is classified into two categories. They are the Primary market (New Issues Market) and the Secondary market (Old (Existing) Issues Market). This classification is done on the basis of the nature of the instrument brought into the market.

On the basis of the types of institutions involved in capital market, it can be classified into various categories such as the Government Securities market or Gilt-edged market, Industrial Securities market, Development Financial Institutions (DFIs) and financial intermediaries.

The structure of the Indian capital market has its distinct features. These different segments of the capital market help to develop the institution of capital market in many dimensions.

The primary market helps to raise fresh capital in the market. In the secondary market, the buying and selling (trading) of capital market instruments takes place.

Primary Market

In the primary market, the securities - shares, bonds and debentures are offered to the public for subscription for the purpose of raising capital. The issue of certificates is regulated by the SEBI and the Companies Act. There are various intermediaries in the primary market such as an issue manager, merchant banker, or a lead arranger. The primary market is further classified into 'public issue market' and 'private issue market'.

Secondary Market

In the secondary market, the securities are purchased and sold once they have already been first offered to the public in the primary market or once they are listed in the stock exchanges. The secondary markets comprises of equity markets and debt markets. It is an avenue where already existing securities are bought and sold amongst the investors. The secondary market can function as an auction market or as a dealer market. Stock exchange is a part of the auction market, where as Over the Counter (OTC) market is a part of the dealer market. The secondary market is a very good platform for the investors to trade their securities.

(a) **Government Securities Market:** This is also known as the Gilt-edged market. It is a market for government and semi-government securities backed by the RBI.

(b) **Industrial Securities Market:** This market is for buying and selling of shares and debentures of the existing and new corporate firms. This market is further classified into two types such as the New Issues Market (Primary) and the Old (Existing) Issues Market (Secondary). In the primary market, fresh capital is raised by companies by issuing new shares, bonds, units of mutual funds and debentures. In the Secondary market, already existing old shares and debentures are traded. This trading takes place through the registered stock exchanges. In India we have three prominent stock exchanges. They are the Bombay Stock Exchange (BSE), the National Stock Exchange (NSE) and Over The Counter Exchange of India (OTCEI).

(c) **Development Financial Institutions (DFIs):** This comprises of various special purposes financial institutions like IFCI, ICICI, SFCs, IDBI, UTI, etc. These financial institutions provide long-term finance for those purposes for which they are set up.

(d) **Financial Intermediaries:** The next important segment of the Indian capital market is the financial intermediaries which comprises of various merchant banking institutions, mutual funds, leasing finance companies, venture capital companies and other financial institutions.

The *Role/Functions* of the Capital Market are as follows:

1. **Capital Market a Link between Savers and Investors:** The capital market functions as a link between savers and investors. It plays an important role in mobilising the savings and diverting them in productive investment. In this way, capital market plays an important role in transferring the financial resources from surplus and wasteful areas to deficit and productive areas, thus increasing the productivity and prosperity of the country.

2. **Encouragement to Saving:** With the development of capital market, the banking and non-banking institutions provide facilities, which encourage people to save more. In the less-developed countries, in the absence of a capital market, there are very little savings and those who save often invest their savings in unproductive and wasteful directions, i.e., in real estate (like land, gold, and jewellery) and conspicuous consumption. Capital market raises resources for longer periods of time. Thus it provides an investment avenue for people who wish to invest resources for a long period of time. It provides suitable interest rate or returns to investors. Capital market provides diverse investment avenues for the public through instruments like bonds, equities, units of mutual funds, insurance policies, etc.

3. **Encouragement to Investment:** The capital market facilitates lending to the businessmen and the government and thus encourages investment. It provides facilities through banks and nonbank financial institutions. Various financial assets, *e.g.*, shares, securities, bonds, etc., induce savers to lend to the government or invest in industry. With the development of financial institutions, capital becomes more mobile, interest rate falls and investment increases.

4. **Capital Formation:** Capital formation implies net addition to the existing stock of capital in the economy. When capital market mobilises idle resources, it generates savings and the mobilised savings are made available to various segments such as agriculture, industry, etc. This helps in increasing capital formation through capital market.

5. **Speed up Economic Growth and Development:** The capital market not only reflects the general condition of the economy, but also smoothens and accelerates the process of economic growth. Various institutions of the capital market, like nonbank financial intermediaries, allocate the resources rationally in accordance with the development needs of the country. The proper allocation of resources results in the expansion of trade and industry in both public and private sectors, thus promoting balanced economic growth in the country. Thus, Capital market enhances production and productivity in the national economy, as it makes funds available for long period of time. It also helps in research and development. This helps in increasing production and productivity in economy by generation of employment and development of infrastructure.

6. **Proper Regulation of Funds:** Capital markets not only helps in fund mobilisation, but it also helps in proper allocation of these resources. It can have regulation over the resources so that it can direct funds in a qualitative manner.

7. **Stability in Security Prices:** The capital market tends to stabilise the values of stocks and securities and reduce the fluctuations in the prices to the minimum. The process of stabilisation is facilitated by providing capital to the borrowers at a lower interest rate and reducing the speculative and unproductive activities.

8. **Benefits to Investors:** The credit market helps the investors, i.e., those who have funds to invest in long-term financial assets, in many ways:

   • It brings together the buyers and sellers of securities and thus ensures the marketability of investments,

   • By advertising security prices, the Stock Exchange enables the investors to keep track of their investments and channelize them into most profitable lines,

   • It safeguards the interests of the investors by compensating them from the Stock Exchange Compensating Fund in the event of fraud and default.

9. **Service Provision:** As an important financial set up, the capital market provides various types of services. It includes long-term and medium-term loans to industry, underwriting services, consultancy services, export finance, etc. These services help the manufacturing sector in a wide spectrum.

To conclude, the role and importance of capital market:

• Capital market plays an extremely important role in promoting and sustaining the growth of an economy.

• It plays a critical role in mobilising savings for investment in productive assets, and thus acts as a major catalyst in transforming the economy into a more efficient, innovative and competitive marketplace within the global arena.

• Capital markets also provide a medium for risk management by allowing the diversification of risk in the economy.

• Capital market has played a crucial role in supporting periods of technological progress and economic development throughout history.

• The existence of deep and broad capital market is absolutely crucial and critical in spurring the growth our country.

• An essential imperative for India has been to develop its capital market to provide alternative sources of funding for companies and thus achieve a more effective mobilisation of investors' savings.

• Capital market also provides a valuable source of external finance. For a long time, the Indian market was considered too small to attract much attention. However, this view has changed rapidly as vast amounts of international investment have poured into our markets over the last decade. The Indian market provides attractive opportunities to the global investing community.

- It facilitates and promotes the process of economic growth in the country by diverting the resources in productive channels.

Thus capital market definitely plays a constructive role in the overall development of an economy. The lack of an advanced and vibrant capital market can lead to underutilisation of financial resources.

Stock Exchanges in India

Let us first know what is meant by – (a) Stock Markets; (b) Stock Exchanges.

(a) Stock Markets: Stock Market is a market where the trading of company stock, both listed securities and unlisted takes place. It is different from stock exchange because it includes all the national stock exchanges of the country. For example, we use the term, "the stock market bubble" has busted.

(b) Stock Exchanges: Stock Exchanges are an organised market place, either corporation or mutual organisation, where members of the organisation gather to trade company stocks or other securities. The members may act either as agents for their customers, or as principals for their own accounts. Stock exchanges also facilitate the issue and redemption of securities and other financial instruments including the payment of income and dividends. The record keeping is central but trade is linked to such physical place because modern markets are computerised. The trade on an exchange is done only by members and stock brokers who have a seat on the exchange.

The BSE and NSE: Most of the trading in the Indian stock market takes place on two stock exchanges: the Bombay Stock Exchange (BSE) and the National Stock Exchange (NSE). The BSE has been in existence since 1875. On the other hand, the NSE was founded in 1992 and started trading in 1994. Both the exchanges follow the same trading mechanism, trading hours, settlement process etc. At the last count, the BSE had about 4,700 listed firms, whereas the NSE had about 1,200. Out of all the listed firms on the BSE, only about 500 firms constitute more than 90% of its market capitalisation; the rest of them consist of highly illiquid shares.

On both the exchanges almost all the significant firms of India are listed. NSE enjoys a dominant share in spot trading, with about 70% of the market share (2009) and almost a complete monopoly in derivatives trading, with about 98% share in this market (2009). Both exchanges compete for the order flow that leads to reduced costs, market efficiency and innovation. The presence of arbitrageurs keeps the prices on the two stock exchanges within a very tight range.

Trading Mechanism at both the exchanges takes place through an open electronic limit order book, in which order matching is done by the trading computer. There are no specialists or market-makers and the entire process is order-driven, which means that the market orders placed by investors are automatically matched with the best limit orders. Hence, the buyers and sellers remain anonymous. The advantage of such an order-driven market is that it brings more transparency, by displaying all buy and sell orders in the trading system. In the absence of market makers, however, there is no guarantee that orders will be executed. All orders in the trading system need to be placed through brokers, many of which provide online trading facility to retail customers. Institutional investors can also take advantage of the direct market access (DMA) option. In this option they use trading terminals provided by brokers for placing orders directly into the stock market trading system.

Trading Hours and Settlement cycle: Equity spot markets follow a T+2 rolling settlement, which implies that any trade taking place on Monday gets settled by Wednesday. All trading on stock exchanges takes place between 09:15 AM and 3:30 PM, IST (GMT+ 5.5 hours), Monday to Friday. It is essential that delivery of shares must be made in dematerialised form, and each exchange has its own clearing house, which assumes all settlement risk, by serving as a central counterparty.

Hours of Operation.

Session	Timing
Pre-open trading session	09:00 – 09:15
Trading Session	09:15 – 15:30
Position Transfer Session	15:30 – 15:50
Closing Session	15:50 – 16:05

The two prominent **Indian Market Indices** are: Sensex and Nifty. Sensex is the oldest market index for equities; it includes shares of 30 firms listed on the BSE, which represent about 45% of the index's free-float market capitalisation. It was created in 1986 and provides time series data from April 1979 onward. Another index is the Nifty, which includes 50 shares listed on the NSE and represents about 62% of its free-float market capitalisation. It was created in 1996 and provides times data from July 1990 onward.

Market Regulation (SEBI): The overall responsibility of development, regulation and supervision of the stock market rests with the Securities and Exchange Board of India (SEBI). It was formed in 1992 as an independent authority. SEBI has consistently tried to lay down market rules in line with the best market practices. In case of a breach SEBI enjoys vast powers of imposing penalties on market participants.

Foreign Investments in India: India started allowing outside investments only in the 1990s. Foreign investments are of two types: (a) Foreign Direct Investment (FDI) and Foreign Portfolio Investment (FPI). FDI implies investments in which an investor takes part in the day-to-day management and operations of the company. On the other hand, FPI implies investments in shares without any control over management and operations.

For making portfolio investment in India, one should be registered either as a foreign institutional investor (FII) or as one of the sub-accounts of one of the registered FIIs. Both registrations are granted by SEBI. FIIs mainly consist of mutual funds, pension funds, endowments, sovereign wealth funds, insurance companies, banks, asset management companies, etc. At present, India does not allow foreign individuals to invest directly into its stock market but high-net-worth individuals – net worth of at least $US50 million- can be registered as sub-accounts of an FII.

FIIs and their sub accounts can invest directly into any of the stocks listed on any of the stock exchanges. They can also invest in unlisted securities outside stock exchanges, subject to approval of the price by the RBI. They can invest in units of mutual funds and derivatives traded on any stock exchange. However, FII's cannot invest or trade in Govt Treasury Bills.

FIIs must invest a minimum of 70% of their investments in equity and the balance of 30% can be invested in debt. Only an FII registered as a debt-only FII can invest 100% of its investment into debt instruments. FIIs must use special non-resident rupee bank accounts to move money in and out of India. The balances held in such an account can be fully repatriated.

Investment Ceilings: The Govt. of India has prescribed the FDI limit and different ceilings for different sectors. The FDI ceilings mostly fall in the range of 26 to 100%. As for the FPI, i.e., portfolio investment, there are two additional restrictions- (i) the aggregate limit of investment by all FIIs, inclusive of their sub-accounts in any particular firm, has been fixed at 24% of the paid-up capital. This can be raised up to the sector cap with the approval of the company's boards and shareholders. (ii) Investment by any single FII in any particular firm should not exceed 10% of the paid-up capital of the company. Regulations allow a separate 10% ceiling on investment for each of the sub-accounts of an FII, in any particular firm. But, in case of foreign corporations or individuals investing as a sub-account, the same ceiling is only 5%.

Investment Opportunities: Foreign entities and individuals can gain access to Indian stock market through institutional investors. Many India-focussed mutual funds are becoming popular among retail investors. There are certain offshore instruments like participatory notes (PNs) and depositary receipts. Investments could also be made through these instruments.

To conclude, emerging markets like India are fast becoming engines for future growth. Currently, only a very low percentage of the household savings of Indians are invested in the domestic stock market, but with GDP growing at 7% to 8% per annum and with a stable financial market, we might see more money joining the race. It's the right time for outside investors to seriously think about joining the Indian bandwagon.

To sum up the Stock Exchanges in India,

National Stock Exchange (NSE): NSE, incorporated in the year 1992, provides trading in the equity as well as debt market. Maximum trading volumes take place on NSE and therefore it enjoys leadership position in the country.

- The NSE is India's leading stock exchange covering 364 cities and towns across the country. NSE was set up by leading institutions to provide a modern, fully automated screen-based trading system with national reach.

- The Exchange has brought about unparalleled transparency, speed and efficiency, safety and market integrity. It has set up facilities that serve as a model for the securities industry in terms of systems, practices and procedures.

- NSE has played a catalytic role in reforming the Indian securities market in terms of microstructure, market practices and trading volumes.

- Today the market uses state-of-art information technology to provide an efficient and transparent trading, clearing and settlement mechanism, and has witnessed several innovations in products and services, such as demutualisation of stock exchange governance, screen based trading, electronic transfer of securities, fine-tuned risk management systems, professionalism of trading members, market of debt and derivative instruments and intensive use of information technology.

- **The NSE was set-up with the following objectives:**
  o Establishing a nation-wide trading facility for equities, debt instruments and hybrids;
  o Ensuring equal access to investors all over the country through an appropriate communication network;
  o Providing a fair, efficient and transparent securities market to investors using electronic trading systems;
  o Enabling shorter settlement cycles and book entry settlement systems; and
  o Meeting the current international standards of securities markets.

- NSE is more than a mere market facilitator. It's that force which is guiding the industry towards new horizons and greater opportunities.

- NSE has been promoted by leading financial institutions, banks, insurance companies and other financial intermediaries

- The NSE model however, does not exclude, but in fact accommodates involvement, support and contribution of trading members in a variety of ways.

- The day-to-day management of the Exchange is delegated to the Managing Director who is supported by a team of professional staff.

Bombay Stock Exchange (BSE): BSE was set up in the year 1875 as "The Native Share and Stock Brokers Association". It is the oldest stock exchange in Asia, older than the Tokyo Stock Exchange (established in 1878). It has evolved in to its present status as the premier stock exchange. BSE has the largest number of scripts which are listed.

BSE is a voluntary non-profit making Association of Persons (AOP) and has converted itself into demutualised and corporate entity. It has evolved over the years into its present status as the Premier Stock Exchange in the country. It was the first Stock Exchange in the country to have obtained permanent recognition in 1956 from the Government of India under the Securities Contracts (Regulation) Act, 1956.

The Exchange, while providing an efficient and transparent market for trading in securities, debt and derivatives upholds the interests of the investors and ensures redressal of their grievances whether against the companies or its own member-brokers. It also strives to educate and enlighten the investors by conducting investor education programmes and making available to them necessary information inputs.

Pune Stock Exchange (PSE): There are many regional stock exchanges in India. The regional stock exchange, i.e., Pune Stock Exchange Limited stands 7th in the country.

- The Exchange was established on 2nd September 1982 to cater to the needs of the growing investor community in the city.
- Beginning small, with 35 members and a few lakhs rupees business to start, the exchange has grown tremendously to over 185 members and undertakes an average of ₹ 15-20 crores of business daily.
- Much of the work is computerised with a smooth settlement system.
- Over 310 companies are listed with the Stock Exchange.
- The Exchange provides an efficient market, upholds investors' interests and ensures redressal of their grievances.
- It strives to educate and enlighten investors by making available necessary information inputs.
- In 1995, PSE opted for the on-line screen-based trading system based on VECTOR (Versatile Engine for Centralised Trading and On-line Reporting).
- The present operations cover 183 broker members and 9 workstations for administration, Market Operations and Surveillance activities of PSE.
- PSE has been looking into the possibilities of widening its activities to different parts of Pune city and to other cities like Satara, Sangli, Solapur, Kolhapur, Ahmednagar, Aurangabad, Nashik and Mumbai.
- Initially the trading was allowed only in the securities which were listed on PSE, but later the trading was also allowed in the securities which were listed on the other stock exchanges, under "Permitted Securities". This increased the turnover substantially.
- From October 1982 to February 1996 the trading was conducted in the traditional fashion, i.e., in the trading ring by way of open cry out system. However, on 15th March 1996 the trading activities were switched over to the most advanced computerised system to fall in the line with the system present in USA and Europe. PSE was the first regional stock exchange to implement the on-line trading system.
- With this new system, the brokers now need not assemble in the trading ring for execution of their orders. They can conduct the trading by sitting in their offices from where their computers are connected to the main computer of the Exchange through

Local Area Network. The orders are compiled by the main system during trading hours and are matched by computers with the principle of "best bid is matched with the best order." The moment trade is matched, it is instantly informed to the members which they can visualise on their computer screens.

- The screen based system has provided transparency to the investors regarding the rates of the securities, the general market trend, liquidity, etc.
- The members are benefitted as far as their data regarding pending orders, day-to-day position about the business recorded since it is being generated expeditiously through the system.

Securities and Exchange Board of India (SEBI)

For the smooth functioning of the capital market a proper coordination among different organisations and segments is a pre-requisite. In order to regulate, promote and direct the progress of the Indian Capital Market, the government has set up "Securities and Exchange Board of India" (SEBI). SEBI is the supreme authority governing and regulating the Capital Market of India. Thus, the Securities and Exchange Board of India, abbreviated SEBI, is the regulator for the securities market in India. It was officially established by the Government of India in the year 1988 and given statutory powers on 12 April 1992 through the SEBI Act, on the recommendations of the Narasimham Committee. SEBI has it's Headquarter at the business district of Bandra-Kurla Complex in Mumbai, and has Northern, Eastern, Southern and Western Regional Offices in New Delhi, Kolkata, Chennai and Ahmedabad respectively.

Initially, SEBI was a non-statutory body without any statutory power but in the year 1995, the SEBI was given additional power by the Government of India through an amendment to the SEBI Act 1992. The role of SEBI in regulating Indian capital market is very important because Government of India can only open or take decision to open new stock exchange in India after getting advice from SEBI. If SEBI thinks that it will be against its rules and regulations, SEBI can ban any stock exchange from trading in shares and stocks.

SEBI has to be responsible to the needs of three groups, which constitute the market: (a) the issuers of securities; (b) the investors; (c) the market intermediaries.

SEBI has three functions rolled into one body: Quasi-legislative; Quasi-judicial and Quasi-executive.

Purposes/Aims of SEBI:

- Registering and regulating the working of stock brokers and other intermediaries associated with the securities market.
- Regulating the business in stock markets and other securities markets.
- Registering and regulating the working of collective investment schemes including mutual funds.
- Prohibiting insider trading in securities.
- Prohibiting fraudulent and unfair trade practices relating to securities market.

- To provide license to brokers for activities in stock exchanges in India.
- To make rules and regulations for controlling the stock exchanges in India.
- To make amendments in the rules and regulations of stock exchanges in India.
- To encourage foreign investors to investment in India.
- To safeguard the interests of investors.
- To develop the stock and share market in India.
- To reduce the fluctuations in the market prices of shares.
- To create good relationships among the large numbers of brokers, finance agents and financers.

For the discharge of its functions efficiently, SEBI has been vested with wide-ranging Powers

- To approve bye-laws of stock exchanges;
- To require the stock exchange to amend their bye-laws;
- Inspect the books of accounts and call for periodical returns from recognized stock exchanges;
- Inspect the books of accounts of a financial intermediaries;
- Compel certain companies to list their shares in one or more stock exchanges;
- Levy fees and other charges on the intermediaries for performing its functions;
- Grant license to any person for the purpose of dealing in certain areas;
- Delegate powers exercisable by it;
- Prosecute and judge directly the violation of certain provisions of the Companies Act;
- Power to impose monetary penalties.

Achievements of SEBI

SEBI has enjoyed success as a regulator by pushing systematic reforms aggressively and successively. SEBI is credited for quick movement by making the markets electronic and paperless. This has been possible by introducing T+5 rolling cycle from July 2001 and T+3 in April 2002 and further to T+2 in April 2003. The rolling cycle of T+2 implies settlement is done in 2 days after Trade date. SEBI has been active in setting up the regulations according to the law. SEBI has been instrumental in taking quick and effective steps in light of the global meltdown and the Satyam failure. In light of the global meltdown, it liberalised the takeover code to facilitate investments by removing regulatory structures. At present SEBI has increased the application limit for retail investors to ₹ 2 lakh from 1 lakh. In the light of Satyam fiasco, in October 2011, it increased the extent and quantity of disclosures to be made by Indian corporate promoters.

SEBI is the regulator to control Indian capital market. Since its establishment in 1992, it has been working hard to protect the interests of Indian investors. SEBI has learnt from past incidents of cheating with naive investors of India such as that were precipitated by Stock brokers like Harshad Mehta and Ketan Parekh. Now, SEBI is stricter with those who commit frauds in capital market.

Points to Remember

- The **Indian money market** comprises – organised sector and unorganised sector. While the organised sector comes under the direct regulation of RBI, the unorganised sector comprises of indigenous bankers, money lenders and unregulated non-banking financial institution.

- There are **two types of financial markets** viz., the money market and the capital market. The money market is that part of a financial market which deals in the borrowing and lending of short-term loans generally for a period of one day to one year.

- Some of the **important players in the money market are:** (i) Government; (ii) Reserve Bank of India; (iii) Discount and Finance House of India; (iv) Banks; (v) Financial Institutions; (vi) Corporate Firms; (vii) Mutual funds; (viii) Non-Banking Finance Companies; (ix) Primary Dealers; (x) Securities Trading Corporation of India; (xi) Provident Funds; (xii) Public Sector Undertakings.

- **Functions of Money Market:** Financing trade; Financing Industry; Self-sufficiency of commercial Bank; Profitable Investment; Help to central Bank.

- **Instruments of Money Market:** Call Money and Notice Money Market; treasury Bills Market; Commercial bills; Certificates of Deposits; Commercial papers; Repos and reverse Repos; Money Market Mutual Funds.

- **Instruments of Unorganised sector:** indigenous bankers; money lenders; unregulated non-bank financial intermediaries.

- **Reforms in Indian Money Market:** Deregulation of interest rates; introduction of new money market instruments; reduction in CRR and SLR; development of inter-bank call and notice money market; minimum lock-in period.

- **RBI:** Note issue; Banker's Bank; Banker to Government; Custodian of Exchange reserves; controller or credit; agricultural finance; promotional and developmental functions.

- **Two types of financial institutions:** banking and non-banking.

- The capital market is a market for financial assets which have a long or indefinite maturity.

- Capital market consists of financial institutions like IDBI, ICICI, UTI, LIC, etc.

- Most of the trading in the Indian stock market takes place on two stock exchanges: the Bombay Stock Exchange (BSE) and the National Stock Exchange (NSE).

- For the smooth functioning of the capital market a proper coordination among different organisations and segments is a pre-requisite. In order to regulate, promote and direct the progress of the Indian Capital Market, the government has set up "Securities and Exchange Board of India" (SEBI).

Questions for Discussion

1. What do you mean by Money Market?
2. Explain Money Market with the help of different definitions.
3. Illustrate with flow-chart the structure of Indian Money Market.
4. Write short notes on: (a) Organised Sector of Indian Money Market; (b) Unorganised Sector of Indian Money Market.
5. Write in detail the functions/role of Money Market.
6. Which are the various instruments used in Indian Money Market?
7. Explain the main components of unorganised money market.
8. Describe the drawbacks of Indian Money Market.
9. What are the various reforms that have taken place in Indian Money Market over the years?
10. Write a note on Reserve Bank of India.
11. Write in detail the functions of the RBI.
12. Explain the relation of RBI with reference to – (a) Currency; (b) Credit Control; (c) Balance of Payment.
13. Explain the meaning of Capital Market. Discuss its role and functions.
14. With the help of flow-chart, explain the structure of Indian Money Market.
15. Write a note on Primary and Secondary Market.
16. Write a detail note on SEBI.
17. Describe the Stock Exchanges in India.

Objective Questions

1. State whether the statement is true or false:

    (a) The Indian money market comprises of organised and unorganised sector.

    (b) Indian money market is a well-developed money market.

    (c) RBI is the apex institution that controls and monitors all organisations in the organised sector of the money market.

    (d) Money market enables commercial banks to use their excess reserves in profitable investments.

    (e) There is no diversity in rates of interest in the Indian money market.

    [Ans.: (a) True, (b) False, (c) True, (d) True, (e) False]

2. Choose the correct alternative:

    (i) Repo is a transaction from the _____ point of view.

    (a) seller's (b) buyer's (c) nation's (d) none of the above.

(ii) Moneylenders is component of ____ market.

(a) capital (b) money (c) organised money (d) unorganised money.

(iii) Money market deals in highly ____ financial instruments.

(a) Liquid (b) illiquid (c) capital (d) none of the above

(iv) RBI has the monopoly of ____ issue in the country.

(a) Currency (b) note (c) gold (d) all of the above.

(v) The overall responsibility of development, regulation and supervision of the stock market rests with ____

(a) Indian money market (b) Indian capital market (c) SEBI (d) none of the above

[Ans.: (i) (a), (ii) (d), (iii) (a), (iv) (b), (v) (c)]

■■■

Chapter 5...

Public Finance Infrastructure

Contents ...

Learning Objectives ...

➢ To learn the various terms and concepts of National Income

➢ To familiarise with the practices related to National Income

➢ To understand the organisation operating at global level

➢ To have knowledge about GATT and WTO

➢ To have knowledge about the Union Budget

➢ To know the components of revenue account, capital account

➢ To know about the fiscal deficit

➢ To know the various plan and non-plan expenditure of government

5.1 Introduction

The economy of India is the tenth-largest in the world by nominal Gross Domestic Product (GDP) and third-largest by Purchasing Power Parity (PPP). India is one of the G-20 major economies and a member of BRICS. According to the IMF, on per capita income (PCI) basis, India ranked 141st by nominal GDP and 130th by GDP (PPP) in 2012. India is the 19th largest exporter and the 10th largest importer in the world. In the fiscal year 2011-12 with economic growth rate was 6.2% which slowed down to 5.0% for the 2012-13 fiscal year. India's GDP grew by an astounding 9.3% in 2010-11 and in three years it has halved down. The government has forecasted a growth of 6.1% to 6.7% for the year 2013-14, whilst the RBI expects the same to be at 5.7%.

The independence-era Indian economy, from 1947 to 1991, was based on a mixed economy concept combining features of capitalism and socialism, resulting in inward-looking interventionist policies and import-substituting economy. However, in 1991, India adopted liberal and free-market principles and liberalised its economy to international trade under the guidance of Shri. Manmohan Singh, the then finance minister from 30th November 2009 to 24 January 2010 and previously under the leadership of P. V. Narsimha Rao, Prime Minister from 1991 to 1996, who eliminated License Raj. Following major economic reforms, and a strong focus on developing national infrastructure such as Golden Quadrilateral project under Mr. Vajpayee, the country's economic growth progressed at a rapid pace, with relatively large increases in per capita incomes.

5.2 National Income

The concept of national income occupies an important place in economic theory. National income is the flow of goods and services which become available to a nation during a year. National income is the aggregate money value of all goods and services produced in a country during one year and deductions made due to wear and tear, depreciation of plants and machinery used in plants to be considered.

According to **A. C. Pigou**, *"the national dividend (national income) is that part of the objective income of the community including, of course, income derived from abroad, which can be measured in money."*

In the words of **Prof. Marshall**, *"The labour and capital of a country, acting upon its natural resources, produce annually a certain net aggregate of commodities, material and immaterial, including services of all kinds. The word 'net' provides for using up of raw and half-finished goods and for wearing out and depreciation of plant which is involved in production; all such waste be deducted from the gross produce before the net income can be found. And net income due on account of foreign investments must be added in. This is the true net annual income or revenue of the country, or the national dividend."*

Elements of National Income:

(i)   National income refers to the income of a country, say, India.

(ii) National income includes all types of goods and services which have an exchange value, counting each one of them *only once*.

Thus, *national income is the aggregate money value of all goods and services produced in a country during a year, avoiding double or multiple counting.*

According to **Prof. J. R.Hicks**, *"the national income consists of a collection of goods and serviced reduced to a common basis by being measured in terms of money."* The total volume of production is then, expressed as a sum of money.

Terms/Concepts of National Income

Gross National Product (GNP): "It is the total market value of all final goods and services produced in a year". GNP is a *monetary* measure because there is no other way of adding up the heterogeneous variety of goods and services produced in a year. While calculating GNP multiple or double-counting must be avoided by using market value of *final* goods only and ignore intermediate goods.

GNP at market price (GNP_{mp}) can be obtained by adding:-

(a) Private consumption expenditure

(b) Gross domestic private investment

(c) Government expenditure on goods and services

(d) Net foreign earnings.

Net National Product (NNP_{mp}): In the production of GNP during a year, we use some capital. The capital goods like plant and machinery wear out or depreciate in value. All this is *depreciation*. When we *minus* depreciation charges from GNP_{mp} we get NNP_{mp}.

$$NNP_{mp} = GNP_{mp} - D \text{ (Where D is the Depreciation)}$$

National Income at Factor Cost: It means sum of all incomes earned by factors of production for their contribution in production of net output. In fact, National Income actually means national income at factor cost.

National Income at market price includes *indirect taxes* and *subsidies*, while NNP at factor cost excludes indirect taxes.

Example: A bottle of syrup is produced at the cost of ₹ 14 in a factory. When it is sold in the market indirect taxes are added and hence the price is now ₹ 16 (₹ 14 +2) per bottle. Thus, **NNP_{fc} + Indirect taxes = NNP_{mp}. (NNP_{fc} is NNP at factor Cost)**

On the other hand, if a subsidy is applied by the government, the subsidy causes the market price to fall. The factors are paid ₹ 14 to produce a bottle of syrup. But, in the market, government sells it at ₹ 12. Thus, the burden of ₹ 2 is borne by the government. In such a case **NNP_{fc} – Subsidies = NNP_{mp}.**

Conversely, National Income or NNP_{fc} is minus indirect taxes plus subsidies.

i.e. $NNP_{fc} = NNP_{mp}$ – Indirect taxes

Or $NNP_{fc} = NNP_{mp}$ + Subsidies

Personal Income (P.I.): P.I. is the sum of all incomes actually received by all individuals or households during a given year.

Thus, **P.I. = N.I. – Social security contributions– Corporate Income taxes– Undistributed Corporate Profits + Transfer Payments.** (Personal Income equals to National Income minus social security contributions minus corporate income taxes minus undistributed corporate profits plus transfer payments).

Disposable Personal Income (D.P.I.): After we deduct personal taxes like income tax and personal property taxes from Personal Income we obtain D.P.I.

Thus, **D.P.I. = P.I. – Personal taxes (direct taxes).**

Gross Domestic Product (GDP): GDP is the *market value* of all officially recognised *final* goods and services produced within a country in a given period of time.

- "The monetary value of all the finished goods and services produced within a country's borders in a specific time period, though GDP is usually calculated on an annual basis. It includes all of private and public consumption, government outlays, investments and exports less imports that occur within a defined territory".

- Symbolically, **GDP = C + G + I + (X-M)**

  Where, C = all private consumption, or consumer spending, in a nation's economy; G = sum of government spending; I = sum of all the country's businesses spending on investment goods; (X-M) = the nation's total 'net' exports, calculated as total exports minus total imports.

- "*Gross*" means that GDP measures production regardless of the various uses to which that production can be put to. Production can be used for immediate consumption, for investment in new fixed assets or inventories, or for replacing depreciated fixed assets. "*Domestic*" means that GDP measures production that takes place within the country's borders. In the equation given above, the 'exports minus imports' term is necessary in order to null out expenditures on things not produced in the country (imports) and add things in things produced but not sold in the country (exports).

- GDP is commonly used as an indicator of the economic health of a country, as well as to gauge of a nation's standard of living. Thus, GDP is one of the primary indicators used to gauge the health of a country's economy. It represents the total rupee value of all goods and services produced over a specific time period. Usually, GDP is expressed as a comparison to the previous year. For example, if the year-to-year GDP increases by 3%, it means that the economy has grown by 3% over the last year.

- To the use of GDP as an economic measure, critics point out that the statistics do not consider the underground economy – transactions that are not reported to the government. It is also pointed out that GDP is not intended to gauge material well-being, but serves as a measure of a nation's productivity, which is unrelated.

- Measuring GDP is complicated but its calculation can be done in one of the three ways, all of which should, in principle, give the same result. They are the product (or output) approach, the income approach and the expenditure approach.

- The most direct of the three is the *product approach*, which totals the outputs of every class of enterprise to arrive at that total. The expenditure approach adds up what everyone has spent. The principle is that all of the product must be bought by somebody; hence the value of the total product must be equal to people's total expenditures in buying things. The income approach adds up what everyone has earned in a year. The principle is that the incomes of the productive factors must be equal to the value of their product, and determines GDP by finding the sum of incomes of all the producers.

- The Income Approach is also referred to as GDP (I) and is calculated by adding up total compensation to employees, gross profits for incorporated and non-corporate firms, and taxes less any subsidies. However, Expenditure Approach is the more common measure and is calculated by adding total consumption, investment, government spending and net exports.

- GDP may represent economic production or economic growth; it has deep impact on nearly everyone within that economy. For example, when the economy is healthy, it implies low unemployment, wages increase as businesses demand labour to meet the growing ·economy. Further, a significant change (rise or fall) in GDP usually has a remarkable effect on the stock market. A bad economy usually means lower profits for companies, which in turn means lower stock prices. A negative GDP growth is one of the factors that economists use to determine whether an economy is in recession.

- GDP measures national income and output for a given country's economy. GDP in India is reported by the World Bank Group. The GDP in India was worth 1847.98 billion US dollars in 2011. The GDP value of India represents 2.98 per cent of the world economy. Historically, from 1960 until 2011, India's GDP averaged 368.8 USD Billion, reaching an all time high of 1848.0 USD billion in December 2011 and a record low of 36.6 USD billion in December of 1960.

- The factor used to convert GDP from current to constant values is called as the GDP deflator. Unlike consumer price index (CPI) which measures inflation or deflation in the price of household consumer goods, the GDP deflator measures changes in the prices of all domestically produced goods and services in an economy including investment goods and government services and household consumption goods.

- The level of GDP in different countries may be compared by converting their value in national currency according to either the current currency exchange rate, or the purchasing power parity exchange rate.

Case Study (Why should policymakers care about GDP – Who wins at the Olympics?)

Every 4 years, the nations of the world compete in the Olympic Games. When the games end, commentators use the number of medals a nation takes home as a measure of success. This measure seems very different from the GDP that economists use to measure success. However, this is not so. Economists Andrew Bernard and Meghan Busse examined the determinants of Olympic success in a study published in the Review of Economics and Statistics in 2004. The most natural explanation is population: countries with more population, other things being equal, have more star athletes. But this is not the full story. India, China, Bangladesh, Pakistan together have more than 40 percent of the world's population, but they typically win only 6 percent of the medals. The reason is that these countries are poor. Despite their large populations, they account for only 5 percent of the world's GDP. Their poverty prevents many gifted athletes from reaching their potential.

Andrew and Meghan find that the best gauge of a nation's ability to produce world-class athletes is total GDP. A large total GDP means more medals, regardless of whether the total comes from high GDP per person or a large number of people. It implies, if two nations have the same total GDP, they can be expected to win the same number of medals, even if one nation (India) has many people and low GDP per person and the other nation (Netherlands) has few people and high GDP per person.

In addition to GDP, two other factors influence the number of medals won. The host country usually earns extra medals, reflecting the benefit that the athletes get from competing on their home turf. Another, the Centrally planned economies like the former communist countries of Eastern Europe, devoted more of the nation's resources to training Olympic athletes than did free-market economies, where people have more control over their own lives.

(**Source:** Principles of Macroeconomics – Mankiw).

Per Unit GDP: GDP is an aggregate figure which does not consider difference in sizes of nations. Therefore, GDP can be stated as GDP per capita (per person) in which total GDP is divided by the resident population on a given date. GDP per capita is not a measure of personal income. GDP per citizen is where total GDP is divided by the numbers of citizens residing in the country on a given date. GDP per citizen is pretty similar to GDP per capita in most nations, however, in nations with very high proportions of temporary foreign workers like in Persian Gulf nations, the two figures – GDP per capita and GDP per citizen – may differ vastly.

Methods of Computing GDP

1. Production Approach: (Inventory Method):

- It is the *market value* of all final goods and services calculated during one year.
- The Production approach is also called Net Product or Value added method.
- This method consists of three stages: (i) Estimating the Gross Value of domestic Output out of the many various economic activities; (ii) Determining the 'intermediate' consumption, i.e., the cost of material, supplies and services used to produce the final goods or services; and finally (iii) Deducting intermediate consumption (Depreciation) from Gross Value to obtain the Net value of Domestic Output.

- Symbolically,

  Net Value Added = Gross Value of Output – Value of Intermediate Consumption.

  Value of Output = Value of the total sales of goods and services + Value of changes in the inventories.

  The sum of Net Value Added in various economic activities is known as GDP at factor cost.

  GDP at factor cost + indirect taxes – subsidies on products is GDP at Producer Price (GDP at Market price).

- For measuring 'gross' output of domestic product, economic activities (i.e. industries) are classified into various sectors – Primary Sector (includes agriculture and allied activities), Secondary Sector (includes manufacturing units) and Tertiary Sector (includes services like banking, insurance, transport, trade). These sectors are further divided into sub-sectors and each sub-sector is further divided into commodity group or service group.

- For an individual unit, we subtract the amount of depreciation from gross output to get net production value added by each unit. By adding net products of all the sub-sectors, we get Net Domestic Product (NDP).

- The final output and intermediate goods is available in terms of market prices and then by subtracting indirect taxes we get NDP at factor costs.

- If we add or subtract net income from abroad, we get Net National Product (NNP) at factor costs which is nothing but National Income.

- **Precautions to be taken in this method:** (a) own account production of fixed assets by government enterprises and households, (b) production for self-consumption, (c) imputed rent of owner occupied houses. All these are not to be counted. Care is to be taken that sale of second-hand machines is not included as they were counted as a part production in the year which they were produced.

- **Difficulties faced in this approach:** The main difficulty is that large areas of production activities are excluded for different reasons. (a) their net product cannot be valued either because there is no acceptable way of valuing them, such as services of housewives or self-services in home or services of friends; (b) difficulty of securing data of subsistence producing units, particularly in under-developed countries; (c) adequate data regarding output, raw material etc., are not often available from many proprietorships, non-profit institutions, partnerships and governments; (d) difficult to ascertain the actual amount of depreciation as fall in the value of Capital stock depends upon many factors which are difficult to measure; (e) lack of adequate and reliable data particularly in under-developed countries.

2. **Income Approach:**

- It is the sum total of incomes of individuals living in a country during one year.

- Another way of measuring GDP is to measure total income and it is referred to as Gross Domestic Income (GDI) or GDP (I). GDI should provide the same amount as the expenditure method and by definition GDI = GDP.

- The incomes accruing to all the factors of production during the process of production are aggregated together to arrive at the national income of the country. This is known as *national income at factor cost.*

- The various factors of production are paid remuneration for the services rendered by them in production. These payments are known as factor payments. They represent the costs of the producers. For the factors of production they constitute factor-incomes which have to be totalled to estimate the national income of the country.

- Thus, in income approach, the national product is obtained by adding up the factor-incomes accruing to the concerned factors during the process of production.

- National Income by Income Method is computed as follows:

  N. I. (NNP at factor cost) = Rent + Wages + Interest + Profit

  + Undistributed profits of joint stock of companies

  + Income from government property

  + Profit from public sector undertakings

  + Direct taxes on companies

  + Net income from abroad

- Transfer payments, government subsidies to business firms and indirect business taxes

- Depreciation

  N.I. (NNP at factor cost) = R + W + I + P + G + (X – M)

  i.e. Rent + Wages + Interest + Profit + Government (Income from govt. property and Profits from public enterprises) + Net income from abroad (X-M).

- This method of estimating national income has the advantage of indicating the distribution of national income among the different income groups such as landlords, capitalists, labourers etc. Hence, it is called as *'national income by distributive shares.'*

- Two adjustments must be made to get GDP: (i) Indirect taxes minus subsidies are added to get from factor cost to market prices; (ii) Depreciation is added to get from NDP to get GDP.

3. Expenditure Method

- In this method it is the sum of all expenditures incurred by individuals during one year.

- In economics, most things produced are produced for sale and are sold. Therefore, measuring the total expenditure of money used to buy things is a way of measuring production. This is expenditure method of calculating GDP.

- Income can be spent either on consumer goods or investment goods, i.e. consumption expenditure or investment expenditure. To the private expenditure on consumer and investment goods, we add government expenditure, i.e., government's purchases of goods and services. Lastly, we add net foreign investments.

- GDP = Consumption expenditure + Investment expenditure + government expenditure + Net exports.

$$Y = C + I + G + (X\text{-}M)$$

- **C = (Consumption):** Consumption is normally the largest GDP component in the economy, consisting of private household final consumption expenditure. These personal expenditures include durable goods, non-durable goods, and services. Examples are food, jewellery, gasoline, medical expenses, rent. It does not include purchase of new housing.

- **I = (Investment):** It includes spending by private firms/entrepreneurs on renewal, replacement, new investments, i.e. depreciation, inventory, new capital assets etc. This is domestic private investment expenditure. Thus, it includes business investment in equipment but does not include exchanges of existing assets. For example, construction of a new factory, purchase of software, or purchase of machinery and equipment. Spending by households, not government spending, on new houses is also included in Investment. 'Investment' in GDP does not mean purchases of financial products. Spending on financial products is grouped as 'saving' which is opposite of investment. This avoids double-counting – if one buys shares in a company (savings) and the company uses the money received to buy equipment etc., (investment) the amount will be counted towards GDP, when the company spends the money on investment; and if we also count it when one gives it to the company it would be to count twice an amount that only corresponds to one group of products. Buying of financial products like bonds or stocks is a swapping of deeds, a transfer of claims on future production, not directly an expenditure on products.

- **G = (Government Spending):** It is the sum of government expenditures on final goods and services. It includes salaries of public servants, purchase of weapons for the military, and any investment expenditure by a government. It does not include any transfer payments, such as social security or unemployment benefits.

- **X = (Exports):** It represents gross exports. GDP captures the amount a country produces, including goods and services produced for other nations' consumption, therefore exports are added.
- **M = (Imports):** It represents gross imports. Imports are subtracted since imported goods will be included in the terms G, I or C and must be deducted to avoid counting foreign supply as domestic.
- Add to the domestic expenditure what the foreign countries spend on the goods and services of the national economy and what this country spends on goods and services of the foreign countries, i.e. exports minus imports (X-M). This is called *net exports*.

  Thus, GDP = final consumption expenditure (C) + gross capital formation (I) + (G) + net exports (X-M).

  Y = C + I + G + (X-M).(Y = National Income).
- Net National Income at factor cost = (NNP at factor cost) =

      Total private consumption expenditure

  +   Total private investment expenditure

  +   Total government expenditure on consumption and investment goods +

  +   Exports Imports + Subsidies – Indirect taxes + Depreciation.
- Note that C, G and I are expenditures on *final* goods and services; expenditures on *intermediate* goods and services do not count. (Intermediate goods and services are those that are used by businesses to produce other goods and services within the accounting year).

Illustrations of GDP component variables- C, I, G, (X-M):

Let us understand the inclusion and exclusion of GDP component variables.

- If an individual spends money to renovate a hotel to increase occupancy rates, the spending represents private investment and will be included in measurement of GDP in 'I' component, but if he buys shares in a consortium to execute the renovation, it is a saving and it is not included in GDP measurement. However, when the consortium conducted its own expenditure on renovation, that expenditure would be included in GDP.
- If a hotel is a private home, spending for renovation would be measured as consumption, but if a government agency converts the hotel into an office for civil servants, the spending would be included in the government spending, i.e.,'G'.
- If the renovation involves the purchase of an art piece from abroad, that spending would be counted as C, G, or I – depends whether it is private, government or a business investment of renovation. But then counted again as an import and subtracted from the GDP so that GDP counts only those goods produced within the country.
- If a domestic producer makes that art piece for a foreign hotel and is paid for it, then this payment would not be counted as C, G, or I, but would be counted as an export.

One of the basic questions that must be addressed in preparing the national economic accounts is how to define the production boundary, i.e., what part of the human activities are to be included in or excluded from the measure of the economic production.

"Market output" is defined as that which is sold for 'economically significant' prices. (Here, significant prices imply prices which have a significant influence on the amounts producers are willing to supply and purchasers wish to buy). An exception is that illegal goods and services are excluded even if they are sold at economically significant prices.

Non-market output is partly excluded and partly included. For example, the growth of trees in an uncultivated forest is not included in production, but the harvesting of the trees from that forest is included. Thus, natural processes without human involvement are excluded but there must be a person or an institution to compensate for the product.

The exclusion and inclusion is further limited by 'functional considerations'. Production that is difficult to value in an economically meaningful way, i.e. difficult to put price-tag is excluded. For example, services provided by people to members of their own families free of charge, such as meal preparation, cleaning, emotional support, care of elderly.

Non-market outputs that are included within the measurement are those which do not have market price but compilers of GDP must impute a value to them, either by the cost of the goods and services used to produce them or the value of a similar item that is sold in the market.

These items are- (i) goods and services produced for own-use by firms are attempted to be included, such as machine constructed by an engineering firm for use in its own plant. (ii) Goods and services provided by government and non-profit organisations free of charge or for economically insignificant prices are included. The value of these goods and services is estimated as equal to their cost of production. For example, government-provided clean water confers substantial benefits above its cost. (iii) Renovations and upkeep by an individual to a home that the individual owns and occupies are included. The value of upkeep is estimated as the rent that the individual could charge for the home if the individual did not occupy it himself. (iv) Agricultural production set aside for self-consumption is included. (v) Services, such as account maintenance and service to borrowers, provided by banks and other financial institutions without charge or for a fee that does not reflect their full value have a value imputed to them by the compilers and are included.

To conclude, of all the above three approaches/practices, it is the output and income method which is largely used. However, in developed countries the income method is extensively used. The expenditure method is difficult to use as there are certain practical difficulties involved in obtaining reliable information of the total expenditure. Whatever may be the method followed for the computation of the GNP, with appropriate adjustments all the three methods should give nearly the same results. The ideal way to arrive at national income will be to employ all these three methods. This would allow cross-checking and ensure greater accuracy.

Externalities

GDP is widely used by economists to measure economic recession and recovery and an economy's general monetary ability to address externalities. However, GDP is not meant to measure externalities, instead it is a neutral measure which merely shows an economy's general ability to pay for externalities such as social and environmental concerns. Examples of externalities include:

(a) **Wealth distribution:** GDP does not account for income inequality of various demographic groups.

(b) **Non-Market transactions:** GDP excludes activities that are not provided through the market, such as household production and volunteer or unpaid services and hence GDP is understated.

(c) **Underground economy:** Official GDP estimates may not take into account the underground economy, in which transactions contributing to production, such as illegal trade and tax avoiding activities, are unreported, causing GDP to be underestimated.

(d) **Asset Value:** GDP does not take into consideration the value of all assets in an economy. It is just like ignoring a company's balance sheet and judging it solely on the basis of its income statement.

(e) **Non-monetary economy:** GDP omits economies where no money comes into play at all, resulting in inaccurate or abnormally low GDP figures. For example, bartering may be more prominent than the use of money. GDP also ignores subsistence production.

(f) **Quality improvements and inclusion of new products:** True economic growth is understated by GDP when it does not adjust for quality improvements and new products. For example, although mobile phones today are less expensive and more featured than mobile phones from the past, GDP treats them as the same product by only accounting for the monetary value.

(g) **What is being produced:** GDP counts work that produces no 'net' change or that result from repairing harm. For instance, rebuilding after a natural disaster may produce a considerable amount of economic activity and thus boost GDP. The economic value of health care is another classic example – it may raise GDP if many people are sick and they are receiving expensive treatment, but it is not a desirable situation.

(h) **Sustainability of growth:** GDP is a measurement of economic historic activity and is not necessarily a projection. A country may achieve a temporarily high GDP from use of natural resources or by misallocating investment.

(i) **Nominal GDP:** Nominal GDP does not measure variations in purchasing power or costs of living by area, so when the GDP figure is deflated overtime, GDP growth can vary greatly depending on the basket of goods used and the relative proportions used to deflate the GDP figure.

(j) **Cross-border comparisons of GDP:** These comparisons can be inaccurate as they do not consider local differences in the quality of goods, even when adjusted for purchasing power parity. This type of adjustment to an exchange rate is controversial due to the difficulties of finding comparable baskets of goods to compare purchasing power across countries. For example, people in country X may consume the same number of locally produced oranges as in country Y, but oranges in country X are of a more tasty variety. This difference in material well being will not show up in GDP statistics.

Growth Rate

Growth rate implies the amount of increase that a specific variable has gained within a specific period and context. For investors, this typically represents the compounded annualised rate of growth of a company's revenues, earnings, dividends and even macro concepts – such as the economy as a whole. Expected forward-looking or trailing growth rates are two common kinds of growth rates used for analysis.

Growth rate may refer to:

- Exponential growth – a growth rate classification.
- Economic growth – the increase in value of the goods and services produced by an economy.
- Population growth rate – change in population over time.
- Compounded annual growth rate – (CAGR) – a measure of financial growth.
- The study of historical growth rates is one of the simplest methods of estimating future growth. However, historically high growth rates do not always mean a high rate of growth looking into the future, because industrial and economic conditions change constantly. For example, the auto industry has higher rates of revenue growth during good economic times. However, in times of recession, consumers would not spend disposable income on a new car.
- The GDP Growth Rate shows a percentage change in the seasonally adjusted GDP value in the certain quarter, compared to the previous quarter. Because of climatic conditions and holidays, the intensity of the production varies throughout the year. This makes a direct comparison of two consecutive quarters difficult and in order to adjust for these conditions many countries calculate the quarterly GDP using so called seasonally adjusted method. The GDP can be determined by using the three different methods- product, the income and the expenditure method which should give the same result.

India and GDP Growth Rate

- India is the world's tenth largest economy and the second most populated country.

- GDP Growth Rate in India is reported by the Organisation for Economic Cooperation and Development (OECD). Besides, OECD and the World Bank there are many organisations that calculate and report GDP growth rates. As far as the official GDP growth rate figures are concerned, in India these are reported by the Ministry of Statistics and Programme Implementation.

- Historically, from 1996 until 2012, India's GDP growth Rate averaged 1.63 percent reaching an all time high of 5.80 percent in December of 2003 and a record low of - 1.70 percent in March of 2009.

- In India, the growth rate in GDP measures the change in the seasonally adjusted value of the goods and services produced by the Indian economy during the quarter.

- The most important and the fastest growing sectors of Indian economy are Services. Trade, Hotels, Transport, Communication Financing, Insurance, Real Estate, Business Services, Community Social and Personal Services account for more than 60 percent of GDP. Although, Agriculture, forestry and fishing constitute around 12 percent of the output, these employ more than 50 percent of the labour force. Apart from these, Manufacturing accounts for 15 percent of GDP, construction for another 8 percent and remaining 5 percent is contributed by mining, quarrying, electricity, gas and water supply.

Purchasing Power Parity (PPP)

- PPP is "an economic theory that estimates the amount of adjustment needed on the exchange rate between countries in order for the exchange to be equivalent to each currency's purchasing power." In other words, PPP is an economic theory and a technique used to determine the relative value of currencies, estimating the amount of adjustment needed on the exchange rate between countries in order for the exchange to be equivalent (or on par with) each currency's purchasing power.

- It asks how much money would be needed to purchase the same goods and services in two countries, and uses that to calculate an implicit foreign exchange rate. Using that PPP rate, an amount of money thus has the same purchasing power in different countries. PPP rates facilitate international comparisons of income, as market exchange rates are often volatile. They are affected by political and financial factors that do not lead to immediate changes in income and tend to systematically understate the standard of living in poor countries, due to the Balassa-Samuelson effect.

- The relative version of PPP is calculated as: $E = \dfrac{P_1}{P_2}$,

- Where E = exchange rate of currency 1 to currency 2; P_1 represents the cost of 'X' in currency 1; P_2 represents the cost of good 'X' in currency 2.

- The exchange rate adjusts so that an identical good in two different countries has the same price when expressed in the same currency.

- Purchasing Power Parities (PPPs) are indicators of price level differences across countries. They indicate how many currency units a particular quantity of goods and services costs in different countries. PPPs can be used as currency conversion rates to convert expenditures expressed in national currencies into an artificial common currency (the Purchasing Power Standard, PPS), thus eliminating the effect of price level.

- Deviations from parity imply differences in purchasing power of a "basket of goods" across countries, which means that for the purposes of many international comparisons, countries' GDPs or other national income statistics need to be "PPP-adjusted" and converted into common units. The best known purchasing power adjustment is the hypothetical *Geary-Khamis dollar* (the "international dollar"). The real exchange rate is then equal to the nominal exchange rate, adjusted for differences in price levels. If purchasing power parity held exactly, then the real exchange rate would always equal to one. However, in practice, the real exchange rates exhibit both short run and long run deviations from this value.

Importance/Uses of PPPs

- It converts national accounts aggregates into comparable volume aggregates. In particular, PPPs can be used to compare the GDP of different countries without the figures being distorted by differing price levels in those countries.

- It analyses relative price levels across countries. For this purpose, the PPPs are divided by the current nominal exchange rate to obtain a price level index (PLI) which expresses the price level of a given country relative to others.

- It helps in data collection. The calculation of PPPs is a multilateral exercise and data is collected involving the National Statistical Institutes of the participating countries, Eurostat and the Organisation for Economic co-operation and Development (OECD). This setup is governed by PPP regulation.

- According to the IMF, in 2009, India's implied Purchasing Power Parity (PPP) conversion rate was reported at 16.28 National currency per U.S. Dollars. In the same year India's economy share of world total GDP, adjusted by PPP, was 5.06 percent. In 2015, India's implied PPP conversion rate is expected to be 19.38 National currency per U.S. dollar and India's share of world total GDP is forecasted to be 6.12 percent.

5.3 GATT

5.3.1 Introduction

The General Agreement on Tariff and Trade (GATT) was established in 1948 in Geneva to pursue the objective of free trade in order to encourage growth and development of all member countries. The principal purpose of GATT was to ensure competition in commodity trade through the removal or reduction of trade barriers. The first seven rounds of negotiations conducted under GATT were aimed at stimulating international trade through reduction in tariff barriers and also by reduction in non-tariff restrictions on imports imposed by member countries. GATT did provide a useful forum for discussion and negotiations on international trade issues.

5.3.2 GATT – The Predecessor to the WTO

In 1947, 23 countries formed the General Agreement on Tariffs and Trade (GATT) under the auspices of the United Nations to abolish quotas and reduce tariffs. By the time the WTO replaced GATT in 1995, 125 nations were members. Many believe that GATT's contribution to trade liberalisation made possible the expansion of world trade in the second half of the 20th century.

The GATT was a permanent international organisation having a permanent Council of representatives with headquarters at Geneva. Its function was to call international conferences to decide on trade liberalisation on multilateral basis.

The fundamental principle of GATT was that each member nation must open its markets equally to every other member nation – any sort of discrimination was prohibited. The principle of "trade without discrimination" was embodied in GATT's **most favoured nation (MFN) clause-** once a country and its trading partners had agreed to reduce a tariff, that tariff cut was automatically extended to every other member country irrespective of whether they were signatory to the agreement. GATT held several major conferences (eventually referred to as "rounds") from 1947 to 1993 to address trade issues. These sessions led to many multilateral reductions in tariffs and non-tariff barriers.

Over time, GATT grappled with the issue of non-tariff barriers in terms of industrial standards, government procurement, subsidies and countervailing duties (duties in response to another country's protectionist measures), licensing, and customs valuation. In each area, GATT members agreed to apply the same product standards for imports as for domestically produced goods, treat bids by foreign companies on a non-discriminatory basis for most large contracts, prohibit export subsidies except on agricultural goods, simplify licensing procedures that allow importation of foreign-made goods, and use a uniform procedure to value imports when assessing duties on them.

Purpose of GATT

The principles contained in the Code of International trade Conduct underlie the objectives of GATT:

(a) To follow unconditional MFN principle.

(b) To carry on trade on the principle of non-discrimination, reciprocity and transparency.

(c) To grant protection to domestic industry through tariffs only.

(d) To liberalise tariff and non-tariff measures through multilateral negotiations.

To achieve these goals, the Agreement provided for: (i) multilateral trade negotiations; (ii) consultation, conciliation and settlement of disputes; and (iii) waivers to be granted in exceptional cases.

Articles of GATT

The Articles of GATT reflects the objectives and basic principles of the Agreement.

1. Most Favoured Nation (MFN): To ensure non-discrimination, Article I dealt with unconditional most favoured nation (MFN) clause for all import and export duties. The principle of MFN implies that tariff preferences accorded by a country to another are extended to all others with which it has trade relations. It also forbade the contracting parties from granting any new preferences.

2. Schedules of Concessions: The basic component of GATT was a negotiated balance of mutual tariff concessions among contracting parties. The contracting parties committed themselves not to raise import tariffs above the negotiated rates "bound" in the schedules of concessions, as incorporated in Article II of the Agreement. The bound tariff rates negotiated were generalised to all contracting parties through the MFN principles. In other words, the GATT stressed reciprocal and mutually advantageous arrangements among contracting parties.

3. Elimination in QRs: Article XI of the Agreement prohibited or restricted the use of quantitative restrictions (QRs) to trade. GATT encouraged countries to fix a ceiling on their import duties at the lowest possible level.

4. Emergency Safeguard Code: Article XIX of the GATT provided emergency safeguard code. Under this, a country could impose a tariff or quota to restrain imports which "caused or threatened serious injury" to domestic producers.

5. Exceptions: Articles XX and XXI provide certain *General* and *Security* exceptions towards the prohibitions of import quotas by contracting parties. These exceptions were: (a) a country in BOP difficulties could introduce temporary quantitative restrictions (QRs), but under MFN rule these must apply equally to imports from all sources. (b) Underdeveloped countries were permitted to apply QRs to further their economic development, but only under procedures approved by the GATT. (c) QRs could not be applied to agricultural or fishery products if domestic production of these articles was subject to equally restrictive production or marketing controls.(d) The GATT allowed a country to take action if products of other countries were 'dumped', or imported at subsidised prices. (e) GATT allowed a country to introduce temporary "safeguard" increases in protection when industries were injured by sudden increase in imports. (f) Article XXIV allowed countries to form customs or free trade areas among themselves, provided they were formed to facilitate trade between the constituent territories and not to raise barriers to trade of other contracting parties.

6. Subsidies and Countervailing Duties: The rules on subsidies and countervailing duties were incorporated in a separate code negotiated in the Tokyo round of the 1970s. According to these rules (a) export duties on manufactured products were banned except for developing nations; (b) export subsidies for primary goods were restricted only by the condition that they could not lead to acquisition or more than an equitable share of world export trade; (c) authorised importing countries to take compensating action against trading partners found to be dumping goods in their markets or increasing rates through exports subsidies; (d) in case of 'dumping', the importing country could impose anti-dumping or countervailing duties to the extent that the sale of imported goods took place in the importing country's market at less than its "normal value" and caused material injury to the domestic industry; (e) in the same way, the agreement authorised an importing country to impose offsetting countervailing duties on goods benefitting from export subsidies in the exporting country, when these resulted in material injury to the domestic industry. But such anti-dumping or countervailing duties should not result in any additional protection of the affected industry in the importing country. It implies that the duties could not be imposed at rates higher than were necessary to offset the margins of dumping or subsidy benefits.

7. Dispute Settlement: Under the GATT dispute settlement procedures, complaints could be brought against actions that violated the rules or impeded the objectives of the Agreement. The GATT relied on panels of 3 or 5 independent experts who made findings and recommendations for adoption by the GATT Council.

GATT "Rounds" Of Global trade Negotiations are shown in Table 5.1.

Table 5.1

Period	Round	Negotiations Outcome
1947	Geneva Round	45,000 tariff concessions representing half of world trade.
1949	Annecy Round	Modest tariff reductions.
1950-51	Torquay Round	In relation to 1948 level 25% tariff reductions.
1955-56	Geneva Round	Tariff reductions slightly.
1961-62	Dillon Round	Tariff reductions.
1963-67	Kennedy Round	Modest reduction of Agricultural goods, anti dumping code, average tariff reduction of 35% on industrial goods.
1973-79	Tokyo Round	34% for industrial goods (tariff reduction), Non-tariff trade barrier code.
1986-94	Uruguay Round	Tariffs, non-tariff measures, rules, services, intellectual property, dispute settlement, creation of WTO.

The Uruguay Round of Negotiations - 8th Round Of GATT

The 8th round of Multilateral Trade Negotiations, popularly known as Uruguay Round (since it was launched at Punta Del Este in Uruguay) was started in September 1986 at a special session of GATT Contracting Parties held at Ministerial level. On December 20, 1991, Arthur Dunkel, the then Director-General of GATT tabled a Draft Final Act of the Uruguay Round, known as the Dunkel draft text. This was a "take-it-or-leave-it" document. The Uruguay Round (UR) contained the mandate to have contained in 15 areas. In Part I, negotiations on trade in Goods were to be conducted in 14 areas and in Part II negotiations on trade in Services were to be carried out.

Part I i.e. trade in Goods declaration in UR contained the following: (i) tariffs; (ii) Non-tariff measures; (iii) Tropical products; (iv) Natural resource-based products; (v) textiles and clothing; (vi) agriculture; (vii) GATT articles; (viii) safeguards; (ix) MTN (multilateral trade negotiations) agreements and arrangements; (x) subsidies and countervailing measures; (xi) dispute settlement; (xii) trade related aspects of Intellectual property rights (TRIPs); (xiii) Trade related Investment measures (TRIMs); (xiv) Functioning of the GATT systems (FOGS).

Besides, the traditional GATT subjects such as tariff and nontariff barriers and improvement in GATT rules and disciplines on subsidies and countervailing measures, anti-dumping measures etc., certain new areas such as TRIPs, TRIMs and Trade in Services were included for the first time for negotiations.

These negotiations were expected to be concluded in 4 years, but due to differences in participating countries on certain critical areas, such as, agriculture, textiles, TRIPs and anti-dumping measures, agreement could not be reached. As pointed above, to break this deadlock, Mr. Arthur Dunkel, complied a very detailed document, popularly known as Dunkel Proposals and presented it before the member-countries as a compromise document. This proposal culminated into the Final Act on December 15, 1993 and India signed the agreement along with 117 nations on April 15, 1994.

Gains from Uruguay Round (UR)

The UR agreements and their implementations would result in following gains:

1. **Income and trade:** The gains in this aspect would be:
   (i) $ 510 billion increase in annual world income by 2005.
   (ii) World trade in **goods** would be higher by $ 745 billion in the year 2005.
   (iii) Largest increase in global trade in goods by 60% in clothing, 20% in agriculture, forestry and fishery products, and 19% in processed food and beverages; and
   (iv) Increase in the exports and imports of the developing countries and transition economies (the erstwhile Communist east European and USSR) as a group by 50% above the average increase for the world trade as a whole.

2. Tariff Reduction: In the UR, developed and developing nations abandoned several of their restrictive and discretionary trade and industrial policy tools. Consequently, there have been higher levels of tariff 'bindings' (i.e. end the freedom to use the protectionist instruments of the past). Tariff reductions and bindings were as follows:

(i) Tariff bindings in developed countries on industrial products increased from 78% to 99% and from 22% to 72% in developing nations.

(ii) In agriculture, the bindings increased from 81% to 100% for developed nations and from 22% to 100% for the developing countries.

(iii) Tariff reduction progressively would benefit developing countries seeking to export more processed primary products.

(iv) Tariffs on industrial goods in developed countries reduced from 6.3% to 3.9%.

(v) Above average tariff cuts for several products of export interest would benefit developing countries.

3. Market Access: Related to tariffs, textiles and garments, and agriculture, the agreements on market access were as follows:

(i) Tariff: In developed countries, industrial tariffs were reduced on an average to 4%, and developing countries also reduced their tariffs considerably. The overall tariff reductions in the UR were on an average of one-third. The value of industrial goods which enter the developed countries duty free under MFN increased from 20% to 44%. The proportion of imports into developed countries from all sources with tariffs above 15%, declined from 7% to 5% and from 9% to 5% for imports from developing countries. The market access also increased through higher levels of tariff bindings on industrial goods from 78% to 99% in developed countries and from 22% to 72% in developing nations.

(ii) Textiles and Clothing: A major achievement of the UR was the commitment to integrate this sector into a multilateral framework. The integration would take place in 4 phases by January 1, 2005 when all goods would be integrated. All Multi Fibre Agreement (MFA) restrictions existing on December 31, 1994 were carried over to the WTO Agreement and would be removed when the products integrated into the GATT by January 1, 2005. This would lead to manifold increase in the exports of textiles and clothing from developing countries, provided they are competitive.

(iii) Agriculture: This agreement contained minimum market access commitment on agricultural products. (a) to open national markets to world competition by replacing non-tariff barriers with normal customs duties; (b) to check overproduction in progressively reducing government aids; and (c) to reduce subsidies along with the volume of subsidised exports. The minimum market access commitments on agricultural products subject to tariffs would create vast market opportunities for such important products as 1.8 million tonnes of coarse grain, 1.1 million tonnes of rice, 0.8 million tonnes of wheat, and 0.7 million tonnes of dairy products. There would be increase in market access with reduction in export subsidies of 36% and an 18% decline in domestic support to agricultural producers. Further, the increase of tariff bindings from 81% to 100% in developed countries and from 22% to 100% in developing countries, and with no tariff-barriers on agricultural goods would increase market access for such goods. In other words, the reductions in tariffs on farm products and with reduction in subsidies to agriculture by the developed countries would make the exports of developing countries more profitable.

4. Rules and Discipline: The UR strengthened multilateral rules and discipline. The most significant of these related to subsidies and countervailing measures, anti-dumping, safeguards and dispute settlement. Rules concerning dispute settlement have been time bound, automatic and judicial in approach under the WTO.

5. GATS: This is the first set of multilateral agreement and legally enforceable rules and discipline relating to international trade in services. Services include financial, telecommunications and services of natural persons. The GATS requires non-discrimination by governments on the basis of MFN clause and transparency in the form of publication of all relevant laws and regulations relating to trade in services.

6. TRIMs: This agreement prohibits investment measures that are inconsistent with national treatment or general elimination of quantitative restrictions. Developing countries have been given 5 years to phase out inconsistent TRIMs and developed countries have been given 2 years. The TRIMs agreement does not impose any obligation to provide access to any particular sector for foreign investment.

7. TRIPs: The UR contained agreement on TRIPs. It provides norms and standards for copyrights and related rights, trademarks, geographical indications, industrial designs, patents, layout designs of integrated circuits, trade secrets and protection of undisclosed information. TRIPs agreement allowed 1 year for developed countries, 5 years for developing and 11 years for least developed countries to change their laws for the implementation of TRIPs. The TRIPs agreement on patents would be able to tap the generic market in the USA and is expected to generate new business worth billions of dollars by the turn of the century and similar opportunities in the EEC (European Economic Countries) for developing countries like India. These countries would gain from the inflow of better technology and create a better climate for research and development in agriculture and pharmaceuticals. This would result in availability of quality products in the market. For instance, if the farmers get better quality seeds from multinationals even at higher prices and improve and increase their produce substantially, they stand to gain. In the same way the national drug manufacturers would gain in developing countries when they establish strategic linkages for development of their new discoveries in drugs.

GATT and Developing Countries

There were very little gains from GATT for developing countries, before the Kennedy Round (1964-67), except that they could use quantitative restrictions to correct disequilibrium in balance of payments and benefitted from tariff reduction by developed countries. But the principle of reciprocity for trade concessions went against the developing countries because they were unable to provide equivalent gains to the developed countries. For example, tariffs on total manufactured imports by developed countries averaged 11% but were 17% on those from developing nations. Further, GATT did not take any initiative on trade barriers on agricultural and tropical products of developing nations.

The concept of "special and preferential" treatment for developing countries was formally introduced into the General Agreement in 1957. According to it, negotiations would keep in mind their needs for a more flexible use of tariff protection to assist their economic development and the special needs of these countries to maintain tariffs for revenue purposes. On recommendations of Haberler's Report, the GATT started an action programme in 1958 which suggested that the developed countries should reduce taxation and trade barriers on industrial and primary products of developing countries.

In 1963, with a more positive attitude the contracting parties agreed and tariffs on some tropical products like tea and timber were reduced or eliminated by the developed countries.

In 1964, a new Part IV on Trade and Development was incorporated into the General Agreement dealing with the principle on non-reciprocity for developing countries.

The Kennedy Round bestowed some benefits on developing countries when 37 developed countries reduced tariffs on manufactured products. But, practically no attention was paid to the problems of the developing nations.

In 1970, the Generalised System of Preferences (GSP) was introduced which allowed developed countries to grant unilateral tariff preference to developing countries for a period of 10 years to the extent needed to grant preferential treatment under GSP which has since then been extended further.

However, the Tokyo Round (1973-79) a number of agreements on subsidies and countervailing duties covering agricultural, fisheries and forestry products; on customs valuation; on government procurement; on technical barriers to trade; on import licensing; on dairy products; on bovine meat; and on civil aircraft were reached. It was a victory for developing countries for these agreements contained special provisions for developing countries. Further, this round also led to trade concessions to the exports of raw, processed and semi-processed tropical products of developing countries by developed nations.

However, special restrictions have been applied on trade in textiles and clothing by the developed countries outside the GATT rules. And, developing countries, being the main exporters of these goods, have been at a disadvantage in this respect.

- The early 1960s witnessed the advent of the Short-term Arrangement on Cotton Textiles in 1961-62 and the Long-term arrangement from 1962-73 restricted trade in cotton textiles on the request that developed countries, which are chief importers, need special protection against "market disruption" by lower-cost developing country suppliers.

- In 1974, the first multi fibre agreement (MFA I) was negotiated between the developed and developing countries for a period of 4 years and was renewed in 1978 (MFA II) and in 1982 it was MFA III. In 1986, it was renewed for 5 years MFA IV.

- The renewed MFA was potentially more restrictive than the previous ones. It allowed the developed importing country to cut imports of specific products from particular developing countries on a selective basis when it was feared that too many imports were capable of "market disruption" for local products.

- The significant change in MFA IV was that it extended its coverage from cotton, wool and man-made fibres to all vegetable fibres as well as silk mixed with cotton, wool or man-made fibres. For the first time, a return to the GATT rules was written into the MFA, with no mention of phasing out the MFA or setting a time limit within which this objective of GATT rules to trade in textiles would be attained.

- Under the UR, textiles and clothing would be integrated into a multilateral framework, and integration of this sector into the GATT rules 1994 would take place in 4 phases by January 1, 2005, when all products would be integrated. That is, all MFA restrictions would be removed by that date.

- Despite preferential treatment for developing countries provided in the GATT rules, they are being discriminated under the "escape clauses" and "safeguard" rules of the GATT. Many other trade restrictions like "voluntary export restraints" and "orderly marketing agreements" go against the interest of the developing countries and dilute the utility of the General Agreement under the Uruguay Round.

Critical Evaluation of GATT

The Agreement has witnessed large scale evasion of GATT rules by contracting parties over the years and hence been criticised on the following grounds:

(a) The increasing use of subsidies had been a factor in side-tracking the GATT. This is because GATT's rules on subsidies are not explicit. The GATT rules allowed domestic subsidies but they led to retaliation if they damaged the trade interests of other countries. The result has been further worsening of open trade.

(b) The "safeguard"rules under Article XIX of the GATT permitted the contracting parties to grant protection in case of need, such as injurious dumped or subsidised imports, or in severe balance of payments difficulties. But all temporary restrictions allowed under the exception clause have become permanent feature of the world trading system.

(c) The GATT's role was being understated by the concluding bilateral, discriminatory and restrictive arrangements outside the GATT rules. The EU and the US have placed many import restrictions on innumerable products from Brazil, Hong Kong, Korea, and a host of other developing countries besides Japan, after bilateral negotiations. At present, over 100 MFA type bilateral agreements are in force in the world which restricts exports of developing countries to the developed ones.

(d) In GATT, from its beginning, agriculture was treated as a special case where GATT rules hardly applied. Because, almost all the developed countries followed such agricultural trade policies which were inconsistent with the GATT agreement. It was only at the Kennedy Round and the Tokyo Round that a few agreements were arrived at relating to agricultural and dairy products. However, trade liberalisation for agricultural products has less to give to the manufacturers. Producers of agricultural products have been resorting to domestic support policies leading to surplus production that can be exported only with the help of heavy subsidies. For instance, European countries have been exporting subsidised wheat and the US has placed import restrictions on dairy products.

(e) It is true that the developed countries have removed most of the tariff barriers, but they have been reluctant to abolish others. Rather, they have devised new trade restrictions under the garb of "voluntary export restraints", "low-cost suppliers", "market disruption" etc. which are outside the GATT rules. They are applied against developing and state trading countries. For example, such restrictions affect over 50% of the French imports and 45% of the US.

(f) The GATT rules in Article XXIV which permitted the formation of customs unions and free-trade areas had been distorted and abused. These rules left many ambiguities which seriously weakened the GATT. "They had set a dangerous precedent for further special deals, fragmentation of the trading system, and damage of the trading interests of non-participants." As a result, the benefits of MFN rule failed to spread uniformly among the contracting parties.

(g) GATT did not possess any mechanism to get its rules implemented by contracting parties. The dispute settlement consisted of a panel of 3 to 5 independent experts whose recommendations had no legal binding. This was, indeed, a serious weakness of the GATT.

Perhaps due to these limitations in the working of GATT as much as 80% of world trade was being conducted outside the GATT rules. Despite the criticisms, 125 countries operated under the GATT agreements and the remaining nations gained under the MFN rule.

Social Clause in GATT

A very startling proposal was made in the context of the finalisation of the GATT agreement towards the end of March 1994. This proposal, referred to as "social clause" was moved by US to be incorporated in the Marrakesh Declaration.

- The US representative proposed under this clause to levy a countervailing duty on imports from developing nations aimed at offsetting the low labour costs prevailing there. To remove this differential advantage, exporters from developing nations to USA would have to pay duty aimed at neutralising the cost advantage. The social cause is motivated by humanitarian concern, that the developing countries adopt proper standards of living for the workers and pay their labour better wages.

- It was a rude shock to the Third World countries, since it aimed at blunting the only competitive edge of these countries. The plight of labour in the third world countries was actually a deep desire to deprive developing countries of their only competitive advantage. They know that as far as technology is concerned, developing nations are at a historical disadvantage. That is, the developing countries have now to pay high price for getting technology from the developed countries. If this clause is introduced, Indian products will become unsaleable in the USA and other countries of the EC. It implies that the poorer nations will be forced to pay for the fact that they are poor.

- Further, the move of the Harkin Bill which calls upon the US department of Labour to annually identify goods made with the use of child labour and the countries exporting them. If this Bill is passed, US government will ban the import of these items, severely affecting India's exports of gems, jewellery, carpets, textiles and garments etc. The social clause, therefore, is aimed at countries like India so that the advantage to the developing world is destroyed and their capacity to export of manufactured goods is crippled. That is, the country will be forced to export raw materials like cotton and iron ore and import garments and steel.

- Mr. Pranab Mukherjee, opposing the linkage between social policy concerns, like labour standards, and trade stated at Marakkesh on April 13, 1994:"I would like to state categorically that while we are strongly committed to internationally recognised labour standards, we see no merit whatsoever in the attempt to force linkages where they do not exist. Trade policy cannot be made the arbiter of all concerns."

- The social clause proposal became the rallying point of G-15 states. They believed that the social clause proposal would hit their economies adversely and aggravate the problems of balance of payments.

- The proposed linkage would negate the benefits of trade liberalisation and aggravate the problems of unemployment and distress. Delhi Declaration came down heavily on the coercive aspect of proposed linkages. The declaration emphasised that the application of unilateral coercive measures by the developed countries aimed at the Third world countries with a view to obtain economic or political advantage which is unacceptable.

- Another proposal to introduce an environmental protection clause with the intention of forcing the developing countries to pay for the alleged destruction of environment. Experts are of the view that this is hard to imagine since three-fourths of the damage to world ecological environment has been caused by the developed world over the last two centuries. And, now the developing countries are being asked to pay for the sins committed by the developed nations.

- There is no end to the innovative machinations which the developed countries initiate to force the developing countries into submission to their proposals. The temporary withdrawal of social clause should not be a cause of triumph for the developing countries; it is quite possible that USA may revive it.

- There is a need to put question as a counterpart: should developing countries on the basis of human considerations, impose countervailing duties on the US goods till such time that the Blacks in America are assured equality of treatment? Thus, the third World Countries must be vigilant to the fact that the enlarged scope of GATT s not used to their disadvantage.

To conclude, there is no doubt that in a world of unequal partners, multilateralism is superior to bilateralism and if some concessions are to be extracted from strong partners belonging to US and European Community, then the combined strength of the developing countries can exercise a stronger pull in their favour. The developed countries are able to pressurise the developing countries by various new devices, more especially through TRIPs and TRIMs. Although the Government of India is claiming that very substantial benefits are likely to accrue as a result of GATT agreement, but it is premature to reach any definite conclusion. The Final Act is such a big document that it has wheels-within-wheels and the thrust of the ACT is to toe the line of the developed nations. In Mr. R. K. Khurana's words, "The consensus, however, is that the Uruguay Round has been a game in which the more powerful nations lay down the rules. Unfortunately, India is not one among the powerful trading nations and is, therefore, doubtful if the country could have achieved anything significantly more than our negotiations have managed."

5.4 World Trade Organisation (WTO)

Introduction

From early times, the need for a world trade body was felt. On the recommendations of the Bretton Woods Conference in 1994, the International Trade Organization (ITO) was proposed to be set up along with the World Bank and the IMF.

The ITO was not set up but in its place, GATT was established by the US, UK and some other countries in 1947.

But it was realised that GATT was based in favour of the developed countries and was slightly called as the 'rich men's club'. Due to it, the developing nations insisted on setting up of ITO, but US opposed to this proposal. To solve the issue, the UN appointed a committee in 1963. The committee recommended the UNCTAD (United Nation Conference on Trade and Development). As such UNCTAD came into being in 1964 and could manage to secure some concessions for the developing nations.

The WTO was established on 1st January 1995. The Uruguay round of GATT negotiations concluded on 15th December 1993 and ministers had given their political backing to the results by signing the Final Act at a meeting in Marrakesh, Morocco in April 1994. India, along with 123 ministers besides the EC countries signed the Final Act incorporating the 8th round of multilateral trade negotiations. The 'Marrakesh Declaration' of 15th April 1994 affirmed that the results of the Uruguay Round would 'strengthen the world economy and lead to more trade, investment, employment and income growth throughout the world'

The Final Act Consists of:

(i)   The WTO Agreement which covers the formation of the organisation and the rules governing its working;

(ii) The Ministerial decisions and declarations which contain important agreements covering subjects like – trade in goods, services, intellectual property, plurilateral trade, dispute settlement rules etc.

WTO is the embodiment of the Uruguay Round results and the success or to the General Agreement of Tariffs and Trade (GATT), the WTO has larger membership than GATT, the present number stands at 151 and India is one of the founder members of WTO.

5.4.1 Objectives of WTO

The WTO reiterates the objectives of GATT, which are as follows:

1. In the area of trade and economy, its efforts shall be conducted with a view to raise standard of living and incomes, promote full employment, expand production and trade in goods and services.

2. To allow for optimum utilisation of world's resources and fulfil the objective of sustainable development, seeking both: (a) protect and preserve the environment; (b) to enhance the means that are consistent with respective needs and concerns at different levels of economic development.

3. To take positive steps to ensure that developing countries, especially 'the least developed ones, secure a better share of growth in world trade commensurate with the needs of their economic development.

4. To ensure linkages between trade policies, environmental policies and sustainable development.

5. To establish procedures for resolving trade disputes among members.

6. WTO aims at promoting trade flows by encouraging nations to adopt non-discriminatory and predictable trade policies.

7. To develop an integrated, more viable and durable multilateral trading system including: (a) the GATT, (b) the results of past liberalisation efforts (c) the results of the 8ᵗʰ Round i.e. the Uruguay Round of multilateral trade negotiations.

5.4.2 Functions of WTO

WTO, based in Geneva, Switzerland performs following functions:

1. WTO provides a forum for multilateral trade negotiations. That is acting as a forum for negotiations among its members concerning their multilateral trade.

2. It administers the Understanding on Rules and Procedures governing the Settlement of Disputes of the Agreement.

3. It co-operates with other international institutions-IMF and the World Bank and its affiliated agencies- involved in global economic policy making.

4. Provision of technical assistance and training for developing countries.

5. WTO acts as a management consultant for world trade. Experts on the panel of WTO scan the world economic environment and make observations on contemporary issues.

6. WTO maintains trade-related database. Members are required to notify in detail various trade measures and statistics.

7. It provides the framework for the implementation, administration and operation of the Plurilateral Trade Agreements relating to trade in civil aircraft, government procurement, trade in dairy products and bovine meat.

8. It oversees national trade policies.

9. WTO acts as a watchdog of international trade, constantly examining the trade regimes of individual members.

From the above mentioned functions it clarifies that WTO does not aim at economic or political integration, but it seeks to promote free trade among member countries.

The WTO Agreement contains some 29 individual legal texts which embody the Trade Negotiations, covering everything from agriculture to textiles and clothing and from services to government procurement, rules of origin and intellectual property.

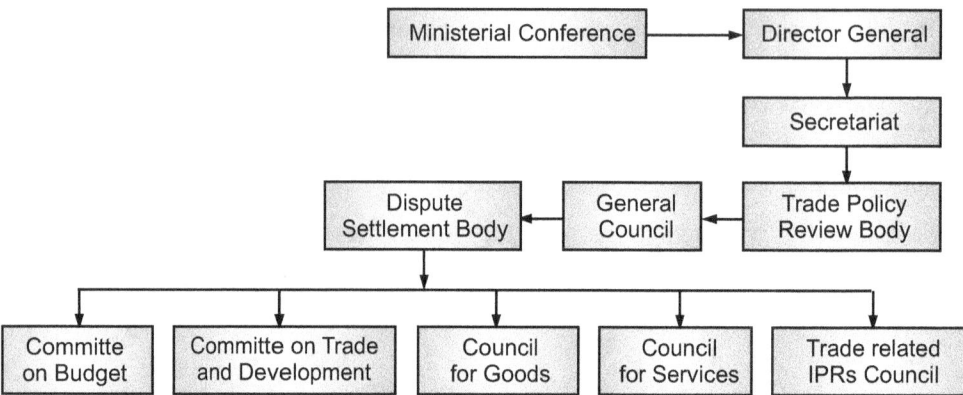

Fig. 5.1: Structure of WTO

(i)   Fig. 5.1 shows the structure of the WTO is dominated by its highest authority-the *Ministerial Conference*. This body is composed of representatives of all WTO members. It meets every two years and is empowered to make decisions on all matters under any of the multilateral trade agreements.

(ii) The day-to-day work of the WTO is entrusted to a member of subsidiary bodies: mainly, the **General Council** also compared of all WTO members, which is required to report to the Ministerial Conference.

(iii) The General Council convenes in two particular Forms: (a) The Dispute Settlement Body and (b) The Trade Policy Review Body.

(iv) The General Council delegates responsibility to three bodies viz. (a) The Council of Trade in Goods, (b) Trade in Services, (c) Trade-Related aspects of Intellectual Property Rights.

(v)   The Council for Goods Supervises the implementation and functioning of all the agreements covering trade in goods. The latter two Councils have responsibility for their respective WTO agreements.

(vi) Three others bodies are set up by the Ministerial Conference who report to the General Council.

    (a) **The Committee on Trade and Development** concerned with issues relating to the developing nations and particularly to the 'least-developed' among them.

    (b) **The Committee on Balance of Payments** concerned with consultations among WTO members and nations that resort to trade restrictive measures to cope with their BOPs difficulties.

    (c) **Committee on Budget, Finance and Administration** relates to WTO's financing and budget.

Each of the plurilateral agreements of the WTO such as civil aircraft, government procurement, dairy products and bovine meat establish their own management bodies, which are required to report the General Council.

5.4.3 Principles of WTO

The WTO is based on the principles as explained below:

1. **Transparency:** WTO aims at achieving transparency in world trade relations by obligating members to publish their respective laws, regulations related to valuation of products for customs, rates of duty, taxes, charges that will affect sale, distribution, transportation, insurance, warehousing etc. The objective is to enable the governments and traders to become familiar with them. This would help the exporters to plan their trade and safeguard them against all difficulties and confusions. To promote transparency, WTO conducts periodic review of trade policies of member countries.

2. **Most Favoured Nation (MFN) Treatment:** Any member country shall not discriminate between its trading partners – all member countries are granted "most favoured nation" (MFN) status.

   According to this status to the nation, every time a member country lowers a trade barrier or opens up a market, that country needs to extend the benefits to all trading partners.

3. **On National Level: Non-Discrimination within a Country:** It means that imported and locally produced goods should be treated equally. Article III of the GATT 1994 states that "the products of the territory of any contracting party imported into the territory of any other contracting party shall be accorded no less favourable treatment than that accorded to like products of national origin in respect of all laws, regulations and requirements affecting their internal sale, offering for sale, purchase, transportation, distribution or use". This stands true to WTO also.

4. **Trade Barriers to be prohibited:** Physical restrictions on the import and export of goods are prohibited under GATT. The member countries can protect domestic industry through tariff. WTO is not a "free trade" institution. In limited circumstances, it does allow tariffs and other forms of protection

5. **Rule based Trading System:** The WTO stands for rule based trading system. As per this system, the WTO sets and enforces rules that are essential for conducting world trade on fair terms. On basis of its automatic and speedier disputes settlement mechanism, the WTO adjudicates on disputes between members. It facilitates in the open trade between countries.

6. **Protection of Environment:** The preamble to the WTO agreement refers to the objective of sustainable development and emphasises the need to preserve the environment. Agreements on Technical Barriers to Trade and Sanitary contain provisions to protect human, animal and plant life, health and the environment. The key subjects of WTO TRIPS and GATS contain provisions relating to the environment.

7. **Principle of Competition:** Removal or reduction of tariffs and subsidies will expose locally produced goods and services to imported goods. As such there will be 'level playing field' between foreign and local goods and services. In other words, it will promote competition between them. The objective of WTO is to promote open and fair competition. The Singapore Ministerial Conference (1996) set up a Working Group on Trade and Competition Policy, which has the mandate to study issues raised by members relating to trade and competition in order to identify areas that may merit further consideration in the WTO framework. The WTO seeks to protect consumer interest by promoting competition among trading members.

8. **Optimal Utilisation of Resources:** The best way to promote trade is by lowering trade barriers, as trade ensures optimum utilisation of resources. Every country, rich or poor have assets in the form of industrial, natural, human and financial. These assets can be employed to produce goods and services for their domestic market or for global market. The principle of 'comparative advantage' implies that nations gain and prosper by taking advantage of their assets and concentrate on production of those goods and services for they are best suited. With enlarged markets, domestic or overseas, will allow the country to produce more and reap the economies of large scale production. And, when free trade or liberal trade policies exist, it allows unrestricted flow of goods and services and in expanded markets.

In contrast, if protectionist policy continuous government subsidies result in inefficient firms supplying consumers with outdated and unattractive goods. As a result, despite protection and subsidies factories close and jobs are lost. And, if other governments pursue policies of protection, markets contract and world economic activity is reduced. Thus, the importance of free and open trade.

5.4.4 WTO Agreements/Key Subjects of WTO

The WTO Agreement consists of the following which embody the results of the Uruguay Round of the Multilateral Trade Negotiations (MTN).

1. Dispute Settlement System: The understanding on rules and procedures governing the settlement of disputes shall apply to consultations and the settlement of disputes between members concerning their rights and obligations under the provisions of the Agreement establishing the WTO. With this objective, a Dispute Settlement Body (DSB) was set up.

In stage one of the dispute settlements; it holds consultations between the members concerned. If the consultation fails, on the agreement of both the parties, the Director General of WTO offers good offices, conciliations and mediation. The complainant member can ask the DSB to establish a panel of three experts within 30 days. The DSB will adopt the report within 30 days which will be unconditionally accepted by the parties to the dispute.

2. Plurilateral Trade Agreements (PTA): The PTA consist of the Agreement on Trade in Civil Aircraft, on Government Procurement, International Dairy Agreement and Agreement on International Bovine Meat . In April 1979 at Geneva was the first Agreement, which has been modified and amended. The latter three agreements were done in 1994, 15th April at Marrakesh.

3. Trade Policy Review Mechanism (TPRM): The establishment of TPRM Body is aimed to carry out reviews of the trade policies and practices under Multilateral Trade Agreements and the PTA. This would facilitate smooth functioning of the multilateral trading system. Each member shall report regularly to the TRPB about the trade policies and practices pursued by it, this ensures full transparency in the multilateral trade system. Further, annual overview of developments in the international trading environment having an effect on the multilateral trading system shall also be undertaken by the TPRB. Then, an annual report by Director General will be issued to assist the above overview and set out major activities of the WTO and also highlight important policy issues having an impact on the multilateral trading system.

4. Agreement on Trade Related Aspects of Intellectual Property Rights (TRIPs): Intellectual property rights may be defined as "information with commercial value". IPRs are the exclusive rights given to persons over the innovations and creations for their use for a certain period of time. IPRs have been characterised as a composite of "ideas, inventions and creative expression" and the "public willingness to bestow the status of property on them".

IPRs include patents, trademarks, copyrights, geographic indications, industrial designs and layout designs of integrated circuits, undisclosed information such as trade secrets, plant variety protection. Special (*sui generis)* forms of protection have also emerged to address specific needs of knowledge-producers as in the case of plant breeder's rights and the protection of layout designs of integrated circuits.

The objectives of IPRs are to encourage and reward creative work; to encourage innovation; to promote fair competition; to help consumer protection to facilitate transfer of technology.

(i)   **Copyright and Related Rights:** This protection with respect to literary and artistic works and the parties are required to comply with the Berne Convention. It includes protection to computer programmes and authors of computer programmes, performers and producers of phonograms i.e. sound recording, broadcasting organisations are to be given the right to authorise or prohibit the commercial rent of their works to the public. It applies to films also.

(ii)   **Trademarks:** Any sign-personal names, letters, numbers, any combination of signs, figurative elements and combination of colours are eligible for registration as trademarks. The owner of a registered trademark has the exclusive right to prevent all third parties not having the owner's consent from using in the course of trade identical or similar signs for goods or services. The registration of a trade mark is renewable indefinitely.

(iii) **Geographical Indications:** It refers to the identity of a good as originating in the territory of a member or a region or locality in that territory where a given quality or reputation of the good is essentially attributed to its geographical origin. Thus, it is required that members provide the legal means for interested parties to prevent the use of any indication which misleads the consumer in relation to the origin of goods and if done would be referred as unfair trade practice.

(iv) **Industrial designs:** Owners of protected designs would be able to prevent the manufacture, sale or import of goods bearing a design which is a copy of the protected design for commercial purpose. The duration of protection is for atleast 10 years.

(v) **Patents:** Any invention-product or process- can be patented. It will be provided in fields of technology, but it must be new has industrial application. The Agreement requires 20-year patent protection. Inventions if involves prohibition in terms of commercial exploitation for public morality will not be patented. Members shall provide for the protection of plant varieties either by patents or by an effective *sui generis* system.

(vi) **Integrated Circuits:** The TRIPs Agreement provides protection to the layout designs-topographies- of integrated circuits for a time period of 10 years.

(vii) **Trade Secrets:** Trade secrets and know-how having commercial value can be provided protection against breach of confidence and other acts.

The Agreement requires a one-year transition period for developed countries to bring their legislation and practices to match the implementation of TRIPs. For developing countries and the erstwhile East-European and USSR countries would have a 5 year transition period and for the least developed nations it would be 11 years.

The major demerit or limitation of a strong regime of IPRs is that they are, particularly the very poor nations, ill-equipped for significant R&D. In a world over where the industrial countries are the major producers of technology and developing countries heavily depend on imports of technology, IPRs turn out to be, generally more beneficial to industrial countries than to developing countries. Industrial nations gain huge amounts of net transfers from TRIPs, developing countries, including India, are expected to experience net outward transfers on account of TRIPs.

However, the developing countries shall take advantage of the IPRs regime by protecting their traditional knowledge and enormous biological resources and investing in human capital and R & D. Further, stronger IPR protection could be expected to give a boost to R&D

in countries like India whose potential intellectual capital may be expected to grow in great width and in depth. Developing nations hold approximately 90% of world biological resources, which are particularly important in the development of new pharmaceuticals. Institutions can be built to protect the collective intellectual property rights for traditional knowledge held by cultural groups.

5. General Agreements on Trade in Services (GATS): This Agreement covers all internationally traded services. Services were included in the MTNs for the first time by the UR. Because of the special characteristics and the socio-economic and political implications of certain services, they have been generally subject to various types of national restrictions-visa requirements, investment regulations, marketing regulations etc.

The GATS defines four modes of international delivery of services:

- Cross-border supply i.e. transborder data flows, transportation services;
- Commercial presence i.e. providing of services abroad through FDI or representative offices;
- Consumption abroad i.e. tourism and
- Movement of personnel i.e. entry and stay of foreign consultants.

In short, services is the supply of a service from the region of one country into the region of any other member (country); in the territory of one member to the service consumer of any other member; by a service supplier of one member, through commercial presence in the territory of any other member or by a service supplier of one member, through presence of natural persons of a member in the territory of any other member.

The framework of GATS includes basic obligation of all member nations on international trade in services, including financial services, telecommunications, transport, audio, visual movement of workers, professional services. The MFN obligation prevents countries from discriminating among foreign suppliers of services. It requires transparency which includes the publication of all relevant laws and regulations relating to services trade. Any liberalisation of trade in services would be progressive in character. It would be through negotiations every five years to review the reduction or removal the adverse effects of measures on trade in services.

As for the *movement of natural persons*, it allows the governments to negotiate specific commitments applicable to the *temporary* stay of people for the purpose of providing a service.

Related to *financial services*, it provides the right to governments to take appropriate measures for the protection of investors, depositors and policy holders which would ensure the integrity and stability of the financial system.

For *Telecommunications*, the Agreement requires a member to establish, construct, acquire, lease, operate or supply telecommunication transport networks and services and make it available to the public. As for the developing nations, to strength its domestic telecommunications infrastructure and service capacity, it can place reasonable conditions on access to and use of public telecommunications, transport networks and services.

The GATS will also apply to *aircraft repair and maintenance services*, marketing of air transport services and computer reservation services.

The governments have agreed to set up working parties on – Trade in services and environment to achieve sustainable development and professional services to ensure that measures like qualifications requirement, technical standards do not constitute unnecessary barriers to trade.

6. Multilateral Agreements on Trade in Goods: This includes various agreements dealing with different aspects related to trade in goods.

   (i) GATT 1994: The WTO Agreement includes the provisions of specified legal instruments, the Marrakesh Protocol to GATT 1994 and other following understandings:

      (a) Transparency of the legal rights and obligations, the nature and level of 'any other charges' levied on bound tariff items in the Schedules of concessions, as given in Article II,1b of GATT 1994.

      (b) To ensure transparency of the activities of state trading enterprises, members need to notify such enterprises to the council- Article XVII of GATT.

      (c) Members imposing restrictions with the aim of balance of payments should do so in the least disruptive manner. They should avoid the imposition of "new" quantitative restrictions and should publicly announce "as soon as possible" time schedules for the removal of restrictive measures for the purposes of Balance Of Payment.

      (d) Article XVIII lays down new procedures for the negotiation of compensation when tariff bindings are modified or withdrawn.

      (e) The Agreement on Customs unions and Free Trade Areas clarifies the criteria and procedures for the review of new or enlarged customs unions or free trade areas or for evaluation of their effects on third parties.

  (ii) Agreement on Agriculture: The Agreement on Agriculture relates to domestic subsidies, export subsidies, minimum market access commitment, domestic support, sanitary and phytosanitary and food aid operations. The Agreement aims at open the national markets to international competition by reducing non-tariff barriers allowing normal custom duties; to check overproduction by progressively reducing government aids that encourage overproduction-this is then disposed off through export subsidies or destroyed; it seeks new disciplines on export competition and reduction in subsidies.

(a) **Domestic Subsidies:** It includes non-product subsidies that is given for all crops and include subsidies on inputs; and product-specific subsidies that is given for specific crops as in India in the form of minimum price support for some agricultural crops.

(b) **Export Subsidies:** WTO members are required to reduce the value of direct export subsidies to a level of 36% below the 1986-90 base period level in 6 year period for implementation. For developing nations the reductions are 2/3rds those of the developed countries over a 10-year period, but no reductions apply to the least developed nations.

(c) **Domestic Support:** Domestic support measures that have a minimum impact on trade, known as "green box" policies and are excluded from reduction commitments. Such measures include general governments services in the areas of research, disease control, infrastructure and food security. It includes direct payments to producers in the form of income support, structural adjustment assistance, direct payments under environmental programmes and under regional assistance programme.

(d) **Sanitary and Phytosanitary measures:** The measures concern food safety and animal and plant health. The agreement recognises that governments have the right to take sanitary and phytosanitary measures to protect human, animal or plant life or health. But they should not arbitrarily discriminate between members where identical or similar conditions are present. The agreement seeks to ensure that animal and plant health and safety measures do not serve as unwarranted trade barriers.

(e) **Food Stocking and Food Aid:** The agreement recognises that during the transition period the least developed and net food importing developing countries may experience negative effects in relation to supplies of food imports. Therefore, it chalks out objectives in relation to the provision of food aid and basic foodstuffs in full grant form and aid for agricultural development.

(f) **Minimum Market Access Commitment:** These measures applies to those countries that maintain restriction of various types on agricultural imports and are required to convert those restrictions into tariffs and reduce those tariffs by 36% over the 6-year period. Such countries are required to allow a minimum market access opportunity of 3% of their domestic consumption for foreign agricultural consumption for 6 years which will rise to 5% after that period.

(iii) **Agreement on Textiles and Clothing:** This Agreement is to secure the integration of the textiles and clothing sector into the GATT 1994 and it would take place in 4 phases. *First*, on January 1, 1995, each party was integrated into GATT products and it should be not less than 16 per cent of its total volume of imports in 1990. *Second,* this phase starting January 1, 1998 products which accounted for not less than 17% of 1990 imports would be integrated from the GATT products from the specific list in the Agreement. *Third,* this phase starting from January 1, 2002, products accounting not less than 18% of 1990 imports would be integrated; *Fourth,* phase starting from January 1, 2005, all remaining products would be integrated at the end of this transition period.

Integration implies that trade in yarn, fabrics, made-up textile products and clothing will be governed by GATT. All Multi-Fibre Agreement (MFA) have been carried over into the new agreement that existed on December 31, 1994. And, in case of non-MFA restrictions maintained by some members would be brought in the scope of GATT 1994 to be phased out progressively by 2005. There is a special transitional safeguard against products that have yet not entered in the integration of GATT 1994. Action can be taken against an individual exporting nation if it is found by the importing country that the overall imports of a product have entered in such large quantities that it can cause serious damage to the relevant domestic industry.

(iv) **Agreement on Technical Barriers to Trade:** It seeks to ensure that technical negotiations, standards, testing and certification procedures do not create unnecessary obstacles to trade. A Code of Good Practice for the preparation, adoption and application of standards by standardising bodies has been included into the Agreement.

(v) **Agreement on Trade Related Aspects of Investment Measures (TRIMs):** It aims at removal of all trade related investment measures like quantitative restrictions and national treatment, within a period of 5 years. It requires foreign investment companies to be treated at par with the national companies. It prevents the imposition of restrictions on areas of investment. The Agreement recognises that certain investment measures restrict and distort trade, thus compulsorily mandatory notification of all non-confirming TRIMs and their removal within 2 years for developed countries, 5 years for developing nations and within 7 years for the least developed nations.

(vi) **Agreement on Anti-Dumping:** If dumped imports cause injury to a domestic industry in the importing member country, thus the Article VI of the GATT provides for the right of contracting parties to apply anti-dumping measures. This Agreement of WTO is an improvement over the Tokyo Round Agreement. It gives greater clarity, detailed rules and criteria to be taken into account for determining injury caused by dumped imports to domestic industry. Under the new rules, an anti-dumping investigation should be immediately terminated if the "margin of dumping" is less than 2% of the export price or the volume (quantity) of dumped imports from a particular country is less than 3% of the total imports of that product.

(vii) Agreement on Subsidies and Countervailing Measures (SCM): This agreement applies to non-agricultural products. It classifies subsidies into three categories- the **prohibitive** (like red traffic signal) **category** includes subsidies with high trade-distorting effects. They are export subsidies and those that favour the use of domestic over imported goods. Developing countries with per capita income of less than $1,000 have been exempted from the export subsidies prohibition. The second category is the **non-actionable** (green traffic light) **category,** they are not specific to an enterprise or industry or a group of enterprises or industries. The third is **actionable** (like amber light at traffic signal) industries that are neither red nor green. These subsidies are actionable by a trading partner if it damages the interests. It can seek remedy by having countervailing duties or follow the dispute-settlement procedures.

For developing countries there is exemption on certain types of subsidy practices like investment subsidies, agricultural input subsidies that becomes available to low income or resource-poor farmers.

WTO and Developing World

Developing countries have not been getting a fair deal in the WTO regime. The Wall Street Journal has reported that while the US and the EC are getting the best pieces of the world trade pie, the developing countries are getting the crumbs.

As pointed out above the Uruguay Round was larger in scope and coverage that the earlier rounds and for the first time covered areas like services, agriculture, intellectual property, environmental policies and sustainable development. The 8th Round took 8 years long of negotiations by the contracting countries and the legal document comprising the Final Act of the results contains 29 Agreements of the Uruguay Round of Multilateral Trade Negotiations.

The WTO contains not only the original GATT as amended by the Uruguay Round but also a number of new Agreements. These Agreements are likely to benefit the developing and the least developed countries in their efforts towards globalisation. However, many loopholes in these agreements have been experienced by the developing and the least developed nations, which are working to their disadvantage.

Textiles and Clothing: International trade in textiles was estimated to be worth $240 billion a year. Estimates were that after the phasing out of MFA (Multi Fibre Agreement), world exports of textiles would rise by $25 billion a year. With a 2.2 per cent share in the world textile trade, as such India's share in additional exports could be $0.55 billion. But the real gain will depend on the country's ability to compete with countries like China, Hong Kong, Taiwan, South Korea etc. which are considered as leaders in the textile trade. Textile and Clothing Agreement claims that the developing countries would mostly benefit out of it during the transitional period. However, the gains to them are likely to be delayed due to the long period of phasing out of the MFA. It is because of two reasons- (i) when a developed country takes certain types of textiles and clothing out of the MFA, it will apply on a non-discriminatory MFN basis to all exporting countries. (ii) only 49% of all products would be integrated into the GATT on the last day of the 10-year transition period.

The "product-coverage" for the phasing out is so large that all items of textiles and clothing which are not covered by quotas are included in it. In other words, there will be little phasing out of quota items till the end of the 10-year phasing out period. As for India, its apparel exports will suffer till 2005 as the US announced a 4-stage phase out programme ending January 2005 under which 90% of the restrictions on Indian apparel exports would remain till 2005.

The effect of the Uruguay Round (UR) is not the same on all countries. For e.g. a measure which is favourable to one developed country may be unfavourable to the other developed country. It is therefore, quite natural that there exists interest conflict both among the developed and developing nations. Latin American countries were perhaps not very interested in liberalising the trade in textiles because they stand to gain if they could gain a direct entry to the NAFTA through some regional arrangement and then could provide them an edge over competitors like India and Pakistan.

Agriculture: It is believed that the liberalisation of agricultural trade and the increase in agricultural prices is due to cut in producer subsidies in the developed countries would benefit agricultural exporters and the increase in food prices due to cut in subsidies may adversely affect the food importers. Now, the reality is that more than 100 developing countries are net food importers (i.e. they are at disadvantageous situation). Again, the increase in food prices is expected to make food production in these countries more competitive leading to an increase in production. The subsidisation of production and export of farm production in the developed countries would have discouraging effect on the production of developing countries where farmers have not been able to compete with the imported stuff having low prices due to subsidies. In other words, the Agreement on agriculture would harm the interests of farmers in developing countries. The Agreement allows only 10% subsidy of the value of the production, it would become almost impossible for the governments of developing countries to provide price support to particular agricultural commodities. It would also be the case with input subsidy given to low income farmers. The reduction and removal in subsidy unaccompanied by a rational price policy would hit farmers in developing countries.

Again, prices in international market are not determined by competition but by corporations of the developed nations which procure and sell them. This will only lead to foreign debt and worsen the balance of payments problem.

The Agreement lays down the application of sanitary and physiosanitary measures against the farm products of developing countries. The Codex Alimentarius, an agency which is not subject to any democratic process sets the rules and may declare as "safe" products of the developed nations and "unsafe" of developing nations.

Further, the opening up of markets as per the WTO Agreement has taken place in developing countries but in turn the developing nations has got little success in getting market access in developed countries. Market access continues to be restricted by tariffs and other barriers such as Sanitary and Physiosanitary standards.

Despite these, the agricultural sector in developing countries is expected to benefit from this Agreement by generating export surpluses. They may gain from higher prices of such crops as food grains, cotton and by diversifying in areas of horticulture, floriculture, dairy products and other allied products.

TRIMS: The Agreement on TRIMs is a weak one. The TRIMs agreement would remove restrictions on foreign investments. Though FDI (Foreign Direct Investment) is not mentioned, yet it is feared that MNCs would try to control high priority areas in developing countries. The Agreement deals with discriminatory imports restrictions. On the whole, the TRIMs Agreement has reduced the decision-making powers of national governments. For e.g. they cannot specify local contents in domestic manufacturing and cannot restrict the percentage of imported inputs in its exported products or the export or particular product.

GATT RULES: The GATT Rules 1994 relating to the phasing out of the *Quantitative Restrictions (QRs)* and preferences are vague. The use of QRs by developing countries to overcome their balance of payments difficulties has been rendered ineffective by providing it only for the least developed countries.

In the Subsidies Agreement, the developing countries have committed to eliminate subsidies having an impact on export prices with the result that they have given up the policy of export-led growth.

The GATT Rules on anti-dumping leave so much at the discretion of national governments that very few actions would qualify as their violations. Thus, partly due to GATT Rules and partly due to economic situations, anti-dumping and countervailing duties are being used for restricting trade by the USA, EEC and other developed nations.

The non-technical barriers to trade like the environmental, health and sanitary considerations can act as non-tariff barriers in developing countries. For e.g. the US has tried to block shrimp exports from India, insisting that they should be caught with devices which do not net turtles.

GATS: Developing countries were very apprehensive about the proposal to liberalise trade in services- financial, transport and communication, health, educational, professional and media services- as developing countries have a distinct advantage in these areas. By liberalising trade in services, the objective of developed countries is to control over the production and use of services in developing countries. The service sectors in developing countries would have to face unequal competition from the vast resources which the firms of developed countries possess. Many developing countries do possess comparative advantage in skilled and unskilled labour, but their mobility is controlled by strict immigration laws of developed countries.

Dispute Settlement: The dispute settlement system of the WTO poses a threat to the sovereignty of countries. For instance, if a request is made to the WTO for setting up a panel in case of a dispute, the WTO Secretariat has been given the authority to propose nominations on the panel and the parties to dispute shall not oppose nominations. The parties to the dispute shall have no say in decision-making. Further, the powerful developed nations like US may adopt cross-retaliatory measures under the cover of the dispute settlement mechanism which may go against the developing countries.

The US Trade Law Section 301 allows individual firms to compel the US government to investigate foreign trade practices that restrict their trade interests. It is doubtful if the WTO's dispute settlement system can resolve complaints arising out of the use of this law.

TRIPs: The TRIPs agreement is patently discriminatory that favours the developed countries and go against the interest of the developing countries.

As developed countries and their MNCs have vast resources and facilities for R&D, they would be at an advantage to invest and patent their process and products. The domestic prices of such goods-drugs and medicines- would rise and burden the consumers. Imports would increase of patented raw materials and products by developing countries, exports would receive a set back and worsen the balance of payments.

The acceptance of TRIPs agreement would necessitate wide-ranging amendments in the patent laws of developing countries. The change would further lead to brain drain which would prove costly for such countries.

The increase in the patent right to 20 years would again be detrimental to the interests of developing countries. Though it is 20 years for developed nations and 10 years for developing countries to change their existing laws. But the TRIPs agreement takes away this concession through the "classical pipeline protection" clause. According to this clause, patent applications for agricultural and pharmaceuticals goods would be accepted by the concerned authorities even after the agreement came into force from January 1, 1995. For e.g. for a pharmaceutical product normally it takes 10 years from the date of filing a patent to market it. As a result, patent protection to such a product would be necessary from the year 2005 onwards. There would be no investments on new products, when the patent would be valid for only 20 years.

The Agreement provides for the grant of "exclusive marketing rights" which is inimical to the interests of developing countries because it grants the patentee the right to prevent the use of his patent product or process being used for the export market. Thus, the patented technology may be provided by MNC to exploit the local market of a developing country.

According to Dr. Deepak Nayyar, the implications of the TRIPs agreement for the absorption, diffusion and adaptation of technologies in developing countries are far reaching. Much needed technologies may no longer be available at affordable costs.

The implications and consequences of the TRIPs agreement suggest that the emerging international system for the protection of intellectual property rights is bound to be inequitable and inimical for the developing countries.

Developing countries have identified various instances of inequalities and imbalances in the UR Agreements and submitted a large number of formal proposals for rectifying them. These proposals have been known as the implementation issues. It is argued that the implementations issues should be urgently resolved and any new round of Multilateral Trade Negotiations (MTN) shall be taken up only after that. However, the developed countries want the new round of MTN soon.

The developed countries deceive developing nations by not implementing several of their commitments in letter and spirit.

Dubey points out that, subsidies normally maintained by developed countries have been made non-actionable. That is, subsidies to farmers maintained by major developed nations have, instead of decreasing, have gone up mainly because these countries were able to switch over to subsidies permissible under the Agreement on Agriculture, before the commencement of its implementation.

Liberal policy towards textiles trade has been claimed as a boon for the developing nations, but here too the developing countries have been deceived as developed importing countries have sought to comply with the targets of liberalisation set out in the Agreement on Textiles and Clothing by taking credit for the items already outside restriction.

The rich countries, according to UNCTAD Report, despite their commitment in the TRIPs agreement, have taken no real steps to share their technology in the interests of reducing poverty. The TRIPs agreement does not provide intellectual property protection for indigenous knowledge such as those used in traditional medicine.

The rich countries have also tilted the playing field for trade. These nations, to varying degrees, pay large subsidies to their domestic food producers. These subsidies are so large that they affect world market prices of agricultural goods, causing direct harm to poor countries. EU-subsidised exports have contributed to the decline of the dairy industries in Brazil and Jamaica and the sugar industry in South Africa.

Various instances of inequalities and imbalances in the UR Agreements have been noticed by the developing countries. The attempt of the developed countries to resolve issues is designed to safeguard their most vital trading interests and to restore balance in WTO agreements.

Implications for India: India was one of the 76 governments that became a member of the WTO on its first day. The following are the views expressed in support and against India becoming a member of the WTO are as follows:

1. India is one of the few developing countries which have succeeded in implementing economic reforms like liberation programmes. Over three-quarters of WTO members are developing countries. These countries have chosen to join WTO after careful deliberations in their respective countries. Obviously, when they decided to be member of WTO, they have perceived economic gains for themselves and India should not be an exception. The criticism that WTO exists only for industrialised countries is not all that valid. In the Uruguay round negotiations it was developing countries and transition economies that took a much more active and influential role. And, with the end of the Uruguay Round, developing countries showed themselves prepared to take on most of the obligations that are required of developed countries. The WTO gave transition periods to adjust to the more unfamiliar provisions of WTO-particularly to the poorest 'least developed countries'. Further, a ministerial decision on measures in favour of least-developed nations, gives extra flexibility to those countries in implementing WTO agreements, calls for speeding in implementation of market access concessions etc.

2. The significance of the WTO to India lies in the role that a dynamic export industry can play in the country's development- both in terms of job creation, skill development and technological evolution. Earlier, there were no incentives to improve technology and productivity as it was a closed system that left no room for evolution. It is only by forcing industries to sell outside the country and compete for export markets that they will have an incentive to evolve. India needs to search for external markets to export more and pay for its imports. The country has for long believed that it is a self sufficient economy. But, from petroleum and fertilisers to capital goods, raw materials and life saving drugs, the Indian economy is vitally dependent on imports. It makes sense in being a part of multilateral trading system, if India needs to export and import. Even a country like China, despite its fiercely-guarded sovereignty and having a status of the world's last major socialist power, has sought and succeeded in joining the WTO.

3. At the request of the developing countries, to help them promote their exports, the International Trade Centre (ITC) was set up by GATT in 1994. And by being a member

of the WTO, India can benefit from the ITC, which is jointly operated by the WTO and the United Nations. ITC, on the request from the developing countries gives following services: (a) formulate and implement export promotion programmes and import operations and techniques, (b) it provides information and advice on export markets and marketing technique, (c) assists in establishing export promotion and marketing services and training personnel required for these services. For the least-developed nations the service is freely provided.

4. The GATT Secretariat projects that the largest increases will be in the areas of clothing (60%), agriculture, forestry and fishery products (20%) and processed food and beverages (19%). As India's existing and potential export competitiveness rests in these products, it is logical to believe that India will obtain large gains in these sectors. To be more concrete in our assumption that India's market share in world exports improves from 0.5% to 1% and assuming that we are able to take advantage of the trade opportunities, then the trade gains may conservatively be placed at 2.7 billion US dollars extra exports per year.

5. India benefits from membership of WTO- that is India is saved from entering into multiple bilateral trade negotiations with other countries. If India was not the member of WTO, then it would be required to enter as many bilateral agreements as the country desires to have trade links. But with WTO membership, India enjoys the advantage of having trade links with all other member countries without the need for bilateral agreements.

6. India benefits from WTO's provisions for a multilateral set of rules. Such rules provide greater protection against bilateral pressures or against trade barriers and restrictions that cannot be experienced under a multilaterally agreed framework. The multilateral set of rules has given greater stability and predictability to international trading system.

7. There are several areas in the Uruguay round package that relate of market access, such as tariffs, textiles and agriculture and India's position in all these sectors is advantageous and the provisions are favourable to the country. GATS is another area, when operationalised benefits India.

Case Study 1: Managing the Challenges of WTO Participation

Protecting the Geographical Indication for Darjeeling Tea

This case study relates to the geographical indication (GI) protection of Darjeeling tea.

It tells the story of the unauthorised use and registration of 'Darjeeling and Darjeeling logo' by Japanese companies already registered in Japan by the Tea Board of India. The study also refers to the unauthorised use and attempted registration of the words 'Darjeeling and Darjeeling logo' by some other developed countries.

Problem

India is the world's largest producer of tea, with a total production of 846 million kg in the year 2002, supplying about 31 per cent of the world's favourite hot drink. Among the teas grown in India, **Darjeeling tea offers distinctive characteristics of quality and flavour, and also a global reputation for more than a century.** Broadly speaking, there are two factors which have contributed to such an exceptional and distinctive taste, namely (i) geographical origin and (ii) processing. Thus Darjeeling tea has been cultivated, grown and produced in tea gardens in a well-known geographical area – the Darjeeling district in the Indian state of West Bengal – for over one and a half centuries.

Legal Backing

Even though the tea industry in India lies in the private sector, it has been statutorily regulated and controlled by the Ministry of Commerce since 1933 under various enactments culminating in the Tea Act, 1953. The Tea Board was set up under this Act. A major portion of the annual production of Darjeeling tea is exported, the key buyers being Japan, Russia, the United States, and the United Kingdom and other European Union (EU) countries such as France, Germany and the Netherlands.

In order **to ensure the supply of genuine Darjeeling tea**, a compulsory system of certifying the authenticity of exported Darjeeling tea was incorporated into the 1953 Tea Act in February 2000. The system makes it compulsory for all the dealers in Darjeeling tea to enter into a licence agreement with the Tea Board of India on payment of an annual licence fee. The terms and conditions of the agreement provide, inter alia, that the licensees must furnish information relating to the production and manufacture of Darjeeling tea and its sale, through auction or otherwise. The Tea Board is thus able to compute and compile the total volume of Darjeeling tea produced and sold in the given period. **No blending with teas of other origin is permitted.** Certificates of origin are then issued for export consignments under the Tea (Marketing and Distribution Control) Order.

Data is entered from the garden invoices (the first point of movement outside the factory) into a database, and the issue of the certificate of origin authenticates the export of each consignment of Darjeeling tea by cross-checking the details. The customs authorities in India have instructed, by circular, all customs checkpoints to check for the certificates of origin accompanying the Darjeeling tea consignments and not to allow the export of any tea as 'Darjeeling' without this certificate. This ensures the sale-chain integrity of Darjeeling tea until consignments leave the country.

Legal Protection at Domestic Level - CTM (Certification Trade Marks) Registration

In order to provide legal protection in India the Tea Board of India registered the 'Darjeeling logo' and also the word 'Darjeeling' as Certification Trade Marks (CTMs) under the (Indian) Trade and Merchandise Marks Act, 1958 (now the Trade Marks Act, 1999).

GI Registration

The Tea Board of India has also applied for the registration of the words 'Darjeeling' and 'Darjeeling logo' under the Geographical Indications of Goods (Registration and Protection) Act, 1999 (the Act) which came into force with effect from 15 September 2003, in addition to the CTMs mentioned above.

Under the Act

(a) No person shall be entitled to institute any proceeding to prevent or recover damages for the infringement of unregistered geographical indications.

(b) A registration of geographical indications shall give to the registered proprietor and all authorised users whose names have been entered in the register the right to obtain relief in respect of infringement of the geographical indications. However, authorised users alone shall have the exclusive right to the use of the geographical indications in relation to the goods in respect of which the geographical indications are registered.

(c) A registered geographical indication is infringed by a person who, not being an authorised user thereof,

   (i) uses such geographical indications by any means in the designation or presentation of goods that indicates or suggests that such goods originate in some other geographical area other than the true place of origin of the goods in a manner which misleads the public; or

   (ii) uses any geographical indications in such a manner which constitutes an act of unfair competition including passing off in respect of registered geographical indications; or

   (iii) uses another geographical indication to the goods which, although literally true as to the territory, region or locality in which the goods originate, falsely represents to the public that the goods originate in the region, territory or locality in respect of which such registered geographical indications relate.

(d) The purpose of the GI Act is to create a public register, and

(e) The GI Act confers public rights.

Advantages of GI Protection at Domestic Level and Export Markets

The reason for the need for additional protection for GI over and above the CTM has been set out by the chair of the Tea Board of India as follows:

• When CTM registration is not accepted in a jurisdiction where protection is sought, for example, France for Darjeeling;

• Because GI registration is necessary to obtain reciprocal protection of a mark mandate under EU Regulation 2081/92; and

• Registration gives clear status to a GI, indicating a direct link with geographical origin.

Quite apart from the aforesaid reasons the GI Act in India has also been enacted in order **to comply with its obligation under the Agreement on Trade-Related Aspects of Intellectual Property Rights (TRIPS)**, which requires WTO members to enact appropriate implementation legislation for GI.

Steps taken at International Level

(a) **Registration of Darjeeling tea and Logo:** In order to protect 'Darjeeling' and 'Darjeeling logo' as GI, the Tea Board of India registered the marks in various countries, including the United States, Canada, Japan, Egypt, and the United Kingdom and some other European countries, as a trade mark/CTM. In this context it is relevant to note that on 3 August 2001 the UK Trade Registry granted registration of the word 'Darjeeling' as of 30 March 1998 under the UK Trade Marks Act 1994. The United States has also accepted the application of the Tea Board for the registration of 'Darjeeling' as a CTM in October 2002.

(b) **The appointment of the International Watch Agency:** In order to prevent the misuse of 'Darjeeling' and the logo, the Tea Board has since 1998 hired the services of Compumark, a World Wide Watch agency. Compumark is required to monitor and report to the Tea Board all cases of unauthorised use and attempted registration.

(c) **The Assistance of Overseas Buyers:** In order to ensure the supply of genuine Darjeeling tea, the Tea Board has sought the help of all overseas buyers, sellers and Tea Council and Associations in so far as they should insist on certificates of origin to accompany all export consignments of Darjeeling tea.

The Role Played by Local and External Players

(a) **The Tea Board of India:** The sole representative of tea producers in India, is responsible for the implementation of the government's regulations and policies. It is vested with the authority to administer all stages of tea cultivation, processing and sale (including the Darjeeling segment) through various orders issued by the government. It works in close co-operation with the

(b) **Darjeeling Planter's Association:** Which is the sole producers' forum for Darjeeling tea.

Both the Tea Board and the Darjeeling Planter's Association (DPA) have been involved at various levels in protecting and defending the 'Darjeeling tea' and 'Darjeeling logo'. The primary objects are (i) to prevent misuse of the word 'Darjeeling' for tea sold worldwide; (ii) to deliver the correct product to the consumer; (iii) to enable the commercial benefit of the equity of the brand to reach the Indian tea industry and ultimately the plantation worker; (iv) to achieve international status similar to champagne or Scotch whisky in terms of both brand and equity and governance/ administration.

The Tea Board of India assumed the role of complainant in making and filing opposition or other legal measures whenever cases of unauthorised use or attempted or actual registration of Darjeeling and Darjeeling logo were brought to its notice. Such legal measures are generally taken where negotiation failed. For instance, in February 2000 in Japan the Tea Board of India filed an opposition against Yutaka Sang Yo Kabushiki Kaisa of Japan for registration of the trade mark 'Darjeeling Tea' with the map of India, and against Mitsui Norin Kabushiki Kaisa for the use in advertising of the 'Divine Darjeeling' logo. These opposing parties defended the invalidation action filed against them.

Some disputes relating to Darjeeling tea have been settled through negotiation undertaken by the Tea Board of India with the foreign companies concerned, with the help of their respective governments. Thus, the Tea Board with the help of the Indian government continues to negotiate with France at various levels over the activities of the French trademark authorities. Moreover Bulgaria, Switzerland agreed to withdraw the legend 'Darjeeling Tea fragrance for men' pursuant to legal notice and negotiations.

In one of the cases in France, the Tea Board of India put the applicant Comptoir des Parfums (which advertised in March 1999) on notice, and drew its attention to the prior rights and goodwill in the name of Darjeeling as the GI for tea, and requiring it to withdraw its application voluntarily. Based on the correspondence, the applicant consented to the amendment of all specifications of goods by the addition of 'all those goods being made of Darjeeling tea or recalling the scent of Darjeeling tea'.

'The Tea Board of India feels that a partnership with the buyers in the major consuming countries such as Germany, Japan and the United Kingdom would be the only long term solution to the problem of possible passing off.'

Challenges

The Tea Board of India has faced a series of hurdles, challenges and difficulties in the protection and enforcement of the word 'Darjeeling' and of the Darjeeling logo. Some of the major challenges faced by the Tea Board's effort to protect 'Darjeeling' and the Darjeeling logo in Japan, France, Russia, the United States and other countries are given below.

(a) Unauthorised use and Registration of Darjeeling Tea and Logo in Japan: In the first case the Tea Board filed an invalidation action against International Tea KK, a Japanese Company, over the registration of the Darjeeling logo mark, namely, Darjeeling women 'serving tea/coffee/coca/soft drinks/fruit juice' in the Japanese Patent Office (JPO) on 29 November 1996 with the trademark registration number 3221237. The impugned registration was made notwithstanding the registration in Japan of the identical Darjeeling logo mark by the Tea Board of India, with the trademark registration number 2153713, dated 31 July 1987. The Tea Board also filed a non-use cancellation action. On 28 August 2002 the JPO Board of Appeal held that the pirate registration was invalid because it was contrary to public order and morality. With regard to the Tea Board's non-use cancellation action, the JPO decided that International Tea KK had not furnished sufficient evidence to substantiate its use of registration and thereby allowed the appeal of the Tea Board.

In the second case, the Tea Board of India opposed the application for 'Divine Darjeeling' in class 30 (Darjeeling tea, coffee and cocoa produced in Darjeeling, India) filed by Mitsui Norin KK of Japan advertised on 29 February 2000. The opposition was mainly on three grounds, namely (i) 'divine' is a laudatory term and accordingly the mark for which protection is sought is merely 'Darjeeling', which is clearly non-distinctive; (ii) 'Divine Darjeeling' is misleading in so far as 'coffee and cocoa produced in Darjeeling' are concerned, all the more so because the district of Darjeeling does not produce coffee or cocoa; (iii) Darjeeling tea qualifies as a geographical indication under international conventions including TRIPS and ought to be protected as such in Japan, a member of TRIPS.

The JPO Opposition Board dismissed the invalidation action filed by the Tea Board of India primarily on the ground that the mark 'Divine Darjeeling' as a whole was not misleading or descriptive of the quality of goods. However, the non-use cancellation action succeeded, because the registered proprietor was not able to place on record adequate evidence to prove the use of the mark in Japan.

In yet another case the Tea Board of India brought an invalidation action against Japanese trade mark registration of 'Darjeeling tea' with a map of India in class 30 by Yutaka Sangyo Kabushiki Kaisa, on the ground that the registration was contrary to public order and morality. This action was rejected on the ground that 'the written English characters "Darjeeling tea" and the map of India for the goods of Darjeeling tea are used as an indication of the origin and quality of Darjeeling tea and will not harm the feelings of the Indian people'. However, the non-use cancellation action filed by the Tea Board succeeded, because the registered proprietor was not able to place on record sufficient evidence to prove the use of the mark in Japan.

A perusal of these decisions reveals that the JPO did not decide the contention of the Tea Board of India relating to the TRIPS Agreement, which requires WTO members to provide the legal means to prevent the use of a GI for goods originating in a geographical area other than the true place of origin in a manner which misleads the public to constitute an act of unfair competition. Indeed, non-disposal of the argument that the procedural guidelines of WTO be followed dilutes the effect of the TRIPS Agreement.

Other Examples of Defending GI Against Developed Countries:

France: While the Indian system protects French GIs, France on the other hand does not extend similar or reciprocal protection to Indian GIs. Thus, French law does not permit any opposition to an application for a trademark similar or identical to a GI, if the goods covered are different from those represented by the GI. The owner of the GI can take appropriate judicial proceedings only after the impunged application has proceeded to registration. The net effect of such a provision has been that despite India's protests, Darjeeling has been misappropriated as a trade mark in respect of several goods in class 25, namely, clothing, shoes and headgear. The French Examiner – even though he found evidence in favour of the Tea Board of India (i) on sufficient proof of use of 'Darjeeling' tea in France, and (ii) that the applicant had slavishly copied the name Darjeeling in its application – held that the respective goods 'clothing, shoes, headgear' and 'tea' are not of the same nature, function and intended use, produced in different places and sold through different networks. The Examiner also held that even if the applicant has slavishly copied the Tea Board's Darjeeling logo (being the prior mark), the difference in the nature of the respective goods is sufficient to hold that the applicant's mark may be adopted without prejudicing the Tea Board's rights in the name 'Darjeeling'.

In another case the Tea Board opposed the application against the advertised marks for Darjeeling in classes 5, 12 and 28 by Dor François Marie in France. The French Examiner rejected the Tea Board's opposition and held that the respective goods did not (i) have the same nature, function and intended use; and (ii) share the same distribution circuits. However, he held that although the applicant's mark constituted a partial reproduction of the Tea Board's prior figurative registration for the Darjeeling logo, the designated goods lacked similarity to that of the Tea Board's prior marks and the logo, therefore, may be used as a trade mark without prejudicing the prior rights of the Tea Board.

Russia: The Tea Board filed an application for unauthorised use by a company of the word 'Darjeeling'. This application was objected to on the ground of conflict with an earlier registration of the identical word by a company named 'Akorus'. The Russian Patent Office overruled the objection and accepted the application of Tea Board of India for the word 'Darjeeling'.

United States: The Tea Board is opposing an application filed by its licensee in United States to register 'Darjeeling nouveau' ('nouveau' is the French for 'new') relating to diverse goods and service such as clothing, lingerie, Internet services, coffee, cocoa and so on in respect of first flush Darjeeling tea. The registration application is under consideration even though 'Darjeeling' is already registered under US CTM law.

Other Countries: Quite apart from the above, in several cases the Tea Board of India opposed attempted registration and unauthorised use of the word 'Darjeeling' in Germany, Israel, Norway and Sri Lanka before the Patent Office of the country concerned.

Costs of Protection and Enforcement for the Industry and the Government

Another major challenge faced by the Tea Board of India relates to legal and registration expenses, costs of hiring an international watch agency and fighting infringements in overseas jurisdictions. Thus during the last four years the Tea Board of India has spent approximately US$200,000 for these purposes. This amount does not include administrative expenses including the relevant personnel working for the Tea Board, the cost of setting up monitoring mechanisms, software development costs and so forth. It is not possible for every geographical indication right holder to incur such expenses for protection. Further, like overseeing, monitoring and implementing GI protection, the high cost of taking legal action can prevent a country from engaging a lawyer to contest the case, however genuine and strong the case may be. Moreover, a lack of expertise in the proper handling of highly complex legal language is another challenge to be met.

Lessons for Others

The Tea Board of India appears to be not satisfied with the policy as well as the approach of the patent authority in Japan and France. In order to deal with the situations described above, India, along with several other member countries of the WTO, wants to extend the proposed register for GI to include products or goods, other than wines and spirits, which may be distinguished by the quality, reputation or other characteristics essentially attributable to their geographical origin. The main advantage would be to develop a multilateral system of notification and registration of all geographical indications. In this connection, a joint paper has recently been submitted to the Two's TRIPS Council.

The Doha Ministerial Declaration under paragraphs 12 and 18 also provides a mandate for the issue of providing a higher level of protection to GIs to products other than 'wines and spirits' to be addressed by the TRIPS Council. According to the Tea Board, (i) extension of protection under Article 23 for products other than wines and spirits is required where no legal platform exists to register a GI or a CTM which is a TRIPS obligation, for example Japan; (ii) once the scope of protection is extended it would not be necessary to establish the credentials/reputation of a GI before fighting the infringement of similar 'types', 'styles', or 'look-alikes'; and (iii) additional protection would rectify the imbalance created by the special protection of wines and spirits

The experience in defending GI in France, the United States and Japan further strengthens the Tea Board's perspective on the subject. Despite a registration of 'Darjeeling' as a GI in France, the Tea Board was unsuccessful in defending it because French law does not permit any opposition to an application for a trade mark, similar or identical to a GI. Likewise, India's efforts to protect 'Darjeeling' in Japan did not succeed because the prefix 'Divine' has not gained currency in the Japanese language.

From the experiences described above it is felt that it is high time to evolve a rule that (i) no application for registration of a GI of the same or similar goods or products or even similar type, style or look-alike already registered in that country be ordinarily entertained by the competent authority of the country concerned. (ii) Further, the GI status and apprehended or actual violation of GI should be published at both domestic and international levels. (iii) adequate steps should be taken to evolve rules and procedures for GI or CTM registration in all the member countries of the WTO. This would prevent conflict to a great extent. (iv) Finally, a vigilance cell should be established to check the violation and misuse of the GI of any product.

Case Study 2: Basmati Rice

Basmati is an aromatic rice grown in Northern India and Pakistan. In September 1997, Rice Tec, a small food technology company based in Texas, U.S., was granted a patent by the US patent office to call an aromatic rice variety developed in USA Basmati. For this India challenged the case. The argument was that basmati is unique aromatic rice grown in Northern India, and not a name Rice Tec could claim. In fact only inventions can be patented. As a result, the US patent office accepted India's basic position, and Rice Tec had to drop 15 of the 20 claims that it had made. On the balance claims, Rice Tec managed to evolve three new varieties of rice. As India had not objected to this, it got a patent from US Patent and Trademarks Office. Thus, the ruling has not handed over Rice Tec the basmati brand, but it provides a patent for superior three strains of basmati developed by cross-breeding a Pakistani basmati with a semi-dwarf American variety.

According to the WTO Agreement, geographical indications (GI) like basmati can be legally protected and their misuse in this way can be prevented. Unfortunately, Government of India has not taken timely steps for protecting our GI and bio-diversity. A Geographical Indication of Goods Bill was introduced in Parliament in 1999, and in 2001 but has not become an Act.

5.5 Sources of Revenue and Expenditure (Centre and State)

The *revenue budget* of the Central Government deals with receipts from taxation and from non-tax sources and expenditure met out of these sources.

Tax revenue comes mainly from 3 sources:

(a) Taxes on income and expenditure;

(b) Taxes on property and capital (property) transactions; and

(c) Taxes on commodities and services.

Non-Tax revenue consists of:

(a) Currency, coinage and mint;

(b) Interest receipts and dividends; and

(c) Other non-tax revenue.

Revenue expenditure is on:

(a) Such general services as general administration including police, judiciary, defence, collection of taxes;

(b) Social and community services; such as education, medical and public health, labour and employment, and

(c) Economic services like agriculture, industries, transportation, trade etc.

Capital Budget of the Government of India also known as capital account consists of capital receipts and capital expenditure.

The **capital receipts** of the Central Government are composed of:

(a) Net recoveries of loans and advances made previously to State Governments, Union territories and public sector undertakings.

(b) Net market borrowings (i.e. gross borrowings from the market less repayments of public debt).

(c) Net small savings collections (gross collections less share of the States) and

(d) Other capital receipts such as provident funds, special deposits, etc.

Capital Expenditure of the Union Government consists of expenditure on capital items, mainly in the form of loans to States and Union Territories for financing plan projects and other capital expenditure on economic development on social and community development and capital expenditure on defence.

The Indian Government can be classified into Central Government and state government.

Taxes imposed on citizens of India can be broadly classified into two categories:

1. Direct Taxes and

2. Indirect Taxes.

1. **Direct taxes** are those taxes which we pay directly to the central government and example of direct tax is Income Tax e.g. tax paid on salary by employees.

    (a) Tax Deducted at Source (TDS): Income tax has now taken the form of TDS. TDS is not only deducted on employees but for all other people who have some business or are in some profession also.

    There is a broad category which is used to deduct TDS at the appropriate rate mentioned on various forms of income earned by people. For e.g.: On Professional TDS @ 10% is deducted, on contractors @ 1% and so on.

    (b) Wealth tax is also paid to the Central Government @1% on wealth exceeding ₹ 30 lakhs.

    (c) CENVAT: Central Value added tax; this tax is on sales of goods and differs from normal VAT. This goes to the Central Government.

2. **Indirect taxes** are those taxes which we do not pay directly to the government but indirectly. For example when we purchase any product, we pay VAT and other taxes levied on it, about which we do not know much as most of the times it is sold to us as including all taxes and levies.

(a) Other form of indirect taxes is Customs duty which is paid on import of any product in India. There are various rates applicable and many duties involved which require detailed explanation.

(b) Excise duty is also a form of indirect tax which is levied at the time of manufacture of any product.

(c) Service tax is paid on the services provided. E.g.: renting, telecom service, internet service, cargo service. All these services when availed also include a component in form of service tax @10.3%.

State Government earns from:

(a) Sales tax or VAT, which is levied on products.

(b) Entertainment tax which is levied on movies and other form of entertainment mediums.

(c) Toll tax for entry into city.

(d) Professional Tax for undertaking any profession in a city like Doctors and Lawyers, etc.

There are also various other taxes levied by the State Government.

Education cess of 3% is a kind of residuary tax which is subdivided into: Education cess (EC) @ 2% and Secondary and Higher Education cess (SHEC) @1%. This tax is levied for the purpose of providing education to the poor, including secondary and higher education.

5.6 Plan and Non-Plan Expenditure

There are two components of expenditure – plan and non-plan.

Plan expenditures are estimated after discussions between each of the ministries concerned and the Planning Commission.

Non-Plan *revenue expenditure* is accounted for by interest payments, subsidies-mainly on food and fertilisers, wage and salary payments to government employees, grants to States and Union Territories governments, pensions, police, economic services in various sectors, other general services such as tax collection, social services and grants to foreign governments. Non-plan capital expenditure mainly includes defence, loans to public enterprises, loans to States, Union Territories and foreign governments.

Forms of Taxes & Subsidies (Incidence & Effects)

Revenues of the Central Government

The Central Government has (a) revenue budget, i.e. estimates of receipts and disbursements on Revenue Account; and (b) a Capital budget which relates to receipts and disbursements on Capital Account.

The total current revenue of the Central Government consists of tax revenue, and non-tax revenue. This has been rising quite fast, partly due to more taxes and higher rates of taxes and partly due to inflation

As said earlier, the total revenue receipts come from two sources: tax-revenue and non-tax revenue.

Tax Revenue: Tax revenue of the Central Government consists of 3 types:

(i) Income taxes on income and expenditure;

(ii) Property taxes or taxes on property (capital assets);

(iii) Commodity taxes, i.e. taxes on goods and services.

The first two types of taxes are known as **direct taxes** and the commodity taxes are **indirect taxes.**

Taxes on Income: The government of India imposes two types of income taxes, viz., personal tax and corporation tax (or tax on company profits).

1. Income Tax

Personal income tax is levied on individuals by the Central Government. The income tax does not fall on all people but only on those people who are better off. Thus, income in India is based on the principle of the "ability to pay", which is that who can pay more should pay more to the government. On the basis of this principle, certain people with low incomes are exempted from paying income tax. The Budget 2011-12 has a threshold limit exemption in case of:

- All assesses at ₹ 1,80,000
- All women assesses at ₹ 2,50,000
- Senior citizen (age 60 years to 80 years) at ₹ 2,50,000 Senior citizen (80 years and above) ₹ 5,00,000

During the last twenty years, there has been continuous reduction in the income tax rates because high rates of income tax were an important reason for extensive evasion of income tax and the rise of black money. It is now accepted that moderate rates of income tax encourages savings, foster growth and motivates voluntary compliance. The marginal rate of tax is now 30 percent and it was as high as 97.25 percent before 1975 and since then there has been continuous reduction in the income tax rates, and has helped to reduce tax evasion and thus, increase tax collection.

Since 2005-06, all forms of concessions previously given to promote savings were dropped and the budget allows every tax payer a consolidated limit of ₹ 1 lakh for savings which will be deducted from the total income before tax is calculated. An additional amount of ₹ 20,000 is allowed over and above the existing limit of ₹ 1 lakh and tax saving for investment in the long term infrastructure bonds as notified by the Central Government.

The 6 deductions, allowed by previous budgets, continue: (i) a deduction on interest paid on housing loan for self-occupied house property; (ii) medical insurance premium; (iii) specified expenditure on disabled dependents; (iv) expense for medical treatment for self or dependent; (v) deduction in respect of interest on loans for pursuing higher studies; (vi) deductions to a person with disability.

In terms of yield, the personal income tax in India is highly productive. The volume of revenue collected from personal income tax amounted to ₹ 140 crores in 1950-51, it rose to ₹ 1,72,026 crores in 2011-12. This huge increase since 1981 has taken place, even though the rates of income tax have been reduced and a large number of people are out of the income tax net.

Corporation Tax: The corporation tax is a tax on the net income of the companies. The Central Government has been imposing a tax on the profits of the large and small companies known as the corporation tax. There was a difference between the rates of corporation tax for domestic companies and for foreign companies.

Since 1990-91, the rates of corporation tax have been gradually reduced. This reduction has been aimed at better compliance and to stimulate the growth process, create multiplier beneficial effects all round and also to attract foreign investments. Besides the basic corporate taxes, there was a surcharge and it was then removed periodically. The 1999-2000 budget reimposed a 10 percent surcharge on corporate tax.

Many companies, even the large ones, with huge profits managed to escape the corporate tax net by taking advantage of using the provisions of exemptions, deductions, incentives, differential rate of deprecation, etc.

In 1996-97, P. C. Chidambaram imposed the Minimum Alternate Tax (MAT). If total income of a company as computed under corporation tax, after availing all eligible deductions, was less than 30 percent of the book profits, then the company would be charged a minimum tax, which would be 12 percent of the book profit. In Budget 2009-10, MAT has been increased to 15 percent. The power, infrastructure sectors, export-oriented units, etc., has been exempted from MAT.

In recent years, the changes in corporate tax structure are:

- Reduction of the tax rate from 30 to 20 percent on royalty and technical services fees payable to foreign companies;
- Modification of the MAT on companies;
- Abolition of tax on dividends in the hands of the shareholders; and
- Imposition of tax on distributed profits at a moderate rate of 10 percent. This is to induce companies to retain the bulk of their profits and plough them into fresh investments.

Under the impact of economic planning and rapid industrialisation, the yield from corporate tax has been rising steadily, about ₹ 3,59,990 crores in 2011-12, reflecting the growing industrialisation in the country. At present, the corporation tax is the single largest revenue-yielding tax in the country.

Interest Tax: The Interest Tax Act 1974 provided for the levy and a special tax on the gross amount of interest accruing to the commercial banks on loans and advances made by them in India. The Government withdrew the interest tax in 1985 but later re-introduced it as an anti-inflationary measure. The tax was levied on the gross interest income of "credit institutions", i.e. banks, public financial institutions, financial companies, etc.

Expenditure Tax: As from November 1987, the government imposed an expenditure tax under the Expenditure Tax Act, 1987. This Act provided for a levy of a tax on expenditure incurred in hotels where the room charges for any unit of residential accommodation were ₹ 400 or more per day per individual. The rates of expenditure tax were revised later from 10 percent to 20 percent and the tax was extended to expenditure incurred in restaurants providing superior facilities of air conditioning, etc.

The yield from personal income tax and corporate income tax has risen over the last few years reflecting clearly the rapid growth of the Indian economy and rise in personal incomes of the middle and higher income groups.

2. Central Government Taxes on Property or Capital Assets

Since Independence, the Central Government has imposed certain taxes on wealth, inheritance of wealth and gifts with the aim of: (a) these taxes would fall on the rich; (b) they would help reduce the inequality of wealth and income in the country. It has been noticed that there have been inefficient implementation and extensive evasions in these taxes.

Wealth Tax: Among property taxes, this is the most important one. It has been imposed on the accumulated wealth or property of every individual. Of course, not all wealth holders are taxed, as wealth below ₹ 2.5 lakhs is exempted. Initially, wealth tax was as high as 15 percent and when combined with progressive income tax, this wealth tax forced the rich to avoid both income and wealth tax. In the 1992-93 budget, Dr. Manmohan Singh withdrew wealth tax on productive assets such as shares and limited tax to unproductive assets such as guest houses, residential houses, jewellery etc. Since 1993, wealth tax is chargeable with respect to the net wealth exceeding ₹ 15 lakhs at 1 percent only. It is interesting to note that the budget estimate and actual realisation of wealth tax had remained constant at ₹ 145 crores for many years, indicating the inefficiency in this tax. It is better to abolish wealth tax as the collection is disgracefully low.

Estate Tax: Formerly, Estate Duty was imposed on the estate of a person which was inherited by his heirs. The collection of this tax was by the Central Government but proceeds went to the State Government. This tax ranged from 4 percent to 40 percent of the value of the estate left behind. Thus, this tax was highly progressive in nature and the burden was to fall heavily on the larger properties. It was meant to reduce the large fortune through inheritance. However, the amount of revenue collected was pitiably low indicating extensive evasions. Since the tax yield was low, while the cost of administration was relatively high, V. P. Singh (former finance minister), abolished the estate duty from mid March 1985.

Gift Tax: As a complement to the 3 taxes – estate duty, wealth tax and expenditure tax – in 1958, the gift tax was imposed by the Government. The gift tax was charged and collected every financial year on gifts purchased during the previous year. A basic weakness of the gift tax was that it was imposed on the donor and the rate was highly progressive according to the value of the gift. This led to huge tax evasions. The 1990-91 budget introduced major changes in the taxation, that is the incidence or burden of this tax would fall on the receiver and not on the donor, the exemption limit was raised, the rate of gift tax was reduced, but unfortunately these changes were not implemented. Mr. Yashwant Singh, in 1998-99, abolished the gift tax on the ground of its low yield. Gifts are now clubbed with income in the hands of their beneficiaries.

The main objective of imposing taxes on property and on transfer of property was to reduce the growing inequalities of income and wealth, which has never been achieved, due to various exemptions allowed over the years, corruption and tax evasions.

3. **Taxes on Commodities and Services**

Commodity taxes have been important sources of revenue for the Central government. Central excise duties and customs duties are 2 important taxes of the Central Government.

Customs Duties: These are duties or taxes imposed on commodities imported into India (import duties) or on those commodities exported from India (export duties). Export duties are removed as they reduce the competitive position of Indian goods in global markets. Import duties have been relatively very productive. The revenue from import duties has increased because of heavy imports of iron and steel, chemicals, drugs and medicines, fertilisers, petroleum products, etc.

The government was expected to collect ₹ 1,51,000 crores from custom duties during 2011-12 budget. In the last few years, the Government has actually rationalised the import duties but yet custom duties are quite significant in India's tax structure and it is the 3rd largest source of tax revenue to the Centre after corporation tax and excise duties.

Excise Duties: The Central Government found excise duties a very good source of additional revenue for the purpose of economic development. These duties are levied by the Centre on commodities which are produced within the country. But commodities on which State Governments impose excise duties, for instance, on liquor and drugs, are exempted from Central Excise Duties. At first, sugar, cotton, mill cloth, tobacco, motor spirit, matches, cement etc., were the goods which yielded most of the excise duties. In recent years, excise duties have been extended to a large number of goods and the duties already levied have been raised. Gross Revenue from Central Excise duties have increased from ₹ 70 crores in 1950-51 to an expected ₹ 1,64,116 crores for 2011-12.

The Constitution 80th Amendment Act, 2000 has prescribed the sharing of all central taxes with the states.

Service Tax: Till 1995, services were never taxed by the Government of India. There was a realisation that if commodities could be taxed on their production and sale, then services too could be taxed as the component of services in GDP is increasing rapidly.

Service tax is one of the fastest growing taxes for the Central government. The yield from service tax had increased from ₹ 407 crores in 1994-95 (the 1st year of collection) to ₹ 2,610 crores in 2001-02 and was expected to be ₹ 82,000 crores in 2011-12.

To sum up, direct taxes on income and property are direct as the assesses have to pay them and it cannot shift to others. Indirect taxes are taxes on commodities and services and the burden can be shifted to others. The over-riding importance of commodity and service taxes (increase from 64 to 84 percent between 1951 and 1991) in the tax structure of the Central Government was a clear indication that the Government found it easy to impose indirect taxes rather than direct taxes (income and property taxes) that declined from 36 percent to 16 percent. But the burden of indirect taxes fell more heavily on the lower and middle income groups than on the richer sections of the community.

5.7 Direct/Indirect Taxes

Direct taxes are those that are levied on the income of individuals or organisations, such as income tax, corporate tax, inheritance tax. *Income tax* is the tax levied on individual income from various sources like salaries, investments, interest, etc. *Corporate tax* is the tax paid by companies or firms on the incomes they earn.

Indirect taxes are the taxes paid by consumers when they buy goods and services. These include excise and customs duties. Customs duty is the charge levied when goods are imported into the country, and is paid by the importer or exporter. Excise duty is a levy paid by the manufacturer on items manufactured within the country. In indirect taxes all charges are passed on to the consumer.

Non-Tax Revenues of the Central Government

The Central Government gets revenue from other sources also, which are collectively called non-tax revenue. Non-tax revenue includes receipts from fiscal services, interest receipts, dividends and profits of government enterprises, general services, etc. In 1950-51, non-tax revenue of the Centre was ₹ 49 crores, increased to ₹ 890 crores in 1970-71 to ₹ 1,25,435 crores for 2011-12.

Interest receipts which constitute an important source of non-tax revenue comprise of interest on loans to states and Union territories, interest payable by Railways and Postal services, and other interest receipts, such as loans to public enterprises, etc.

Profits and dividends relate to profits of the RBI, profits of nationalised banks, LIC, public enterprises, etc.

Fiscal services relate to revenue received by the Central Government from:

(i)   currency, coinage and mint;

(ii) other fiscal services related to India Security Press, Nasik, Hyderabad, etc., and

(iii) general services include social community services, economic services and grants-in-aid and contributions.

Expenditure of the Central Government

The Central Government adopted a new classification of public expenditure from the 1987-88 budget. According to this, all public expenditure is classified into:

1.   Non-Plan Expenditure, and 2. Plan Expenditure.

1. **Non-Plan expenditure:** This is further divided into *revenue* expenditure and *capital* expenditure.

   Revenue expenditure is financed out of revenue receipts, both tax and non-tax revenue. Under revenue expenditure the following are included:

   (a) Interest payments, defence revenue expenditure, major subsidies (food, fertilisers and export promotion), other subsidies, debt relief to farmers, postal deficit, police, pensions, other general services (organs of state, tax collection, external affairs etc.)

   (b) Social services (education, health, broadcasting etc.)

   (c) Economic services (agriculture, industry, power, transport, communications, science and technology etc.)

   (d) Grants to states and Union territories and grants to foreign governments.

   Capital (non-plan) expenditure includes items such as defence capital expenditure, loans to public enterprises, loans to States and Union territories and loans to foreign Governments. In a period of 12 years, the non-plan expenditure increased by 13 times from ₹ 64,500 crores in 1989-90 to ₹ 8,16,182 crores in 2011-12.

2. **Plan Expenditure:** This is composed of:

   (a) Central plans, such as on agriculture, rural development, irrigation and flood control, energy, industry and minerals, transport, communications, science and technology and environment, social services and others, and

   (b) Central assistance for Plans of the States and Union territories.

   Plan expenditure on both revenue and capital accounts was ₹ 28,400 crores in 1989-90 and was expected to touch ₹ 4,41,547 crores in 2011-12, i.e. a rise of 15.6 times in 12 years.

Thus, the *capital expenditure* (non-plan and plan) of the Central government consists of:

(i) Loans to states and union territories for financing Plan projects, and loans to foreign governments;

(ii) Capital expenditure on economic development;

(iii) Capital expenditure on social and community development;

(iv) Capital expenditure on defence; and

(iv) Capital expenditure on general services.

The *capital receipts,* from which capital expenditure is incurred, consists of:

(i) Net recoveries of loans and advances to State Governments and Union Territories and public sector enterprises;

(ii) Net market borrowings (i.e. gross borrowings less repayments);

(iii) Net small savings collections (gross small savings less State's share); and

(iv) Other capital receipts which include provident funds, special deposits, etc.

- Revenue expenditure has increased due to the Government's participation in nation-building activities like education, public health, rise in prices etc.

- Defence, debt services and administrative expenses are responsible for keeping the non-development expenditure at a high level.

- Subsidies on food, fertilisers and on export promotion, have become an integral part of the Central Government expenditure and despite the Government's frequent promise to reduce them, they are continuing to rise, year after year.
  Total subsidies rose from ₹ 4,900 crores in 1985-86 to ₹ 12,160 crores in 1990-91 to an expected ₹ 1,43,570 crores in 2011-12.

- The Centre assists the states and the union territories with grants and assistance for national calamities. The tremendous rise in expenses on administration is a matter of great concern.

- Interest payments has now become the single largest item of expenditure due to extensive borrowing from the market, banks and financial institutions for the purpose of development and other needs, as a result it has increased the burden of debt services.

- The second largest item of Government expenditure is on subsidies / grants. Some subsidies are to protect the poor and ensure a minimum quality of life for the poor. *Subsidies can be defined as the difference between the cost of goods and services provided publicly and the actual recoveries made from those using those goods and services.*

- There are two types of subsidies viz., *direct* (transparent subsidies) and *indirect* (hidden subsidies). In the case of direct subsidies, there is a clear identification of beneficiaries and budgetary allocation. Indirect subsidies arise on account of non-recovery of user charges for services provided by the Government and it also includes non-recovery of loans given to public sector undertakings, co-operative societies, farmers etc.

• To conclude, in recent years, the Government is burdened with the ever-increasing burden of subsidies and general administration.

State Government

In India, each State Government prepares its own budget of income and expenditure every year. An important fact is that the receipts and expenditure of the States on the revenue account have been continuously increasing. In 1951-52, the current revenue of the States was ₹ 396 crores, which increased to ₹ 16,290 crores in 1980-81 and was expected to exceed ₹ 8,04,943 crores in 2009-10.

The main reason for this huge increase in state revenue is the necessity to finance the continuously rising expenditure of states which has gone up from ₹ 392 crores in 1951-52 to ₹ 9,37,408 crores in 2010-11. Increase in state revenues over the last 50 years are imposition of new taxes, especially on commodities, rise in the rate of taxes, greater share in Central Government taxes and increasing receipts from the Central Government by way of general and particular grants, etc.

Likewise, there are many reasons for the increase in the expenditure of the States over the years. For example, expansion in civil administration, higher salaries and wages due to rise in the price level and cost of living, increase in the provision of government services in the form of education, public health, etc., and the increased expenditure on development.

The First part of the State's Budget- revenue receipts and revenue expenditures: In the past, States had a regular surplus of revenue over current expenditure. For example, in 1951-52 current account surpluses was ₹ 4 crores and it increased to ₹ 1,480 crores in 1980-81. However, since 1986-87, the states, like the Centre have been incurring heavy deficits. In 2010-11, the states expected a revenue deficit ₹ 24,370 crores.

The Second part of the state budget consists of capital receipts of states and disbursements out of them: Capital receipts consist of market loans, borrowings from the Central Government, collecting small savings of the public and provident fund contributions. The capital expenditure or outlays (disbursement) are on various development projects like river valley projects, schemes for agricultural development, etc. The states experienced capital account deficit in the first 40 years since 1951-52, for the reason that the capital revenue was less than capital disbursal.

The over-all surplus/deficit of the states is the revenue surplus and deficits + capital deficits and surpluses. In the 2010-11 budget, the states anticipate a revenue deficit of ₹ 24,370 crores, but capital surplus of ₹ 5,684 crores and so the net over-all deficit is ₹ 18,686 crores.

Current Revenue of State Governments: In India, the State Governments collect revenue from different sources to meet their revenue expenditure. These sources are:

(a) States own taxes, states' share in Central taxes;

(b) States' share in the tax proceeds of the Central government;

(c) Grants-in-aid and other contributions from the Centre, and

(d) States' own non-tax revenue.

The tax revenue of the States consists of 2 parts:

(a) revenue from States' taxes, comprising of taxes on income, taxes on property and capital transactions and taxes on commodities and services, and

(b) share in Central taxes.

In the 2010-11 budget, revenue from states' own taxes was ₹ 4,18,151 crores and the states' share in central taxes was ₹ 2,08,997 crores (total ₹ 6,27,148 crores).

The second source of current revenue to the states is known as *non-tax revenue*, which consists of:

(a) grants from the Central Government, and

(b) states' own non-tax revenue, consisting of interest receipts, dividends and profits, general services (of which state lotteries are the most important for most of the states), social services and economic services.

The State government depends heavily on the Centre for their revenue receipts:

• Till 1999-2000, the Centre imposed and collected personal taxes and excise duties, but shared proceeds with the States. Between 2000 and 2005, States got 29.5 percent of all the tax collections of the Centre. This share was increased to 30.5 per cent of all Central taxes for the 5 year period 2005-2010.

• The States receive grants from the Central Government on the recommendations of the finance commissions. Grants from the Centre are made for State Plan schemes, Central Plan schemes, centrally sponsored schemes, special plan schemes and non-plan grants which consist of:

    (i)   statutory grants;

    (ii)   grants for natural calamities; and

    (iii) non-plan no-statutory grants.

    During 2010-11, the States hope to receive ₹ 3,92,279 crores as total transfers from the Centre (₹ 2,08,997 crores for share in taxes and ₹ 1,83,282 crores for grants-in-aid). Thus, 57.5 percent of the total revenue receipts of the Central Government show the states' dependence on the Centre for their current revenue.

- Now, States' own sources of tax revenue- taxes on income of the people and property taxes and taxes on property transactions, taxes on commodities and services.

- The State Governments have been getting revenue from taxes on income in 2 ways: agricultural income tax and profession tax. These are collected by the States themselves. The proceeds from these 2 taxes are relatively insignificant. For example, agricultural income tax yields ₹ 20 crores to ₹ 22 crores in a year for all the states. Profession tax – trade and employment- yield more revenue as for instance, about ₹ 3,000 crores in 2007-08. When we consider all the states and union territories, this collection is surely insignificant. Before 2000, States had a large share in the personal income tax imposed and collected by the Centre. About 85 percent of the proceeds of the personal income tax were transferred to the states at one time. This system of transfer was an important share to the states. This share to the states has been reduced to 30.5 percent for the period 2005-10.

- **Taxes on Property and Property transactions:** The main sources are land revenue, stamps and registration and tax on urban immovable property. Land revenue used to be an important source of revenue to the states but it is not so now. The rate of land revenue differs from state to state, the rate ranges between 25 and 50 percent of the net produce (one-sixth of the gross produce). At present, stamps and registration on transfer of property occupy an important position in revenue receipts. The collection from stamps and registration has been steadily increasing as property transactions are extensive in these years. However, there is extensive evasion of stamp duties as the rates are high and most property transactions are under-valued to escape paying high stamp duties. Some state governments impose urban immovable property tax, which is meagre, about ₹ 22 crores in 1990-91 and about ₹ 160 crores in 2007-08. The Centre, till 1985, imposed and collected tax on the inheritance of property known as estate duty and the proceeds transferred to the States. This tax was to reduce inequality of income and wealth and raise revenue for the states but it has been discontinued due to extensive evasion.

- **Taxes on Commodities and Services:** Sales tax is the most important source of revenue raised by the states. The sales tax accounted to about 71.6 percent in 2010-11. Under sales tax, proceeds from general sales tax, Central sales tax, sales tax on motor spirit and purchase tax on sugarcane are included. There has been considerable opposition to the levy of sales tax in India. The tax rates are different in different states. The tax burden is heavy from goods that move from one state to another. There was considerable criticism on the levy and collection of sales taxes in different states-general sales tax, specific sales tax and central sales tax. States' Excise Duties are on alcoholic liquors, opium, Indian hemp and other narcotics. In recent years, almost all states have given up prohibition and are raising large resources from State excise duties. Other important taxes on commodities and services include taxes on vehicles, taxes on passengers and goods, taxes on electricity, and entertainment tax. In fact, electricity duties have been an important source of revenue to states.

- **VAT:** Indian Constitution has empowered the States with exclusive powers to tax sales and purchases of goods other than newspapers. On the other hand, Central Government has exclusive powers to tax sales and purchase of goods in the course of inter-state trade but proceeds of such a tax will be collected and retained by the States in which the movement of the goods in inter-state commences.

  An argument has been forwarded that sales tax in India is the easiest to pay and the least hard on incentives to work and save. The sales tax plays an important role in a federal structure like USA or India. The Central Government depends heavily on income taxes, but the States depend upon sales tax to obtain a considerable portion of their income.

- **Criticism:** Sales tax has been blamed to be regressive in character, i.e. paid by people with low and middle incomes and more by large families - lower income families spend a large percentage of their income on consumption. If sales tax is levied on food items and necessaries, the sales tax becomes much more regressive in nature.

  o Sales tax often tends to have a cascading effect – it means that the tax is collected at all stages and at every time, a commodity is bought and sold.

  o Sales tax on high priced goods is easily evaded by the consumers by not insisting for cash receipts. The State Governments lose tax revenue because of extensive corruption in the sales tax department.

  To overcome these defects, the Government proposed to introduce a value-added-tax (VAT) in place of States sales taxes. India showed great interest in replacing States sales tax with VAT, after the European Economic Community (EEC) adopted VAT as the major sales tax in the EEC countries.

- **Calculation of VAT:** When a garments' seller buys a shirt from the mill for ₹ 100 and sells it for ₹ 120, he has added ₹ 20 to the value of the shirt. It means that the value of the garment sellers' service is ₹ 20. The value added by a firm is the difference between the price of its product and the cost of the product to the firm.

  A firm can calculate the value added by it in any one of the ways:

  (i) Subtract the cost of goods purchased from sales;

  (ii) Add together the various elements that make up the value-added, viz., payment of wages, rent, interest and profit.

  VAT (value-added-tax), as the name indicates, is a tax on the value added to goods in the process of production and distribution. For example, if the government wants to tax the sale of an air-conditioner, it can do so at the manufacturing stage, at the wholesale stage or as retail sales tax at the final stage of sale to the consumer. An alternative is to levy a tax of say 10 percent of the value-added at each stage on the chain of production. Thus, the value-added at each stage adds up to the total value added (i.e. final price). In the same way, a tax on the value added at each stage will add up to the same as tax on the final stage. Thus, a value added tax (VAT) is simply another way of levying a sales tax.

Illustration: Let us suppose that VAT is 12 percent. Firm A has total revenue of ₹ 1 crore and has input cost of ₹ 60 lakhs. The VAT liability of the Firm A is:

Sales revenue	₹	1,00,00,000
Cost of input	₹	60,00,000
Value added by the Firm A	₹	40,00,000
VAT (at 12%)	₹	4,80,000

This method of calculating VAT is known as deduction of cost method or substitution method. The limitation of this method is *evasion of taxation through exaggeration of cost*. Like in the above example, the firm may state its cost of input at ₹ 80 lakhs and as such value of output added by Firm A will come down to ₹ 20 lakhs and VAT will reduce to ₹ 2,40,000, i.e. 12% of ₹ 20 lakhs.

"Tax method" or "invoice method" is the second method of calculating VAT. Firm A calculates VAT as follows:

Sales revenue	₹	1,00,00,000
Cost of input	₹	60,00,000
Total tax liability (at 12% of sales revenue)	₹	12,00,000
Less tax paid on input of (` 60,00,000) =	₹	7,20,000
Net tax liability	₹	4,80,000

In the 2nd method, firm A has to produce vouchers of tax paid already, viz., ₹ 7,20,000 to those from whom firm A has purchased the input valued at ₹ 60 lakhs; and thus there is no possibility of tax evasion. This method is far better and is used in EEC countries and in England. It is being adopted in India.

Merits: The Merits *of VAT* are as follows:

VAT is a neutral tax since it does not influence the organization of production.

VAT cannot be easily evaded and there is minimum loss of revenue.

VAT is easier to enforce through cross-checking, since tax paid by one firm is reported as a deduction by a subsequent firm.

VAT is spread over a large number of firms, instead of being concentrated on a single point in the chain of production as is the case of sales tax.

Producer (capital) goods can be easily excluded under VAT and thus, there is an incentive to invest and produce more.

VAT system encourages exports since VAT is identifiable and is fully rebated on exports. Goods under VAT are exported tax-free and are thus, competitive internationally.

Difficulties: Difficulties in application of VAT in India are stated as follows:

1. The collection of VAT demands that all producers, distributors, traders and everyone in the chain of production and distributors undertake:
    (i)   to keep accounts,
    (ii) keep proper accounts of all their transactions, and
    (iii) they also undertake to calculate the gross revenue, assess the tax already paid and calculate the tax liability.

2. VAT implies accounting discipline. But, in India, traders and intermediaries do not keep accounts and so far have managed by using malpractices with sales tax officers. Further, the government has to simplify VAT procedures for small traders and artisans.

3. From the start, the BJP-led NDA government at the Centre had shown keen interest in implementing VAT. States had agreed in principle to convert sales taxes to a uniform VAT by the end of March 2001. A final decision was taken that all States and Union territories would introduce VAT from April 2003. The decision taken was that every State legislation on VAT should have a minimum set of common features. Accordingly, a model VAT Bill was circulated to all the States. It was decided that :

    • The VAT legislations of all States and Union Territories (UTs) would have common provisions with respect to all important matters.

    • With the introduction of VAT, the origin based Central Sales Tax would be phased out.

    • The Additional Duties of Excise (goods of special importance) Act would be suitably amended to empower States to levy sales tax/VAT on sugar, textiles and tobacco with a ceiling rate of 4 percent. This would be done without affecting the existing levy of Additional Duties of Excise on these items by the government.

    • In the initial years of introduction of VAT many States expressed possible revenue losses and the Central Government agreed to compensate the States to the extent of 100 percent of revenue loss in the first year, 75 percent in the second year and 50 percent in the third year.

The VAT, after approval of the President of India, was introduced on April 1, 2005. By 2006-07, as many as 27 out of 28 States and Union Territories had replaced sales tax with VAT; the exception was Uttar Pradesh, which adopted VAT later.

In recent years, State Governments have expanded the taxpayer base, better compliance, rationalization of tax rates, improving the efficiency of tax administration, simplification of tax laws and introducing a modern and improved tax system.

• **States' share in Central Excise duties:** The share of the states in central excise duties was not much, ₹ 1 crore in 1951-52, but since 1956-57 this share has increased (in fact it is the second most important source of revenue to the states after sales tax). The 2 reasons are: more commodities were brought under the central excise tax net, and the share increased from 20 to 45 percent. Under the recommendation of the Eleventh Finance Commission, States do not get a share in Central excise duties, but they get a share in the total tax revenue of the Centre, 29.5 percent in 2000-05 and is 30.5 percent during 2005-2010.

- **Non-tax revenue of the States:** These are grants-in-aid from the Central Government (statutory grants awarded by the Finance Commission and discretionary grants sanctioned by the Planning Commission to finance plan outlays, expected to be ₹ 1,83,282 crores in the 2010-11 budget) and other non-tax revenue. States own non-tax revenues include interest receipts, dividends from state enterprises and income from general services, social, community and economic services. In 2010-11, the states' own non-tax revenue would come to ₹ 1,02,609 crores.

Revenue Expenditure of State Governments: The State Governments, under the Indian Constitution, have been entrusted with the important functions of maintaining law and order and also with many nation-building activities such as education, public health and medicine, irrigation, agriculture, etc. The State Governments have adopted the policy of building up Welfare States i.e., raising agricultural and industrial prosperity of the States and looking after the needs of the poor and the downtrodden.

- Since 1951-52, development and non-development expenditure of the states accounted for 50 percent each of the total expenditure. In 2010-11, development expenditure of the states accounted for nearly 59.7 percent of the total expenditure and non-development expenditure constituted only 37.5 percent.
- **Non-development Expenditure:** This expenditure of the States include:
  (i)   the organs of States;
  (ii)   fiscal services;
  (iii) interest payments, and servicing of debt which include appropriations for reduction or avoidance of debt;
  (iv)   administrative services;
  (v)   pensions and miscellaneous general services.

  The single largest non-development expenditure of the states is payment of interest (36.6 percent of the total non-development expenditure). These payments are partly to the Central Government and partly to the market for the loans raised. The second largest item of non-development expenditure is pensions, ₹ 1,00,357 crores (31.7 percent of the total non-plan expenditure). The third largest item of expenditure is on administrative services (23.5 percent of total non-development expenditure).
- **Development Expenditure:** This includes expenditure on: (a) social and community services and (b) economic services. Expenditure on social and community services include services like education, family planning and public health, housing, labour employment, social security and welfare and natural calamities. Social services confer

a positive advantage on the community, and the more developed these services are, the happier and better off would be the people in the country. On economic services, the expenditure consists of expenditure on agriculture, veterinary and co-operation, irrigation, electricity, rural and community development projects, civil works, industries and minerals etc. The single most important item of development expenditure is education which accounts for about 34 to 35 percent of the total development expenditure. The next item is agriculture and allied services including irrigation.

5.8 Union Budget

The dictionary meaning of *budget is a systematic plan for the expenditure of a usually fixed resource during a given period.* Thus, Union Budget, which is a yearly affair, is a comprehensive display of the government's finances. It is the most significant economic and financial event in India. The Finance Minister puts down a report that contains Government of India's revenue and expenditure for one fiscal year. The fiscal year runs from April 01 to March 31.

The Union budget is preceded by an Economic Survey which outlines the broad direction of the budget and the economic performance of the country.

The Budget is the most extensive account of the Government's finances, in which revenues from all sources and expenses of all activities undertaken are aggregated. It comprises the revenue budget and the capital budget. It also contains estimates for the next fiscal year called budgeted estimates.

Barring a few exceptions, like elections, Finance Minister presents the annual Budget in the Parliament on the last working day of February. The budget has to be passed by the Lok Sabha before it can come into effect on April '01.

Revenue Budget

The revenue budget consists of revenue receipts of the government (revenues from tax and other sources) and the expenditure undertaken from these revenues. Revenue receipts are divided into tax and non-tax revenue. *Tax revenues* are made up of taxes such as income tax, corporate tax, excise, customs and other duties which the government levies. Non-tax revenue consists of interest and dividend on investments made by government, fees and other receipts for services rendered by Government. Revenue expenditure is the payment incurred for the normal day-to-day running of government departments and various services that it offers to its citizens. The government also has other expenditure like servicing interest on its borrowings, subsidies, etc.

The difference between revenue receipts and revenue expenditure is usually negative. This means that the government spends more than it earns. The difference is called the revenue deficit.

Capital Budget

It consists of capital receipts and payments. The main items of *capital receipts* are loans raised by Government from public called as Market Loans. Borrowings by Government from Reserve Bank and other parties through sale of Treasury Bills, loans received from foreign Governments and recoveries of loans granted by Central Government to State and Union Territory Governments and other parties. Capital payments consist of capital expenditure on acquisition of assets like land, buildings, machinery, equipment, investments in shares, etc., and loans and advances granted by Central Government to State and Union Territory Governments, Government companies, Corporations and other parties. Capital Budget also incorporates transactions in the Public Account.

Types of Budget Deficits

Deficit financing has been used by the Government of India for acquiring funds to finance economic development. Governments sometimes run budget deficits, especially when the unexpected happens. When the government cannot raise enough financial resources through taxation, it finances its development expenditures through

(a) by running down its cash balances with RBI;

(b) borrowing from the market; and

(c) borrowing from RBI.

In this way, the government acquires the necessary finance to secure real resources for economic development.

A budget is essential for any organization if it wants to meet its financial obligations. Meeting these financial obligations is especially difficult for governments that have to manage billions of rupees in revenue and expenditures every year. It is a constant struggle to maintain a balanced budget especially when unexpected expenses such as closures of large organizations and natural disasters such as hurricanes occur. When a government spends beyond its revenue, it results in a budget deficit.

1. Revenue Deficit

A revenue deficit occurs when the amount of revenue Government receipts falls short of the amount expected. Based on the previous year's budget, the government projects' expected revenues and expenditures to determine how much revenue they will make at the end of the current year. For example, a government can project revenues of ₹ 1,000,000 for 2010 and project expenditures of ₹ 7,50,000 for a net gain of ₹ 2,50,000. At the end of the year, if the government's actual revenue is ₹ 8,50,000 and its actual expenditure is ₹ 7,50,000, then the net amount collected is ₹ 1,00,000. The government would then have created a revenue deficit of ₹ 1,50,000,00 (the difference between the projected and actual revenue).

Revenue Deficit: Since 1950-51, the government of India recognised only 2 types of deficits, viz., revenue deficit and over-all budgetary deficit.

Revenue Deficit = Revenue Receipts – Revenue Expenditure

The concept of revenue deficit is a simple one. **Current revenue** expenditure of the Central Government is met out of current revenue receipts (including tax and non-tax revenue of the Government). In 1990-91:

Total revenue receipts = ₹ 54,950 crores

Total revenue expenditure = ₹ 73,510 crores

Revenue Deficit = Revenue receipts – revenue expenditure

= ₹ 54,950 crores – ₹ 73,510 crores = ₹ 18,560 crores.

For the year 2011-12, revenue deficit is –

Revenue receipts = ₹ 7,89,892 crores

Revenue expenditure = ₹ 10,97,162 crores

Revenue deficit for 2011-12 = ₹ 7,89,892 crores – ₹ 10,97,162 crores = ₹ – 3,07,270 crores. (Negative revenue deficit reflects failure of the Government of India to meet its current expenditure from current revenue).

In fact, on the recommendations of the Taxation Enquiry Commission, the Government of India had adopted, at the time of the First Plan, *a deliberate budgetary policy of revenue surplus* which implied *creating excess of current receipts over current expenditure*. Revenue surplus is created by widening the tax base and increasing tax revenue on one side and strict control of revenue expenditure under check on the other side. This revenue surplus is to be utilised for economic development under the five Year Plans.

During the period 1951-75, the objective of revenue surplus had gradually ended because of continuous expansion of current expenditure, particularly of the non-plan category, i.e. defence, general administration, interest payments and subsidies of major and minor types. Accordingly, revenue deficit became a special feature of Central Government budgeting from the middle of the 1970s.

2. Budget Deficit

Budget deficit = Total receipts – Total expenditure

Total receipts include total *current* receipts and total *capital* receipts. Likewise, total expenditure includes total current expenditure and total capital expenditure or disbursements. In the year 1990-91,

Total receipts (current + capital) = ₹ 93,960 crores

Total expenditure (current + capital) = ₹ 105,310 crores

Budget deficit = Total receipts – Total expenditure

i.e

₹ 93,960 crores – ₹ 105,310 crores = ₹ (–) 11,350 crores

For the year 2011-12, budget deficit

= ₹ 12,57,729 crores – ₹ 12,57,729 crores = ₹ Nil.

Budget deficit is sometimes also referred to as the over-all budget deficit. It occurs when the total expenditure *exceeds* total receipts, and this was called as deficit financing by the Ministry of Finance.

The whole concept of budget deficit or over-all budget deficit since 1950-51 and the method of covering it by borrowing from RBI through the sale of Treasury Bills was wrong. "Capital receipts" are the sum of (i) recoveries of loans, (ii) other receipts, and (iii) borrowing and other liabilities. In reality, the 3rd source – borrowing and other liabilities – are not the receipts of the Government and should not be included under capital receipts. They are liabilities of the Government, payable to the public. They also form a part of the over-all budget deficit.

The actual extent of deficit financing in any given year should include: (i) over-all budgetary deficit, + (ii) market borrowings, small savings collections and other capital receipts (which are really liabilities). The Chakravarty Committee defined that 'deficit' of the fiscal operations include not only budgetary deficit but also market borrowings and other liabilities. Thus, from 1997-98, the Government accepted the recommendations of the Committee and (i) gave up the conventional concept of deficit financing and (ii) started the calculation of a third concept of deficit, known as fiscal deficit.

3. Fiscal Deficit

Fiscal deficits happen as a result of revenue deficits. After the government projects its net gain for the year, its leaders presume that they will have a certain net amount of funds for their operational needs. At the end of the fiscal year, if the *actual total expenditure surpasses the projected revenue*, then the government will experience a fiscal deficit. Unexpected expenses such as assistance to areas affected by natural disasters or allocations to struggling organizations are reasons for the increase in expenditures.

In simple terms, *fiscal deficit is budgetary deficit + market borrowings and other liabilities of the Government of India.*

Fiscal Deficit = Revenue Receipts + Capital receipts (only recoveries of loans and other receipts) minus Total expenditure. **(OR)** Fiscal deficit = Budget deficit + Government's market borrowings and liabilities.

For the year 1990-91, Fiscal deficit (1990-91) = revenue receipts for the year 1990-91 = ₹ 54,950 crores + Capital receipts in the form of recoveries of loans and receipts in 1990-91 = ₹ 5,710 crores; total revenue in 1990-91= ₹ 60,660 crores minus Total expenditure in 1990-91 = ₹ 1,05,310 crores. Fiscal deficit = ₹ 44,650 crores.

(OR) Fiscal deficit in 1990-91 (Budget deficit in 1990-91 = i.e. ₹ 11,350 crores + Market borrowing and other liabilities in 1990-91, i.e. ₹ 33,300 crores = ₹ 44,650 crores.

Thus, fiscal deficit indicates the total borrowing requirements of the Government from all sources. From the economy point of view, fiscal deficit is important as (i) it shows the gap between government receipts and government expenditure; (ii) it reflects the true extent of borrowing by the Government in a fiscal year, and the traditional concept of budgetary deficit reflects only the Government's borrowing from the RBI.

4. Primary Deficit

Now, when the government has a fiscal deficit, it needs to borrow money from an institution such as a bank to cover its expenditures. Interest on the loans has to be paid to the bank. The interest payment is subtracted from the amount of the fiscal deficit and is referred to as the primary deficit.

The Finance Ministry, in recent years, has introduced 'primary deficit', though it does not have any policy significance.

Primary Deficit = Fiscal Deficit – Interest payments

In the 2011-12 budget, fiscal deficit was ₹ 4,12,817 crores and interest payments was ₹ 2,67,936 crores, then primary deficit for 2011-12

= ₹ 4,12,817 crores – ₹ 2,67,936 crores = ₹ 1,44,831 crores.

Fiscal Policy

Fiscal policy is a change in government spending or taxing designed to influence economic activity. These changes are designed to control the level of aggregate demand in the economy. Governments usually bring about changes in taxation, volume of spending, and size of the budget deficit or surplus to affect public expenditure.

Fiscal Deficit

As mentioned earlier, Fiscal deficit is an economic phenomenon, where the Government's total expenditure surpasses the revenue generated. It is the difference between the government's total receipts (excluding borrowing) and total expenditure.

Components of Fiscal Deficit

The primary component of fiscal deficit includes revenue deficit and capital expenditure.

Revenue deficit: It is an economic phenomenon, where the net amount received fails to meet the predicted net amount to be received.

Capital expenditure: It is the fund used by an establishment to produce physical assets like property, equipments or industrial buildings. Capital expenditure is made by the establishment to consistently maintain the operational activities.

In India, the fiscal deficit is financed by obtaining funds from the Reserve Bank of India, called deficit financing. The fiscal deficit is also financed by obtaining funds from the money market (primarily from banks).

CONCEPTS: (explained above in types of deficits).

Trends of Deficit

(a) Revenue deficit has been rising quite fast, from ₹ 18,560 crores to ₹ 3,07,270 crores between 1991 and 2012. As compared to the proportion of GDP, revenue deficit had ranged between 3.5 to 4.7 percent, which is quite high. Such high revenue deficit pointed out that the government had been living beyond their means and hence, had to cut its current expenditure (particularly non-plan expenditure) instead of looking for sources of additional taxation.

(b) Originally, budget deficit was calculated to show RBI lending to the government. Since 1997, RBI lending to Government through ad hoc treasury bills was given up.

(c) The Finance Ministry has so estimated that the *total capital receipts of the Government are exactly equal to the total expenditure*. Thus, there is no over-all budget deficit.

(d) Fiscal deficit has been growing rapidly and dangerously, from ₹ 27,040 crores in 1988-89 to ₹ 44,630 crores in 1990-91 and ₹ 4,00,996 crores in the 2007-08 budget. The international financial institutions like the World Bank and the IMF objected to the high rate of fiscal deficit (7.7% of GDP) in 1990-91 and asked the Government of India to reduce it over the next few years.

(e) The RBI has been warning the government regularly of the impending debt trap. It was only when the World Bank and International institutions refused to bail out India in 1990-91 unless it reduced its fiscal deficit, that the Government was compelled to take strict measures to control non-plan expenditure.

It was the NDA government that made a two-point attack in reducing revenue and fiscal deficits through increasing revenue on one side and controlling the non-plan expenditure on the other. According to the 2008-09 budget, fiscal deficit was projected to be 2.5 percent of GDP but it turned to be 6.0 percent of GDP. For Budget 2011-12, Fiscal deficit has been at 4.6 percent of GDP.

Controls of Deficit

In order to place fiscal discipline on a statutory basis,

- The Government has introduced the Fiscal Responsibility Bill in the Parliament.

- The statutory liquidity ratio (SLR) for banks has been reduced to 25 percent from the high of 38.5% and banks are holding government securities far in excess over the SLR requirements, the estimated excess being of the order of ₹ 1,00,000 crore. Thus, the banks hold government securities not only on account of statutory prescriptions and lowest risk weight for capital adequacy purposes but also as a profitable investment.

- The development of secondary market for government securities is closely related to successful public debt management. Bank has, therefore, been taking initiative to develop the necessary institutional structure for the government securities market.

- The development of the institutional structure may be traced to the formation of Securities Trading Corporation of India Ltd. The efforts of the Bank gained further momentum with the institution of the system of primary dealers and satellite dealers. Further, Bank has taken a supportive stand to the evolution of mutual funds dedicated to investment in government securities. This is expected to help in widening the government securities market.

Need to control the monetisation of government debt

As per the supplementary agreement that the Reserve Bank entered with Government of India in March 1997, a scheme of Ways and Means advances has been put in place for the Central government. When the Ways and Means advances reach 75 percent of the limit, Reserve Bank can trigger a fresh borrowing from the market. Under this agreement, surplus cash in the account of the Central Government with the Bank should be invested in central government securities. This operation helps reduce the level of monetised debt temporarily. Operationally, the Bank addresses the problem of monetisation of debt by adopting strategic conduct of market borrowing programme. This involves timing of private placements and public issues in such a way as to take advantage of the liquidity conditions in the market both for raising the borrowing and for selling securities earlier subscribed by the Bank in the primary auctions.

Need to have a optimum maturity profile of the outstanding government debt

The central government debt of maturities above 10 years formed 85.8 percent in 1990-91. It has been substantially altered in favour of short-term over the last few years. The government debt maturing within the next 5 years constitute roughly 45 percent of the marketable debt. Bunching of maturities would result in the need to raise commensurately larger gross borrowing and this may exert pressure on both resources and interest rates.

Need to ensure that the interest rates structure thrown up by the Market Borrowing Programme does not come in conflict with the Stance of Monetary Policy

The compulsions of the monetary policy management and internal debt management are attempted to be harmonised through the Bank's Open Market Operations (OMO). By conducting liquidity adjustments in the system through OMO, Bank is able to bring about orderly conditions in the short-term money market. As the interest rate structure is driven by expectations, management of the short-term liquidity has a wholesome effect on the formation of the term structure of interest rates. RBI has put in place a system of Liquidity Adjustment Facility (LAF) to bring about orderly conditions in the short end of the market.

Expert Recommendation

Financial advisors recommend that the Government should not promote disinvestment to reduce fiscal deficits. Fiscal deficit can be reduced by bringing up revenues or by lowering expenditure.

Fiscal deficit reduction has an impact over the agricultural and social sector. The Government's investments in these sectors will be reduced.

Points to Remember

- The economy of India is the tenth-largest in the world by nominal Gross Domestic Product (GDP) and third-largest by purchasing power parity (PPP).

- India is one of the G-20 major economies and a member of BRICS (Brazil, Russia, India, China, South Africa).

- India's GDP grew by an astounding 9.3% in 2010-11 and in three years it has halved down.

- The government has forecasted a growth of 6.1% to 6.7% for the year 2013-14, whilst the RBI expects the same to be at 5.7%.

- In 1991, India adopted liberal and free-market principles and liberalised its economy to international trade under the guidance of Shri Manmohan Singh, the then finance minister from 30th November 2009 to 24 January 2010 and previously under the leadership of P. V. Narsimha Rao, Prime Minister from 1991 to 1996, who eliminated License Raj.

- National income is the flow of goods and services which become available to a nation during a year.

- **Gross National Product (GNP):** "It is the total market value of all final goods and services produced in a year".

- When we *minus* depreciation charges from GNP_{mp} we get NNP_{mp}.

- **National Income at Factor Cost:** It means sum of all incomes earned by factors of production for their contribution in production of net output. In fact, National Income actually means national income at factor cost.

- National Income at market price includes **indirect taxes** and **subsidies**, while NNP at factor cost excludes indirect taxes.

- **Personal Income (P.I.):** P.I. is the sum of all incomes actually received by all individuals or households during a given year.

- **Gross Domestic Product (GDP):** GDP is the *market value* of all officially recognised *final* goods and services produced within a country in a given period of time.

- Symbolically, **GDP = C + G + I + (X – M)**

- GDP is one of the primary indicators used to gauge the health of a country's economy.

- **Methods of Computing GDP:**
    1. **Production Approach:** (Inventory Method):

        It is the *market value* of all final goods and services calculated during one year.

2. **Income Approach:** It is the sum total of incomes of individuals living in a country during one year.

   N.I. (NNP at factor cost) = R + W + I + P + G + (X – M)

3. **Expenditure Method:** In this method it is the sum of all expenditures incurred by individuals during one year.

   Y = C + I + G + (X – M).

- **Growth Rate:** Growth rate implies the amount of increase that a specific variable has gained within a specific period and context.

- PPP is "an economic theory that estimates the amount of adjustment needed on the exchange rate between countries in order for the exchange to be equivalent to each currency's purchasing power."

Question for Discussion

1. Explain the different methods of national income measurement.
2. Define national income.
3. Explain the terms (i) PPP; (ii) Growth rate.
4. How do you differentiate between direct and indirect taxes?
5. What is GATT? State its objectives.
6. What are the different provisions of GATT?
7. Critically evaluate GATT's achievements.
8. Discuss the achievements of the Uruguay Round of the GATT.
9. How far the developing countries have benefited from the GATT?
10. What is WTO and state its objectives?
11. Discuss the functions of WTO.
12. Write in detail the principles of WTO.
13. Write a note on WTO and Developing world.
14. What are the implications of WTO for India?
15. What do you mean by plan and non-plan expenditure?
16. Explain fiscal deficit.
17. What are the different types of budget deficits?
18. Enumerate the methods of deficit control.
19. Write a detailed note on budget.
20. Differentiate between WTO and GATT.

Objective Questions

1. List the four components of GDP. Give an example of each.

2. What components of GDP (if any) would each of the following transactions affect? Explain.

    (a) A family buys a new television set.

    (b) Aunt Mary buys a new house.

    (c) Ford sells an Ikon from its inventory,

    (d) You buy a pizza.

    (e) Honda expands its factory in Faridabad.

3. Choose the correct alternative:

    (i) In a four sector economy national income is measured as:

    (a) $Y = C + I + G + X - M$;

    (b) $Y = C + I + G + T$;

    (c) $Y = C + I + G - X + M$;

    (d) $Y = C + I + T + X - M$.

    [Ans.: (a)]

    (ii) Which of the following is not considered in calculation of national income?

    (a) Interest on bank deposits.

    (b) Dividend earned on share of Adani Energy Limited.

    (c) Salary of employees of State Electricity Board.

    (d) Pension received by government employees.

    [Ans.: (d)]

    (iii) Which of the following is not a final good?

    (a) Airplane (b) Chair (c) Alumina (d) Book.

    [Ans.: (c)]

■■■

BIBLIOGRAPHY

1. Economics – Lipsey & Chrystal (11th Edition)- Oxford (Indian Edition).
2. Economics – Samuelson Nordhaus (18th Edition) – TATA McGRAW-HILL Edition.
3. Managerial Economics- P. L.Mehta – Sultan Chand & Sons. (Analysis, Problems and Cases)
4. Managerial Economics – H. L. Ahuja – (3rd Revised Edition) – (Analysis of Managerial Decision Making).
5. Managerial Economics – Dominick Salvatore – (Adapted by – Ravikesh Srivastava) – 6th Edition. (Principles & Worldwide Applications).
6. Economics –Mrs.Kiran Jotwani – Nirali Prakashan.
7. Macro Economics – M.L. Seth – Lakshmi Narain Agarwal.
8. Macro Economic Analysis – Mrs. Kiran Jotwani, Dr. Mukund Mahajan – Nirali Prakashan.
9. Micro Economic Analysis – Mrs. Kiran Jotwani, Dr. Mukund Mahajan – Nirali Prakashan.
10. http:/kalian-city.blogspot.com/2010/09/what-is-capital-market-meaning.html
11. Managerial Economics – R. L. Varshney, K.Maheshwari – (20th revised & enlarged edition) – Sultan Chand & Sons.
12. Managerial Economics – Geetika, Piyali Ghosh, Purba Roy Choudhury- Tata McGraw Hill Education Private Limited.
13. Indian Economy – Himalaya Publishing House – (30th Revised Edition) – Misra Puri.
14. www.svtuition.org/2010/05-role of sebi in indian capital market html.
15. www.sircoficwai.com-sebi.
16. Wikipedia.org/wiki/securities and exchange-board-of-india.
17. http://shodhganga.inflibnet.ac.in/bitstream/10603/2027/7/07_chapter%202.pdf.

■■■